English-French Parallel Text Bilingual Edition

The Hound of the Baskervilles

Le Chien des Baskerville

ARTHUR CONAN DOYLE

The Hound of the Baskervilles
was published in 1902 by
Arthur Conan Doyle

It was translated from English to French by
Adrien de Jassaud in 1905

This bilingual edition was produced in 2022 for
Smart Books
by
Raul Kask

Original illustrations by
Sidney Paget

Cover and interior design by
Raul Kask

SMART BOOKS
Learn languages by reading
your favourite books

TABLE OF CONTENTS

Chapter 1	Mr. Sherlock Holmes	7
Chapter 2	The Curse of the Baskervilles	14
Chapter 3	The Problem	26
Chapter 4	Sir Henry Baskerville	35
Chapter 5	Three Broken Threads	48
Chapter 6	Baskerville Hall	59
Chapter 7	The Stapletons of Merripit House	70
Chapter 8	First Report of Dr. Watson	84
Chapter 9	The Light upon the Moor [Second Report of Dr. Watson]	94
Chapter 10	Extract from the Diary of Dr. Watson	114
Chapter 11	The Man on the Tor	125
Chapter 12	Death on the Moor	138
Chapter 13	Fixing the Nets	152
Chapter 14	The Hound of the Baskervilles	163
Chapter 15	A Retrospection	176

TABLE DES MATIÈRES

Chapitre 1	M. Sherlock Holmes	7
Chapitre 2	La Malédiction des Baskerville	14
Chapitre 3	Le problème	26
Chapitre 4	Sir Henry Baskerville	35
Chapitre 5	Fils cassés	48
Chapitre 6	Le chateau de Baskerville	59
Chapitre 7	M. Stapleton, de Merripit house	70
Chapitre 8	Premier rapport du docteur Watson	84
Chapitre 9	La lumière sur la lande [Deuxième rapport du docteur Watson]	94
Chapitre 10	Extraits du journal de Watson	114
Chapitre 11	L'homme du pic noir	125
Chapitre 12	Mort sur la lande	138
Chapitre 13	Filets tendus	152
Chapitre 14	Le Chien des Baskerville	163
Chapitre 15	Détails rétrospectifs	176

ARTHUR CONAN DOYLE

Sir Arthur Ignatius Conan Doyle (22 May 1859 – 7 July 1930) was a British writer and physician. He created the character Sherlock Holmes in 1887 for A Study in Scarlet, the first of four novels and fifty-six short stories about Holmes and Dr. Watson. The Sherlock Holmes stories are milestones in the field of crime fiction. Doyle was a prolific writer; other than Holmes stories, his works include fantasy and science fiction stories about Professor Challenger and humorous stories about the Napoleonic soldier Brigadier Gerard, as well as plays, romances, poetry, non-fiction, and historical novels.

Doyle was born in Edinburgh, Scotland in 1859. He had a difficult childhood because of his father's alcoholism. Supported by wealthy uncles, Doyle was sent to school in England at the age of nine. Then he went on to Stonyhurst College, which he attended until 1875. From 1875 to 1876, he was educated at the Jesuit school Stella Matutina in Feldkirch, Austria. His family decided that he would spend a year there in order to perfect his German and broaden his academic horizons.

Photo: Arnold Genthe / Wikimedia Commons

Arthur Conan Doyle in June 1914.

From 1876 to 1881, Doyle studied medicine at the University of Edinburgh Medical School. While studying, Doyle began writing short stories. His earliest extant fiction, "The Haunted Grange of Goresthorpe", was unsuccessfully submitted to Blackwood's Magazine. His first published piece, "The Mystery of Sasassa Valley", a story set in South Africa, was printed in Chambers's Edinburgh Journal on 6 September 1879.

After graduating with Bachelor of Medicine and Master of Surgery degrees from the University of Edinburgh in 1881, he served as a ship's surgeon on the SS Mayumba during a voyage to the West African coast. He completed his Doctor of Medicine degree with a dissertation on *tabes dorsalis* in 1885.

In 1882 Doyle tried to practice medicine when he opened a medical practice, first with his former classmate and later alone. Both practices were unsuccessful. While waiting for patients, he returned to writing fiction. In 1891 he studied ophthalmology in Vienna and in Paris. After returning to London he opened a small office and consulting room, but yet again his efforts as an ophthalmologist was a failure.

Photo: Kim Traynor / Wikimedia Commons

Sherlock Holmes statue in Edinburgh, erected opposite the birthplace of Doyle, which was demolished c. 1970.

Doyle struggled to find a publisher. His first work featuring Sherlock Holmes and Dr. Watson, A Study in Scarlet, was written in three weeks when he was 27 and was accepted for publication by Ward Lock & Co on 20 November 1886, which gave Doyle £25 (equivalent to £2,900 in 2019) in exchange for all rights to the story. The piece appeared a year later in the Beeton's Christmas Annual and received good reviews in The Scotsman and the Glasgow Herald.

Sherlock Holmes was partially modeled on Doyle's former university teacher Joseph Bell. Other authors sometimes suggest additional influences – for instance, Edgar Allan Poe's character C. Auguste Dupin. Dr. (John) Watson owes his surname, but not any other obvious characteristic, to a Portsmouth medical colleague of Doyle's, Dr. James Watson.

A sequel to A Study in Scarlet was commissioned, and The Sign of the Four appeared in Lippincott's Magazine in February 1890.

Doyle's attitude towards his most famous creation was ambivalent. He was thinking of killing the character and in an attempt to deflect publishers' demands for more Holmes stories, he raised his price to a level intended to discourage them, but found they were willing to pay even the large sums he asked.] As a result, he became one of the best-paid authors of his time.

In December 1893, to dedicate more of his time to his historical novels, Doyle had Holmes and Professor Moriarty plunge to their deaths together down the Reichenbach Falls in the story "The Final Problem". Public outcry, however, led him to feature Holmes in 1901 in the novel The Hound of the Baskervilles. Holmes was ultimately featured in a total of 56 short stories—the last published in 1927—and four novels by Doyle, and has since appeared in many novels and stories by other authors.

The Hound of the Baskervilles is one of the most famous stories ever written, in 2003, the book was listed as number 128 of 200 on the BBC's The Big Read poll of the UK's "best-loved novel". In 1999, a poll of "Sherlockians" ranked it as the best of the four Holmes novels.

Originally serialised in The Strand Magazine from August 1901 to April 1902, it is set largely on Dartmoor in Devon in England's West Country and tells the story of an attempted murder inspired by the legend of a fearsome, diabolical hound of supernatural origin. Sherlock Holmes and his companion Dr. Watson investigate the case.

Portrait of Sherlock Holmes by Sidney Paget, 1904.

The cover of the first edition.

The shadow of Sherlock Holmes.
L'ombre de Sherlock Holmes.

CHAPTER 1. MR. SHERLOCK HOLMES

Mr. Sherlock Holmes, who was usually very late in the mornings, save upon those not infrequent occasions when he was up all night, was seated at the breakfast table. I stood upon the hearth-rug and picked up the stick which our visitor had left behind him the night before. It was a fine, thick piece of wood, bulbous-headed, of the sort which is known as a "Penang lawyer."

Just under the head was a broad silver band nearly an inch across. "To James Mortimer, M.R.C.S., from his friends of the C.C.H.," was engraved upon it, with the date "1884."

It was just such a stick as the old-fashioned family practitioner used to carry—dignified, solid, and reassuring.

"Well, Watson, what do you make of it?"

Holmes was sitting with his back to me, and I had given him no sign of my occupation.

"How did you know what I was doing? I believe you have eyes in the back of your head."

"I have, at least, a well-polished, silver-plated coffee-pot in front of me," said he. "But, tell me, Watson, what do you make of our visitor's stick? Since we have been so unfortunate as to miss him and have no notion of his errand, this accidental souvenir becomes of importance. Let me hear you reconstruct the man by an examination of it."

"I think," said I, following as far as I could the methods of my companion, "that Dr. Mortimer is a successful, elderly medical man, well-esteemed since those who know him give him this mark of their appreciation."

"Good!" said Holmes. "Excellent!"

"I think also that the probability is in favour of his being a country practitioner who does a great deal of his visiting on foot."

"Why so?"

"Because this stick, though originally a very handsome one has been so knocked about that I can hardly imagine a town practitioner carrying it.

CHAPITRE 1. M. SHERLOCK HOLMES

Ce matin-là, M. Sherlock Holmes qui, sauf les cas assez fréquents où il passait les nuits, se levait tard, était assis devant la table de la salle à manger. Je me tenais près de la cheminée, examinant la canne que notre visiteur de la veille avait oubliée. C'était un joli bâton, solide, terminé par une boule — ce qu'on est convenu d'appeler «une permission de minuit».

Immédiatement au-dessous de la pomme, un cercle d'or, large de deux centimètres, portait l'inscription et la date suivantes: «À M. James Mortimer, ses amis du C. C. H. — 1884».

Cette canne, digne, grave, rassurante, ressemblait à celles dont se servent les médecins «vieux jeu».

«Eh bien, Watson, me dit Holmes, quelles conclusions en tirez-vous?»

Holmes me tournait le dos et rien ne pouvait lui indiquer mon genre d'occupation.

«Comment savez-vous ce que je fais? Je crois vraiment que vous avez des yeux derrière la tête.

— Non; mais j'ai, en face de moi, une cafetière en argent, polie comme un miroir. Allons, Watson, communiquez-moi les réflexions que vous suggère l'examen de cette canne. Nous avons eu la malchance de manquer hier son propriétaire et, puisque nous ignorons le but de sa visite, ce morceau de bois acquiert une certaine importance.

— Je pense, répondis-je, suivant de mon mieux la méthode de mon compagnon, que le docteur Mortimer doit être quelque vieux médecin, très occupé et très estimé, puisque ceux qui le connaissent lui ont donné ce témoignage de sympathie.

— Bien, approuva Holmes… très bien!

— Je pense également qu'il y a de grandes probabilités pour que le docteur Mortimer soit un médecin de campagne qui visite la plupart du temps ses malades à pied.

— Pourquoi?

— Parce que cette canne, fort jolie quand elle était neuve, m'apparaît tellement usée que je ne la vois pas entre les mains d'un médecin de ville.

The thick-iron ferrule is worn down, so it is evident that he has done a great amount of walking with it."

"Perfectly sound!" said Holmes.

"And then again, there is the 'friends of the C.C.H.' I should guess that to be the Something Hunt, the local hunt to whose members he has possibly given some surgical assistance, and which has made him a small presentation in return."

"Really, Watson, you excel yourself," said Holmes, pushing back his chair and lighting a cigarette. "I am bound to say that in all the accounts which you have been so good as to give of my own small achievements you have habitually underrated your own abilities. It may be that you are not yourself luminous, but you are a conductor of light. Some people without possessing genius have a remarkable power of stimulating it. I confess, my dear fellow, that I am very much in your debt."

He had never said as much before, and I must admit that his words gave me keen pleasure, for I had often been piqued by his indifference to my admiration and to the attempts which I had made to give publicity to his methods. I was proud, too, to think that I had so far mastered his system as to apply it in a way which earned his approval.

He now took the stick from my hands and examined it for a few minutes with his naked eyes. Then with an expression of interest he laid down his cigarette, and carrying the cane to the window, he looked over it again with a convex lens.

"Interesting, though elementary," said he as he returned to his favourite corner of the settee. "There are certainly one or two indications upon the stick. It gives us the basis for several deductions."

"Has anything escaped me?" I asked with some self-importance. "I trust that there is nothing of consequence which I have overlooked?"

"I am afraid, my dear Watson, that most of your conclusions were erroneous. When I said that you stimulated me I meant, to be frank, that in not-

L'usure du bout en fer témoigne de longs services.

— Parfaitement exact! approuva Holmes.

— Et puis, il y a encore ces mots: «Ses amis du C. C. H.». Je devine qu'il s'agit d'une société de chasse… Le docteur aura soigné quelques-uns de ses membres qui, en reconnaissance, lui auront offert ce petit cadeau.

— En vérité, Watson, vous vous surpassez, fit Holmes, en reculant sa chaise pour allumer une cigarette. Je dois avouer que, dans tous les rapports que vous avez bien voulu rédiger sur mes humbles travaux, vous ne vous êtes pas assez rendu justice. Vous n'êtes peut-être pas lumineux par vous-même; mais je vous tiens pour un excellent conducteur de lumière. Il existe des gens qui, sans avoir du génie, possèdent le talent de le stimuler chez autrui. Je confesse, mon cher ami, que je suis votre obligé.»

Auparavant, Holmes ne m'avait jamais parlé ainsi. Ces paroles me firent le plus grand plaisir, car, jusqu'alors, son indifférence aussi bien pour mon admiration que pour mes efforts tentés en vue de vulgariser ses méthodes, m'avait vexé. De plus, j'étais fier de m'être assimilé son système au point de mériter son approbation quand il m'arrivait de l'appliquer.

Holmes me prit la canne des mains et l'examina à son tour pendant quelques minutes. Puis, soudainement intéressé, il posa sa cigarette, se rapprocha de la fenêtre et la regarda de nouveau avec une loupe.

«Intéressant, quoique élémentaire, fit-il, en retournant s'asseoir sur le canapé, dans son coin de prédilection. J'aperçois sur cette canne une ou deux indications qui nous conduisent à des inductions.

— Quelque chose m'aurait-il échappé? dis-je d'un air important. Je ne crois pas avoir négligé de détail essentiel.

— Je crains, mon cher Watson, que la plupart de vos conclusions ne soient erronées. Quand je prétendais que vous me stimuliez, cela signifiait qu'en ing your fallacies I was occasionally guided towards the truth. Not that you are entirely wrong in this instance. The man is certainly a country practitioner. And he walks a good deal."

"Then I was right."

"To that extent."

"But that was all."

"No, no, my dear Watson, not all—by no means all. I would suggest, for example, that a presentation to a doctor is more likely to come from a hospital than from a hunt, and that when the initials 'C.C.' are placed before that hospital the words 'Charing Cross' very naturally suggest themselves."

"You may be right."

"The probability lies in that direction. And if we take this as a working hypothesis we have a fresh basis from which to start our construction of this unknown visitor."

"Well, then, supposing that 'C.C.H.' does stand for 'Charing Cross Hospital,' what further inferences may we draw?"

"Do none suggest themselves? You know my methods. Apply them!"

"I can only think of the obvious conclusion that the man has practised in town before going to the country."

"I think that we might venture a little farther than this. Look at it in this light. On what occasion would it be most probable that such a presentation would be made? When would his friends unite to give him a pledge of their good will? Obviously at the moment when Dr. Mortimer withdrew from the service of the hospital in order to start a practice for himself. We know there has been a presentation. We believe there has been a change from a town hospital to a country practice. Is it, then, stretching our inference too far to say that the presentation was on the occasion of the change?"

"It certainly seems probable."

"Now, you will observe that he could not have been on the staff of the hospital, since only a man well-established in a London practice could hold such a position, and such a one would not drift into the country. What was he, then? If he was in the hospital and yet not on the staff he could only have been a house-surgeon or a house-physician—little more than a senior student. And he left five years ago—the date is on the stick. So your grave, middle-aged family practitioner vanishes into thin air, my dear Watson, and there emerges a young

relevant vos erreurs j'étais accidentellement amené à découvrir la vérité.... Oh! dans l'espèce, vous ne vous trompez pas complètement. L'homme est certainement un médecin de campagne... et il marche beaucoup.

— J'avais donc raison.

— Oui, pour cela.

— Mais c'est tout?

— Non, non, mon cher Watson... pas tout – tant s'en faut. J'estime, par exemple, qu'un cadeau fait à un docteur s'explique mieux venant d'un hôpital que d'une société de chasse. Aussi, lorsque les initiales «C. C.» sont placées avant celle désignant cet hôpital, les mots «Charing Cross» s'imposent tout naturellement.

— Peut-être.

— Des probabilités sont en faveur de mon explication. Et, si nous acceptons cette hypothèse, nous avons une nouvelle base qui nous permet de reconstituer la personnalité de notre visiteur inconnu.

— Alors, en supposant que C. C. H. signifie «Charing Cross Hospital», quelles autres conséquences en déduirons-nous?

— Vous ne les trouvez-pas?... Vous connaissez ma méthode.... Appliquez-la!

— La seule conclusion évidente est que notre homme pratiquait la médecine à la ville avant de l'exercer à la campagne.

— Nous devons aller plus loin dans nos suppositions. Suivez cette piste. À quelle occasion est-il le plus probable qu'on ait offert ce cadeau? Quand les amis du docteur Mortimer se seraient-ils cotisés pour lui donner un souvenir? Certainement au moment où il quittait l'hôpital pour s'établir.... Nous savons qu'il y a eu un cadeau.... Nous croyons qu'il y a eu passage d'un service d'hôpital à l'exercice de la médecine dans une commune rurale. Dans ce cas, est-il téméraire d'avancer que ce cadeau a eu lieu à l'occasion de ce changement de situation?

— Cela semble très plausible.

— Maintenant vous remarquerez que le docteur Mortimer ne devait pas appartenir au service régulier de l'hôpital. On n'accorde ces emplois qu'aux premiers médecins de Londres – et ceux-là ne vont jamais exercer à la campagne. Qu'était-il alors? Un médecin auxiliaire.... Il est parti, il y a cinq ans... lisez la date sur la canne. Ainsi votre médecin, grave, entre deux âges, s'évanouit en fumée, mon cher Watson, et, à sa place, nous voyons apparaître un garçon de trente ans, aimable, modeste, distrait et possesseur d'un chien que je défellow under thirty, amiable, unambitious, absent-minded, and the possessor of a favourite dog, which I should describe roughly as being larger than a terrier and smaller than a mastiff."

I laughed incredulously as Sherlock Holmes leaned back in his settee and blew little wavering rings of smoke up to the ceiling.

"As to the latter part, I have no means of checking you," said I, "but at least it is not difficult to find out a few particulars about the man's age and professional career."

From my small medical shelf I took down the Medical Directory and turned up the name. There were several Mortimers, but only one who could be our visitor.

I read his record aloud.

"Mortimer, James, M.R.C.S.[1], 1882, Grimpen, Dartmoor, Devon. House-surgeon, from 1882 to 1884, at Charing Cross Hospital. Winner of the Jackson prize for Comparative Pathology, with essay entitled 'Is Disease a Reversion?' Corresponding member of the Swedish Pathological Society. Author of 'Some Freaks of Atavism' (Lancet 1882). 'Do We Progress?' (Journal of Psychology, March, 1883). Medical Officer for the parishes of Grimpen, Thorsley, and High Barrow."

"No mention of that local hunt, Watson," said Holmes with a mischievous smile, "but a country doctor, as you very astutely observed. I think that I am fairly justified in my inferences. As to the adjectives, I said, if I remember right, amiable, unambitious, and absent-minded. It is my experience that it is only an amiable man in this world who receives testimonials, only an unambitious one who abandons a London career for the country, and only an absent-minded one who leaves his stick and not his visiting-card after waiting an hour in your room."

"And the dog?"

"Has been in the habit of carrying this stick behind his master. Being a heavy stick the dog has held it tightly by the middle, and the marks of his teeth are very plainly visible. The dog's jaw, as shown in the space between these marks, is too broad in my opinion for a terrier and not broad enough for a mastiff. It may have been—yes, by Jove, it is a curly-haired spaniel."

He had risen and paced the room as he spoke. Now he halted in the recess of the window. There

peindrai vaguement plus grand qu'un terrier et plus petit qu'un mastiff.»

Je souris d'un air incrédule, tandis que Holmes se renversait sur le canapé, en lançant au plafond quelques bouffées de fumée.

«Je ne puis contrôler cette dernière assertion, dis-je; mais rien n'est plus facile que de nous procurer certains renseignements sur l'âge et les antécédents professionnels de notre inconnu.»

Je pris sur un rayon de la bibliothèque l'annuaire médical et je courus à la lettre M. J'y trouvai plusieurs Mortimer. Un seul pouvait être notre visiteur.

Je lus à haute voix:

— «Mortimer, James, M. R. C. S.[1] 1882; Grimpen, Dartmoor, Devon. Interne de 1882 à 1884 à l'hôpital de Charing Cross. Lauréat du prix Jackson pour une étude de pathologie comparée, intitulée: «L'hérédité est-elle une maladie?» Membre correspondant de la Société pathologique suédoise. Auteur de «Quelques caprices de l'atavisme» (The Lancet, 1882), «Progressons-nous?» (Journal de Pathologie, 1883). Médecin autorisé pour les paroisses de Grimpen, Thornsley et High Barrow.»

— Hé! Watson, il n'est nullement question de société de chasse, fit Holmes avec un sourire narquois; mais bien d'un médecin de campagne, ainsi que vous l'aviez finement pronostiqué, d'ailleurs. Mes déductions se confirment. Quant aux qualificatifs dont je me suis servi, j'ai dit, si je me souviens bien: aimable, modeste et distrait. Or, on ne fait de cadeaux qu'aux gens aimables; un modeste seul abandonne Londres pour se retirer à la campagne et il n'y a qu'un distrait pour laisser sa canne au lieu de sa carte de visite, après une attente d'une heure dans notre salon.

— Et le chien? repris-je.

— Le chien porte ordinairement la canne de son maître. Comme elle est lourde, il la tient par le milieu, fortement. Regardez la marque de ses crocs! Elle vous indiquera que la mâchoire est trop large pour que le chien appartienne à la race des terriers et trop étroite pour qu'on le range dans celle des mastiffs. C'est peut-être,... oui, parbleu! c'est un épagneul!»

Tout en parlant, Holmes s'était levé et arpentait la pièce. Il s'arrêta devant la fenêtre. Sa voix avait

[1] Member of royal college Surgeons. (Membre du collège royal des chirurgiens.)

was such a ring of conviction in his voice that I glanced up in surprise.

"My dear fellow, how can you possibly be so sure of that?"

"For the very simple reason that I see the dog himself on our very door-step, and there is the ring of its owner. Don't move, I beg you, Watson. He is a professional brother of yours, and your presence may be of assistance to me. Now is the dramatic moment of fate, Watson, when you hear a step upon the stair which is walking into your life, and you know not whether for good or ill. What does Dr. James Mortimer, the man of science, ask of Sherlock Holmes, the specialist in crime? Come in!"

The appearance of our visitor was a surprise to me, since I had expected a typical country practitioner. He was a very tall, thin man, with a long nose like a beak, which jutted out between two keen, grey eyes, set closely together and sparkling brightly from behind a pair of gold-rimmed glasses. He was clad in a professional but rather slovenly fashion, for his frock-coat was dingy and his trousers frayed. Though young, his long back was already bowed, and he walked with a forward thrust of his head and a general air of peering benevolence.

As he entered his eyes fell upon the stick in Holmes's hand, and he ran towards it with an exclamation of joy.

"I am so very glad," said he. "I was not sure whether I had left it here or in the Shipping Office. I would not lose that stick for the world."

"A presentation, I see," said Holmes.

"Yes, sir."

"From Charing Cross Hospital?"

"From one or two friends there on the occasion of my marriage."

"Dear, dear, that's bad!" said Holmes, shaking his head.

Dr. Mortimer blinked through his glasses in mild astonishment.

"Why was it bad?"

"Only that you have disarranged our little deductions. Your marriage, you say?"

"Yes, sir. I married, and so left the hospital, and with it all hopes of a consulting practice. It was necessary to make a home of my own."

"Come, come, we are not so far wrong, after all," said Holmes. "And now, Dr. James Mortimer—"

"Mister, sir, Mister—a humble M.R.C.S."

un tel accent de conviction que la surprise me fit lever la tête.

«Comment, mon cher ami, dis-je, pouvez-vous affirmer cela?

— Pour la raison bien simple que j'aperçois le chien à notre porte et que voilà le coup de sonnette de son maître.... Restez, Watson; le docteur Mortimer est un de vos confrères, votre présence me sera peut-être utile.... Que vient demander le docteur Mortimer, homme de science, à Sherlock Holmes, le spécialiste en matière criminelle?... Entrez!»

M'attendant à voir le type du médecin de campagne que j'avais dépeint, l'apparition de notre visiteur me causa une vive surprise. Le docteur Mortimer était grand, mince, avec un long nez crochu qui débordait entre deux yeux gris, perçants, rapprochés l'un de l'autre et étincelants derrière des lunettes d'or. Il portait le costume traditionnel – mais quelque peu négligé – adopté par ceux de sa profession; sa redingote était de couleur sombre et son pantalon frangé. Quoique jeune, son dos se voûtait déjà: il marchait la tête penchée en avant et son visage respirait un air de grande bonhomie.

En entrant, il aperçut sa canne dans les mains de Holmes et il se précipita avec une expression joyeuse:

«Quel bonheur! fit-il. Je ne me souvenais plus où je l'avais laissée.... Je ne voudrais pas perdre cette canne pour tout l'or du monde.

— Un cadeau, n'est-ce pas? interrogea Holmes.

— Oui monsieur.

— De l'hôpital de Charing Cross?

— De quelques amis que j'y comptais... à l'occasion de mon mariage.

— Ah! fichtre! c'est ennuyeux, répliqua Holmes, en secouant la tête.»

Le docteur Mortimer, légèrement étonné, cligna les yeux.

«Qu'y a-t-il d'ennuyeux?

— Vous avez dérangé nos petites déductions.... Vous dites: votre mariage?

— Oui. Pour me marier, j'ai quitté l'hôpital.... Je désirais me créer un intérieur.

— Allons, fit Holmes, après tout, nous ne nous sommes pas trompés de beaucoup.... Et maintenant, docteur Mortimer....

— Non, monsieur! M. Mortimer, tout bonnement!... Un humble M. R. C. S.

"And a man of precise mind, evidently."

"A dabbler in science, Mr. Holmes, a picker up of shells on the shores of the great unknown ocean. I presume that it is Mr. Sherlock Holmes whom I am addressing and not—"

"No, this is my friend Dr. Watson."

"Glad to meet you, sir. I have heard your name mentioned in connection with that of your friend. You interest me very much, Mr. Holmes. I had hardly expected so dolichocephalic a skull or such well-marked supra-orbital development. Would you have any objection to my running my finger along your parietal fissure? A cast of your skull, sir, until the original is available, would be an ornament to any anthropological museum. It is not my intention to be fulsome, but I confess that I covet your skull."

Sherlock Holmes waved our strange visitor into a chair.

"You are an enthusiast in your line of thought, I perceive, sir, as I am in mine," said he. "I observe from your forefinger that you make your own cigarettes. Have no hesitation in lighting one."

The man drew out paper and tobacco and twirled the one up in the other with surprising dexterity. He had long, quivering fingers as agile and restless as the antennæ of an insect.

Holmes was silent, but his little darting glances showed me the interest which he took in our curious companion.

"I presume, sir," said he at last, "that it was not merely for the purpose of examining my skull that you have done me the honour to call here last night and again today?"

"No, sir, no; though I am happy to have had the opportunity of doing that as well. I came to you, Mr. Holmes, because I recognized that I am myself an unpractical man and because I am suddenly confronted with a most serious and extraordinary problem. Recognizing, as I do, that you are the second highest expert in Europe—"

"Indeed, sir! May I inquire who has the honour to be the first?" asked Holmes with some asperity.

"To the man of precisely scientific mind the work of Monsieur Bertillon must always appeal strongly."

"Then had you not better consult him?"

"I said, sir, to the precisely scientific mind. But

— Et, évidemment, un homme d'un esprit pratique.

— Oh! un simple minus habens, un ramasseur de coquilles sur le rivage du grand océan inconnu de la science. C'est à M. Sherlock Holmes que je parle?....

— Oui; et voici mon ami, le docteur Watson.

— Très heureux de faire votre connaissance, monsieur. J'ai souvent entendu prononcer votre nom avec celui de votre ami. Vous m'intéressez vivement, monsieur Holmes. J'ai rarement vu un crâne aussi dolichocéphalique que le vôtre, ni des bosses supra-orbitales aussi développées. Voulez-vous me permettre de promener mon doigt sur votre suture pariétale? Un moulage de votre crâne, monsieur, en attendant la pièce originale, ferait l'ornement d'un musée d'anthropologie. Loin de moi toute pensée macabre! Mais je convoite votre crâne.»

Holmes montra une chaise à cet étrange visiteur.

«Vous êtes un enthousiaste de votre profession, comme je le suis de la mienne, dit-il. Je devine à votre index que vous fumez la cigarette... ne vous gênez pas pour en allumer une.»

Notre homme sortit de sa poche du papier et du tabac, et roula une cigarette avec une surprenante dextérité. Il avait de longs doigts, aussi agiles et aussi mobiles que les antennes d'un insecte.

Holmes demeurait silencieux; mais ses regards, obstinément fixés sur notre singulier compagnon, me prouvaient à quel point celui-ci l'intéressait.

Enfin Holmes parla. «Je présume, monsieur, dit-il, que ce n'est pas seulement pour examiner mon crâne que vous m'avez fait l'honneur de venir me voir hier et de revenir aujourd'hui?

— Non, monsieur, non,... bien que je me réjouisse de cet examen. Je suis venu, monsieur Holmes, parce que je reconnais que je ne suis pas un homme pratique et ensuite parce que les circonstances m'ont placé en face d'un problème aussi grave que mystérieux. Je vous considère comme le second parmi les plus habiles experts de l'Europe....

— Vraiment! Puis-je vous demander le nom de celui que vous mettez en première ligne? fit Holmes avec un peu d'amertume.

— L'œuvre de M. Bertillon doit fort impressionner l'esprit de tout homme amoureux de précision scientifique.

— Alors, pourquoi ne le consultez-vous pas?

— J'ai parlé de précision scientifique. Mais, en

as a practical man of affairs it is acknowledged that you stand alone. I trust, sir, that I have not inadvertently—"

"Just a little," said Holmes. "I think, Dr. Mortimer, you would do wisely if without more ado you would kindly tell me plainly what the exact nature of the problem is in which you demand my assistance."

ce qui concerne la science pratique, il n'y a que vous.... J'espère, monsieur, que je n'ai pas involontairement....

— Un peu, interrompit Holmes. Il me semble, docteur, que, laissant ceci de côté, vous feriez bien de m'expliquer exactement le problème pour la solution duquel vous réclamez mon assistance.»

CHAPTER 2. THE CURSE OF THE BASKERVILLES

"I have in my pocket a manuscript," said Dr. James Mortimer.

"I observed it as you entered the room," said Holmes.

"It is an old manuscript."

"Early eighteenth century, unless it is a forgery."

"How can you say that, sir?"

"You have presented an inch or two of it to my examination all the time that you have been talking. It would be a poor expert who could not give the date of a document within a decade or so. You may possibly have read my little monograph upon the subject. I put that at 1730."

"The exact date is 1742." Dr. Mortimer drew it from his breast-pocket. "This family paper was committed to my care by Sir Charles Baskerville, whose sudden and tragic death some three months ago created so much excitement in Devonshire. I may say that I was his personal friend as well as his medical attendant. He was a strong-minded man, sir, shrewd, practical, and as unimaginative as I am myself. Yet he took this document very seriously, and his mind was prepared for just such an end as did eventually overtake him."

Holmes stretched out his hand for the manuscript and flattened it upon his knee.

"You will observe, Watson, the alternative use of the long s and the short. It is one of several indications which enabled me to fix the date."

I looked over his shoulder at the yellow paper and the faded script. At the head was written: "Baskerville Hall," and below in large, scrawling figures: "1742."

"It appears to be a statement of some sort."

"Yes, it is a statement of a certain legend which runs in the Baskerville family."

"But I understand that it is something more modern and practical upon which you wish to consult me?"

"Most modern. A most practical, pressing matter, which must be decided within twenty-four hours. But the manuscript is short and is intimate-

CHAPITRE 2. LA MALÉDICTION DES BASKERVILLE

«J'ai dans ma poche un manuscrit, commença le docteur.

— Je l'ai aperçu quand vous êtes entré, dit Holmes.

— Il est très vieux.

— Du xviiie siècle — à moins qu'il ne soit faux.

— Comment le savez-vous?

— Pendant que vous parliez, j'en ai entrevu cinq ou six centimètres. Il serait un piètre expert celui qui, après cela, ne pourrait préciser la date d'un document à une dizaine d'années près. Avez-vous lu ma petite monographie sur ce sujet?... Je place le vôtre en 1730.

— Il est exactement de 1742, répondit Mortimer, en sortant le manuscrit de sa poche. Ces papiers m'ont été confiés par sir Charles Baskerville, dont la mort tragique a causé dernièrement un si grand émoi dans le Devonshire. J'étais à la fois son médecin et son ami. D'un esprit supérieur, pénétrant, pratique, il se montrait aussi peu imaginatif que je le suis beaucoup moi-même. Cependant il ajoutait très sérieusement foi au récit contenu dans ce document, et cette foi le préparait admirablement au genre de mort qui l'a frappé.»

Holmes prit le manuscrit et le déplia sur son genou.

«Vous remarquerez, Watson, me dit-il, que les s sont indifféremment longs et courts. C'est une des quelques indications qui m'ont permis de préciser la date.»

Par-dessus son épaule, je regardai le papier jauni et l'écriture presque effacée. En tête, on avait écrit: «Baskerville Hall», et, au-dessous, en gros chiffres mal formés: «1742».

«Je vois qu'il s'agit de sortilège, fit Holmes.

— Oui; c'est la narration d'une légende qui court sur la famille de Baskerville.

— Je croyais que vous désiriez me consulter sur un fait plus moderne et plus précis?

— Très moderne.... Et sur un point précis, urgent, qu'il faut élucider dans les vingt-quatre heures. Mais ce manuscrit est court et intimement ly connected with the affair. With your permission I will read it to you."

Holmes leaned back in his chair, placed his finger-tips together, and closed his eyes, with an air of resignation.

Dr. Mortimer turned the manuscript to the light and read in a high, cracking voice the following curious, old-world narrative:

"Of the origin of the Hound of the Baskervilles there have been many statements, yet as I come in a direct line from Hugo Baskerville, and as I had the story from my father, who also had it from his, I have set it down with all belief that it occurred even as is here set forth. And I would have you believe, my sons, that the same Justice which punishes sin may also most graciously forgive it, and that no ban is so heavy but that by prayer and repentance it may be removed. Learn then from this story not to fear the fruits of the past, but rather to be circumspect in the future, that those foul passions whereby our family has suffered so grievously may not again be loosed to our undoing.

"Know then that in the time of the Great Rebellion (the history of which by the learned Lord Clarendon I most earnestly commend to your attention) this Manor of Baskerville was held by Hugo of that name, nor can it be gainsaid that he was a most wild, profane, and godless man. This, in truth, his neighbours might have pardoned, seeing that saints have never flourished in those parts, but there was in him a certain wanton and cruel humour which made his name a by-word through the West.

"It chanced that this Hugo came to love (if, indeed, so dark a passion may be known under so bright a name) the daughter of a yeoman who held lands near the Baskerville estate. But the young maiden, being discreet and of good repute, would ever avoid him, for she feared his evil name.

"So it came to pass that one Michaelmas this Hugo, with five or six of his idle and wick-

lié à l'affaire. Avec votre permission, je vais vous le lire.»

Holmes s'enfonça dans son fauteuil, joignit les mains et ferma les yeux, dans une attitude résignée.

Le docteur Mortimer exposa le document à la lumière et lut d'une voix claire et sonore le curieux récit suivant:

«On a parlé souvent du chien des Baskerville. Comme je descends en ligne directe de Hugo Baskerville et que je tiens cette histoire de mon père, qui la tenait lui-même du sien, je l'ai écrite avec une conviction sincère en sa véracité. Je voudrais que mes descendants crussent que la même justice qui punit le péché sait aussi le pardonner miséricordieusement, et qu'il n'existe pas de si terrible malédiction que ne puissent racheter le repentir et les prières. Je voudrais que, pour leur salut, mes petits enfants apprissent, non pas à redouter les suites du passé, mais à devenir plus circonspects dans l'avenir et à réprouver les détestables passions qui ont valu à notre famille de si douloureuses épreuves.

«Au temps de notre grande révolution, le manoir de Baskerville appartenait à Hugo, de ce nom, homme impie et dissolu. Ses voisins lui auraient pardonné ces défauts, car la contrée n'a jamais produit de saints; mais sa cruauté et ses débauches étaient devenues proverbiales dans la province.

«Il arriva que Hugo s'éprit d'amour (si, dans ce cas, l'emploi de ce mot ne constitue pas une profanation) pour la fille d'un cultivateur voisin. La demoiselle, réservée et de bonne réputation, l'évitait, effrayée par son mauvais renom.

«Une veille de Saint-Michel, Hugo, de concert avec cinq ou six de ses compagnons de ed companions, stole down upon the farm and carried off the maiden, her father and brothers being from home, as he well knew. When they had brought her to the Hall the maiden was placed in an upper chamber, while Hugo and his friends sat down to a long carouse, as was their nightly custom.

"Now, the poor lass upstairs was like to have her wits turned at the singing and shouting and terrible oaths which came up to her from below, for they say that the words used by Hugo Baskerville, when he was in wine, were such as might blast the man who said them. At last in the stress of her fear she did that which might have daunted the bravest or most active man, for by the aid of the growth of ivy which covered (and still covers) the south wall she came down from under the eaves, and so homeward across the moor, there being three leagues betwixt the Hall and her father's farm.

"It chanced that some little time later Hugo left his guests to carry food and drink—with other worse things, perchance—to his captive, and so found the cage empty and the bird escaped. Then, as it would seem, he became as one that hath a devil, for, rushing down the stairs into the dining-hall, he sprang upon the great table, flagons and trenchers flying before him, and he cried aloud before all the company that he would that very night render his body and soul to the Powers of Evil if he might but overtake the wench. And while the revellers stood aghast at the fury of the man, one more wicked or, it may be, more drunken than the rest, cried out that they should put the hounds upon her.

"Whereat Hugo ran from the house, crying to his grooms that they should saddle his mare and unkennel the pack, and giving the hounds a kerchief of the maid's, he swung them to the line, and so off full cry in the moonlight over the moor.

"Now, for some space the revellers stood agape, unable to understand all that had been done in such haste. But anon their bemused wits awoke to the nature of the deed which was like to be done upon the moorlands. Everything was now in an uproar, some calling for their pistols, some for their horses, and some for another flask of wine. But at length some sense came back to their crazed minds,

plaisir, se rendit à la ferme et enleva la jeune fille, en l'absence de son père et de ses frères. Ils la conduisirent au château et l'enfermèrent dans un donjon; puis ils descendirent pour achever la nuit en faisant ripaille, selon leur coutume.

«De sa prison, la pauvre enfant frissonnait, au bruit des chants et des blasphèmes qui montaient jusqu'à elle. Dans sa détresse, elle tenta ce qui aurait fait reculer les plus audacieux: à l'aide du lierre qui garnissait le mur, elle se laissa glisser le long de la gouttière et s'enfuit par la lande vers la maison de son père, distante d'environ trois lieues.

«Quelque temps après, Hugo quitta ses amis pour monter un peu de nourriture à sa prisonnière. Il trouva la cage vide et l'oiseau envolé. Alors, on l'aurait dit possédé du démon. Dégringolant l'escalier, il entra comme un fou dans la salle à manger, sauta sur la table et jura devant toute la compagnie que, si cette nuit même il pouvait s'emparer de nouveau de la fugitive, il se donnerait au diable corps et âme. Tous les convives le regardaient, ahuris. À ce moment l'un deux, plus méchant — ou plus ivre — que les autres, proposa de lancer les chiens sur les traces de la jeune fille.

«Hugo sortit du château, ordonna aux valets d'écurie de seller sa jument, aux piqueurs de lâcher la meute et, après avoir jeté aux chiens un mouchoir de la prisonnière, il les mit sur le pied. L'homme, en jurant, les bêtes, en hurlant, dévalèrent vers la plaine, sous la clarté morne de la lune.

«Tout ceci s'était accompli si rapidement que, tout d'abord, les convives ne comprirent pas. Mais bientôt la lumière se fit dans leur esprit. Ce fut alors un vacarme infernal; les uns demandaient leurs pistolets, les autres leur cheval, ceux-ci de nouvelles bouteilles de vin. Enfin, le calme rétabli, la poursuite commença. Les chevaux couraient ventre à terre sur la route que la jeune fille avait dû prendre pour and the whole of them, thirteen in number, took horse and started in pursuit. The moon shone clear above them, and they rode swiftly abreast, taking that course which the maid must needs have taken if she were to reach her own home.

"They had gone a mile or two when they passed one of the night shepherds upon the moorlands, and they cried to him to know if he had seen the hunt. And the man, as the story goes, was so crazed with fear that he could scarce speak, but at last he said that he had indeed seen the unhappy maiden, with the hounds upon her track.

"'But I have seen more than that,' said he, 'for Hugo Baskerville passed me upon his black mare, and there ran mute behind him such a hound of hell as God forbid should ever be at my heels.'

"So the drunken squires cursed the shepherd and rode onward. But soon their skins turned cold, for there came a galloping across the moor, and the black mare, dabbled with white froth, went past with trailing bridle and empty saddle.

"Then the revellers rode close together, for a great fear was on them, but they still followed over the moor, though each, had he been alone, would have been right glad to have turned his horse's head.

"Riding slowly in this fashion they came at last upon the hounds. These, though known for their valour and their breed, were whimpering in a cluster at the head of a deep dip or goyal, as we call it, upon the moor, some slinking away and some, with starting hackles and staring eyes, gazing down the narrow valley before them.

"The company had come to a halt, more sober men, as you may guess, than when they started. The most of them would by no means advance, but three of them, the boldest, or it may be the most drunken, rode forward down the goyal. Now, it opened into a broad space in which stood two of those great stones, still to be seen there, which were set by certain forgotten peoples in the days of old. The moon was shining bright upon the clearing, and there in the centre lay the unhappy maid where she had fallen, dead of fear and of fatigue.

"But it was not the sight of her body, nor yet was it that of the body of Hugo Baskerville

rentrer directement chez elle.

«Les amis de Hugo galopaient depuis deux kilomètres, quand ils rencontrèrent un berger qui faisait paître son troupeau sur la lande. En passant, ils lui crièrent s'il avait vu la bête de chasse. On raconte que la peur empêcha l'homme de répondre immédiatement. Cependant il finit par dire qu'il avait aperçu l'infortunée jeune fille poursuivie par les chiens.

«— J'ai vu plus que cela, ajouta-t-il; j'ai vu galoper en silence, sur les talons du sire de Baskerville, un grand chien noir, que je prie le ciel de ne jamais découpler sur moi.»

«Les ivrognes envoyèrent le berger à tous les diables et continuèrent leur course. Mais le sang se figea bientôt dans leurs veines. Le galop d'un cheval résonna sur la lande et la jument de Hugo, toute blanche d'écume, passa près d'eux, les rênes flottantes, la selle vide.

«Dominés par la peur, les cavaliers se serrèrent les uns contre les autres; mais ils ne cessèrent pas la poursuite, quoique chacun, s'il eût été seul, eût volontiers tourné bride.

«Ils arrivèrent enfin sur les chiens. La meute était réputée, pour sa vaillance et ses bonnes qualités de race; cependant les chiens hurlaient lugubrement autour d'un buisson poussé sur le bord d'un profond ravin. Quelques-uns faisaient mine de s'éloigner, tandis que d'autres, le poil hérissé, les yeux en fureur, regardaient en bas, dans la vallée.

«La compagnie, complètement dégrisée, s'arrêta. Personne n'osant avancer, les trois plus audacieux descendirent le ravin. La lune éclairait faiblement l'étroite vallée formée par le fond de la gorge. Au milieu, la pauvre jeune fille gisait inanimée, à l'endroit où elle était tombée, morte de fatigue ou de peur.

«Ce ne fut ni son cadavre, ni celui de Hugo, étendu sans mouvement à quelques pas de là,

There in the centre lay the unhappy maid where she had fallen
Au milieu, la pauvre jeune fille gisait inanimée, à l'endroit où elle était tombée

lying near her, which raised the hair upon the heads of these three dare-devil roysterers, but it was that, standing over Hugo, and plucking at his throat, there stood a foul thing, a great, black beast, shaped like a hound, yet larger than any hound that ever mortal eye has rested upon.

"And even as they looked the thing tore the throat out of Hugo Baskerville, on which, as it turned its blazing eyes and dripping jaws upon them, the three shrieked with fear and rode for dear life, still screaming, across the moor.

"One, it is said, died that very night of what he had seen, and the other twain were but broken men for the rest of their days.

"Such is the tale, my sons, of the coming of the hound which is said to have plagued the family so sorely ever since. If I have set it down it is because that which is clearly known hath less terror than that which is but hinted at and guessed.

"Nor can it be denied that many of the family have been unhappy in their deaths, which have been sudden, bloody, and mysterious. Yet may we shelter ourselves in the infinite goodness of Providence, which would not forever punish the innocent beyond that third or fourth generation which is threatened in Holy Writ.

"To that Providence, my sons, I hereby commend you, and I counsel you by way of caution to forbear from crossing the moor in those dark hours when the powers of evil are exalted.

"[This from Hugo Baskerville to his sons Rodger and John, with instructions that they say nothing thereof to their sister Elizabeth.]"

qui effraya le plus les trois sacripants. Ce fut une horrible bête, noire, de grande taille, ressemblant à un chien, mais à un chien ayant des proportions jusqu'alors inconnues.

«La bête tenait ses crocs enfoncés dans la gorge de Hugo. Au moment où les trois hommes s'approchaient, elle arracha un lambeau de chair du cou de Baskerville et tourna vers eux ses prunelles de feu et sa gueule rouge de sang.... Le trio, secoué par la peur, s'enfuit en criant.

«On prétend que l'un des trois hommes mourut dans la nuit; les deux autres restèrent frappés de folie jusqu'à leur mort.

«C'est ainsi, mes enfants, que l'on raconte la première apparition du chien qui, depuis cette époque, a, dit-on, si cruellement éprouvé notre famille. J'ai écrit cette histoire, parce que les amplifications et les suppositions inspirent toujours plus de terreur que les choses parfaitement définies.

«Plusieurs membres de la famille, on ne peut le nier, ont péri de mort violente, subite et mystérieuse. Aussi devons-nous nous confier à l'infinie bonté de la Providence qui punit rarement l'innocent au delà de la troisième ou de la quatrième génération, ainsi qu'il est dit dans l'Écriture sainte.

«Je vous recommande à cette Providence, mes chers enfants, et je vous conseille d'éviter, par mesure de prudence, de traverser la lande aux heures obscures où l'esprit du mal chemine.»

(De Hugo Baskerville à ses fils Roger et John, sous la recommandation expresse de n'en rien dire à leur sœur Élisabeth.)

When Dr. Mortimer had finished reading this singular narrative he pushed his spectacles up on his forehead and stared across at Mr. Sherlock Holmes. The latter yawned and tossed the end of his cigarette into the fire.

"Well?" said he.

"Do you not find it interesting?"

"To a collector of fairy tales."

Dr. Mortimer drew a folded newspaper out of his pocket.

Lorsque le docteur Mortimer eut achevé sa lecture, il remonta ses lunettes sur son front et regarda Sherlock Holmes. Ce dernier bâilla, jeta le bout de sa cigarette dans le feu et demanda laconiquement:

«Eh bien?

— Vous ne trouvez pas ce récit intéressant?

— Si; pour un amateur de contes de fées.»

Mortimer sortit de sa poche un journal soigneusement plié.

"Now, Mr. Holmes, we will give you something a little more recent. This is the Devon County Chronicle of May 14th of this year. It is a short account of the facts elicited at the death of Sir Charles Baskerville which occurred a few days before that date."

My friend leaned a little forward and his expression became intent. Our visitor readjusted his glasses and began:

«Maintenant, monsieur Holmes, fit-il, je vais vous lire quelque chose de plus récent. C'est un numéro de la Devon County Chronicle, publié le 14 mai de cette année et contenant les détails de la mort de sir Charles Baskerville, survenue quelques jours avant cette date.»

Mon ami prit une attitude moins indifférente. Le docteur rajusta ses lunettes et commença:

"The recent sudden death of Sir Charles Baskerville, whose name has been mentioned as the probable Liberal candidate for Mid-Devon at the next election, has cast a gloom over the county. Though Sir Charles had resided at Baskerville Hall for a comparatively short period his amiability of character and extreme generosity had won the affection and respect of all who had been brought into contact with him.

"In these days of *nouveaux riches* it is refreshing to find a case where the scion of an old county family which has fallen upon evil days is able to make his own fortune and to bring it back with him to restore the fallen grandeur of his line.

"Sir Charles, as is well known, made large sums of money in South African speculation. More wise than those who go on until the wheel turns against them, he realised his gains and returned to England with them. It is only two years since he took up his residence at Baskerville Hall, and it is common talk how large were those schemes of reconstruction and improvement which have been interrupted by his death. Being himself childless, it was his openly expressed desire that the whole countryside should, within his own lifetime, profit by his good fortune, and many will have personal reasons for bewailing his untimely end. His generous donations to local and county charities have been frequently chronicled in these columns.

"The circumstances connected with the death of Sir Charles cannot be said to have been entirely cleared up by the inquest, but at least enough has been done to dispose of those rumours to which local superstition has given rise. There is no reason whatever to suspect foul play, or to imagine that death could be from any but natural causes.

"Sir Charles was a widower, and a man who

«La mort récente de sir Charles Baskerville, désigné comme le candidat probable du parti libéral aux prochaines élections du Mid-Devon, a attristé tout le comté. Quoique sir Charles n'ait résidé à Baskerville Hall que peu de temps, l'amabilité de ses manières et sa grande générosité lui avaient gagné l'affection et le respect de tous ceux qui le connaissaient.

«En ces temps de «nouveaux riches», il est réconfortant de voir des rejetons d'anciennes familles ayant traversé de mauvais jours reconstituer leur fortune et restaurer l'antique grandeur de leur maison.

«On sait que sir Charles avait gagné beaucoup d'argent dans l'Afrique du Sud. Plus sage que ceux qui poursuivent leurs spéculations jusqu'à ce que la chance tourne contre eux, il avait réalisé ses bénéfices et était revenu en Angleterre. Il habitait Baskerville depuis deux ans et nourrissait le grandiose projet de reconstruire le château et d'améliorer le domaine, projet que la mort vient d'interrompre. N'ayant pas d'enfants, il voulait que tout le pays profitât de sa fortune, et ils sont nombreux ceux qui déplorent sa fin prématurée. Nous avons souvent relaté dans ces colonnes ses dons généreux à toutes les œuvres charitables du comté.

«L'enquête n'a pu préciser les circonstances qui ont entouré la mort de sir Charles Baskerville; mais, au moins, elle a dissipé certaines rumeurs engendrées par la superstition publique.

«Sir Charles était veuf; il passait pour

may be said to have been in some ways of an eccentric habit of mind. In spite of his considerable wealth he was simple in his personal tastes, and his indoor servants at Baskerville Hall consisted of a married couple named Barrymore, the husband acting as butler and the wife as housekeeper. Their evidence, corroborated by that of several friends, tends to show that Sir Charles's health has for some time been impaired, and points especially to some affection of the heart, manifesting itself in changes of colour, breathlessness, and acute attacks of nervous depression. Dr. James Mortimer, the friend and medical attendant of the deceased, has given evidence to the same effect.

"The facts of the case are simple. Sir Charles Baskerville was in the habit every night before going to bed of walking down the famous yew alley of Baskerville Hall. The evidence of the Barrymores shows that this had been his custom.

"On the fourth of May Sir Charles had declared his intention of starting next day for London, and had ordered Barrymore to prepare his luggage. That night he went out as usual for his nocturnal walk, in the course of which he was in the habit of smoking a cigar.

"He never returned.

"At twelve o'clock Barrymore, finding the hall door still open, became alarmed, and, lighting a lantern, went in search of his master.

"The day had been wet, and Sir Charles's footmarks were easily traced down the alley. Halfway down this walk there is a gate which leads out on to the moor. There were indications that Sir Charles had stood for some little time here. He then proceeded down the alley, and it was at the far end of it that his body was discovered.

"One fact which has not been explained is the statement of Barrymore that his master's footprints altered their character from the time that he passed the moor-gate, and that he appeared from thence onward to have been walking upon his toes.

"One Murphy, a gipsy horse-dealer, was on the moor at no great distance at the time, but he appears by his own confession to have been the worse for drink. He declares that he heard cries but is unable to state from what direction they came. No signs of violence were to be discovered upon Sir Charles's person, and though

quelque peu excentrique. Malgré sa fortune considérable, il vivait très simplement. Son personnel domestique consistait en un couple, nommé Barrymore: le mari servant de valet de chambre et la femme, de bonne à tout faire. Leur témoignage, confirmé par celui de plusieurs amis, tend à montrer que, depuis quelque temps, la santé de sir Charles était fort ébranlée. Il souffrait de troubles cardiaques se manifestant par des altérations du teint, de la suffocation et des accès de dépression nerveuse. Le docteur Mortimer, ami et médecin du défunt, a témoigné dans le même sens.

«Les faits sont d'une grande simplicité. Tous les soirs, avant de se coucher, sir Charles avait l'habitude de se promener dans la fameuse allée des Ifs, de Baskerville Hall. La déposition des époux Barrymore l'a pleinement établi.

«Le 4 mai, sir Charles fît part de son intention bien arrêtée de partir le lendemain pour Londres. Il donna l'ordre à Barrymore de préparer ses bagages. Le soir, il sortit pour sa promenade nocturne, pendant laquelle il fumait toujours un cigare.

«On ne le vit pas revenir.

«À minuit, Barrymore, trouvant encore ouverte la porte du château, s'alarma et, allumant une lanterne, il se mit à la recherche de son maître.

«Il avait plu dans la journée; les pas de sir Charles s'étaient imprimés dans l'allée. Au milieu de cette allée, une porte conduit sur la lande. Des empreintes plus profondes indiquaient que sir Charles avait stationné à cet endroit. Ensuite il avait dû reprendre sa marche, car on ne retrouva son cadavre que beaucoup plus loin.

«Il est un point de la déclaration de Barrymore qui reste encore inexplicable: il paraîtrait que la forme des empreintes s'était modifiée à partir du moment où sir Charles Baskerville avait repris sa promenade. Il semble n'avoir plus marché que sur la pointe des pieds.

«Un certain Murphy — un bohémien — se trouvait à cette heure tout près de là, sur la lande; mais, d'après son propre aveu, il était complètement ivre. Il déclare cependant avoir entendu des cris, sans pouvoir indiquer d'où ils venaient. On n'a découvert sur le corps de sir Charles aucune trace de violence, quoique the doctor's evidence pointed to an almost incredible facial distortion—so great that Dr. Mortimer refused at first to believe that it was indeed his friend and patient who lay before him—it was explained that that is a symptom which is not unusual in cases of dyspnœa and death from cardiac exhaustion. This explanation was borne out by the post-mortem examination, which showed long-standing organic disease, and the coroner's jury returned a verdict in accordance with the medical evidence.

"It is well that this is so, for it is obviously of the utmost importance that Sir Charles's heir should settle at the Hall and continue the good work which has been so sadly interrupted. Had the prosaic finding of the coroner not finally put an end to the romantic stories which have been whispered in connection with the affair, it might have been difficult to find a tenant for Baskerville Hall.

"It is understood that the next of kin is Mr. Henry Baskerville, if he be still alive, the son of Sir Charles Baskerville's younger brother. The young man when last heard of was in America, and inquiries are being instituted with a view to informing him of his good fortune."

le rapport du médecin mentionne une convulsion anormale de la face — convulsion telle que le docteur Mortimer s'est refusé tout d'abord à reconnaître dans le cadavre le corps de son ami. On a remarqué fréquemment ce symptôme dans les cas de dyspnée et de mort occasionnée par l'usure du cœur. L'autopsie a corroboré ce diagnostic, et le jury du coroner a rendu un verdict conforme aux conclusions du rapport médical.

«Nous applaudissons à ce résultat. Il est, en effet, de la plus haute importance que l'héritier de sir Charles s'établisse au château et continue l'œuvre de son prédécesseur si tristement interrompue. Si la décision prosaïque du coroner n'avait pas définitivement détruit les histoires romanesques murmurées dans le public à propos de cette mort, on n'aurait pu louer Baskerville Hall.

«L'héritier du défunt — s'il vit encore — est M. Henry Baskerville, fils du plus jeune frère de sir Charles. Les dernières lettres du jeune homme étaient datées d'Amérique; on a télégraphié dans toutes les directions pour le prévenir de l'héritage qui lui échoit.»

Dr. Mortimer refolded his paper and replaced it in his pocket.

"Those are the public facts, Mr. Holmes, in connection with the death of Sir Charles Baskerville."

"I must thank you," said Sherlock Holmes, "for calling my attention to a case which certainly presents some features of interest. I had observed some newspaper comment at the time, but I was exceedingly preoccupied by that little affair of the Vatican cameos, and in my anxiety to oblige the Pope I lost touch with several interesting English cases. This article, you say, contains all the public facts?"

"It does."

"Then let me have the private ones."

He leaned back, put his finger-tips together, and assumed his most impassive and judicial expression.

"In doing so," said Dr. Mortimer, who had begun to show signs of some strong emotion, "I am telling that which I have not confided to anyone. My motive for withholding it from the coroner's inquiry is that a man of science shrinks from plac-

Le docteur Mortimer replia son journal et le replaça dans sa poche.

«Tels sont les faits de notoriété publique, monsieur Holmes, dit-il.

— Je vous remercie, dit Sherlock, d'avoir appelé mon attention sur ce cas, certainement intéressant par quelques points.... Ainsi donc cet article résume tout ce que le public connaît?

— Oui.

— Apprenez-moi maintenant ce qu'il ne connaît pas.»

Holmes se renversa de nouveau dans son fauteuil et son visage reprit son expression grave et impassible.

«En obtempérant à votre désir, fit le docteur Mortimer, qui commençait déjà à donner les signes d'une violente émotion, je vais vous raconter ce que je n'ai confié à personne. Je me suis tu devant le coroner, parce qu'un homme de science y ing himself in the public position of seeming to indorse a popular superstition. I had the further motive that Baskerville Hall, as the paper says, would certainly remain untenanted if anything were done to increase its already rather grim reputation. For both these reasons I thought that I was justified in telling rather less than I knew, since no practical good could result from it, but with you there is no reason why I should not be perfectly frank.

"The moor is very sparsely inhabited, and those who live near each other are thrown very much together. For this reason I saw a good deal of Sir Charles Baskerville. With the exception of Mr. Frankland, of Lafter Hall, and Mr. Stapleton, the naturalist, there are no other men of education within many miles.

"Sir Charles was a retiring man, but the chance of his illness brought us together, and a community of interests in science kept us so. He had brought back much scientific information from South Africa, and many a charming evening we have spent together discussing the comparative anatomy of the Bushman and the Hottentot.

"Within the last few months it became increasingly plain to me that Sir Charles's nervous system was strained to the breaking point. He had taken this legend which I have read you exceedingly to heart—so much so that, although he would walk in his own grounds, nothing would induce him to go out upon the moor at night. Incredible as it may appear to you, Mr. Holmes, he was honestly convinced that a dreadful fate overhung his family, and certainly the records which he was able to give of his ancestors were not encouraging.

"The idea of some ghastly presence constantly haunted him, and on more than one occasion he has asked me whether I had on my medical journeys at night ever seen any strange creature or heard the baying of a hound. The latter question he put to me several times, and always with a voice which vibrated with excitement.

"I can well remember driving up to his house in the evening some three weeks before the fatal event. He chanced to be at his hall door. I had descended from my gig and was standing in front of him, when I saw his eyes fix themselves over my shoulder and stare past me with an expression of the most dreadful horror. I whisked round and had just time to catch a glimpse of something which I took to be a large black calf passing at the head of

regarde à deux fois avant d'endosser une superstition populaire... Moi aussi, je crois qu'il serait impossible de louer Baskerville Hall, si quelque chose venait en augmenter l'horrible réputation. Pour ces deux raisons, j'en ai dit moins que je n'en savais — il ne pouvait en résulter pratiquement rien de bon. Mais, avec vous, je n'ai plus les mêmes motifs de garder le silence.»

Et Mortimer nous fit le récit suivant:

«La lande est presque inhabitée, et ceux qui vivent dans le voisinage les uns des autres sont étroitement liés ensemble. Voilà la raison de mon intimité avec sir Charles Baskerville. À l'exception de M. Frankland, de Lafter Hall, et de M. Stapleton, le naturaliste, il n'y a pas, à plusieurs milles à la ronde, de gens bien élevés.

«Sir Charles se plaisait dans la retraite, mais sa maladie opéra entre nous un rapprochement qu'un commun amour de la science cimenta rapidement. Il avait apporté du sud de l'Afrique un grand nombre d'observations scientifiques et nous avons passé ensemble plus d'une bonne soirée à discuter l'anatomie comparée du Bushman et du Hottentot.

«Pendant les derniers mois de sa vie, je constatai la surexcitation progressive de son système nerveux. La légende que je viens de vous lire l'obsédait à tel point que rien au monde n'aurait pu l'amener à franchir la nuit la grille du château. Quelque incroyable que cela vous paraisse, il était sincèrement convaincu qu'une terrible fatalité pesait sur sa famille, et, malheureusement, les archives de sa maison étaient peu encourageantes.

«La pensée d'une présence occulte, incessante, le hantait. Bien souvent il me demanda si, au cours de mes sorties nocturnes, je n'avais jamais aperçu d'être fantastique ni entendu d'aboiements de chien. Il renouvela maintes fois cette dernière question — et toujours d'une voix vibrante d'émotion.

«Je me souviens parfaitement d'un incident qui a précédé sa mort de quelques semaines. Un soir, j'arrivai au château en voiture. Par hasard, sir Charles se trouvait sur sa porte. J'étais descendu de mon tilbury et je lui faisais face. Tout à coup ses regards passèrent par-dessus mon épaule et j'y lus aussitôt une expression de terreur. Je me retournai juste à temps pour distinguer confusément, au détour de la route, quelque chose que je pris pour un the drive.

"So excited and alarmed was he that I was compelled to go down to the spot where the animal had been and look around for it. It was gone, however, and the incident appeared to make the worst impression upon his mind.

"I stayed with him all the evening, and it was on that occasion, to explain the emotion which he had shown, that he confided to my keeping that narrative which I read to you when first I came. I mention this small episode because it assumes some importance in view of the tragedy which followed, but I was convinced at the time that the matter was entirely trivial and that his excitement had no justification.

"It was at my advice that Sir Charles was about to go to London. His heart was, I knew, affected, and the constant anxiety in which he lived, however chimerical the cause of it might be, was evidently having a serious effect upon his health. I thought that a few months among the distractions of town would send him back a new man. Mr. Stapleton, a mutual friend who was much concerned at his state of health, was of the same opinion. At the last instant came this terrible catastrophe.

"On the night of Sir Charles's death Barrymore the butler, who made the discovery, sent Perkins the groom on horseback to me, and as I was sitting up late I was able to reach Baskerville Hall within an hour of the event.

"I checked and corroborated all the facts which were mentioned at the inquest. I followed the footsteps down the yew alley, I saw the spot at the moor-gate where he seemed to have waited, I remarked the change in the shape of the prints after that point, I noted that there were no other footsteps save those of Barrymore on the soft gravel, and finally I carefully examined the body, which had not been touched until my arrival.

"Sir Charles lay on his face, his arms out, his fingers dug into the ground, and his features convulsed with some strong emotion to such an extent that I could hardly have sworn to his identity.

"There was certainly no physical injury of any kind. But one false statement was made by Barrymore at the inquest. He said that there were no traces upon the ground round the body. He did not observe any. But I did—some little distance off, but fresh and clear."

"Footprints?"

"Footprints."

énorme veau noir.

«Cette apparition émut tellement sir Charles qu'il courut à l'endroit où il avait vu l'animal et qu'il le chercha partout des yeux. Mais la bête avait disparu. Cet incident produisit une déplorable impression sur son esprit.

«Je passai toute la soirée avec lui, et ce fut pour expliquer l'émotion ressentie qu'il confia à ma garde l'écrit que je vous ai lu. Ce petit épisode n'a d'importance que par la tragédie qui a suivi; sur le moment, je n'y en attachai aucune et je jugeai puérile l'exaltation de mon ami.

«Enfin, sur mes instances, sir Charles se décida à partir pour Londres. Le cœur était atteint, et la constante angoisse qui le poignait — quelque chimérique qu'en fût la cause — avait une répercussion sur sa santé. Je pensais que les distractions de la ville le remettraient promptement. M. Stapleton, consulté, opina dans le même sens. Au dernier instant, la terrible catastrophe se produisit.

«La nuit du décès de sir Charles Baskerville, Barrymore, le valet de chambre qui avait fait la lugubre découverte, m'envoya chercher par un homme d'écurie. Je n'étais pas encore couché et, une heure plus tard, j'arrivais au château.

«Je contrôlai tous les faits mentionnés dans l'enquête: je suivis la trace des pas dans l'allée des Ifs et je vis à la grille l'endroit où le défunt s'était arrêté. À partir de cet endroit, je remarquai la nouvelle forme des empreintes. Sur le sable fin, il n'y avait d'autres pas que ceux de Barrymore; puis j'examinai attentivement le cadavre, auquel on n'avait pas encore touché.

«Sir Charles était étendu, la face contre terre, les bras en croix, les doigts crispés dans le sol et les traits tellement convulsés sous l'empire d'une violente émotion que j'aurais à peine osé certifier son identité.

«Le corps ne portait aucune blessure…. Mais la déposition de Barrymore était incomplète. Il a dit qu'auprès du cadavre il n'existait nulle trace de pas…. Il n'en avait pas vu…. Elles ne m'ont pas échappé, à moi… nettes et fraîches… à quelque distance du lieu de la scène!…

— Des empreintes de pas?

— Oui, des empreintes de pas.

"A man's or a woman's?"

Dr. Mortimer looked strangely at us for an instant, and his voice sank almost to a whisper as he answered.

"Mr. Holmes, they were the footprints of a gigantic hound!"

— D'homme ou de femme?»

Mortimer nous considéra une seconde d'une façon étrange. Sa voix n'était plus qu'un faible murmure, quand il répondit:

«Monsieur Holmes, j'ai reconnu l'empreinte d'une patte de chien gigantesque!»

CHAPTER 3. THE PROBLEM

I confess at these words a shudder passed through me. There was a thrill in the doctor's voice which showed that he was himself deeply moved by that which he told us. Holmes leaned forward in his excitement and his eyes had the hard, dry glitter which shot from them when he was keenly interested.

"You saw this?"

"As clearly as I see you."

"And you said nothing?"

"What was the use?"

"How was it that no one else saw it?"

"The marks were some twenty yards from the body and no one gave them a thought. I don't suppose I should have done so had I not known this legend."

"There are many sheep-dogs on the moor?"

"No doubt, but this was no sheep-dog."

"You say it was large?"

"Enormous."

"But it had not approached the body?"

"No."

"What sort of night was it?'

"Damp and raw."

"But not actually raining?"

"No."

"What is the alley like?"

"There are two lines of old yew hedge, twelve feet high and impenetrable. The walk in the centre is about eight feet across."

"Is there anything between the hedges and the walk?"

"Yes, there is a strip of grass about six feet broad on either side."

"I understand that the yew hedge is penetrated at one point by a gate?"

"Yes, the wicket-gate which leads on to the moor."

"Is there any other opening?"

"None."

"So that to reach the yew alley one either has to come down it from the house or else to enter it by

CHAPITRE 3. LE PROBLÈME

Je confesse que ces mots me causèrent un frisson. Il y avait dans la voix du docteur Mortimer un tremblement qui prouvait que son propre récit l'avait profondément ému. Penché en avant, Holmes l'écoutait avec, dans les yeux, cette lueur qui décèle toujours chez lui un vif intérêt.

«Vous avez vu cela? interrogea-t-il.

— Aussi nettement que je vous vois.

— Et vous n'en avez rien dit?

— Pourquoi en aurais-je parlé?

— Comment expliquez-vous que vous soyez le seul à avoir remarqué ces empreintes?

— Elles commençaient seulement à une vingtaine de mètres du cadavre... personne n'y avait fait attention. Si je n'avais pas connu la légende, il est probable que j'aurais agi comme tout le monde.

— Y a-t-il beaucoup de chiens de berger sur la lande?

— Beaucoup.... Mais celui-là n'était pas un chien de berger.

— Vous dites que vous le jugez de grande taille?

— Énorme.

— Et qu'il n'avait pas approché le cadavre?

— Non.

— Quelle nuit faisait-il?

— Humide et froide.

— Pleuvait-il?

— Non.

— Décrivez-moi l'allée des Ifs.

— Elle est formée par une double rangée de vieux ifs, hauts de douze pieds et absolument impénétrables. On se promène sur la partie comprise entre les arbustes, large de huit pieds.

— Entre les ifs et cette partie, sablée sans doute, n'y a-t-il rien?

— Si. Il existe, de chaque côté, une bande de gazon d'environ six pieds.

— La bordure d'ifs, m'avez-vous dit, est coupée par une porte?

— Oui... qui donne accès sur la lande.

— Il n'y a pas d'autre ouverture?

— Aucune.

— De telle sorte qu'on n'arrive à l'allée des Ifs que par la maison ou par cette porte?

the moor-gate?"

"There is an exit through a summer-house at the far end."

"Had Sir Charles reached this?"

"No; he lay about fifty yards from it."

"Now, tell me, Dr. Mortimer—and this is important—the marks which you saw were on the path and not on the grass?"

"No marks could show on the grass."

"Were they on the same side of the path as the moor-gate?"

"Yes; they were on the edge of the path on the same side as the moor-gate."

"You interest me exceedingly. Another point. Was the wicket-gate closed?"

"Closed and padlocked."

"How high was it?"

"About four feet high."

"Then anyone could have got over it?"

"Yes."

"And what marks did you see by the wicket-gate?"

"None in particular."

"Good heaven! Did no one examine?"

"Yes, I examined, myself."

"And found nothing?"

"It was all very confused. Sir Charles had evidently stood there for five or ten minutes."

"How do you know that?"

"Because the ash had twice dropped from his cigar."

"Excellent! This is a colleague, Watson, after our own heart. But the marks?"

"He had left his own marks all over that small patch of gravel. I could discern no others."

Sherlock Holmes struck his hand against his knee with an impatient gesture.

"If I had only been there!" he cried. "It is evidently a case of extraordinary interest, and one which presented immense opportunities to the scientific expert. That gravel page upon which I might have read so much has been long ere this smudged by the rain and defaced by the clogs of curious peasants. Oh, Dr. Mortimer, Dr. Mortimer, to think that you should not have called me in!

— On peut également s'y rendre par une serre construite à l'extrémité de l'allée.

— Sir Charles a-t-il poussé sa promenade jusque-là?

— Non, cinquante mètres le séparaient encore de cette serre.

— Maintenant, voudriez-vous me dire, docteur Mortimer, — et ce détail a son importance — si les empreintes que vous avez relevées se trouvaient sur le sable de l'allée ou sur le gazon?

— Je n'ai pu distinguer aucune empreinte sur le gazon.

— Existaient-elles seulement sur le même côté que la porte?

— Oui, sur le bord de l'allée sablée, du même côté que la porte.

— Vous m'intéressez excessivement.... Autre chose, cette porte était-elle fermée?

— Fermée et cadenassée.

— Quelle est sa hauteur?

— Quatre pieds.

— Alors, quelqu'un aurait pu la franchir?

— Facilement.

— Près de la porte, y avait-il des marques particulières?

— Non.

— Ah!... A-t-on fait des recherches de ce côté?

— Personne autre que moi.

— Et vous n'avez rien découvert?

— Sir Charles avait dû piétiner sur place. Évidemment, il était resté en cet endroit cinq ou dix minutes.

— Comment le savez-vous?

— Parce que, deux fois, les cendres de son cigare se sont détachées.

— Très bien déduit, approuva Holmes. Watson, reprit-il, voici un collègue selon notre cœur.... Mais ces marques?

— Le piétinement les avait rendues confuses. En dehors de l'empreinte des pas de sir Charles, il m'a été impossible d'en distinguer d'autres.»

De sa main, Sherlock Holmes frappa son genou dans un geste d'impatience.

«Encore si j'avais été là! s'écria-t-il. Le cas m'apparaît d'un intérêt palpitant. Cette page de gravier sur laquelle j'aurais pu lire tant de choses, la pluie et le sabot des paysans curieux l'auront faite indéchiffrable. Ah! docteur Mortimer, pourquoi ne m'avez-vous pas appelé? Vous êtes bien coupable!

You have indeed much to answer for."

"I could not call you in, Mr. Holmes, without disclosing these facts to the world, and I have already given my reasons for not wishing to do so. Besides, besides—"

"Why do you hesitate?"

"There is a realm in which the most acute and most experienced of detectives is helpless."

"You mean that the thing is supernatural?"

"I did not positively say so."

"No, but you evidently think it."

"Since the tragedy, Mr. Holmes, there have come to my ears several incidents which are hard to reconcile with the settled order of Nature."

"For example?"

"I find that before the terrible event occurred several people had seen a creature upon the moor which corresponds with this Baskerville demon, and which could not possibly be any animal known to science. They all agreed that it was a huge creature, luminous, ghastly, and spectral. I have cross-examined these men, one of them a hard-headed countryman, one a farrier, and one a moorland farmer, who all tell the same story of this dreadful apparition, exactly corresponding to the hell-hound of the legend. I assure you that there is a reign of terror in the district, and that it is a hardy man who will cross the moor at night."

"And you, a trained man of science, believe it to be supernatural?"

"I do not know what to believe."

Holmes shrugged his shoulders.

"I have hitherto confined my investigations to this world," said he. "In a modest way I have combated evil, but to take on the Father of Evil himself would, perhaps, be too ambitious a task. Yet you must admit that the footmark is material."

"The original hound was material enough to tug a man's throat out, and yet he was diabolical as well."

— Je ne pouvais vous appeler, monsieur Holmes, sans révéler tous ces faits, et je vous ai déjà donné les raisons pour lesquelles je désirais garder le silence. D'ailleurs… d'ailleurs….

— Pourquoi cette hésitation?

— Dans certain domaine, le détective le plus expérimenté et le plus subtil demeure impuissant.

— Insinuez-vous que ces faits appartiennent au domaine surnaturel?

— Je ne le dis pas positivement.

— Mais vous le pensez évidemment.

— Depuis le drame, monsieur Holmes, on m'a raconté divers incidents qu'il est malaisé de classer parmi les événements naturels.

— Par exemple?

— J'ai appris qu'avant la terrible nuit plusieurs personnes ont vu sur la lande un animal dont le signalement se rapportait à celui du démon des Baskerville…. L'animal ne rentre dans aucune espèce cataloguée. On convient qu'il avait un aspect épouvantable, fantastique, spectral. J'ai questionné ces gens, un paysan obtus, un maréchal ferrant et un fermier. Aucun n'a varié sur le portrait de la sinistre apparition. Elle incarnait bien exactement le chien vomi par l'enfer, d'après la légende. La terreur règne dans le district en souveraine maîtresse, et il pourrait se vanter d'être téméraire celui qui s'aventurerait la nuit sur la lande.

— Et vous, un homme de science, vous admettez une manifestation surnaturelle?

— Je ne sais que croire.»

Holmes haussa les épaules.

«Jusqu'ici, dit-il, j'ai borné mes investigations aux choses de ce monde. Dans la limite de mes faibles moyens, j'ai combattu le mal… mais ce serait une tâche bien ambitieuse que de s'attaquer au démon lui-même. Cependant, il vous faut bien admettre la matérialité des empreintes!

— Le chien originel était assez matériel pour déchiqueter le cou d'un homme, et néanmoins il était bien d'essence infernale!

"I see that you have quite gone over to the supernaturalists. But now, Dr. Mortimer, tell me this. If you hold these views, why have you come to consult me at all? You tell me in the same breath that it is useless to investigate Sir Charles's death, and that you desire me to do it."

"I did not say that I desired you to do it."

"Then, how can I assist you?"

"By advising me as to what I should do with Sir Henry Baskerville, who arrives at Waterloo Station"—Dr. Mortimer looked at his watch—"in exactly one hour and a quarter."

"He being the heir?"

"Yes. On the death of Sir Charles we inquired for this young gentleman and found that he had been farming in Canada. From the accounts which have reached us he is an excellent fellow in every way. I speak now not as a medical man but as a trustee and executor of Sir Charles's will."

"There is no other claimant, I presume?"

"None. The only other kinsman whom we have been able to trace was Rodger Baskerville, the youngest of three brothers of whom poor Sir Charles was the elder. The second brother, who died young, is the father of this lad Henry. The third, Rodger, was the black sheep of the family. He came of the old masterful Baskerville strain and was the very image, they tell me, of the family picture of old Hugo. He made England too hot to hold him, fled to Central America, and died there in 1876 of yellow fever. Henry is the last of the Baskervilles. In one hour and five minutes I meet him at Waterloo Station. I have had a wire that he arrived at Southampton this morning. Now, Mr. Holmes, what would you advise me to do with him?"

"Why should he not go to the home of his fathers?"

"It seems natural, does it not? And yet, consider that every Baskerville who goes there meets with an evil fate. I feel sure that if Sir Charles could have spoken with me before his death he would have warned me against bringing this, the last of the old race, and the heir to great wealth, to that deadly place. And yet it cannot be denied that the prosperity of the whole poor, bleak countryside depends upon his presence. All the good work which has been done by Sir Charles will crash to the ground if there is no tenant of the Hall. I fear

— Je vois que vous avez passé aux partisans du surnaturel.... Maintenant, répondez encore à ceci: Puisque vous pensez ainsi, pourquoi êtes-vous venu me consulter? Vous me demandez en même temps de ne pas rechercher les causes de la mort de sir Charles Baskerville et vous me priez de m'occuper de ces recherches.

— Je ne vous en ai pas prié.

— Alors en quoi puis-je vous aider?

— En m'indiquant l'attitude que je dois garder vis-à-vis de sir Henry Baskerville, qui arrive à Waterloo station — ici le docteur Mortimer tira sa montre — dans une heure un quart.

— Est-ce lui qui hérite?

— Oui. À la mort de sir Charles, nous avons fait une enquête sur ce jeune homme et nous avons appris qu'il se livrait à l'agriculture, au Canada. Les renseignements fournis sur son compte sont excellents à tous égards.... Je ne parle pas à cette heure comme le médecin, mais comme l'exécuteur testamentaire de sir Charles Baskerville.

— Il n'y a pas d'autres prétendants à la fortune du défunt, je présume?

— Pas d'autres, le seul parent dont nous ayons pu retrouver la trace se nomme — ou mieux se nommait Roger Baskerville, il était le troisième frère de sir Charles. Le second frère, mort jeune, n'a eu qu'un fils, Henry; on considérait le troisième frère, Roger, comme la brebis galeuse de la famille. Il perpétuait l'ancien type des Baskerville et continuait, m'a-t-on affirmé, les errements du vieil Hugo. Le séjour de l'Angleterre lui paraissant malsain, il s'expatria dans l'Amérique centrale, où il mourut de la fièvre jaune, en 1876, Henry est donc le dernier des Baskerville.... Dans une heure cinq minutes, je le rencontrerai à Waterloo station.... Il m'a télégraphié de Southampton qu'il arriverait ce matin.... Que dois-je faire, monsieur Holmes?

— Pourquoi n'irait-il pas dans la demeure de ses ancêtres?

— Cela semble tout naturel, n'est-ce pas? Et cependant il faut se souvenir que les Baskerville qui ont habité le château ont tous péri de mort violente. J'ai la conviction que, si sir Charles avait pu me parler avant son décès, il m'aurait instamment recommandé de ne pas y conduire le dernier représentant de sa race et l'héritier de sa grande fortune. D'autre part, il est incontestable que la prospérité de ce misérable pays dépend absolument de la présence de sir Henry. Tout le bien commencé par sir Charles sera perdu, si le château reste délest I should be swayed too much by my own obvious interest in the matter, and that is why I bring the case before you and ask for your advice."

Holmes considered for a little time.

"Put into plain words, the matter is this," said he. "In your opinion there is a diabolical agency which makes Dartmoor an unsafe abode for a Baskerville—that is your opinion?"

"At least I might go the length of saying that there is some evidence that this may be so."

"Exactly. But surely, if your supernatural theory be correct, it could work the young man evil in London as easily as in Devonshire. A devil with merely local powers like a parish vestry would be too inconceivable a thing."

"You put the matter more flippantly, Mr. Holmes, than you would probably do if you were brought into personal contact with these things. Your advice, then, as I understand it, is that the young man will be as safe in Devonshire as in London. He comes in fifty minutes. What would you recommend?"

"I recommend, sir, that you take a cab, call off your spaniel who is scratching at my front door, and proceed to Waterloo to meet Sir Henry Baskerville."

"And then?"

"And then you will say nothing to him at all until I have made up my mind about the matter."

"How long will it take you to make up your mind?"

"Twenty-four hours. At ten o'clock tomorrow, Dr. Mortimer, I will be much obliged to you if you will call upon me here, and it will be of help to me in my plans for the future if you will bring Sir Henry Baskerville with you."

"I will do so, Mr. Holmes."

He scribbled the appointment on his shirt-cuff and hurried off in his strange, peering, absent-minded fashion.

Holmes stopped him at the head of the stair.

"Only one more question, Dr. Mortimer. You say that before Sir Charles Baskerville's death several people saw this apparition upon the moor?"

"Three people did."

"Did any see it after?"

"I have not heard of any."

"Thank you. Good-morning."

Holmes returned to his seat with that quiet look of inward satisfaction which meant that he

sert. Je suis venu vous demander un avis, monsieur Holmes, parce que je crains de me laisser entraîner par mon intérêt, trop évident en l'espèce.»

Holmes resta songeur pendant un moment.

Puis il dit: «En d'autres termes, voici quelle est votre opinion: Vous estimez qu'une influence diabolique rend le séjour de Dartmoor insalubre aux Baskerville. Ai-je bien exprimé votre pensée?

— Ne suis-je pas fondé à le prétendre?

— J'en conviens. Mais, si votre théorie sur le surnaturel est exacte, notre jeune homme peut aussi bien en subir les effets à Londres que dans le Devonshire. J'ai peine à admettre un diable dont les pouvoirs s'arrêteraient aux limites d'une paroisse – tout comme ceux d'un conseil de fabrique.

— Vous traiteriez probablement la question plus sérieusement, monsieur Holmes, si vous viviez en contact permanent avec ces choses-là. Ainsi, d'après vous, ce jeune homme ne courrait pas plus de dangers dans le Devonshire qu'à Londres?... Il arrivera dans cinquante minutes. Que me conseillez-vous de faire?

— Je vous conseille de prendre un cab, d'appeler votre caniche qui gratte à ma porte d'entrée et d'aller au-devant de sir Henry Baskerville, à Waterloo station.

— Et ensuite?

— Ensuite vous ne lui direz rien jusqu'à ce que j'aie réfléchi.

— Combien de temps comptez-vous réfléchir?

— Vingt-quatre heures. Docteur Mortimer, je vous serais très reconnaissant de revenir me voir ici, demain matin, à dix heures. Pour mes dispositions futures, j'aurais besoin que vous ameniez avec vous sir Henry.

— Comptez-y, monsieur Holmes.»

Le docteur Mortimer griffonna le rendez-vous sur sa manchette et sortit.

Holmes l'arrêta sur le haut de l'escalier.

«Encore une question, docteur Mortimer. Vous m'avez dit qu'avant la mort de sir Charles Baskerville plusieurs personnes avaient aperçu sur la lande l'étrange apparition?

— Oui; trois personnes.

— L'a-t-on revue après?

— Je n'en ai plus entendu parler.

— Merci. Au revoir.»

Holmes retourna s'asseoir avec cet air de satisfaction interne qui signifiait qu'il entrevoyait une had a congenial task before him.

"Going out, Watson?"

"Unless I can help you."

"No, my dear fellow, it is at the hour of action that I turn to you for aid. But this is splendid, really unique from some points of view. When you pass Bradley's, would you ask him to send up a pound of the strongest shag tobacco? Thank you. It would be as well if you could make it convenient not to return before evening. Then I should be very glad to compare impressions as to this most interesting problem which has been submitted to us this morning."

I knew that seclusion and solitude were very necessary for my friend in those hours of intense mental concentration during which he weighed every particle of evidence, constructed alternative theories, balanced one against the other, and made up his mind as to which points were essential and which immaterial.

I therefore spent the day at my club and did not return to Baker Street until evening.

It was nearly nine o'clock when I found myself in the sitting-room once more.

My first impression as I opened the door was that a fire had broken out, for the room was so filled with smoke that the light of the lamp upon the table was blurred by it.

As I entered, however, my fears were set at rest, for it was the acrid fumes of strong coarse tobacco which took me by the throat and set me coughing. Through the haze I had a vague vision of Holmes in his dressing-gown coiled up in an armchair with his black clay pipe between his lips.

Several rolls of paper lay around him.

"Caught cold, Watson?" said he.

"No, it's this poisonous atmosphere."

"I suppose it is pretty thick, now that you mention it."

"Thick! It is intolerable."

"Open the window, then! You have been at your club all day, I perceive."

"My dear Holmes!"

"Am I right?"

"Certainly, but how?"

He laughed at my bewildered expression.

"There is a delightful freshness about you,

tâche agréable.

«Sortez-vous, Watson? me demanda-t-il.

— Oui; à moins que je ne vous sois de quelque utilité.

— Non, mon cher ami; je ne réclame votre concours qu'au moment d'agir. Savez-vous que cette affaire est superbe, unique en son genre à certains points de vue.... Lorsque vous passerez devant la boutique de Bradley, priez-le donc de m'envoyer une livre de son tabac le plus fort... Vous seriez bien aimable de me laisser seul jusqu'à ce soir.... Nous nous communiquerons alors nos impressions sur le très intéressant problème que nous a soumis ce matin le docteur Mortimer.»

Holmes aimait à s'isoler ainsi pendant les heures de contention mentale au cours desquelles il pesait le pour et le contre des choses. Il édifiait alors des théories contradictoires, les discutait et fixait son esprit sur les points essentiels.

Je passai mon après-midi au cercle et ne repris que le soir le chemin de Baker street.

Il était près de neuf heures, lorsque je me retrouvai assis dans le salon de Sherlock Holmes.

En ouvrant la porte, ma première impression fut qu'il y avait le feu à la maison. La fumée obscurcissait tellement la pièce qu'on voyait à peine la flamme de la lampe placée sur la table.

Je fis quelques pas dans le salon et mes craintes s'apaisèrent aussitôt: ce n'était que la fumée produite par un tabac grossier. Elle me saisit à la gorge et me fit tousser. Enfin, à travers cet épais nuage, je finis par découvrir Holmes, enveloppé dans sa robe de chambre, enfoui dans un large fauteuil et tenant entre ses dents le tuyau d'une pipe en terre très culottée.

Plusieurs rouleaux de papier jonchaient le tapis autour de lui.

«Pris froid, Watson? dit-il.

— Non... c'est cette atmosphère empoisonnée.

— Elle doit être, en effet, un peu épaisse.

— Épaisse! Elle est irrespirable!

— Eh bien, ouvrez la fenêtre. Je parie que vous n'avez pas bougé de votre cercle!

— Mon cher Holmes.... Certainement. Mais comment....»

Sherlock Holmes se moqua de mon ahurissement.

«Vous êtes d'une naïveté délicieuse, fit-il. Cela

Watson, which makes it a pleasure to exercise any small powers which I possess at your expense. A gentleman goes forth on a showery and miry day. He returns immaculate in the evening with the gloss still on his hat and his boots. He has been a fixture therefore all day. He is not a man with intimate friends. Where, then, could he have been? Is it not obvious?"

"Well, it is rather obvious."

"The world is full of obvious things which nobody by any chance ever observes. Where do you think that I have been?"

"A fixture also."

"On the contrary, I have been to Devonshire."

"In spirit?"

"Exactly. My body has remained in this armchair and has, I regret to observe, consumed in my absence two large pots of coffee and an incredible amount of tobacco. After you left I sent down to Stamford's for the Ordnance map of this portion of the moor, and my spirit has hovered over it all day. I flatter myself that I could find my way about."

"A large-scale map, I presume?"

"Very large."

He unrolled one section and held it over his knee.

"Here you have the particular district which concerns us. That is Baskerville Hall in the middle."

"With a wood round it?"

"Exactly. I fancy the yew alley, though not marked under that name, must stretch along this line, with the moor, as you perceive, upon the right of it. This small clump of buildings here is the hamlet of Grimpen, where our friend Dr. Mortimer has his headquarters. Within a radius of five miles there are, as you see, only a very few scattered dwellings. Here is Lafter Hall, which was mentioned in the narrative. There is a house indicated here which may be the residence of the naturalist—Stapleton, if I remember right, was his name. Here are two moorland farmhouses, High Tor and Foulmire. Then fourteen miles away the great convict prison of Princetown. Between and around these scattered points extends the desolate, lifeless moor. This, then, is the stage upon which tragedy has been played, and upon which we may help to play it again."

"It must be a wild place."

me réjouit d'exercer à vos dépens les modestes dons que je possède. Voyons, un monsieur auquel on ne connaît pas d'amis intimes sort par un temps pluvieux, boueux.... Il revient le soir, immaculé, le chapeau et les bottines aussi luisants que le matin.... Qu'en concluriez vous? Qu'il a été cloué quelque part toute la journée.... N'est-ce pas évident?

— En effet, c'est plutôt évident.

— Il y a de par le monde une foule de choses évidentes que personne n'observe. Et moi, où croyez-vous que je sois allé?

— Vous êtes également resté cloué ici.

— Erreur!... J'ai visité le Devonshire.

— Par la pensée?

— Oui. Mon corps n'a pas quitté ce fauteuil et a consommé en l'absence de ma pensée — j'ai le regret de le constater — la valeur de deux grands bols de café et une incroyable quantité de tabac. Après votre départ, j'ai envoyé chercher à Stamford la carte officielle de la lande de Dartmoor et mon esprit l'a parcourue en tous sens. À cette heure, je me flatte de pouvoir y retrouver mon chemin sans guide.

— Cette carte est donc établie à une grande échelle?

— Très grande.»

Holmes en déplia une partie qu'il tint ouverte sur ses genoux.

— Voici le district qui nous intéresse, fit-il. Là, au centre, vous apercevez Baskerville Hall.

— Avec cette ceinture de bois?

— Oui. Bien que l'allée des Ifs ne soit désignée par aucun nom, je jurerais qu'elle s'étend le long de cette ligne, avec la lande à droite. Ici, cet amas de maisons représente le hameau de Grimpen où notre ami, le docteur Mortimer, a installé son quartier général. Constatez que, dans un rayon de six kilomètres, il n'y a que de rares habitations. Voici encore Lafter Hall, dont il est question dans le vieux grimoire. La construction indiquée plus loin doit abriter le naturaliste... Stapleton, si je me souviens bien de son nom. Enfin, j'aperçois deux fermes: Iligh Tor et Foulmire. À quatorze milles de là, se dresse la prison de Princetown. Autour et entre ces quelques maisons se déroule la lande, morne, désolée. C'est là que se passa le drame; c'est là que nous essayerons de le reconstituer.

— L'endroit est sauvage?

"Yes, the setting is a worthy one. If the devil did desire to have a hand in the affairs of men—"

"Then you are yourself inclining to the supernatural explanation."

"The devil's agents may be of flesh and blood, may they not? There are two questions waiting for us at the outset. The one is whether any crime has been committed at all; the second is, what is the crime and how was it committed? Of course, if Dr. Mortimer's surmise should be correct, and we are dealing with forces outside the ordinary laws of Nature, there is an end of our investigation. But we are bound to exhaust all other hypotheses before falling back upon this one. I think we'll shut that window again, if you don't mind. It is a singular thing, but I find that a concentrated atmosphere helps a concentration of thought. I have not pushed it to the length of getting into a box to think, but that is the logical outcome of my convictions. Have you turned the case over in your mind?"

"Yes, I have thought a good deal of it in the course of the day."

"What do you make of it?"

"It is very bewildering."

"It has certainly a character of its own. There are points of distinction about it. That change in the footprints, for example. What do you make of that?"

"Mortimer said that the man had walked on tiptoe down that portion of the alley."

"He only repeated what some fool had said at the inquest. Why should a man walk on tiptoe down the alley?"

"What then?"

"He was running, Watson—running desperately, running for his life, running until he burst his heart—and fell dead upon his face."

"Running from what?"

"There lies our problem. There are indications that the man was crazed with fear before ever he began to run."

"How can you say that?"

"I am presuming that the cause of his fears came to him across the moor. If that were so, and it seems most probable, only a man who had lost his wits would have run from the house instead

— Plutôt. Si le diable désirait se mêler des affaires des hommes....

— Ainsi donc, vous aussi, vous penchez vers une intervention surnaturelle?

— Le diable ne peut-il pas se servir d'agents en chair et en os?... Dès le début, deux questions se dressent devant nous. La première: Y a-t-il eu crime? La seconde: Quel est ce crime et comment l'a-t-on commis? Si les conjectures du docteur Mortimer sont fondées et si nous nous trouvons en présence de forces échappant aux lois ordinaires de la nature, certes le mieux est de ne pas pousser plus loin nos investigations, Mais nous devons épuiser toutes les autres hypothèses, avant de nous arrêter à celle-ci.... Nous ferions bien de fermer cette fenêtre, qu'en pensez-vous? Je reconnais que je suis bizarre, mais il me semble qu'une concentration d'atmosphère favorise toujours une concentration de pensée. Je ne vais pas jusqu'à m'enfermer dans une boîte pour réfléchir.... Ce serait cependant la conséquence logique de mes convictions.... De votre côté, avez-vous creusé l'affaire?

— Oui, beaucoup, pendant le courant de la journée.

— Quelle est votre opinion?

— Je me déclare fort embarrassé.

— Cette affaire ne ressemble pas, en effet, à toutes les autres.... Elle en diffère par plusieurs points.... Ce changement dans les empreintes de pas, par exemple.... Comment l'expliquez-vous?

— Mortimer dit que sir Charles Baskerville a parcouru une partie de l'allée sur la pointe des pieds.

— Il n'a fait que répéter la déclaration de quelque imbécile au cours de l'enquête. Pourquoi se promènerait-on dans une allée sur la pointe des pieds?

— Alors?

— Il courait, Watson!... Sir Charles courait désespérément!... Il courait pour se sauver, jusqu'au moment où la rupture d'un anévrisme l'a jeté la face contre terre.

— Pourquoi fuyait-il?

— Là gît le problème. Des indices me portent à croire qu'il était déjà terrassé par la peur, avant même de commencer à courir.

— Sur quelles preuves appuyez-vous ce raisonnement?

— J'admets que la cause de sa peur se trouvait sur la lande. S'il en était ainsi — et cela paraît probable — seul un homme affolé aurait couru en tournant le dos à sa maison, au lieu de se diof towards it. If the gipsy's evidence may be taken as true, he ran with cries for help in the direction where help was least likely to be. Then, again, whom was he waiting for that night, and why was he waiting for him in the yew alley rather than in his own house?"

"You think that he was waiting for someone?"

"The man was elderly and infirm. We can understand his taking an evening stroll, but the ground was damp and the night inclement. Is it natural that he should stand for five or ten minutes, as Dr. Mortimer, with more practical sense than I should have given him credit for, deduced from the cigar ash?"

"But he went out every evening."

"I think it unlikely that he waited at the moorgate every evening. On the contrary, the evidence is that he avoided the moor. That night he waited there. It was the night before he made his departure for London. The thing takes shape, Watson. It becomes coherent. Might I ask you to hand me my violin, and we will postpone all further thought upon this business until we have had the advantage of meeting Dr. Mortimer and Sir Henry Baskerville in the morning."

riger vers elle. Si l'on tient pour véridique le récit du bohémien, sir Charles courait, en appelant au secours, dans la direction où il était le plus improbable qu'il lui en arrivât… Et puis, qu'attendait-il, cette nuit-là? Pourquoi attendait-il dans l'allée des Ifs plutôt qu'au château?

— Vous croyez qu'il attendait quelqu'un?

— Le docteur Mortimer nous a montré un sir Charles Baskerville vieux et infirme. Nous pouvons accepter les promenades vespérales… mais, ce soir-là, le sol était humide et la nuit froide. Est-il admissible qu'il se soit arrêté pendant cinq ou dix minutes, ainsi que le docteur Mortimer, avec une sagacité que je ne lui soupçonnais pas, l'a déduit très logiquement de la chute des cendres de son cigare?

— Puisqu'il sortait tous les soirs.

— Il ne me paraît pas très vraisemblable qu'il s'attardât tous les soirs à la porte donnant sur la lande. Toutes les dépositions, au contraire, indiquent qu'il évitait cette lande. Or, cette nuit-là, il s'était posté à cet endroit… Il partait le lendemain pour Londres… La chose prend corps, Watson; elle devient cohérente!… Voulez-vous me passer mon violon?… Ne pensons plus à cette affaire pour le moment, et attendons la visite du docteur Mortimer et de sir Henry Baskerville.»

CHAPTER 4. SIR HENRY BASKERVILLE

Our breakfast table was cleared early, and Holmes waited in his dressing-gown for the promised interview. Our clients were punctual to their appointment, for the clock had just struck ten when Dr. Mortimer was shown up, followed by the young baronet. The latter was a small, alert, dark-eyed man about thirty years of age, very sturdily built, with thick black eyebrows and a strong, pugnacious face.

He wore a ruddy-tinted tweed suit and had the weather-beaten appearance of one who has spent most of his time in the open air, and yet there was something in his steady eye and the quiet assurance of his bearing which indicated the gentleman.

"This is Sir Henry Baskerville," said Dr. Mortimer.

"Why, yes," said he, "and the strange thing is, Mr. Sherlock Holmes, that if my friend here had not proposed coming round to you this morning I should have come on my own account. I understand that you think out little puzzles, and I've had one this morning which wants more thinking out than I am able to give it."

"Pray take a seat, Sir Henry. Do I understand you to say that you have yourself had some remarkable experience since you arrived in London?"

CHAPITRE 4. SIR HENRY BASKERVILLE

Ce matin-là, nous déjeunâmes de bonne heure. Sherlock Holmes, en robe de chambre, attendait l'arrivée de nos visiteurs. Ils furent exacts au rendez-vous: dix heures sonnaient à peine, quand on introduisit le docteur Mortimer, suivi du jeune baronnet.

Il pouvait avoir trente ans. Petit, alerte, les yeux noirs, il était très solidement bâti. Il avait des sourcils très fournis qui donnaient à son visage une expression énergique.

Il portait un vêtement complet de couleur rougeâtre. Son teint hâlé attestait de nombreuses années passées au grand air, et cependant le calme de son regard et la tranquille assurance de son maintien dénotaient un homme bien élevé.

«Voici sir Henry Baskerville», dit Mortimer.

— Lui-même, ajouta le jeune homme. Et ce qu'il y a de plus étrange, monsieur Holmes, c'est que, si mon ami ici présent ne m'avait pas proposé de me présenter à vous, je serais venu de mon propre mouvement. Vous aimez les énigmes.... Eh bien, j'en ai reçu une, ce matin, qui exige, pour la deviner, plus de temps que je ne puis lui consacrer.»

Holmes s'inclina.

«Veuillez vous asseoir, sir Henry, fit-il. Dois-je comprendre que depuis votre court séjour à Londres, vous avez été l'objet de quelque aventure?

"Nothing of much importance, Mr. Holmes. Only a joke, as like as not. It was this letter, if you can call it a letter, which reached me this morning."

He laid an envelope upon the table, and we all bent over it. It was of common quality, greyish in colour.

The address, "Sir Henry Baskerville, Northumberland Hotel," was printed in rough characters; the post-mark "Charing Cross," and the date of posting the preceding evening.

"Who knew that you were going to the Northumberland Hotel?" asked Holmes, glancing keenly across at our visitor.

"No one could have known. We only decided after I met Dr. Mortimer."

"But Dr. Mortimer was no doubt already stopping there?"

"No, I had been staying with a friend," said the doctor.

"There was no possible indication that we intended to go to this hotel."

"Hum! Someone seems to be very deeply interested in your movements."

Out of the envelope he took a half-sheet of foolscap paper folded into four.

This he opened and spread flat upon the table.

Across the middle of it a single sentence had been formed by the expedient of pasting printed words upon it.

It ran:

As you value your life or your reason keep away from the moor.

The word "moor" only was printed in ink.

"Now," said Sir Henry Baskerville, "perhaps you will tell me, Mr. Holmes, what in thunder is the meaning of that, and who it is that takes so much interest in my affairs?"

"What do you make of it, Dr. Mortimer? You must allow that there is nothing supernatural about this, at any rate?"

"No, sir, but it might very well come from someone who was convinced that the business is supernatural."

"What business?" asked Sir Henry sharply. "It seems to me that all you gentlemen know a great deal more than I do about my own affairs."

"You shall share our knowledge before you

— Oh! rien de bien important, monsieur Holmes. Une plaisanterie, si je ne me trompe... cette lettre — mérite-t-elle ce nom? — qui m'a été remise ce matin.»

Et sir Henry posa une enveloppe sur la table. Nous nous approchâmes tous pour la regarder. Le papier était de couleur grisâtre et de qualité commune.

Une main malhabile avait écrit l'adresse suivante: «Sir Henry Baskerville, Northumberland hotel». La lettre portait le timbre du bureau de Charing Cross et avait été mise à la poste la veille au soir.

«Qui savait que vous descendiez à Northumberland hotel?» demanda Holmes en regardant attentivement notre visiteur.

— Personne. Je m'y suis seulement décidé après ma rencontre avec le docteur Mortimer.

— Sans doute M. Mortimer y logeait déjà?

— Non; j'étais descendu chez un ami, répondit le docteur.

— Il était impossible de prévoir que nous irions dans cet hôtel.

— Hum! fit Sherlock. Quelqu'un me paraît très au courant de vos mouvements».

Holmes tira de l'enveloppe la moitié d'une feuille de papier écolier pliée en quatre.

Il l'ouvrit et la développa sur la table.

Au milieu, des caractères imprimés, réunis ensemble et collés, formaient une seule phrase.

Elle était ainsi conçue:

«Si vous attachez de la valeur à votre raison ou à votre vie, prenez garde à la lande.»

Seul, le mot «lande», était écrit à la main.

«Peut-être m'apprendrez-vous, monsieur Holmes dit sir Henry Baskerville, ce que signifie tout cela et quel est l'homme qui s'intéresse tant à moi?

— Qu'en pensez-vous, docteur Mortimer? Vous conviendrez, en tout cas, qu'il n'y a là rien de surnaturel.

— J'en conviens, monsieur. Mais cet avis ne peut-il être envoyé par une personne convaincue que nous sommes en présence de faits surnaturels?

— Quels faits? demanda vivement sir Henry. Il me semble, messieurs, que vous connaissez mieux mes affaires que je ne les connais moi-même.

— Avant de sortir de cette pièce, répliqua Sherleave this room, Sir Henry. I promise you that," said Sherlock Holmes. "We will confine ourselves for the present with your permission to this very interesting document, which must have been put together and posted yesterday evening. Have you yesterday's Times, Watson?"

"It is here in the corner."

"Might I trouble you for it—the inside page, please, with the leading articles?"

He glanced swiftly over it, running his eyes up and down the columns.

"Capital article this on free trade. Permit me to give you an extract from it.

'You may be cajoled into imagining that your own special trade or your own industry will be encouraged by a protective tariff, but it stands to reason that such legislation must in the long run keep away wealth from the country, diminish the value of our imports, and lower the general conditions of life in this island.'

"What do you think of that, Watson?" cried Holmes in high glee, rubbing his hands together with satisfaction. "Don't you think that is an admirable sentiment?"

Dr. Mortimer looked at Holmes with an air of professional interest, and Sir Henry Baskerville turned a pair of puzzled dark eyes upon me.

"I don't know much about the tariff and things of that kind," said he, "but it seems to me we've got a bit off the trail so far as that note is concerned."

"On the contrary, I think we are particularly hot upon the trail, Sir Henry. Watson here knows more about my methods than you do, but I fear that even he has not quite grasped the significance of this sentence."

"No, I confess that I see no connection."

"And yet, my dear Watson, there is so very close a connection that the one is extracted out of the other. 'You,' 'your,' 'your,' 'life,' 'reason,' 'value,' 'keep away,' 'from the.' Don't you see now whence these words have been taken?"

"By thunder, you're right! Well, if that isn't smart!" cried Sir Henry.

"If any possible doubt remained it is settled by the fact that 'keep away' and 'from the' are cut out in one piece."

"Well, now—so it is!"

"Really, Mr. Holmes, this exceeds anything

lock Holmes, vous en saurez autant que nous, je vous le promets. Pour le moment — et avec votre permission — nous allons nous renfermer dans l'examen de ce fort intéressant document. Il a été probablement confectionné hier soir et mis à la poste aussitôt. Avez-vous le Times d'hier, Watson?

— Il est là, sur le coin de votre table.

— Ayez l'obligeance de me le passer… la page intérieure, s'il vous plaît… celle qui contient les leading articles.»

Holmes parcourut rapidement les colonnes du journal de la Cité.

«Le principal article traite la question de la liberté de commerce, fit-il. Permettez-moi de vous en lire un passage:

«C'est un leurre de croire que les tarifs protecteurs encouragent votre commerce et votre industrie nationale. Si vous attachez de la valeur à vos importations, prenez garde à une trop longue application de cette législation, qui aura vite abaissé les conditions générales de la vie dans cette île… La raison vous en démontrera tout le danger.»

«Quel est votre avis sur ceci, Watson?» s'écria joyeusement Holmes, en se frottant les mains, avec une satisfaction manifeste.

Le docteur Mortimer considéra Holmes avec un air d'intérêt professionnel, tandis que sir Henry tourna vers moi des regards étonnés.

«Je n'entends pas grand'chose aux questions de tarifs et d'économie politique, dit ce dernier. D'ailleurs il me semble que cette lettre nous a un peu détournés de notre sujet.

— Au contraire, sir Henry, je crois que nous y sommes en plein. Watson est plus initié que vous à ma méthode, et cependant je crains qu'il n'ait pas saisi l'importance de cette citation.

— Non, répliquai-je, je ne vois pas quel rapport…

— Il en existe un — et très intime. «Vous», «votre», «votre», «vie», «raison», «attachez de la valeur», «prenez garde à»… Comprenez-vous maintenant où l'on a pris ces mots?

— Mais oui! s'écria sir Henry. C'est très adroit.

— Et s'il me restait un doute, continua Holmes, le seul fait que les mots «prenez garde», et «attachez de la valeur» sont détachés d'un seul coup de ciseaux les dissiperait».

— Réellement, monsieur Holmes, ceci dépasse

which I could have imagined," said Dr. Mortimer, gazing at my friend in amazement. "I could understand anyone saying that the words were from a newspaper; but that you should name which, and add that it came from the leading article, is really one of the most remarkable things which I have ever known. How did you do it?"

"I presume, Doctor, that you could tell the skull of a negro from that of an Esquimau?"

"Most certainly."

"But how?"

"Because that is my special hobby. The differences are obvious. The supra-orbital crest, the facial angle, the maxillary curve, the—"

"But this is my special hobby, and the differences are equally obvious. There is as much difference to my eyes between the leaded bourgeois type of a Times article and the slovenly print of an evening half-penny paper as there could be between your negro and your Esquimau. The detection of types is one of the most elementary branches of knowledge to the special expert in crime, though I confess that once when I was very young I confused the Leeds Mercury with the Western Morning News. But a Times leader is entirely distinctive, and these words could have been taken from nothing else. As it was done yesterday the strong probability was that we should find the words in yesterday's issue."

"So far as I can follow you, then, Mr. Holmes," said Sir Henry Baskerville, "someone cut out this message with a scissors—"

"Nail-scissors," said Holmes. "You can see that it was a very short-bladed scissors, since the cutter had to take two snips over 'keep away.'"

"That is so. Someone, then, cut out the message with a pair of short-bladed scissors, pasted it with paste—"

"Gum," said Holmes.

"With gum on to the paper. But I want to know why the word 'moor' should have been written?"

"Because he could not find it in print. The other words were all simple and might be found in any issue, but 'moor' would be less common."

"Why, of course, that would explain it. Have you read anything else in this message, Mr. Holmes?"

"There are one or two indications, and yet the utmost pains have been taken to remove all clues.

tout ce que j'aurais pu imaginer, dit Mortimer, en examinant mon ami avec stupéfaction. Je comprendrais qu'on eût deviné que ces mots avaient été découpés dans un journal.... Mais indiquer lequel et ajouter qu'ils proviennent d'un leading article, c'est vraiment étonnant! Comment l'avez-vous découvert?

— Je présume, docteur, que vous savez distinguer le crâne des nègres de celui des Esquimaux?

— Très certainement.

— Pourquoi?

— C'est mon métier. Les différences sautent aux yeux.... L'os frontal, l'angle facial, la courbe des maxillaires, le....

— Eh bien, le reste est mon métier, à moi! Les différences me sautent également aux yeux. Je trouve tout autant de dissemblance entre les caractères du Times et ceux d'une méchante feuille de chou qu'entre vos nègres et vos Esquimaux. Pouvoir reconnaître les uns des autres les caractères d'imprimerie, voilà la science la plus élémentaire d'un expert en crime. J'avoue néanmoins qu'au temps de ma jeunesse je confondis le Leeds Mercury avec les Western Morning News. Un premier-Londres du Times est absolument reconnaissable, et ces mots ne pouvaient avoir été pris que là. La lettre étant d'hier, il devenait donc presque certain que je les trouverais dans le numéro paru à cette date.

— Ainsi, demanda sir Henry Baskerville, quelqu'un les a découpés avec des ciseaux?...

— Avec des ciseaux à ongles, précisa Holmes. Remarquez que la lame en était très courte, puisque celui qui les maniait s'y est pris à deux fois pour les mots «prenez garde à» et «attachez de la valeur».

— En effet. Ainsi quelqu'un a découpé les mots avec de petits ciseaux à ongles et les a fixés ensuite à l'aide de colle....

— Non, de gomme, rectifia Holmes.

— ... À l'aide de gomme, sur le papier, continua sir Henry. Expliquez-moi aussi pourquoi le mot «lande» est écrit à la main?

— Parce que l'article ne le contient pas. Les autres mots sont usuels; on peut les rencontrer dans tous les journaux plus facilement que «lande» beaucoup moins commun.

— J'accepte votre explication, monsieur Holmes. Avez-vous lu autre chose dans ce message?

— J'y ai puisé une ou deux indications, bien qu'on ait pris toutes sortes de précautions pour

The address, you observe is printed in rough characters. But the Times is a paper which is seldom found in any hands but those of the highly educated. We may take it, therefore, that the letter was composed by an educated man who wished to pose as an uneducated one, and his effort to conceal his own writing suggests that that writing might be known, or come to be known, by you. Again, you will observe that the words are not gummed on in an accurate line, but that some are much higher than others. 'Life,' for example is quite out of its proper place. That may point to carelessness or it may point to agitation and hurry upon the part of the cutter. On the whole I incline to the latter view, since the matter was evidently important, and it is unlikely that the composer of such a letter would be careless. If he were in a hurry it opens up the interesting question why he should be in a hurry, since any letter posted up to early morning would reach Sir Henry before he would leave his hotel. Did the composer fear an interruption—and from whom?"

"We are coming now rather into the region of guesswork," said Dr. Mortimer.

"Say, rather, into the region where we balance probabilities and choose the most likely. It is the scientific use of the imagination, but we have always some material basis on which to start our speculation. Now, you would call it a guess, no doubt, but I am almost certain that this address has been written in a hotel."

"How in the world can you say that?"

"If you examine it carefully you will see that both the pen and the ink have given the writer trouble. The pen has spluttered twice in a single word and has run dry three times in a short address, showing that there was very little ink in the bottle. Now, a private pen or ink-bottle is seldom allowed to be in such a state, and the combination of the two must be quite rare. But you know the hotel ink and the hotel pen, where it is rare to get anything else. Yes, I have very little hesitation in saying that could we examine the waste-paper baskets of the hotels around Charing Cross until we found the remains of the mutilated Times leader we could lay our hands straight upon the person who sent this singular message. Halloa! Halloa! What's this?"

He was carefully examining the foolscap, upon

donner le change. Observez que l'adresse — d'une écriture mal formée — est mise à la main. Or, le Times est le journal des intelligences cultivées. Nous pouvons en conclure que la lettre a été composée par un homme instruit, qui désirait passer pour quelqu'un qui ne le serait pas. Ensuite les efforts pour déguiser l'écriture suggèrent l'idée que vous connaissez cette écriture ou que vous pourrez la connaître un jour. Vous observerez en outre que les mots ne sont pas collés suivant une ligne droite; il y en a de placés plus haut que d'autres. «Vie», par exemple, est tout à fait hors de la ligne. Faut-il attribuer ce manque de soin à la négligence du découpeur ou bien à son agitation ou à sa précipitation? Je penche pour cette dernière interprétation. Ce message était important et vraisemblablement celui qui le composait y apportait toute son attention. Si nous admettons la précipitation, il faut chercher quelle en était la cause, car la même lettre jetée à la boîte le matin de bonne heure au lieu du soir, aurait touché quand même sir Henry avant sa sortie de l'hôtel. Le correspondant de sir Henry craignait-il d'être interrompu?… Et par qui?

— Nous entrons à présent dans le domaine des hypothèses, fit le docteur Mortimer.

— Disons plutôt, répliqua Holmes, dans le domaine des probabilités… et choisissons la plus vraisemblable. Cela s'appelle appliquer l'imagination à la science. N'avons-nous pas toujours à notre disposition quelque fait matériel pour asseoir nos spéculations? Vous allez m'accuser encore de me livrer à des hypothèses, mais j'ai la certitude que cette lettre a été écrite dans un hôtel.

— Qu'est-ce qui vous fait dire cela? s'écria Mortimer.

— Si vous examinez attentivement cette lettre, vous verrez que la plume et l'encre laissaient à désirer. La plume a craché deux fois dans un même mot et elle a couru trois fois à sec dans l'adresse — courte cependant…. La plume était donc mauvaise et l'encrier contenait peu d'encre. Or, la plume et l'encrier d'un particulier sont rarement dans cet état, et il est plus rare encore qu'ils le soient simultanément…. Tandis que vous connaissez les plumes et les encriers d'hôtels? Aussi je n'hésite pas à dire que nous devons fouiller les corbeilles à papier des hôtels qui avoisinent Charing Cross, jusqu'à ce que nous ayons retrouvé le numéro mutilé du Times. Grâce à lui, nous mettrons la main sur l'expéditeur de ce singulier message…. Tiens! tiens!

Holmes avait élevé à la hauteur de ses yeux le

which the words were pasted, holding it only an inch or two from his eyes.

"Well?"

"Nothing," said he, throwing it down. "It is a blank half-sheet of paper, without even a water-mark upon it. I think we have drawn as much as we can from this curious letter; and now, Sir Henry, has anything else of interest happened to you since you have been in London?"

"Why, no, Mr. Holmes. I think not."

"You have not observed anyone follow or watch you?"

"I seem to have walked right into the thick of a dime novel," said our visitor. "Why in thunder should anyone follow or watch me?"

"We are coming to that. You have nothing else to report to us before we go into this matter?"

"Well, it depends upon what you think worth reporting."

"I think anything out of the ordinary routine of life well worth reporting."

Sir Henry smiled.

"I don't know much of British life yet, for I have spent nearly all my time in the States and in Canada. But I hope that to lose one of your boots is not part of the ordinary routine of life over here."

"You have lost one of your boots?"

"My dear sir," cried Dr. Mortimer, "it is only mislaid. You will find it when you return to the hotel. What is the use of troubling Mr. Holmes with trifles of this kind?"

"Well, he asked me for anything outside the ordinary routine."

"Exactly," said Holmes, "however foolish the incident may seem. You have lost one of your boots, you say?"

"Well, mislaid it, anyhow. I put them both outside my door last night, and there was only one in the morning. I could get no sense out of the chap who cleans them. The worst of it is that I only bought the pair last night in the Strand, and I have never had them on."

"If you have never worn them, why did you put them out to be cleaned?"

"They were tan boots and had never been varnished. That was why I put them out."

"Then I understand that on your arrival in Lon-

papier sur lequel on avait collé les mots et il l'examinait avec soin.

«Eh bien? demandai-je.

— Rien, dit il, en reposant le feuillet sur la table. Ce papier est tout blanc, sans même de filigrane.... Je crois que nous avons tiré de cette curieuse lettre tous les indices qu'elle pouvait fournir. Maintenant, sir Henry, vous est-il arrivé quelque chose depuis votre descente du train?

— Non, monsieur Holmes.... Je ne me souviens pas.

— N'avez-vous pas remarqué que quelqu'un vous ait observé ou suivi?

— Il me semble marcher à travers les ténèbres d'un sombre feuilleton, répondit notre visiteur. Pourquoi diable m'aurait-on surveillé ou suivi?

— Ça m'en a tout l'air cependant. N'avez-vous pas autre chose à nous communiquer, avant que nous entrions dans l'étude de cette sorte de surveillance qui vous entoure?

— Cela dépend de ce que vous jugez digne de vous être communiqué.

— Tout ce qui sort de la marche ordinaire de la vie en vaut la peine.»

Sir Henry sourit.

«Je ne connais presque rien de la vie anglaise, dit-il, puisque j'ai passé la majeure partie de mon existence aux États-Unis ou au Canada. Je ne pense pas toutefois que la perte d'une bottine soit ici un événement qui sorte de la «marche ordinaire de la vie».

— Vous avez perdu une de vos bottines?

— Seulement égaré, intervint Mortimer... Vous la retrouverez en rentrant à l'hôtel. Quelle nécessité d'ennuyer M. Holmes avec de semblables futilités?

— Il m'a interrogé, je réponds, repartit sir Henry.

— Parfaitement, dit Holmes. Dites-moi tout, quelque négligeables que ces incidents puissent vous paraître. Ainsi, vous avez perdu une bottine?

— Tout au moins égaré. J'ai placé la paire à la porte de ma chambre, la nuit dernière, et, ce matin, il ne m'en restait plus qu'une. Questionné, le garçon n'a pu me donner aucune explication. Le pire, c'est que je les avais achetées la veille, dans le Strand, et que je ne les avais jamais portées.

— Si vous ne les avez jamais portées pourquoi les faire nettoyer?

— Le cuir, fauve, n'avait pas encore été poli... Je désirais qu'il le fût.

— Ainsi hier, dès votre arrivée à Londres, vous

don yesterday you went out at once and bought a pair of boots?"

"I did a good deal of shopping. Dr. Mortimer here went round with me. You see, if I am to be squire down there I must dress the part, and it may be that I have got a little careless in my ways out West. Among other things I bought these brown boots—gave six dollars for them—and had one stolen before ever I had them on my feet."

"It seems a singularly useless thing to steal," said Sherlock Holmes. "I confess that I share Dr. Mortimer's belief that it will not be long before the missing boot is found."

"And, now, gentlemen," said the baronet with decision, "it seems to me that I have spoken quite enough about the little that I know. It is time that you kept your promise and gave me a full account of what we are all driving at."

"Your request is a very reasonable one," Holmes answered. "Dr. Mortimer, I think you could not do better than to tell your story as you told it to us."

Thus encouraged, our scientific friend drew his papers from his pocket and presented the whole case as he had done upon the morning before.

Sir Henry Baskerville listened with the deepest attention and with an occasional exclamation of surprise.

"Well, I seem to have come into an inheritance with a vengeance," said he when the long narrative was finished. "Of course, I've heard of the hound ever since I was in the nursery. It's the pet story of the family, though I never thought of taking it seriously before. But as to my uncle's death—well, it all seems boiling up in my head, and I can't get it clear yet. You don't seem quite to have made up your mind whether it's a case for a policeman or a clergyman."

"Precisely."

"And now there's this affair of the letter to me at the hotel. I suppose that fits into its place."

"It seems to show that someone knows more than we do about what goes on upon the moor," said Dr. Mortimer.

"And also," said Holmes, "that someone is not ill-disposed towards you, since they warn you of danger."

"Or it may be that they wish, for their own purposes, to scare me away."

"Well, of course, that is possible also. I am very much indebted to you, Dr. Mortimer, for introduc-

êtes sorti immédiatement et vous avez acheté des bottines?

— J'ai acheté différentes choses.... Le docteur Mortimer m'a accompagné. Dame! Si je dois jouer au grand seigneur, il faut bien que j'en aie les habits... Dans le Far-West, je ne soignais pas beaucoup ma tenue... Parmi mes emplettes, figurait cette paire de bottines jaunes... Je les ai payées six dollars... et on m'en a volé une avant même que j'aie pu m'en servir.

— Je ne vois pas l'utilité de ce vol, dit Holmes. Je partage l'avis du docteur Mortimer... vous les retrouverez bientôt.

— Il me semble, messieurs, dit le baronnet, que nous avons assez causé de moi. Le moment est venu de me dire, à votre tour, tout ce que vous savez.

— Ce désir est très légitime, répondit Sherlock Holmes. Docteur Mortimer, recommencez donc pour sir Henry votre récit d'hier matin.»

Ainsi encouragé, notre ami tira ses papiers de sa poche et narra toute l'histoire que le lecteur connaît déjà.

Sir Henry Baskerville l'écouta avec la plus profonde attention. De temps en temps un cri de surprise lui échappait.

Lorsque le docteur Mortimer cessa de parler, il s'écria:

«J'ai donc recueilli un héritage maudit!... Certes, dès ma plus tendre enfance, j'ai entendu parler de ce chien. C'est l'histoire favorite de la famille, mais je ne pensai jamais à la prendre au sérieux. Quant à la mort de mon oncle... Il me semble que ma tête bout... je ne puis lier deux idées... Je me demande si ce que vous venez de m'apprendre exige une enquête judiciaire ou un exorcisme.

— Précisément.

— Puis, il y a cette lettre adressée à mon hôtel... Elle tombe à propos.

— Elle montre que quelqu'un connaît mieux que nous ce qui se passe sur la lande, dit Mortimer.

— Et aussi que ce quelqu'un vous veut du bien, puisqu'il vous prévient du danger, ajouta Holmes.

— Ma présence là-bas contrarie peut-être certains projets...

— C'est encore possible... Merci, docteur Mortimer, de m'avoir soumis un problème qui ing me to a problem which presents several interesting alternatives. But the practical point which we now have to decide, Sir Henry, is whether it is or is not advisable for you to go to Baskerville Hall."

"Why should I not go?"

"There seems to be danger."

"Do you mean danger from this family fiend or do you mean danger from human beings?"

"Well, that is what we have to find out."

"Whichever it is, my answer is fixed. There is no devil in hell, Mr. Holmes, and there is no man upon earth who can prevent me from going to the home of my own people, and you may take that to be my final answer."

His dark brows knitted and his face flushed to a dusky red as he spoke.

It was evident that the fiery temper of the Baskervilles was not extinct in this their last representative.

"Meanwhile," said he, "I have hardly had time to think over all that you have told me. It's a big thing for a man to have to understand and to decide at one sitting. I should like to have a quiet hour by myself to make up my mind. Now, look here, Mr. Holmes, it's half-past eleven now and I am going back right away to my hotel. Suppose you and your friend, Dr. Watson, come round and lunch with us at two. I'll be able to tell you more clearly then how this thing strikes me."

"Is that convenient to you, Watson?"

"Perfectly."

"Then you may expect us. Shall I have a cab called?"

"I'd prefer to walk, for this affair has flurried me rather."

"I'll join you in a walk, with pleasure," said his companion.

"Then we meet again at two o'clock. Au revoir, and good-morning!"

We heard the steps of our visitors descend the stair and the bang of the front door.

In an instant Holmes had changed from the languid dreamer to the man of action.

"Your hat and boots, Watson, quick! Not a moment to lose!"

He rushed into his room in his dressing-gown and was back again in a few seconds in a frock-coat.

renferme un aussi grand nombre d'intéressantes alternatives. Maintenant, sir Henry Baskerville, il ne nous reste plus qu'un seul point à décider: oui ou non, devez-vous aller au château?

— Pourquoi n'irais-je pas?

— Il paraît y avoir du danger.

— Un danger provenant du démon familial ou d'êtres humains?

— C'est ce qu'il faut éclaircir.

— Quelle que soit votre décision, mon parti est pris. Il n'existe en enfer aucun diable, monsieur Holmes, ni sur terre aucun homme capables de m'empêcher d'aller dans la demeure de mes ancêtres. Voilà mon dernier mot.»

Les sourcils de sir Henry se froncèrent et son visage, pendant qu'il parlait, tourna au rouge pourpre.

Il était évident que le dernier rejeton des Baskerville avait hérité le caractère emporté de ses aïeux.

Il reprit:

«J'ai besoin de méditer plus longuement sur tout ce que vous m'avez appris. Il est malaisé de se décider aussi rapidement. Accordez-moi une heure de recueillement…. Onze heures et demie sonnent, je retourne directement à mon hôtel…. Acceptez, ainsi que M. Watson, une invitation à déjeuner pour deux heures. Je vous répondrai alors plus clairement.

— Cela vous convient-il, Watson? me demanda Holmes.

— Parfaitement.

— Dans ce cas, attendez-nous…. Faut-il faire avancer une voiture?

— Je vous accompagnerai dans votre promenade, fit Mortimer.

— À deux heures,… c'est entendu? répéta sir Henry.

— Oui, à bientôt», répondîmes-nous, Holmes et moi.

Nous entendîmes le pas de nos visiteurs résonner dans l'escalier et la porte de la rue se refermer sur eux.

Aussitôt Holmes abandonna son attitude rêveuse et se réveilla homme d'action.

«Vite! votre chapeau, Watson!» dit-il.

Il courut en robe de chambre vers son cabinet de toilette, d'où il ressortit quelques secondes après en redingote.

There's our man, Watson! Come along!
Voilà notre homme! S'écria Holmes. Venez vite!

We hurried together down the stairs and into the street.

Dr. Mortimer and Baskerville were still visible about two hundred yards ahead of us in the direction of Oxford Street.

"Shall I run on and stop them?"

"Not for the world, my dear Watson. I am perfectly satisfied with your company if you will tolerate mine. Our friends are wise, for it is certainly a very fine morning for a walk."

He quickened his pace until we had decreased the distance which divided us by about half.

Then, still keeping a hundred yards behind, we followed into Oxford Street and so down Regent Street.

Once our friends stopped and stared into a shop window, upon which Holmes did the same. An instant afterwards he gave a little cry of satisfaction, and, following the direction of his eager eyes, I saw that a hansom cab with a man inside which had halted on the other side of the street was now proceeding slowly onward again.

"There's our man, Watson! Come along! We'll have a good look at him, if we can do no more."

At that instant I was aware of a bushy black beard and a pair of piercing eyes turned upon us through the side window of the cab. Instantly the trapdoor at the top flew up, something was screamed to the driver, and the cab flew madly off down Regent Street.

Holmes looked eagerly round for another, but no empty one was in sight. Then he dashed in wild pursuit amid the stream of the traffic, but the start was too great, and already the cab was out of sight.

"There now!" said Holmes bitterly as he emerged panting and white with vexation from the tide of vehicles. "Was ever such bad luck and such bad management, too? Watson, Watson, if you are an honest man you will record this also and set it against my successes!"

"Who was the man?"

"I have not an idea."

"A spy?"

"Well, it was evident from what we have heard that Baskerville has been very closely shadowed by someone since he has been in town. How else could it be known so quickly that it was the Northumberland Hotel which he had chosen? If they

Nous descendîmes l'escalier quatre à quatre, et nous nous précipitâmes dans la rue.

À deux cents mètres devant nous, nous aperçûmes le docteur Mortimer et sir Henry Baskerville se dirigeant vers Oxford street.

Je demandai à mon ami:

«Voulez-vous que je coure et que je les arrête?

— Gardez-vous-en bien, Watson. Votre compagnie me suffit, si la mienne ne vous déplaît pas… Ces messieurs avaient raison… il fait très bon marcher ce matin.»

Holmes hâta le pas, jusqu'à ce que nous eussions diminué de moitié la distance qui nous séparait de nos nouveaux amis.

Alors, laissant entre eux et nous un intervalle d'environ cent mètres, nous parcourûmes Oxford street, puis Regent street.

Bientôt Holmes poussa un cri de joie. Je suivis la direction de son regard et je vis un hansom-cab, rangé le long du trottoir, reprendre sa marche en avant. Un voyageur l'occupait…

«Voilà notre homme! s'écria Holmes. Venez vite! Nous pourrons au moins le dévisager, faute de mieux!»

Comme dans un éclair, je vis une barbe noire broussailleuse et des yeux perçants qui nous regardaient à travers la glace du cab. Aussitôt la trappe par laquelle on communique de l'intérieur avec le cocher s'ouvrit et un ordre fut donné. Le véhicule partit à fond de train vers Trafalgar square.

Holmes chercha immédiatement autour de lui une voiture vide et n'en trouva pas. Dans une course folle, il se jeta au milieu des embarras de la rue. Mais le cab avait trop d'avance sur mon ami, qui le perdit de vue peu après.

«Sapristi! dit Holmes, avec amertume, en se dégageant tout haletant des files de voitures, quelle malchance et aussi quelle imprévoyance de ma part! Si vous êtes juste, Watson, vous enregistrerez cet échec à mon passif.»

J'interrogeai Sherlock:

«Quel homme était-ce?

— Je n'en ai pas la moindre idée.

— Un espion?

— D'après ce que nous avons entendu, il est certain qu'une ombre a marché dans les pas de Baskerville depuis son arrivée à Londres. Comment aurait-on su rapidement qu'il avait choisi Northumberland hotel? Si on l'a espionné le prehad followed him the first day I argued that they would follow him also the second. You may have observed that I twice strolled over to the window while Dr. Mortimer was reading his legend."

"Yes, I remember."

"I was looking out for loiterers in the street, but I saw none. We are dealing with a clever man, Watson. This matter cuts very deep, and though I have not finally made up my mind whether it is a benevolent or a malevolent agency which is in touch with us, I am conscious always of power and design. When our friends left I at once followed them in the hopes of marking down their invisible attendant. So wily was he that he had not trusted himself upon foot, but he had availed himself of a cab so that he could loiter behind or dash past them and so escape their notice. His method had the additional advantage that if they were to take a cab he was all ready to follow them. It has, however, one obvious disadvantage."

"It puts him in the power of the cabman."

"Exactly."

"What a pity we did not get the number!"

"My dear Watson, clumsy as I have been, you surely do not seriously imagine that I neglected to get the number?"

"No. 2704 is our man. But that is no use to us for the moment."

"I fail to see how you could have done more."

"On observing the cab I should have instantly turned and walked in the other direction. I should then at my leisure have hired a second cab and followed the first at a respectful distance, or, better still, have driven to the Northumberland Hotel and waited there. When our unknown had followed Baskerville home we should have had the opportunity of playing his own game upon himself and seeing where he made for. As it is, by an indiscreet eagerness, which was taken advantage of with extraordinary quickness and energy by our opponent, we have betrayed ourselves and lost our man."

We had been sauntering slowly down Regent Street during this conversation, and Dr. Mortimer, with his companion, had long vanished in front of us.

"There is no object in our following them," said Holmes. "The shadow has departed and will not

mier jour, j'en conclus qu'on l'espionnera le second. Vous vous souvenez bien que, tout à l'heure, pendant la lecture des papiers du docteur Mortimer, je me suis approché deux fois de la fenêtre?

— Oui, je me le rappelle.

— Je regardais si personne ne flânait dans la rue. Je n'avais rien remarqué de suspect. Ah! nous avons affaire avec un homme habile, Watson! La chose se complique. Bien qu'il me soit encore impossible de démêler si nous nous trouvons en présence d'une intervention amicale ou hostile, je reconnais qu'il en existe une. Quand nos amis nous ont quittés, je les ai suivis pour découvrir leur invisible surveillant. Cet homme est si rusé qu'au lieu d'aller à pied, il a préféré prendre un cab. Il pouvait ainsi rester en arrière de ceux qu'il observait ou les devancer pour échapper à leur attention. Ce procédé offrait aussi l'avantage de conserver leur contact, si l'envie leur venait de monter en cab; mais il avait un désavantage évident.

— Celui de livrer son auteur à la discrétion du cocher?

— Évidemment.

— Quel malheur que nous n'ayons pas son numéro!

— Mon cher Watson, j'ai été maladroit, j'en conviens.... Toutefois, vous n'imaginez pas sérieusement que j'aie oublié, de l'inscrire là!»

Et Holmes se frappa le front.

Il reprit:

«J'ai lu sur le cab le numéro 2 704. Mais cela nous importe peu pour le moment.

— Qu'auriez-vous pu faire de plus?

— Si j'avais remarqué le cab, j'aurais tourné sur mes talons et pris une autre direction. J'aurais eu alors toute facilité pour en héler un autre, et, à une distance respectueuse, j'aurais trotté dans les pas du premier jusqu'à Northumberland hotel. Là, j'aurais attendu. Puis, lorsque notre inconnu aurait accompagné sir Henry Baskerville chez lui, nous l'aurions filé à notre tour. Tandis que, par une précipitation intempestive, dont notre adversaire a su profiter avec une décision rare, nous nous sommes trahis et nous avons perdu sa trace.»

Tout en causant et en flânant devant les magasins de Regent street, nous avions cessé de voir le docteur Mortimer et son compagnon.

«Il est inutile que nous les suivions plus loin, dit Holmes. L'ombre s'est évanouie et ne reparaîreturn. We must see what further cards we have in our hands and play them with decision. Could you swear to that man's face within the cab?"

"I could swear only to the beard."

"And so could I—from which I gather that in all probability it was a false one. A clever man upon so delicate an errand has no use for a beard save to conceal his features. Come in here, Watson!"

He turned into one of the district messenger offices, where he was warmly greeted by the manager.

"Ah, Wilson, I see you have not forgotten the little case in which I had the good fortune to help you?"

"No, sir, indeed I have not. You saved my good name, and perhaps my life."

"My dear fellow, you exaggerate. I have some recollection, Wilson, that you had among your boys a lad named Cartwright, who showed some ability during the investigation."

"Yes, sir, he is still with us."

"Could you ring him up?—thank you! And I should be glad to have change of this five-pound note."

A lad of fourteen, with a bright, keen face, had obeyed the summons of the manager. He stood now gazing with great reverence at the famous detective.

"Let me have the Hotel Directory," said Holmes. "Thank you! Now, Cartwright, there are the names of twenty-three hotels here, all in the immediate neighbourhood of Charing Cross. Do you see?"

"Yes, sir."

"You will visit each of these in turn."

"Yes, sir."

"You will begin in each case by giving the outside porter one shilling. Here are twenty-three shillings."

"Yes, sir."

"You will tell him that you want to see the waste-paper of yesterday. You will say that an important telegram has miscarried and that you are looking for it. You understand?"

"Yes, sir."

"But what you are really looking for is the centre page of the Times with some holes cut in it with scissors. Here is a copy of the Times. It is this page. You could easily recognize it, could you not?"

tra plus. D'autres cartes nous restent encore dans les mains, jouons-les avec résolution. Reconnaîtriez-vous l'homme assis dans le cab?

— Je ne reconnaîtrais que sa barbe.

— Moi aussi.... Mais je jurerais bien qu'elle est fausse. Un homme, engagé dans une «filature» aussi délicate, ne peut porter une telle barbe que pour dissimuler ses traits.... Entrons ici, Watson.»

Holmes pénétra dans un de ces bureaux de quartier où des commissionnaires se tiennent à toute heure du jour et de la nuit à la disposition du public.

Le directeur le reçut avec force salutations.

«Ah! Wilson, fit mon ami, je vois avec plaisir que vous n'avez pas oublié le léger service que je vous ai rendu.

— Certes non, monsieur. Vous avez sauvé ma réputation et peut-être même ma vie.

— Vous exagérez, mon garçon. Je me souviens que vous aviez, parmi vos boys, un gamin nommé Cartwright, qui fit preuve d'une certaine adresse, au cours de l'enquête.

— Oui, monsieur; il est toujours ici.

— Faites-le monter... Pouvez-vous me procurer la monnaie de ce billet de cinq livres?»

Un jeune garçon de quatorze ans, à la mine intelligente et futée, répondit au coup de sonnette du directeur. Il vint se placer devant Holmes, qu'il regarda respectueusement.

«Donne-moi l'Annuaire des hôtels, lui dit mon ami. Voici, Cartwright, le nom des vingt-trois hôtels qui sont dans le voisinage immédiat de Charing Cross... Tu les vois bien?

— Oui, monsieur.

— Tu les visiteras tous, les uns après les autres.

— Oui, monsieur.

— Tu commenceras par donner au concierge de chacun d'eux un shilling... Voici vingt-trois shillings.

— Oui, monsieur.

— Tu leur demanderas de te remettre les corbeilles à papier d'hier. Tu leur diras qu'on a laissé à une mauvaise adresse un télégramme important que tu tiens à retrouver... Comprends-tu?

— Oui, monsieur.

— Ce qu'il te faudra réellement chercher, ce n'est pas un télégramme, mais une page intérieure du Times dans laquelle on aura pratiqué des coupures à l'aide de ciseaux. Voilà ce numéro du Times et la page en question... Tu la reconnaîtras

"Yes, sir."

"In each case the outside porter will send for the hall porter, to whom also you will give a shilling. Here are twenty-three shillings. You will then learn in possibly twenty cases out of the twenty-three that the waste of the day before has been burned or removed. In the three other cases you will be shown a heap of paper and you will look for this page of the Times among it. The odds are enormously against your finding it. There are ten shillings over in case of emergencies. Let me have a report by wire at Baker Street before evening. And now, Watson, it only remains for us to find out by wire the identity of the cabman, No. 2704, and then we will drop into one of the Bond Street picture galleries and fill in the time until we are due at the hotel."

facilement, n'est-ce pas?

— Oui, monsieur.

— Dans chaque hôtel, le concierge te renverra au garçon du hall, auquel tu donneras aussi un shilling.... Je te remets encore vingt-trois autres shillings. Probablement, dans vingt hôtels sur vingt-trois, on te répondra que le contenu des corbeilles de la veille a été jeté ou brûlé. Dans les trois derniers hôtels, on te conduira à des tas de papiers parmi lesquels tu devras rechercher cette page du Times. Tu as très peu de chances de la retrouver.... Voici dix shillings de plus pour faire face à l'imprévu. Envoie-moi à Baker street, avant ce soir, le résultat de tes investigations. Maintenant, Watson, procurons-nous par télégramme l'identité du cocher qui conduit le cab 2 704. Puis, en attendant l'heure de nous présenter à Northumberland hotel, nous entrerons dans une des expositions de peinture de Bond street.»

CHAPTER 5. THREE BROKEN THREADS

Sherlock Holmes had, in a very remarkable degree, the power of detaching his mind at will.

For two hours the strange business in which we had been involved appeared to be forgotten, and he was entirely absorbed in the pictures of the modern Belgian masters. He would talk of nothing but art, of which he had the crudest ideas, from our leaving the gallery until we found ourselves at the Northumberland Hotel.

"Sir Henry Baskerville is upstairs expecting you," said the clerk. "He asked me to show you up at once when you came."

"Have you any objection to my looking at your register?" said Holmes.

"Not in the least."

The book showed that two names had been added after that of Baskerville. One was Theophilus Johnson and family, of Newcastle; the other Mrs. Oldmore and maid, of High Lodge, Alton.

"Surely that must be the same Johnson whom I used to know," said Holmes to the porter. "A lawyer, is he not, grey-headed, and walks with a limp?"

"No, sir, this is Mr. Johnson, the coal-owner, a very active gentleman, not older than yourself."

"Surely you are mistaken about his trade?"

"No, sir! he has used this hotel for many years, and he is very well known to us."

"Ah, that settles it. Mrs. Oldmore, too; I seem to remember the name. Excuse my curiosity, but often in calling upon one friend one finds another."

"She is an invalid lady, sir. Her husband was once mayor of Gloucester. She always comes to us when she is in town."

"Thank you; I am afraid I cannot claim her acquaintance. We have established a most important fact by these questions, Watson," he continued in a low voice as we went upstairs together.

"We know now that the people who are so

CHAPITRE 5. FILS CASSÉS

Sherlock Holmes possédait à un suprême degré la faculté de détacher son esprit des pensées les plus absorbantes.

Pendant deux heures, il parut avoir oublié l'étrange affaire à laquelle nous étions mêlés, et il se plongea dans l'examen des peintures de l'école belge. Il ne voulut même parler que d'art — dont il n'avait d'ailleurs que des no-tions très imparfaites — pendant le trajet qui séparait Bond street de Northumberland hotel.

«Sir Henry Baskerville vous attend dans sa chambre, nous dit le commis de l'hôtel. Il a bien recommandé qu'on le prévienne dès que vous serez arrivé.

— Y aurait-il de l'indiscrétion à parcourir votre registre? demanda Holmes.

— Pas du tout.»

À la suite du nom de Baskerville, le livre ne contenait que celui de deux voyageurs; Théophile Johnson et sa famille, de Newcastle, et Mme Oldmore et sa fille, de High Lodge, Alton.

— C'est certainement le Johnson que je connais, dit Holmes au portier.... Un avocat, n'est-ce pas?... Avec toute la barbe grise... atteint d'une légère claudication?

— Non, monsieur. Ce Johnson est un gros marchand de charbon, très ingambe, à peu près de votre âge.

— Vous devez faire erreur sur sa profession.

— Non, monsieur. Depuis plusieurs années, il descend dans cet hôtel et nous le connaissons tous.

— Alors, c'est différent. Et Mme Oldmore? Je crois me rappeler ce nom. Excusez ma curiosité; mais souvent, en venant voir un ami, on en rencontre un autre.

— Elle est impotente. Son mari a exercé pendant quelques années les fonctions de maire à Gloucester. Nous la comptons parmi nos meilleurs clients.

— Merci de votre explication. Je regrette de ne pouvoir me recommander auprès de vous de son amitié.» Tout en montant l'escalier, Sherlock Holmes reprit à voix basse:

«Nous avons fixé un point important: nous

He held an old and dusty boot in one of his hands.
Il tenait à la main une vieille bottine toute poudreuse.

interested in our friend have not settled down in his own hotel. That means that while they are, as we have seen, very anxious to watch him, they are equally anxious that he should not see them. Now, this is a most suggestive fact."

savons que ceux qui s'occupent si activement de notre ami ne sont point logés dans le même hôtel que lui. Cela prouve que quelque intérêt qu'ils aient à l'espionner, ainsi que nous l'avons constaté, ils ne désirent pas être vus par lui. Ceci est très suggestif.

"What does it suggest?"

"It suggests—halloa, my dear fellow, what on earth is the matter?"

— En quoi?

— En ceci.... Mon Dieu! mais que diable arrive-t-il?»

As we came round the top of the stairs we had run up against Sir Henry Baskerville himself.

Comme nous tournions dans le corridor de l'hôtel, nous nous heurtâmes à sir Henry Baskerville lui-même.

His face was flushed with anger, and he held an old and dusty boot in one of his hands.

Le visage rouge de colère, il tenait à la main une vieille bottine toute poudreuse.

So furious was he that he was hardly articulate, and when he did speak it was in a much broader and more Western dialect than any which we had heard from him in the morning.

Il paraissait si furieux qu'il avait peine à parler. Quand il put donner un libre cours à son emportement, il s'exprima, en accentuant davantage le jargon du Far-West dont il s'était servi le matin.

"Seems to me they are playing me for a sucker in this hotel," he cried. "They'll find they've started in to monkey with the wrong man unless they are careful. By thunder, if that chap can't find my missing boot there will be trouble. I can take a joke with the best, Mr. Holmes, but they've got a bit over the mark this time."

«On se paye donc ma tête dans cet hôtel, criait-il. S'ils n'y prennent garde, je leur montrerai qu'on ne se moque pas du monde de la sorte! Sacrebleu! si le garçon ne retrouve pas la bottine qui me manque, il m'entendra! Certes, monsieur Holmes, je comprends la plaisanterie; mais celle-ci dépasse les bornes!...

"Still looking for your boot?"

"Yes, sir, and mean to find it."

— Vous cherchez encore votre bottine?

— Oui, monsieur,... et je prétends qu'il faudra bien qu'on la retrouve.

"But, surely, you said that it was a new brown boot?"

— Vous disiez qu'il s'agissait d'une bottine en cuir fauve?

"So it was, sir. And now it's an old black one."

— Oui.... Mais, maintenant, c'est une noire qu'on a égarée.

"What! you don't mean to say—?"

"That's just what I do mean to say. I only had three pairs in the world—the new brown, the old black, and the patent leathers, which I am wearing. Last night they took one of my brown ones, and today they have sneaked one of the black. Well, have you got it? Speak out, man, and don't stand staring!"

— Non?

— Je dis ce que dis. Je n'en ai que trois paires: des jaunes, neuves; des noires, vieilles, et celles que je porte aux pieds. La nuit dernière, on m'a pris une bottine jaune et, ce matin, on m'en a pris une noire. Eh bien! l'avez-vous? Parlerez-vous, idiot, au lieu de rester là à me regarder?»

An agitated German waiter had appeared upon the scene.

"No, sir; I have made inquiry all over the hotel, but I can hear no word of it."

Un domestique, Allemand d'origine, venait d'apparaître:

«Non, monsieur, répondit-il; je ne l'ai pas.... Je l'ai demandée dans tout l'hôtel.

"Well, either that boot comes back before sundown or I'll see the manager and tell him that I go right straight out of this hotel."

— On retrouvera cette bottine avant ce soir ou je préviendrai le gérant que je quitte immédiatement sa boîte.

"It shall be found, sir—I promise you that if you will have a little patience it will be found."

— On la retrouvera, monsieur,... je vous le promets, si vous daignez prendre patience.

"Mind it is, for it's the last thing of mine that I'll lose in this den of thieves. Well, well, Mr. Holmes, you'll excuse my troubling you about such a tri-

— Faites bien attention que c'est la dernière chose que je consens à perdre dans cette caverne de voleurs Je vous demande pardon, M. Holmes, fle—"

"I think it's well worth troubling about."

"Why, you look very serious over it."

"How do you explain it?"

"I just don't attempt to explain it. It seems the very maddest, queerest thing that ever happened to me."

"The queerest perhaps—" said Holmes thoughtfully.

"What do you make of it yourself?"

"Well, I don't profess to understand it yet. This case of yours is very complex, Sir Henry. When taken in conjunction with your uncle's death I am not sure that of all the five hundred cases of capital importance which I have handled there is one which cuts so deep. But we hold several threads in our hands, and the odds are that one or other of them guides us to the truth. We may waste time in following the wrong one, but sooner or later we must come upon the right."

We had a pleasant luncheon in which little was said of the business which had brought us together. It was in the private sitting-room to which we afterwards repaired that Holmes asked Baskerville what were his intentions.

"To go to Baskerville Hall."

"And when?"

"At the end of the week."

"On the whole," said Holmes, "I think that your decision is a wise one. I have ample evidence that you are being dogged in London, and amid the millions of this great city it is difficult to discover who these people are or what their object can be. If their intentions are evil they might do you a mischief, and we should be powerless to prevent it. You did not know, Dr. Mortimer, that you were followed this morning from my house?"

Dr. Mortimer started violently.

"Followed! By whom?"

"That, unfortunately, is what I cannot tell you. Have you among your neighbours or acquaintances on Dartmoor any man with a black, full beard?"

"No—or, let me see—why, yes. Barrymore, Sir Charles's butler, is a man with a full, black beard."

"Ha! Where is Barrymore?"

"He is in charge of the Hall."

de vous ennuyer de ces futilités.

— Pas du tout,… la chose en vaut la peine.

— Est-ce vraiment votre avis?

— Certainement. Mais comment expliquez-vous ceci? questionna Holmes.

— Je ne cherche même pas à l'expliquer. C'est bien la chose la plus curieuse, la plus folle qui me soit jamais arrivée.

— La plus curieuse… peut-être, répliqua Holmes, pensif.

— Qu'en concluez-vous, vous même? demanda à son tour sir Henry.

— Rien encore. Votre cas est très compliqué. Si je rapproche de la mort de votre oncle les événements qui vous sont personnels, je ne crois pas que, sur les cinq cents affaires dont j'ai dû m'occuper, il y en ait une plus ardue. Mais nous tenons plusieurs fils, et il faut espérer que les uns et les autres nous conduiront à la solution. Peu importe que nous perdions du temps à débrouiller nos nombreux écheveaux…. Tôt ou tard nous mettrons la main sur le bon.»

Pendant le déjeuner, il fut peu question de ce qui nous avait réunis. Lorsque nous retournâmes au salon, Holmes demanda à Baskerville quelles étaient ses intentions.

«Retourner au château?

— Quand?

— À la fin de la semaine.

— À tout prendre, dit Holmes, je considère que c'est le parti le plus sage. J'ai la conviction qu'on vous espionne à Londres. Or, au milieu de cette population de plusieurs millions d'habitants, il n'est pas facile de savoir en face de qui nous nous trouvons, pas plus que de découvrir le dessein que l'on poursuit. Puis, si l'on vous veut du mal, nous serons impuissants à l'empêcher…. Avez-vous remarqué, docteur Mortimer, qu'on vous suivait ce matin, depuis le moment où vous êtes sortis de l'hôtel jusqu'à celui où vous y êtes revenus?»

Mortimer fit un soubresaut.

«Suivis! Par qui?

— Ça, je ne puis malheureusement pas vous l'apprendre. Existe-t-il, parmi vos voisins ou vos connaissances de Dartmoor, un homme portant une longue barbe noire?

— Non. Attendez!… Si; Barrymore, le valet de chambre de sir Charles, porte toute sa barbe… elle est noire.

— Ah!… Où habite ce Barrymore?

— On lui a confié la garde du château.

"We had best ascertain if he is really there, or if by any possibility he might be in London."

"How can you do that?"

"Give me a telegraph form.

'Is all ready for Sir Henry?' That will do. Address to Mr. Barrymore, Baskerville Hall. What is the nearest telegraph-office? Grimpen. Very good, we will send a second wire to the postmaster, Grimpen: 'Telegram to Mr. Barrymore to be delivered into his own hand. If absent, please return wire to Sir Henry Baskerville, Northumberland Hotel.' That should let us know before evening whether Barrymore is at his post in Devonshire or not."

"That's so," said Baskerville. "By the way, Dr. Mortimer, who is this Barrymore, anyhow?"

"He is the son of the old caretaker, who is dead. They have looked after the Hall for four generations now. So far as I know, he and his wife are as respectable a couple as any in the county."

"At the same time," said Baskerville, "it's clear enough that so long as there are none of the family at the Hall these people have a mighty fine home and nothing to do."

"That is true."

"Did Barrymore profit at all by Sir Charles's will?" asked Holmes.

"He and his wife had five hundred pounds each."

"Ha! Did they know that they would receive this?"

"Yes; Sir Charles was very fond of talking about the provisions of his will."

"That is very interesting."

"I hope," said Dr. Mortimer, "that you do not look with suspicious eyes upon everyone who received a legacy from Sir Charles, for I also had a thousand pounds left to me."

"Indeed! And anyone else?"

"There were many insignificant sums to individuals, and a large number of public charities. The residue all went to Sir Henry."

"And how much was the residue?"

"Seven hundred and forty thousand pounds."

Holmes raised his eyebrows in surprise.

"I had no idea that so gigantic a sum was involved," said he.

— Il faut que nous sachions s'il est là ou si, par hasard, il n'aurait pas déserté son poste pour venir à Londres.

— Comment faire?

— Donnez-moi une feuille de télégramme.»

Sherlock Holmes griffonna quelques mots. Il lut:

«Tout est-il préparé pour recevoir sir Henry?» Cela suffira. J'envoie cette dépêche à M. Barrymore, château de Bas-kerville. Quel est le bureau de poste le plus proche? Grimpen… Très bien. Nous allons expédier au directeur de ce bureau un télégramme ainsi conçu: «Remettez en mains propres la dépêche destinée à M. Barrymore. Si absent, retournez-la à sir Henry Baskerville, Northumberland hotel.» Nous apprendrons ainsi, avant ce soir, si, oui ou non, Barrymore est à son poste dans le Devonshire.

— Parfait, dit sir Henry. À propos, docteur Mortimer, parlez-nous un peu de ce Barrymore.

— Il est le fils d'un vieil intendant des Baskerville. Ils habitent le château depuis quatre générations. D'après ce que l'on m'a dit, sa femme et lui sont des gens très honorables.

— Il n'en est pas moins vrai, dit Baskerville, que tant qu'aucun membre de la famille ne résidera au château, ces gens-là y trouveront un bon gîte et n'auront rien à faire.

— C'est exact.

— Les Barrymore figuraient-ils sur le testament de sir Charles? demanda Holmes.

— Pour cinq cents livres sterling chacun.

— Ah! Connaissaient-ils cette libéralité?

— Oui. Sir Charles aimait à parler de ses dispositions testamentaires.

— C'est très intéressant.

— J'aime à croire, fit Mortimer, que vos soupçons ne s'étendent pas à tous ceux qui ont reçu un legs de sir Charles… il m'a laissé mille livres.

— Vraiment!… Et à qui encore?

— Il a légué à des particuliers des sommes insignifiantes et d'autres, très considérables, à des œuvres de bien-faisance.

— À combien s'élevait le montant de sa fortune?

— À sept cent quarante mille livres.»

Holmes ouvrit de grands yeux étonnés.

«Je ne me figurais pas que sir Charles possédât une somme aussi gigantesque.

"Sir Charles had the reputation of being rich, but we did not know how very rich he was until we came to examine his securities. The total value of the estate was close on to a million."

"Dear me! It is a stake for which a man might well play a desperate game. And one more question, Dr. Mortimer. Supposing that anything happened to our young friend here—you will forgive the unpleasant hypothesis!—who would inherit the estate?"

"Since Rodger Baskerville, Sir Charles's younger brother died unmarried, the estate would descend to the Desmonds, who are distant cousins. James Desmond is an elderly clergyman in Westmoreland."

"Thank you. These details are all of great interest. Have you met Mr. James Desmond?"

"Yes; he once came down to visit Sir Charles. He is a man of venerable appearance and of saintly life. I remember that he refused to accept any settlement from Sir Charles, though he pressed it upon him."

"And this man of simple tastes would be the heir to Sir Charles's thousands."

"He would be the heir to the estate because that is entailed. He would also be the heir to the money unless it were willed otherwise by the present owner, who can, of course, do what he likes with it."

"And have you made your will, Sir Henry?"

"No, Mr. Holmes, I have not. I've had no time, for it was only yesterday that I learned how matters stood. But in any case I feel that the money should go with the title and estate. That was my poor uncle's idea. How is the owner going to restore the glories of the Baskervilles if he has not money enough to keep up the property? House, land, and dollars must go together."

"Quite so. Well, Sir Henry, I am of one mind with you as to the advisability of your going down to Devonshire without delay. There is only one provision which I must make. You certainly must not go alone."

"Dr. Mortimer returns with me."

"But Dr. Mortimer has his practice to attend to, and his house is miles away from yours. With all the goodwill in the world he may be unable to help you. No, Sir Henry, you must take with you someone, a trusty man, who will be always by your side."

— Sir Charles passait pour être riche, mais jusqu'au jour de l'inventaire, nous ne soupçonnions pas l'étendue de sa fortune, dont le montant total approchait bien d'un million de livres.

— Peste! Voilà un magot pour lequel un homme peut risquer son va-tout.... Encore une question, docteur Morti-mer. En supposant qu'il arrive malheur à notre jeune ami — pardonnez-moi, sir Henry, cette désagréable hypothèse — à qui reviendra cette fortune?

— Roger Baskerville, le plus jeune frère de sir Charles, étant mort garçon, cette fortune irait à des cousins éloignés, les Desmond. James Desmond est un vieux clergyman du Westmoreland.

— Merci. Ces détails sont du plus grand intérêt. Connaissez-vous M. James Desmond?

— Oui, je l'ai aperçu une fois chez sir Charles. Il a un aspect vénérable et mène, dit-on, une vie exemplaire. Je me souviens qu'il a résisté aux sollicitations de sir Charles, qui insistait pour lui faire accepter une donation assez im-portante.

— Ainsi, cet homme, simple de goûts, deviendrait l'héritier des millions de sir Charles?

— Certainement.... D'après l'ordre des successions, il hériterait du domaine. Il recueillerait également toutes les valeurs, à moins qu'il n'en soit décidé autrement par le précédent propriétaire qui peut, par testament, en disposer à son gré.

— Avez-vous fait votre testament, sir Henry? demanda Sherlock Holmes.

— Non. Je n'en ai pas eu encore le temps, puisque je ne sais que d'hier comment sont les choses. Mais, en tout cas, les valeurs mobilières suivront le domaine et le titre.... Telle était la volonté de mon pauvre oncle. Comment le propriétaire de Baskerville, s'il était pauvre, entretiendrait-il le château? Maison, terres, argent doivent se confondre sur la même tête.

— Parfaitement.... J'approuve votre départ immédiat pour le Devonshire. Je ne mets qu'une restriction à ce projet: vous ne pouvez partir seul.

— Le docteur Mortimer m'accompagne.

— Mais le docteur Mortimer a ses occupations et sa maison est située à plusieurs milles du château. Avec la meilleure volonté du monde, il lui serait impossible de vous porter secours. Non, sir Henry, il faut que vous em-meniez avec vous une personne de confiance qui restera sans cesse à vos côtés.

"Is it possible that you could come yourself, Mr. Holmes?"

"If matters came to a crisis I should endeavour to be present in person; but you can understand that, with my extensive consulting practice and with the constant appeals which reach me from many quarters, it is impossible for me to be absent from London for an indefinite time. At the present instant one of the most revered names in England is being besmirched by a blackmailer, and only I can stop a disastrous scandal. You will see how impossible it is for me to go to Dartmoor."

"Whom would you recommend, then?"

Holmes laid his hand upon my arm.

"If my friend would undertake it there is no man who is better worth having at your side when you are in a tight place. No one can say so more confidently than I."

The proposition took me completely by surprise, but before I had time to answer, Baskerville seized me by the hand and wrung it heartily.

"Well, now, that is real kind of you, Dr. Watson," said he. "You see how it is with me, and you know just as much about the matter as I do. If you will come down to Baskerville Hall and see me through I'll never forget it."

The promise of adventure had always a fascination for me, and I was complimented by the words of Holmes and by the eagerness with which the baronet hailed me as a companion.

"I will come, with pleasure," said I. "I do not know how I could employ my time better."

"And you will report very carefully to me," said Holmes. "When a crisis comes, as it will do, I will direct how you shall act. I suppose that by Saturday all might be ready?"

"Would that suit Dr. Watson?"

"Perfectly."

"Then on Saturday, unless you hear to the contrary, we shall meet at the ten-thirty train from Paddington."

We had risen to depart when Baskerville gave a cry of triumph, and diving into one of the corners of the room he drew a brown boot from under a cabinet.

"My missing boot!" he cried.

— Pouvez-vous venir, monsieur Holmes?

— Au moment critique, je tâcherai de me trouver là. Mais vous comprendrez qu'avec les consultations qu'on me demande de tous côtés et les appels qu'on m'adresse de tous les quartiers de Londres, je ne puisse m'absenter pour un temps indéterminé. Ainsi, à cette heure, un des noms les plus honorés de l'Angleterre se trouve en butte aux attaques d'un maître chanteur, et je suis seul capable d'arrêter ce scandale. Dans ces conditions, comment aller à Dartmoor?

— Alors, qui me recommanderiez-vous?»

Holmes posa sa main sur mon bras.

«Si mon ami consentait à accepter cette mission, dit-il, personne ne serait plus digne que lui de la remplir. Il possède toute ma confiance.»

Cette proposition me prit au dépourvu et, sans me donner le temps de répondre, sir Henry saisit ma main, qu'il serra chaleureusement.

«Je vous remercie de votre obligeance, docteur Watson, dit-il. Vous me connaissez maintenant et vous en savez autant que moi sur cette affaire. Si vous acceptez de m'accompagner au château de Baskerville et de me tenir com-pagnie là-bas, je ne l'oublierai jamais.»

Les expéditions aventureuses ont toujours exercé sur moi une irrésistible fascination; de plus, les paroles élogieuses prononcées par Holmes à mon adresse, ainsi que la précipitation du baronnet à m'agréer pour compagnon, me dé-cidèrent rapidement.

«Je viendrai avec plaisir, répondis-je. Je trouverai difficilement un meilleur emploi de mon temps.

— Vous me tiendrez exactement au courant de tout, dit Holmes. Lorsque la crise arrivera — et elle arrivera cer-tainement — je vous dicterai votre conduite. J'espère que vous serez en mesure de partir samedi, n'est-ce pas, sir Henry?

— Cette date convient-elle au docteur Watson? demanda ce dernier.

— Absolument.

— Alors, à samedi! À moins d'avis contraire, nous nous retrouverons à la gare de Paddington, au train de dix heu-res trente.»

Nous nous levions pour prendre congé, quand Baskerville poussa un cri de triomphe. Il se baissa dans un des coins de la chambre et tira une bottine jaune de dessous une armoire.

«La bottine qui me manquait! s'écria-t-il.

"May all our difficulties vanish as easily!" said Sherlock Holmes.

"But it is a very singular thing," Dr. Mortimer remarked. "I searched this room carefully before lunch."

"And so did I," said Baskerville.

"Every inch of it."

"There was certainly no boot in it then."

"In that case the waiter must have placed it there while we were lunching."

The German was sent for but professed to know nothing of the matter, nor could any inquiry clear it up.

Another item had been added to that constant and apparently purposeless series of small mysteries which had succeeded each other so rapidly.

Setting aside the whole grim story of Sir Charles's death, we had a line of inexplicable incidents all within the limits of two days, which included the receipt of the printed letter, the black-bearded spy in the hansom, the loss of the new brown boot, the loss of the old black boot, and now the return of the new brown boot.

Holmes sat in silence in the cab as we drove back to Baker Street, and I knew from his drawn brows and keen face that his mind, like my own, was busy in endeavouring to frame some scheme into which all these strange and apparently disconnected episodes could be fitted.

All afternoon and late into the evening he sat lost in tobacco and thought.

Just before dinner two telegrams were handed in.

The first ran:

Have just heard that Barrymore is at the Hall. BASKERVILLE.

The second:

Visited twenty-three hotels as directed, but sorry to report unable to trace cut sheet of Times. CARTWRIGHT.

"There go two of my threads, Watson. There is nothing more stimulating than a case where everything goes against you. We must cast round for another scent."

"We have still the cabman who drove the spy."

— Puissent toutes vos difficultés s'aplanir aussi aisément! dit Sherlock Holmes.

— C'est très curieux, intervint le docteur Mortimer; avant le déjeuner, j'ai soigneusement cherché par toute la pièce.

— Moi, aussi, fit Baskerville.

— Je l'ai bouleversée de fond en comble. Il n'y avait pas la moindre bottine.

— Dans ce cas, le garçon l'aura rapportée pendant que nous déjeunions.»

On appela le domestique, qui déclara ne rien savoir et ne put fournir aucun renseignement.

Un nouvel incident venait donc de s'ajouter à cette série de petits mystères qui s'étaient succédé si rapidement.

En négligeant la mort tragique de sir Charles, nous nous trouvions en présence de faits inexplicables survenus dans l'espace de deux jours: la réception de la lettre découpée dans le Times, l'espion à barbe noire blotti dans le cab, la perte de la bottine jaune, puis de la vieille bottine noire, et enfin la trouvaille de la bottine jaune.

Durant notre retour à Baker street, Holmes demeura silencieux. Je voyais à ses sourcils froncés, à sa mine préoccu-pée, que son esprit, — comme le mien, d'ailleurs — s'efforçait à relier entre eux ces épisodes étranges et en appar-ence incohérents.

Tout l'après-midi et jusqu'à bien avant dans la soirée, Holmes s'abîma dans ses pensées et s'enveloppa de nuages de fumée.

À l'heure du dîner, on lui apporta deux télégrammes.

Le premier contenait ceci:

«Le directeur de la poste de Grimpen m'annonce que Barrymore est au château. Baskerville.»

Le second était ainsi conçu:

«Selon votre ordre, j'ai visité vingt-trois hôtels; je n'ai découvert dans aucun le numéro découpé du Times. Cartwright.»

Le visage d'Holmes exprima une vive contrariété.

«Voici déjà deux fils qui se brisent dans nos mains, fit-il. Rien ne me passionne plus qu'une affaire dans laquelle tout se retourne contre moi. Il nous faut chercher une autre piste.

— Nous avons encore celle du cocher qui

"Exactly. I have wired to get his name and address from the Official Registry. I should not be surprised if this were an answer to my question."

The ring at the bell proved to be something even more satisfactory than an answer, however, for the door opened and a rough-looking fellow entered who was evidently the man himself.

"I got a message from the head office that a gent at this address had been inquiring for No. 2704," said he. "I've driven my cab this seven years and never a word of complaint. I came here straight from the Yard to ask you to your face what you had against me."

"I have nothing in the world against you, my good man," said Holmes. "On the contrary, I have half a sovereign for you if you will give me a clear answer to my questions."

"Well, I've had a good day and no mistake," said the cabman with a grin. "What was it you wanted to ask, sir?"

"First of all your name and address, in case I want you again."

"John Clayton, 3 Turpey Street, the Borough. My cab is out of Shipley's Yard, near Waterloo Station."

Sherlock Holmes made a note of it.

"Now, Clayton, tell me all about the fare who came and watched this house at ten o'clock this morning and afterwards followed the two gentlemen down Regent Street."

The man looked surprised and a little embarrassed.

"Why, there's no good my telling you things, for you seem to know as much as I do already," said he. "The truth is that the gentleman told me that he was a detective and that I was to say nothing about him to anyone."

"My good fellow; this is a very serious business, and you may find yourself in a pretty bad position if you try to hide anything from me. You say that your fare told you that he was a detective?"

"Yes, he did."

"When did he say this?"

"When he left me."

"Did he say anything more?"

"He mentioned his name."

Holmes cast a swift glance of triumph at me.

"Oh, he mentioned his name, did he? That

conduisait l'espion.

— Oui. J'ai télégraphié au bureau de la police pour qu'on m'envoyât son nom et son adresse.... Tenez, je ne serais pas surpris que ce fût la réponse à ma demande.»

Un coup de sonnette retentissait en effet à la porte d'entrée. Bientôt après, on introduisit dans le salon un homme qui était le cocher lui-même. Il s'avança, en roulant son chapeau entre ses doigts.

«J'ai reçu du bureau central, dit-il, un message m'avertissant que, dans cette maison, un bourgeois avait pris des renseignements sur le 2 704. Je conduis depuis sept ans sans avoir mérité un seul reproche... J'arrive tout droit de la remise pour que vous m'expliquiez bien en face ce que vous avez contre moi.

— Je n'ai rien contre vous, mon brave homme, dit Holmes. Au contraire, si vous répondez clairement à mes ques-tions, je tiens un demi-souverain à votre disposition.

— Alors, y a pas d'erreur, dit le cocher, j'aurai fait une bonne journée. Que voulez-vous savoir?

— D'abord votre nom et votre adresse, pour le cas où j'aurais encore besoin de vous.

— John Clayton, 3, Turpey street. Je remise à Shipley, près de Waterloo station.»

Sherlock Holmes nota ces renseignements.

«Maintenant, Clayton, reprit-il, parlez-moi du voyageur qui est venu ce matin surveiller cette maison et qui, ensuite, a suivi deux messieurs dans Regent street.»

Le cocher parut étonné et quelque peu embarrassé.

«Je ne vois pas la nécessité de vous parler d'une chose que vous connaissez déjà aussi bien que moi, dit-il. La vérité, c'est que ce voyageur m'avoua être un détective et me recommanda de ne souffler mot de lui à personne.

— Mon ami, reprit Holmes gravement, l'affaire est très sérieuse et vous vous mettriez dans un très vilain cas si vous cherchiez à me cacher quoi que ce soit. Ainsi ce monsieur vous a dit qu'il était détective?

— Oui.

— Quand vous l'a-t-il dit?

— En me quittant.

— Vous a-t-il dit autre chose?

— Il s'est nommé.»

Holmes me jeta un regard triomphant.

«Vraiment!... Il s'est nommé!... Quelle impruwas imprudent. What was the name that he mentioned?"

"His name," said the cabman, "was Mr. Sherlock Holmes."

Never have I seen my friend more completely taken aback than by the cabman's reply.

For an instant he sat in silent amazement. Then he burst into a hearty laugh.

"A touch, Watson—an undeniable touch!" said he. "I feel a foil as quick and supple as my own. He got home upon me very prettily that time. So his name was Sherlock Holmes, was it?"

"Yes, sir, that was the gentleman's name."

"Excellent! Tell me where you picked him up and all that occurred."

"He hailed me at half-past nine in Trafalgar Square. He said that he was a detective, and he offered me two guineas if I would do exactly what he wanted all day and ask no questions. I was glad enough to agree. First we drove down to the Northumberland Hotel and waited there until two gentlemen came out and took a cab from the rank. We followed their cab until it pulled up somewhere near here."

"This very door," said Holmes.

"Well, I couldn't be sure of that, but I dare say my fare knew all about it. We pulled up halfway down the street and waited an hour and a half. Then the two gentlemen passed us, walking, and we followed down Baker Street and along—"

"I know," said Holmes.

"Until we got three-quarters down Regent Street. Then my gentleman threw up the trap, and he cried that I should drive right away to Waterloo Station as hard as I could go. I whipped up the mare and we were there under the ten minutes. Then he paid up his two guineas, like a good one, and away he went into the station. Only just as he was leaving he turned round and he said: 'It might interest you to know that you have been driving Mr. Sherlock Holmes.' That's how I come to know the name."

"I see. And you saw no more of him?"

"Not after he went into the station."

"And how would you describe Mr. Sherlock Holmes?"

The cabman scratched his head.

"Well, he wasn't altogether such an easy gentleman to describe. I'd put him at forty years of age,

dence!... Et quel nom vous a-t-il donné?

— Son nom? répéta le cocher... Sherlock Holmes.»

Jamais réponse ne démonta mon ami comme celle qui venait de lui être faite.

Pendant un instant, il sembla ahuri.

«Touché, Watson!... bien touché!... Le coup a été bien envoyé, et je sens devant moi une arme aussi rapide et aussi souple que celle que je manie... Ainsi donc votre voyageur s'appelait Sherlock Holmes?

— Oui, monsieur, il m'a donné ce nom-là.

— Parfait. Où l'avez-vous «chargé» et qu'est-il arrivé ensuite?

— Il m'a hélé à neuf heures et demie, dans Trafalgar square. Il m'a dit qu'il était détective et m'a offert deux guinées pour la journée. Je devais aller où bon lui semblerait, sans jamais lui poser de questions. Je me suis bien gardé de refuser cette offre. Je l'ai conduit près de Northumberland hotel, où nous avons attendu la sortie de deux messieurs qui sont montés dans un cab à la station voisine. Nous avons suivi cette voiture jusqu'à ce qu'elle se soit arrêtée près d'ici.

— À ma porte? dit Holmes.

— Je n'en suis pas certain; mais le bourgeois, lui, savait où les autres allaient. Il est descendu à peu près au milieu de la rue et j'ai «poireauté» une heure et demie. Alors les deux messieurs sont repassés à pied, et nous les avons suivis de nouveau dans Baker street et dans...

— Je sais, interrompit Holmes.

— Nous avions remonté les trois quarts de Regent street... À ce moment, à travers la trappe, mon voyageur m'a crié de filer vers Waterloo station aussi vite que possible. J'ai fouetté la jument et, dix minutes plus tard, nous étions rendus à destination. Il m'a payé deux guinées, comme un «bon zigue», et il est entré dans la gare. En me quittant, il s'est retourné et m'a dit: «Vous serez peut-être content d'apprendre que vous avez conduit M. Sherlock Holmes». Voilà comment j'ai appris son nom.

— Je comprends... Et vous ne l'avez plus revu?

— Non... Il avait disparu dans la gare.

— Faites-moi le portrait de M. Sherlock Holmes.»

Le cocher se gratta la tête:

«Il n'est pas facile à peindre. Il paraît quarante ans... Il est de taille moyenne... cinq ou six centi-

and he was of a middle height, two or three inches shorter than you, sir. He was dressed like a toff, and he had a black beard, cut square at the end, and a pale face. I don't know as I could say more than that."

"Colour of his eyes?"

"No, I can't say that."

"Nothing more that you can remember?"

"No, sir; nothing."

"Well, then, here is your half-sovereign. There's another one waiting for you if you can bring any more information. Good-night!"

"Good-night, sir, and thank you!"

John Clayton departed chuckling, and Holmes turned to me with a shrug of his shoulders and a rueful smile.

"Snap goes our third thread, and we end where we began," said he. "The cunning rascal! He knew our number, knew that Sir Henry Baskerville had consulted me, spotted who I was in Regent Street, conjectured that I had got the number of the cab and would lay my hands on the driver, and so sent back this audacious message. I tell you, Watson, this time we have got a foeman who is worthy of our steel. I've been checkmated in London. I can only wish you better luck in Devonshire. But I'm not easy in my mind about it."

"About what?"

"About sending you. It's an ugly business, Watson, an ugly dangerous business, and the more I see of it the less I like it. Yes, my dear fellow, you may laugh, but I give you my word that I shall be very glad to have you back safe and sound in Baker Street once more."

mètres de moins que vous. Il était habillé comme un gommeux et portait une barbe noire coupée en carré... Il m'a semblé très pâle... Je ne puis vous en dire plus long.

— La couleur de ses yeux?»

Le cocher parut chercher dans ses souvenirs et répondit:

«Je ne me la rappelle pas.

— D'autres détails vous ont-ils frappé?

— Non.

— Bien, fit Holmes. Voici votre demi-souverain. Vous en aurez un autre, si vous m'apportez de nouveaux rensei-gnements. Bonne nuit.

— Bonne nuit, monsieur, et merci.»

John Clayton partit très satisfait. Holmes se retourna vers moi avec un haussement d'épaules et un sourire découragé.

«Voilà un troisième fil qui casse et nous ne sommes pas plus avancés qu'au début, dit-il. Le rusé coquin!... Il con-naissait le numéro de ma maison et la visite projetée par sir Henry Baskerville!... Dans Regent street, il a flairé qui j'étais... il s'est douté que j'avais pris le numéro de sa voiture et que je rechercherais le cocher!... Ah! Watson, cette fois nous aurons à lutter contre un adversaire digne de nous. Il m'a fait mat à Londres; je vous souhaite meilleure chance dans le Devonshire... Mais je ne suis plus aussi tranquille.

— Sur quoi?

— Sur votre sort, là-bas. C'est une vilaine affaire, Watson,... vilaine et dangereuse... Plus je l'examine et moins elle me plaît. Oui, oui, mon cher ami, riez à votre aise!... Je vous jure que je serai très heureux de vous revoir sain et sauf dans notre logis de Baker street.»

CHAPTER 6. BASKERVILLE HALL

Sir Henry Baskerville and Dr. Mortimer were ready upon the appointed day, and we started as arranged for Devonshire. Mr. Sherlock Holmes drove with me to the station and gave me his last parting injunctions and advice.

"I will not bias your mind by suggesting theories or suspicions, Watson," said he; "I wish you simply to report facts in the fullest possible manner to me, and you can leave me to do the theorizing."

"What sort of facts?" I asked.

"Anything which may seem to have a bearing however indirect upon the case, and especially the relations between young Baskerville and his neighbours or any fresh particulars concerning the death of Sir Charles. I have made some inquiries myself in the last few days, but the results have, I fear, been negative. One thing only appears to be certain, and that is that Mr. James Desmond, who is the next heir, is an elderly gentleman of a very amiable disposition, so that this persecution does not arise from him. I really think that we may eliminate him entirely from our calculations. There remain the people who will actually surround Sir Henry Baskerville upon the moor."

"Would it not be well in the first place to get rid of this Barrymore couple?"

"By no means. You could not make a greater mistake. If they are innocent it would be a cruel injustice, and if they are guilty we should be giving up all chance of bringing it home to them. No, no, we will preserve them upon our list of suspects. Then there is a groom at the Hall, if I remember right. There are two moorland farmers. There is our friend Dr. Mortimer, whom I believe to be entirely honest, and there is his wife, of whom we know nothing. There is this naturalist, Stapleton, and there is his sister, who is said to be a young lady of attractions. There is Mr. Frankland, of Lafter Hall, who is also an unknown factor, and

CHAPITRE 6. LE CHATEAU DE BASKERVILLE

Au jour indiqué, sir Henry Baskerville et le docteur Mortimer se trouvèrent prêts, et nous partîmes pour le Devon-shire, ainsi que cela avait été convenu. Sherlock Holmes m'accompagna à la gare, afin de me donner en voiture ses dernières instructions.

«Je ne vous troublerai pas, me dit-il, par l'exposé de mes théories ou par la confidence de mes soupçons. Je désire simplement que vous me teniez au courant des faits jusque dans leurs plus petits détails. Reposez-vous sur moi du soin d'en tirer les déductions qu'ils comporteront.

— Quelle espèce de faits dois-je vous communiquer? demandai-je.

— Tous ceux qui vous paraîtront toucher à l'affaire — même de loin… Renseignez-moi sur les relations du jeune Baskerville avec ses voisins et sur tout ce que vous pourrez recueillir de nouveau concernant la mort de sir Charles. Je me suis livré, ces jours derniers, à quelques enquêtes dont le résultat, je le crains fort, aura été négatif. Une seule chose me semble certaine: M. James Desmond, l'héritier présomptif, est un parfait galant homme; cette persécution n'émane pas de lui. Nous devons donc éliminer ce clergyman de nos calculs. Il ne reste plus que les personnes qui entoureront sir Henry Baskerville sur la lande.

— Ne pensez-vous pas qu'il serait bon de se débarrasser immédiatement du couple Barrymore?

— Non, nous commettrions une faute. Innocents, ce serait une cruelle injustice; coupables, ce serait renoncer à la possibilité de les confondre. Non, non, conservons-les sur notre liste de suspects. Si je me souviens bien, il y a au château un cocher et, sur la lande, deux fermiers. Nous y trouvons également notre ami le docteur Mortimer — que je tiens pour absolument honnête — et sa femme — sur laquelle nous manquons de renseignements. Il y a aussi le naturaliste Stapleton et sa sœur, qu'on dit très attrayante; puis c'est M. Frankland, de Lafter Hall, qui représente un facteur inconnu, ainsi que deux ou trois autres voisins. Vous there are one or two other neighbours. These are the folk who must be your very special study."

"I will do my best."

"You have arms, I suppose?"

"Yes, I thought it as well to take them."

"Most certainly. Keep your revolver near you night and day, and never relax your precautions."

Our friends had already secured a first-class carriage and were waiting for us upon the platform.

"No, we have no news of any kind," said Dr. Mortimer in answer to my friend's questions. "I can swear to one thing, and that is that we have not been shadowed during the last two days. We have never gone out without keeping a sharp watch, and no one could have escaped our notice."

"You have always kept together, I presume?"

"Except yesterday afternoon. I usually give up one day to pure amusement when I come to town, so I spent it at the Museum of the College of Surgeons."

"And I went to look at the folk in the park," said Baskerville. But we had no trouble of any kind."

"It was imprudent, all the same," said Holmes, shaking his head and looking very grave. "I beg, Sir Henry, that you will not go about alone. Some great misfortune will befall you if you do. Did you get your other boot?"

"No, sir, it is gone forever."

"Indeed. That is very interesting. Well, goodbye," he added as the train began to glide down the platform.

"Bear in mind, Sir Henry, one of the phrases in that queer old legend which Dr. Mortimer has read to us, and avoid the moor in those hours of darkness when the powers of evil are exalted."

I looked back at the platform when we had left it far behind and saw the tall, austere figure of Holmes standing motionless and gazing after us.

The journey was a swift and pleasant one, and I spent it in making the more intimate acquaintance of my two companions and in playing with Dr. Mortimer's spaniel.

In a very few hours the brown earth had become ruddy, the brick had changed to granite, and red cows grazed in well-hedged fields where the lush grasses and more luxuriant vegetation spoke

devrez porter vos investigations sur ces gens-là.

— J'agirai de mon mieux.

— Je suppose que vous emportez des armes?

— Oui, j'ai cru bien faire de m'en munir.

— Certainement. Jour et nuit ayez votre revolver à portée de la main, et ne vous relâchez jamais de vos mesures de prudence.»

Nos amis avaient déjà retenu un wagon de 1re classe et nous attendaient sur le quai.

«Non, nous n'avons rien de neuf à vous apprendre, fit le docteur Mortimer, en répondant à une question de mon ami. Je ne puis vous affirmer qu'une chose: personne ne nous a suivis depuis deux jours. Nous ne sommes jamais sortis sans avoir regardé de tous côtés, et un espion n'aurait pas échappé à notre vigilance.

— Vous ne vous êtes pas quittés, je présume?

— Seulement hier, après midi. Quand je suis à Londres, je consacre toujours quelques heures aux distractions... je les ai passées au musée de l'Académie de chirurgie.

— Et moi, je suis allé voir le beau monde, à Hyde Park, dit Baskerville. Il ne s'est rien produit d'extraordinaire.

— C'était tout de même imprudent, répliqua gravement Holmes, en secouant la tête. Je vous prie, sir Henry, de ne plus vous absenter seul, si vous ne voulez pas vous exposer à de grands malheurs. Avez-vous retrouvé votre bottine?

— Non; elle est bien perdue.

— C'est vraiment très curieux. Allons, adieu!» ajouta-t-il, comme le train commençait à glisser le long du quai.

Puis il reprit:

«Souvenez-vous, sir Henry, de l'une des phrases de la légende que le docteur Mortimer nous a lue: «Évitez la lande à l'heure où l'esprit du mal chemine».

Je passai la tête par la portière pour regarder encore le quai, que nous avions déjà laissé bien loin derrière nous, et j'aperçus la grande silhouette de Sherlock Holmes, immobile et tournée vers nous.

Le voyage me parut court et agréable. J'employai le temps à faire plus ample connaissance avec mes compagnons et à jouer avec le caniche de Mortimer.

Peu d'heures après notre départ, le sol changea de couleur; de brun, il devint rougeâtre. Le granit avait remplacé la pierre calcaire. Des vaches rousses ruminaient dans de gras pâturages, dénoof a richer, if a damper, climate.

Young Baskerville stared eagerly out of the window and cried aloud with delight as he recognized the familiar features of the Devon scenery.

"I've been over a good part of the world since I left it, Dr. Watson," said he; "but I have never seen a place to compare with it."

"I never saw a Devonshire man who did not swear by his county," I remarked.

"It depends upon the breed of men quite as much as on the county," said Dr. Mortimer. "A glance at our friend here reveals the rounded head of the Celt, which carries inside it the Celtic enthusiasm and power of attachment. Poor Sir Charles's head was of a very rare type, half Gaelic, half Ivernian in its characteristics. But you were very young when you last saw Baskerville Hall, were you not?"

"I was a boy in my teens at the time of my father's death and had never seen the Hall, for he lived in a little cottage on the South Coast. Thence I went straight to a friend in America. I tell you it is all as new to me as it is to Dr. Watson, and I'm as keen as possible to see the moor."

"Are you? Then your wish is easily granted, for there is your first sight of the moor," said Dr. Mortimer, pointing out of the carriage window.

Over the green squares of the fields and the low curve of a wood there rose in the distance a grey, melancholy hill, with a strange jagged summit, dim and vague in the distance, like some fantastic landscape in a dream.

Baskerville sat for a long time, his eyes fixed upon it, and I read upon his eager face how much it meant to him, this first sight of that strange spot where the men of his blood had held sway so long and left their mark so deep. T

here he sat, with his tweed suit and his American accent, in the corner of a prosaic railway-carriage, and yet as I looked at his dark and expressive face I felt more than ever how true a descendant he was of that long line of high-blooded, fiery, and masterful men.

tant un pays plus fertile, mais plus humide.

Le jeune Baskerville, le visage collé aux vitres du wagon, contemplait avec intérêt le paysage et s'enthousiasmait à la vue des horizons familiers du Devonshire.

«Depuis que j'ai quitté l'Angleterre, dit-il, j'ai parcouru la moitié du monde, mais je n'ai jamais rien trouvé de com-parable à ceci.

— Il est rare de rencontrer un habitant du Devonshire, fis-je observer, qui ne soit pas épris de son comté.

— Cela dépend tout autant de l'individu que du comté, repartit Mortimer. Un examen superficiel de notre ami révèle chez lui la tête du Celte où sont fortement développées les bosses de l'enthousiasme et de l'attachement. Le crâne du pauvre sir Charles présentait les particularités d'un type très rare, moitié gaélique et moitié hibernien.... Vous étiez fort jeune, n'est-ce pas, sir Henry, lorsque vous vîntes au château de Baskerville pour la dernière fois?

— À la mort de mon frère, j'avais une dizaine d'années et je ne suis jamais venu au château. Nous habitions un petit cottage sur la côte méridionale de l'Angleterre. Je suis parti de là pour rejoindre un ami en Amérique. La con-trée que nous traversons est aussi nouvelle pour moi que pour le docteur Watson; cela vous explique l'extrême curi-osité que la lande excite en moi.

— Vous allez pouvoir la satisfaire, dit Mortimer, en désignant la fenêtre du wagon... Vous devez l'apercevoir d'ici.»

Dans le lointain, au-dessus de la verdure des champs et dominant une pente boisée, se dressait une colline grise, mélancolique, terminée par une cime dentelée dont les arêtes, à cette distance, perdaient de leur netteté et de leur vigueur. Cela ressemblait à quelque paysage fantastique entrevu à travers un rêve.

Baskerville tint longtemps les yeux fixés sur ce coin du ciel, et je lus sur son visage mobile l'impression que faisait sur son esprit la vue de cette contrée où ceux de sa race avaient vécu si longtemps et avaient laissé de si profondes traces de leur passage.

Il était assis en face de moi, dans le coin d'un prosaïque wagon, vêtu de son complet gris, parlant avec cet accent américain fortement prononcé, et, pendant que je détaillais sa figure énergique, je pressentais plus que jamais qu'il était vraiment le descendant de cette longue lignée d'hommes ardents et courageux.

There were pride, valour, and strength in his thick brows, his sensitive nostrils, and his large hazel eyes.

If on that forbidding moor a difficult and dangerous quest should lie before us, this was at least a comrade for whom one might venture to take a risk with the certainty that he would bravely share it.

Il y avait de l'orgueil, de la vaillance et de la force sous ces épais sourcils, ainsi que dans ces narines mobiles et dans ces yeux couleur de noisette.

Si, sur cette lande d'aspect sauvage, nous devions entreprendre une enquête difficile et périlleuse, nous aurions dans sir Henry un compagnon avec lequel on pouvait tenter l'aventure, certains qu'il saurait en partager bravement tous les dangers.

The train pulled up at a small wayside station and we all descended. Outside, beyond the low, white fence, a wagonette with a pair of cobs was waiting.

Our coming was evidently a great event, for station-master and porters clustered round us to carry out our luggage.

Le train stoppa à une petite station. Nous descendîmes. Dehors, au delà d'une petite barrière peinte en blanc, attendait une voiture attelée de deux cobs.

Notre arrivée constituait sûrement un grand événement, car le chef de gare et les hommes d'équipe se précipitèrent au-devant de nous pour prendre nos bagages.

It was a sweet, simple country spot, but I was surprised to observe that by the gate there stood two soldierly men in dark uniforms who leaned upon their short rifles and glanced keenly at us as we passed.

The coachman, a hard-faced, gnarled little fellow, saluted Sir Henry Baskerville, and in a few minutes we were flying swiftly down the broad, white road. Rolling pasture lands curved upward on either side of us, and old gabled houses peeped out from amid the thick green foliage, but behind the peaceful and sunlit countryside there rose ever, dark against the evening sky, the long, gloomy curve of the moor, broken by the jagged and sinister hills.

The wagonette swung round into a side road, and we curved upward through deep lanes worn by centuries of wheels, high banks on either side, heavy with dripping moss and fleshy hart's-tongue ferns. Bronzing bracken and mottled bramble gleamed in the light of the sinking sun. Still steadily rising, we passed over a narrow granite bridge and skirted a noisy stream which gushed swiftly down, foaming and roaring amid the grey boulders. Both road and stream wound up through a valley dense with scrub oak and fir.

At every turn Baskerville gave an exclamation of delight, looking eagerly about him and asking countless questions. To his eyes all seemed beautiful, but to me a tinge of melancholy lay upon the countryside, which bore so clearly the mark of the waning year. Yellow leaves carpeted the lanes and fluttered down upon us as we passed. The rattle of our wheels died away as we drove through drifts of rotting vegetation—sad gifts, as it seemed to me,

C'était une simple halte au milieu de la campagne. Je fus donc très surpris de remarquer que, de chaque côté de la porte, deux soldats se tenaient appuyés sur leur fusil. Quand nous passâmes auprès d'eux, ils nous dévisagèrent avec insistance.

Le cocher, petit, trapu, salua sir Henry Baskerville, et, quelques minutes plus tard, nous roulions sur la route blanche et poudreuse. Nous traversions un pays vallonné, couvert de pâturages. Le toit de quelques maisons s'élevait au-dessus des frondaisons épaisses des arbres; mais au-delà de cette campagne paisible, illuminée par les rayons du soleil couchant, la longue silhouette de la lande se détachait en noir sur l'azur du ciel. La voiture s'engagea dans un chemin de traverse.

Nous gravîmes ainsi des sentiers abrupts, bordés de hauts talus tapissés de mousse et de scolopendres, où, pendant des siècles, le passage des roues avait creusé de profondes ornières. Des fougères rouillées par la rosée, des ronces aux baies sanglantes étincelaient aux derniers feux du soleil. Nous franchîmes un petit pont de granit et nous côtoyâmes un ruisseau qui fuyait rapidement sur un lit de cailloux grisâtres. La route et le ruisseau suivaient une vallée plantée de chênes rabougris et de sapins étiques.

Baskerville saluait chaque tournant du chemin par une exclamation de surprise. Tout lui semblait beau, tandis que j'éprouvais une indéfinissable tristesse à l'aspect de cette campagne qui portait les stigmates irrécusables de l'hiver déjà prochain.

for Nature to throw before the carriage of the returning heir of the Baskervilles.

"Halloa!" cried Dr. Mortimer, "what is this?"

A steep curve of heath-clad land, an outlying spur of the moor, lay in front of us. On the summit, hard and clear like an equestrian statue upon its pedestal, was a mounted soldier, dark and stern, his rifle poised ready over his forearm. He was watching the road along which we travelled.

"What is this, Perkins?" asked Dr. Mortimer.

Our driver half turned in his seat.

"There's a convict escaped from Princetown, sir. He's been out three days now, and the warders watch every road and every station, but they've had no sight of him yet. The farmers about here don't like it, sir, and that's a fact."

"Well, I understand that they get five pounds if they can give information."

"Yes, sir, but the chance of five pounds is but a poor thing compared to the chance of having your throat cut. You see, it isn't like any ordinary convict. This is a man that would stick at nothing."

"Who is he, then?"

"It is Selden, the Notting Hill murderer."

I remembered the case well, for it was one in which Holmes had taken an interest on account of the peculiar ferocity of the crime and the wanton brutality which had marked all the actions of the assassin. The commutation of his death sentence had been due to some doubts as to his complete sanity, so atrocious was his conduct. Our wagonette had topped a rise and in front of us rose the huge expanse of the moor, mottled with gnarled and craggy cairns and tors.

A cold wind swept down from it and set us shivering. Somewhere there, on that desolate plain, was lurking this fiendish man, hiding in a burrow like a wild beast, his heart full of malignancy against the whole race which had cast him out.

It needed but this to complete the grim suggestiveness of the barren waste, the chilling wind, and the darkling sky. Even Baskerville fell silent and pulled his overcoat more closely around him.

We had left the fertile country behind and be-

Tout à coup Mortimer s'écria: «Regardez donc ça!»

Une petite colline, une sorte d'éperon formé par la lande et s'avançant dans la vallée, se dressait devant nous. Sur la cime, semblable à une statue équestre, nous aperçûmes un soldat à cheval, le fusil appuyé sur son bras gauche, prêt à faire feu. Il gardait la route par laquelle nous arrivions.

«Que signifie ceci, Perkins?» demanda Mortimer au cocher.

Celui-ci se retourna à demi sur son siège.

«Un condamné s'est échappé, il y a trois jours, de la prison de Princetown. On a placé des sentinelles sur tous les chemins et dans toutes les gares. On ne l'a pas encore retrouvé, et les fermiers des environs sont bien ennuyés.

— Je comprends,…. ils toucheraient cinq livres de récompense en échange d'un petit renseignement.

— Oui, monsieur. Mais cinq livres de récompense représentent bien peu de chose en comparaison du danger qu'ils courent d'avoir le cou coupé. Ah! ce n'est pas un condamné ordinaire! Il est capable de tout.

— Qui est-ce?

— Selden, l'assassin de Notting Hill.»

Je me souvenais parfaitement de ce crime. Il était un de ceux qui avaient le plus intéressé Sherlock Holmes, en rai-son des circonstances particulièrement féroces qui entourèrent le crime et de l'odieuse brutalité avec laquelle l'assassin accomplit son forfait. Cependant on avait commué la sentence de mort prononcée contre le coupable, sur des doutes conçus à propos de sa responsabilité mentale.

Notre voiture avait gravi une pente et, devant nous, se déroulait l'immense étendue de la lande. Un vent glacial qui la balayait nous fit frissonner. Ainsi donc, quelque part sur cette plaine désolée, se terrait comme une bête sauvage, cette infernale créature dont le cœur devait maudire l'humanité qui l'avait rejetée de son sein.

Il ne manquait plus que cela pour compléter la lugubre impression produite par cette vaste solitude, cette bise glacée et ce ciel qui s'assombrissait davantage à chaque instant. Sir Henry Baskerville lui-même devint taciturne et serra plus étroitement autour de lui les pans de son manteau.

Maintenant, les plaines fertiles s'étendaient

neath us. We looked back on it now, the slanting rays of a low sun turning the streams to threads of gold and glowing on the red earth new turned by the plough and the broad tangle of the woodlands.

derrière et au-dessous de nous. Nous voulûmes les contempler une dernière fois. Les rayons obliques du soleil abaissés sur l'horizon teintaient d'or les eaux du ruisseau et faisaient briller la terre rouge fraîchement remuée par le soc de la charrue.

The road in front of us grew bleaker and wilder over huge russet and olive slopes, sprinkled with giant boulders. Now and then we passed a moorland cottage, walled and roofed with stone, with no creeper to break its harsh outline.

Devant nous, la route, avec ses pentes rudes parsemées d'énormes rochers roussâtres, prenait un aspect de plus en plus sauvage. De loin en loin, nous passions près d'un cottage, construit et couvert en pierres, dont aucune plante grimpante n'atténuait la rigidité des lignes.

Suddenly we looked down into a cuplike depression, patched with stunted oaks and firs which had been twisted and bent by the fury of years of storm. Two high, narrow towers rose over the trees.

Soudain, nous vîmes une dépression de terrain, ayant la forme d'un entonnoir, où croissaient des chênes entr'ouverts, ainsi que des sapins échevelés et tordus par des siècles de rafale. Deux hautes tours effilées pointaient au-dessus des arbres.

The driver pointed with his whip.

"Baskerville Hall," said he.

Le cocher les désigna avec son fouet.

«Le château de Baskerville», dit-il.

Its master had risen and was staring with flushed cheeks and shining eyes.

A few minutes later we had reached the lodge-gates, a maze of fantastic tracery in wrought iron, with weather-bitten pillars on either side, blotched with lichens, and surmounted by the boars' heads of the Baskervilles.

Les joues empourprées, les yeux enflammés, sir Henry s'était levé et regardait.

Quelques minutes après, nous atteignîmes la grille du château, enchâssée dans des piliers rongés par le temps, mou-chetés de lichens et surmontés de têtes de sangliers, armes de Baskerville.

The lodge was a ruin of black granite and bared ribs of rafters, but facing it was a new building, half constructed, the first fruit of Sir Charles's South African gold.

Le pavillon du portier n'était plus qu'une ruine de granit noir au-dessus de laquelle s'enchevêtrait un réseau de chevrons dépouillés du toit qu'ils supportaient jadis. En face, s'élevait un nouveau bâtiment dont la mort de sir Charles avait arrêté l'achèvement.

Through the gateway we passed into the avenue, where the wheels were again hushed amid the leaves, and the old trees shot their branches in a sombre tunnel over our heads.

La porte s'ouvrait sur une avenue où les roues de la voiture s'enfoncèrent dans un lit de feuilles mortes. Les branch-es des arbres séculaires qui la bordaient se rejoignaient au-dessus de nos têtes pour former comme un sombre tun-nel.

Baskerville shuddered as he looked up the long, dark drive to where the house glimmered like a ghost at the farther end.

"Was it here?" he asked in a low voice.

"No, no, the yew alley is on the other side."

The young heir glanced round with a gloomy face.

"It's no wonder my uncle felt as if trouble were

Baskerville frissonna, en apercevant cette lugubre allée à l'extrémité de laquelle on découvrait le château.

«Est-ce ici? demanda-t-il à voix basse.

— Non; l'allée des Ifs se trouve de l'autre côté.

— Je ne m'étonne pas que, dans un endroit pareil, l'esprit de mon oncle se soit détraqué.

Il n'en faut pas davantage pour déprimer un

coming on him in such a place as this," said he. "It's enough to scare any man. I'll have a row of electric lamps up here inside of six months, and you won't know it again, with a thousand candle-power Swan and Edison right here in front of the hall door."

homme. Avant six mois j'aurai installé là, ainsi que devant le château, une double rangée de lampes électriques.»

The avenue opened into a broad expanse of turf, and the house lay before us. In the fading light I could see that the centre was a heavy block of building from which a porch projected.

L'avenue aboutissait à une large pelouse au delà de laquelle on distinguait le château. À la clarté pâlissante de ce soir d'automne, je vis que le centre était formé par une construction massive, avec un portail formant saillie.

The whole front was draped in ivy, with a patch clipped bare here and there where a window or a coat of arms broke through the dark veil. From this central block rose the twin towers, ancient, crenelated, and pierced with many loopholes. To right and left of the turrets were more modern wings of black granite. A dull light shone through heavy mullioned windows, and from the high chimneys which rose from the steep, high-angled roof there sprang a single black column of smoke.

La façade disparaissait sous les lierres. Les fenêtres et quelques écussons aux armes des Baskerville coupaient çà et là l'uniformité de cette sombre verdure. De cette partie centrale, montaient les deux tours, antiques, crénelées, percées de nombreuses meurtrières. À droite et à gauche de ces tours, on avait ajouté une aile d'un style plus moderne.

"Welcome, Sir Henry! Welcome to Baskerville Hall!"

A tall man had stepped from the shadow of the porch to open the door of the wagonette. The figure of a woman was silhouetted against the yellow light of the hall. She came out and helped the man to hand down our bags.

"You don't mind my driving straight home, Sir Henry?" said Dr. Mortimer. "My wife is expecting me."

"Surely you will stay and have some dinner?"

"No, I must go. I shall probably find some work awaiting me. I would stay to show you over the house, but Barrymore will be a better guide than I. Good-bye, and never hesitate night or day to send for me if I can be of service."

«Soyez le bienvenu au château de Baskerville, sir Henry», dit une voix.

Un homme de haute taille s'était avancé pour ouvrir la portière de la voiture. Une silhouette de femme se profilait dans l'encadrement de la porte. Elle sortit à son tour et aida l'homme à descendre les bagages.

«Je vous demande la permission de rentrer directement chez moi, sir Henry, dit Mortimer. Ma femme m'attend!

— Vous ne voulez pas dîner avec nous?

— Non; il faut que je m'en aille. Je dois avoir des malades qui me réclament. J'aurais été heureux de vous montrer le château, mais Barrymore sera un meilleur guide que moi. Au revoir, et, si je puis vous rendre service, n'hésitez pas à me faire appeler à toute heure du jour ou de la nuit.»

The wheels died away down the drive while Sir Henry and I turned into the hall, and the door clanged heavily behind us. It was a fine apartment in which we found ourselves, large, lofty, and heavily raftered with huge baulks of age-blackened oak.

Le roulement de la voiture qui emmenait le docteur s'éteignit bientôt dans le lointain. Sir Henry et moi nous entrâmes dans le château et la porte se referma lourdement sur nous. Nous nous trouvâmes dans une grande pièce, dont le plafond, très élevé, était soutenu par de fortes solives de chêne noircies par le temps.

In the great old-fashioned fireplace behind the high iron dogs a log-fire crackled and snapped. Sir Henry and I held out our hands to it, for we were numb from our long drive.

Dans une cheminée monumentale, un feu de bois pétillait sur de hauts chenets. Nous en approchâmes nos mains engourdies par le froid du voyage.

Then we gazed round us at the high, thin window of old stained glass, the oak panelling, the stags' heads, the coats of arms upon the walls, all dim and sombre in the subdued light of the central lamp.

Nous examinâmes curieusement les hautes et longues fenêtres aux vitraux multicolores, les lambris de chêne, les têtes de cerf et les armes accrochées aux murs — le tout triste et sombre sous la

Welcome, Sir Henry! Welcome to Baskerville Hall!
Soyez le bienvenu au château de Baskerville, sir Henry!

"It's just as I imagined it," said Sir Henry. "Is it not the very picture of an old family home? To think that this should be the same hall in which for five hundred years my people have lived. It strikes me solemn to think of it."

I saw his dark face lit up with a boyish enthusiasm as he gazed about him. The light beat upon him where he stood, but long shadows trailed down the walls and hung like a black canopy above him.

Barrymore had returned from taking our luggage to our rooms. He stood in front of us now with the subdued manner of a well-trained servant. He was a remarkable-looking man, tall, handsome, with a square black beard and pale, distinguished features.

"Would you wish dinner to be served at once, sir?"

"Is it ready?"

"In a very few minutes, sir. You will find hot water in your rooms. My wife and I will be happy, Sir Henry, to stay with you until you have made your fresh arrangements, but you will understand that under the new conditions this house will require a considerable staff."

"What new conditions?"

"I only meant, sir, that Sir Charles led a very retired life, and we were able to look after his wants. You would, naturally, wish to have more company, and so you will need changes in your household."

"Do you mean that your wife and you wish to leave?"

"Only when it is quite convenient to you, sir."

"But your family have been with us for several generations, have they not? I should be sorry to begin my life here by breaking an old family connection."

I seemed to discern some signs of emotion upon the butler's white face.

"I feel that also, sir, and so does my wife. But to tell the truth, sir, we were both very much attached to Sir Charles, and his death gave us a shock and made these surroundings very painful to us. I fear that we shall never again be easy in our minds at Baskerville Hall."

lumière atténuée d'une lampe ac-crochée au milieu du plafond.

«C'est bien ainsi que je me représentais le château, me dit sir Henry. Cela ne ressemble-t-il pas à quelque vieux tableau d'intérieur? La demeure n'a pas changé depuis cinq cents ans qu'y vivent mes ancêtres!»

Tandis qu'il jetait les yeux autour de lui, son visage bronzé s'éclaira d'un enthousiasme juvénile. Mais, à un mo-ment, la lumière le frappa directement, alors que de longues traînées d'ombre couraient contre les murs, formant au-dessus de sa tête et derrière lui comme un dais funéraire.

Barrymore était revenu de porter les bagages dans nos chambres. Il se tenait devant nous dans l'attitude respec-tueuse d'un domestique de grande maison. Il avait très bonne apparence, avec sa haute taille, sa barbe noire coupée en carré et sa figure qui ne manquait pas d'une certaine distinction.

«Désirez-vous qu'on vous serve immédiatement, monsieur? demanda-t-il.

— Est-ce prêt?

— Dans quelques minutes. Vous trouverez de l'eau chaude dans vos chambres.... Ma femme et moi, sir Henry, nous serons heureux de rester auprès de vous jusqu'à ce que vous ayez pris vos nouvelles dispositions. Maintenant l'entretien de cette maison va exiger un personnel plus nombreux.

— Pourquoi «maintenant»?

— Je veux dire que sir Charles menait une existence très retirée et que nous suffisions à son service. Vous, — c'est tout naturel — vous recevrez davantage et, nécessairement, vous devrez augmenter votre domesticité.

— Dois-je en conclure que vous avez l'intention de me quitter?

— Oui, mais seulement lorsque vous nous y autoriserez.

— Votre famille n'est elle pas au service des Baskerville depuis plusieurs générations? Je regretterais de commencer ma vie ici en me séparant de serviteurs tels que vous.»

Je crus découvrir quelques traces d'émotion sur le pâle visage du valet de chambre.

«Ma femme et moi nous partageons ce sentiment, reprit Barrymore. Mais à dire vrai, nous étions très attachés à sir Charles; sa mort nous a donné un coup et nous a rendu pénible la vue de tous ces objets qui lui appartenaient. Je crains que nous ne puissions plus supporter le séjour du château.

"But what do you intend to do?"

"I have no doubt, sir, that we shall succeed in establishing ourselves in some business. Sir Charles's generosity has given us the means to do so. And now, sir, perhaps I had best show you to your rooms."

A square balustraded gallery ran round the top of the old hall, approached by a double stair. From this central point two long corridors extended the whole length of the building, from which all the bedrooms opened.

My own was in the same wing as Baskerville's and almost next door to it. These rooms appeared to be much more modern than the central part of the house, and the bright paper and numerous candles did something to remove the sombre impression which our arrival had left upon my mind.

But the dining-room which opened out of the hall was a place of shadow and gloom. It was a long chamber with a step separating the dais where the family sat from the lower portion reserved for their dependents.

At one end a minstrel's gallery overlooked it. Black beams shot across above our heads, with a smoke-darkened ceiling beyond them.

With rows of flaring torches to light it up, and the colour and rude hilarity of an old-time banquet, it might have softened; but now, when two black-clothed gentlemen sat in the little circle of light thrown by a shaded lamp, one's voice became hushed and one's spirit subdued. A dim line of ancestors, in every variety of dress, from the Elizabethan knight to the buck of the Regency, stared down upon us and daunted us by their silent company.

We talked little, and I for one was glad when the meal was over and we were able to retire into the modern billiard-room and smoke a cigarette.

"My word, it isn't a very cheerful place," said Sir Henry. "I suppose one can tone down to it, but I feel a bit out of the picture at present. I don't wonder that my uncle got a little jumpy if he lived all alone in such a house as this. However, if it suits you, we will retire early tonight, and perhaps things may seem more cheerful in the morning."

I drew aside my curtains before I went to bed and looked out from my window. It opened upon the grassy space which lay in front of the hall door. Beyond, two copses of trees moaned and swung in

— Qu'avez-vous l'intention de faire?

— Nous sommes décidés à entreprendre quelque petit commerce; la générosité de sir Charles nous en a procuré les moyens.... Ces messieurs veulent-ils que je les conduise à leur chambre?»

Une galerie courait autour du hall. On y accédait par un escalier à double révolution. De ce point central, deux corridors, sur lesquels s'ouvraient les chambres, traversaient toute la longueur du château.

Ma chambre était située dans la même aile que celle de sir Henry et presque porte à porte. Ces pièces étaient meublées d'une façon plus moderne que le reste de la maison; le papier, clair, et les innombrables bougies, allumées un peu partout, effacèrent en partie la sombre impression ressentie dés notre arrivée.

Mais la salle à manger, qui communiquait avec le hall, était pleine d'ombre et de tristesse. On dressait encore la table sur une espèce d'estrade autour de laquelle devaient autrefois se tenir les domestiques.

À l'une des extrémités de la pièce, une loggia, réservée pour des musiciens, dominait la salle.

À la lueur des torches et avec la haute liesse des banquets du bon vieux temps, cet aspect pouvait être adouci. Mais de nos jours, en présence de deux messieurs vêtus de noir, assis dans le cercle de lumière projeté par une lampe voilée d'un abat-jour, la voix détonnait et l'esprit devenait inquiet. Toute une lignée d'ancêtres habillés de tous les costumes des siècles passés, depuis le chevalier du règne d'Élisabeth jusqu'au petit maître de la Régence, nous fixait du haut de ses cadres et nous gênait par sa muette présence.

Nous parlâmes peu et je me sentis soulagé, une fois le repas terminé, quand nous allâmes fumer une cigarette dans la salle de billard.

«Vrai! ça n'est pas un endroit folâtre, dit sir Henry. Je crois qu'on peut s'y faire, mais je me sens encore dépaysé. Je ne m'étonne pas qu'à vivre seul dans cette maison, mon oncle soit devenu un peu toqué... Vous plaît-il que nous nous retirions de bonne heure dans nos chambres?... Demain matin, les choses nous sembleront peut-être plus riantes.»

Avant de me coucher, j'ouvris mes rideaux pour jeter un coup d'œil sur la campagne. Ma fenêtre donnait sur la pelouse, devant la porte du hall. Au delà, deux bouquets d'arbres s'agitaient en a rising wind.

A half moon broke through the rifts of racing clouds. In its cold light I saw beyond the trees a broken fringe of rocks, and the long, low curve of the melancholy moor.

I closed the curtain, feeling that my last impression was in keeping with the rest.

And yet it was not quite the last.

I found myself weary and yet wakeful, tossing restlessly from side to side, seeking for the sleep which would not come.

Far away a chiming clock struck out the quarters of the hours, but otherwise a deathly silence lay upon the old house.

And then suddenly, in the very dead of the night, there came a sound to my ears, clear, resonant, and unmistakable.

It was the sob of a woman, the muffled, strangling gasp of one who is torn by an uncontrollable sorrow.

I sat up in bed and listened intently. The noise could not have been far away and was certainly in the house.

For half an hour I waited with every nerve on the alert, but there came no other sound save the chiming clock and the rustle of the ivy on the wall.

gémissant sous le souffle du vent.

Une partie du disque de la lune apparaissait dans une déchirure des nuages. À cette pâle clarté, je vis, derrière les arbres, la dentelure des roches, ainsi que l'interminable et mélancolique déclivité de la lande.

Je refermai mon rideau avec la sensation que cette dernière impression ne le cédait en rien à celles déjà éprouvées.

Et cependant elle devait être suivie d'une autre non moins pénible!

La fatigue me tenait éveillé. Je me retournais dans mon lit, à la recherche d'un sommeil qui me fuyait sans cesse.

Dans le lointain, une horloge à carillon sonnait tous les quarts; elle rompait seule le silence de mort qui pesait sur la maison.

Tout à coup un bruit parvint à mon oreille, distinct, sonore, reconnaissable.

C'était un gémissement de femme — le gémissement étouffé de quelqu'un en proie à un inconsolable chagrin.

Je me dressai sur mon séant et j'écoutai avidement. Le bruit était proche et venait certainement de l'intérieur du château.

Les nerfs tendus, je demeurai ainsi plus d'une demi-heure; mais je ne perçus plus que le carillon de l'horloge et le frôlement des branches de lierre contre les volets de ma fenêtre.

CHAPTER 7. THE STAPLETONS OF MERRIPIT HOUSE

The fresh beauty of the following morning did something to efface from our minds the grim and grey impression which had been left upon both of us by our first experience of Baskerville Hall.

As Sir Henry and I sat at breakfast the sunlight flooded in through the high mullioned windows, throwing watery patches of colour from the coats of arms which covered them. The dark panelling glowed like bronze in the golden rays, and it was hard to realise that this was indeed the chamber which had struck such a gloom into our souls upon the evening before.

"I guess it is ourselves and not the house that we have to blame!" said the baronet. "We were tired with our journey and chilled by our drive, so we took a grey view of the place. Now we are fresh and well, so it is all cheerful once more."

"And yet it was not entirely a question of imagination," I answered. "Did you, for example, happen to hear someone, a woman I think, sobbing in the night?"

"That is curious, for I did when I was half asleep fancy that I heard something of the sort. I waited quite a time, but there was no more of it, so I concluded that it was all a dream."

"I heard it distinctly, and I am sure that it was really the sob of a woman."

"We must ask about this right away."

He rang the bell and asked Barrymore whether he could account for our experience. It seemed to me that the pallid features of the butler turned a shade paler still as he listened to his master's question.

"There are only two women in the house, Sir Henry," he answered. "One is the scullery-maid, who sleeps in the other wing. The other is my wife, and I can answer for it that the sound could not have come from her."

And yet he lied as he said it, for it chanced that after breakfast I met Mrs. Barrymore in the long corridor with the sun full upon her face. She was

CHAPITRE 7. M. STAPLETON, DE MERRIPIT HOUSE

Le lendemain, la splendeur du matin dissipa un peu l'impression de tristesse laissée dans nos esprits par notre première inspection du château de Baskerville.

Pendant que je déjeunais avec sir Henry, le soleil éclaira les fenêtres à meneaux, arrachant des teintes d'aquarelle à tous les vitraux armoriés qui les garnissaient; sous ses rayons dorés, les sombres lambris prenaient l'éclat du bronze. On aurait difficilement reconnu la même pièce qui, la veille, nous avait mis tant de mélancolie à l'âme.

«Je crois, dit le baronnet, que nous ne devons nous en prendre qu'à nous-mêmes de ce que nous avons éprouvé hier. La maison n'y était pour rien... Le voyage nous avait fatigués; notre promenade en voiture nous avait gelés...; tout cela avait influé sur notre imagination. Ce matin, nous voilà reposés, bien portants et tout nous paraît plus gai.

— Je ne suis pas de votre avis, répondis-je, en ce qui concerne le jeu de notre imagination. Ainsi n'avez-vous pas entendu quelqu'un — une femme, je crois — pleurer toute la nuit?

— Oui, dans un demi-sommeil, il me semble bien avoir entendu ce bruit. J'ai écouté un instant; mais, le silence s'étant rétabli, j'en ai conclu que je rêvais.

— Moi, je l'ai perçu très distinctement et je jurerais que c'étaient des gémissements de femme... Il faut que nous éclaircissions ce fait.»

Sir Henry sonna Barrymore et lui demanda quelques explications. Aux questions de son maître, je crus voir le visage, déjà pâle, du valet de chambre, pâlir encore davantage.

«Il n'y a que deux femmes dans la maison, sir Henry, dit-il: la fille de cuisine, qui couche dans l'autre aile du château, et ma femme. Or, je puis vous affirmer qu'elle est absolument étrangère au bruit dont vous parlez.»

Le domestique mentait certainement, car, après le déjeuner, je rencontrai Mme Barrymore dans le corridor. Elle se trouvait en pleine lumière. C'était a large, impassive, heavy-featured woman with a stern set expression of mouth. But her telltale eyes were red and glanced at me from between swollen lids.

It was she, then, who wept in the night, and if she did so her husband must know it. Yet he had taken the obvious risk of discovery in declaring that it was not so. Why had he done this? And why did she weep so bitterly?

Already round this pale-faced, handsome, black-bearded man there was gathering an atmosphere of mystery and of gloom.

It was he who had been the first to discover the body of Sir Charles, and we had only his word for all the circumstances which led up to the old man's death. Was it possible that it was Barrymore, after all, whom we had seen in the cab in Regent Street? The beard might well have been the same.

The cabman had described a somewhat shorter man, but such an impression might easily have been erroneous.

How could I settle the point forever?

Obviously the first thing to do was to see the Grimpen postmaster and find whether the test telegram had really been placed in Barrymore's own hands. Be the answer what it might, I should at least have something to report to Sherlock Holmes.

Sir Henry had numerous papers to examine after breakfast, so that the time was propitious for my excursion.

It was a pleasant walk of four miles along the edge of the moor, leading me at last to a small grey hamlet, in which two larger buildings, which proved to be the inn and the house of Dr. Mortimer, stood high above the rest.

The postmaster, who was also the village grocer, had a clear recollection of the telegram.

"Certainly, sir," said he, "I had the telegram delivered to Mr. Barrymore exactly as directed."

"Who delivered it?"

"My boy here. James, you delivered that telegram to Mr. Barrymore at the Hall last week, did you not?"

"Yes, father, I delivered it."

"Into his own hands?" I asked.

une grande femme, impassible, aux traits accentués, ayant, sur les lèvres, un pli amer; Elle avait les yeux rouges et, à travers ses paupières gonflées, son regard se posa sur moi.

Elle avait dû pleurer toute la nuit, et, s'il en était ainsi, son mari ne pouvait l'ignorer. Alors pourquoi avait-il accepté le risque de cette découverte en déclarant le contraire? Pourquoi ce ton affirmatif? Et pourquoi — surtout — sa femme pleurait-elle si convulsivement?

Déjà une atmosphère de mystère et d'obscurité se formait autour de cet homme au teint pâle, porteur d'une superbe barbe noire.

N'était-ce pas lui qui, le premier, avait découvert le cadavre de sir Charles Baskerville? N'était-il pas le seul témoin qui pût nous renseigner sur les circonstances de la mort du vieux gentilhomme? Qu'y avait-il d'impossible à ce qu'il fût le voyageur entrevu dans le cab, à Londres? Sa barbe ressemblait étonnamment à celle de l'inconnu.

Le cocher nous avait bien dépeint son client comme un homme plutôt petit... Mais ne pouvait-il pas s'être trompé?

Comment tirer cette affaire au clair?

Évidemment le plus pressé était d'interroger le directeur du bureau de poste de Grimpen et de savoir si le télégramme adressé à Barrymore lui avait été remis en mains propres. Quelle que fût la réponse, j'aurais au moins un détail à communiquer à Sherlock Holmes.

Sir Henry avait de nombreux documents à compulser; je mis à profit ce temps pour exécuter mon projet.

Une promenade très agréable sur la lande me conduisit à un petit hameau au milieu duquel s'élevaient deux constructions de meilleure apparence que les autres. L'une était l'auberge; l'autre, la maison du docteur Mortimer.

Le directeur de la poste, qui se livrait également au commerce de l'épicerie, se souvenait fort bien du télégramme.

«Certainement, monsieur, me dit-il, on a remis la dépêche à Barrymore, ainsi que l'indiquait l'adresse.

— Qui l'a remise?

— Mon fils, ici présent.»

Le fonctionnaire épicier interpella un gamin qui baguenaudait dans un coin.

«James, demanda-t-il, la semaine dernière, tu as bien remis une dépêche à M. Barrymore?

— Oui, papa.

— À M. Barrymore lui-même? insistai-je.

"Well, he was up in the loft at the time, so that I could not put it into his own hands, but I gave it into Mrs. Barrymore's hands, and she promised to deliver it at once."

— À ce moment-là, il était au grenier et je n'ai pu la donner à lui-même; mais je l'ai remise à Mme Barrymore, qui m'a promis de la lui porter aussitôt.

"Did you see Mr. Barrymore?"

"No, sir; I tell you he was in the loft."

— As-tu vu M. Barrymore?

— Non, monsieur; je vous ai dit qu'il était au grenier.

"If you didn't see him, how do you know he was in the loft?"

— Puisque tu ne l'as pas vu, comment sais-tu qu'il se trouvait au grenier?

"Well, surely his own wife ought to know where he is," said the postmaster testily. "Didn't he get the telegram? If there is any mistake it is for Mr. Barrymore himself to complain."

— Sa femme devait savoir où il était, intervint le directeur de la poste. N'aurait-il pas reçu le télégramme? S'il y a erreur, que M. Barrymore se plaigne!»

It seemed hopeless to pursue the inquiry any farther, but it was clear that in spite of Holmes's ruse we had no proof that Barrymore had not been in London all the time.

Il me semblait inutile de poursuivre plus loin mon enquête. Ainsi, malgré la ruse inventée par Sherlock Holmes, nous n'avions pas acquis la preuve du séjour de Barrymore au château pendant la semaine précédente.

Suppose that it were so—suppose that the same man had been the last who had seen Sir Charles alive, and the first to dog the new heir when he returned to England.

Supposons le contraire..., Supposons que l'homme qui, le dernier, avait vu sir Charles vivant, ait été le premier à espionner son héritier dès son arrivée en Angleterre.

What then?

Alors, quoi?

Was he the agent of others or had he some sinister design of his own? What interest could he have in persecuting the Baskerville family?

Était il l'instrument de quelqu'un ou nourrissait-il de sinistres projets pour son propre compte? Quel intérêt avait il à persécuter la famille Baskerville?

I thought of the strange warning clipped out of the leading article of the Times. Was that his work or was it possibly the doing of someone who was bent upon counteracting his schemes?

Je pensai à l'étrange avertissement découpé dans les colonnes du Times. Était-ce l'œuvre de Barrymore ou bien celle d'un tiers qui s'évertuait à contrecarrer ses desseins?

The only conceivable motive was that which had been suggested by Sir Henry, that if the family could be scared away a comfortable and permanent home would be secured for the Barrymores.

Sir Henry avait émis la version la plus plausible: si on éloignait les Baskerville du château, Barrymore et sa femme y trouveraient un gîte confortable et pour un temps indéfini.

But surely such an explanation as that would be quite inadequate to account for the deep and subtle scheming which seemed to be weaving an invisible net round the young baronet.

Certes, une semblable explication ne suffisait pas pour justifier le plan qui paraissait enserrer le baronnet comme dans les mailles d'un invisible filet.

Holmes himself had said that no more complex case had come to him in all the long series of his sensational investigations.

Holmes lui-même avait convenu que jamais, au cours de ses sensationnelles enquêtes, on ne lui avait soumis de cas plus complexe.

I prayed, as I walked back along the grey, lonely road, that my friend might soon be freed from his preoccupations and able to come down to take this heavy burden of responsibility from my shoulders.

Tout en retournant au château par cette route solitaire, je faisais des vœux pour que mon ami, enfin débarrassé de ses préoccupations, revînt vite me relever de la lourde responsabilité qui pesait sur moi.

Suddenly my thoughts were interrupted by the sound of running feet behind me and by a voice which called me by name.

Soudain je fus tiré de mes réflexions par un bruit de pas. Quelqu'un courait derrière moi, en m'appelant par mon nom.

I turned, expecting to see Dr. Mortimer, but to my surprise it was a stranger who was pursuing

Croyant voir le docteur Mortimer, je me retournai; mais, à ma grande surprise, un inconnu me.

He was a small, slim, clean-shaven, prim-faced man, flaxen-haired and lean-jawed, between thirty and forty years of age, dressed in a grey suit and wearing a straw hat. A tin box for botanical specimens hung over his shoulder and he carried a green butterfly-net in one of his hands.

"You will, I am sure, excuse my presumption, Dr. Watson," said he as he came panting up to where I stood. "Here on the moor we are homely folk and do not wait for formal introductions. You may possibly have heard my name from our mutual friend, Mortimer. I am Stapleton, of Merripit House."

"Your net and box would have told me as much," said I, "for I knew that Mr. Stapleton was a naturalist. But how did you know me?"

"I have been calling on Mortimer, and he pointed you out to me from the window of his surgery as you passed. As our road lay the same way I thought that I would overtake you and introduce myself. I trust that Sir Henry is none the worse for his journey?"

"He is very well, thank you."

"We were all rather afraid that after the sad death of Sir Charles the new baronet might refuse to live here. It is asking much of a wealthy man to come down and bury himself in a place of this kind, but I need not tell you that it means a very great deal to the countryside. Sir Henry has, I suppose, no superstitious fears in the matter?"

"I do not think that it is likely."

"Of course you know the legend of the fiend dog which haunts the family?"

"I have heard it."

"It is extraordinary how credulous the peasants are about here! Any number of them are ready to swear that they have seen such a creature upon the moor."

He spoke with a smile, but I seemed to read in his eyes that he took the matter more seriously.

"The story took a great hold upon the imagination of Sir Charles, and I have no doubt that it led to his tragic end."

"But how?"

"His nerves were so worked up that the appear-

me poursuivait.

J'aperçus un homme de taille moyenne, mince, élancé, blond, la figure rasée, âgé de trente-cinq ans environ, vêtu d'un complet gris et coiffé d'un chapeau de paille. Il portait sur le dos la boîte en fer-blanc des naturalistes et tenait à la main un grand filet vert à papillons.

«Je vous prie d'excuser mon indiscrétion, docteur Watson, dit-il, en s'arrêtant tout haletant devant moi. Sur la lande, pas n'est besoin des présentations ordinaires. Mortimer, notre ami commun, a dû vous parler de moi… Je suis Stapleton, de Merripit house.

— Votre filet et votre boîte me l'auraient appris, répliquai-je, car je sais que M. Stapleton est un savant naturaliste. Mais comment me connaissez-vous?

— Je suis allé faire une visite à Mortimer et, tandis que vous passiez sur la route, il vous a montré à moi par la fenêtre de son cabinet. Comme nous suivions le même chemin, j'ai pensé que je vous rattraperais et que je me présenterais moi-même. J'aime à croire que le voyage n'a pas trop fatigué sir Henry?

— Non, merci; il est en excellente santé.

— Tout le monde ici redoutait qu'après la mort de sir Charles le nouveau baronnet ne vînt pas habiter le château. C'est beaucoup demander à un homme jeune et riche de s'enterrer dans un pareil endroit, et je n'ai pas à vous dire combien cette question intéressait la contrée; sir Henry, je suppose, ne partage par les craintes superstitieuses du populaire?

— Je ne le pense pas.

— Vous connaissez certainement la légende de ce maudit chien que l'on accuse d'être le fléau de la famille?

— On me l'a contée.

— Les paysans de ces parages sont extraordinairement crédules. Beaucoup jureraient avoir rencontré sur la lande ce fantastique animal.»

Stapleton parlait, le sourire sur les lèvres, mais il me sembla lire dans ses yeux qu'il prenait la chose plus au sérieux.

Il reprit:

«Cette histoire hantait l'imagination de sir Charles, et je suis sûr qu'elle n'a pas été étrangère à sa fin tragique.

— Comment cela?

— Ses nerfs étaient tellement exacerbés que

ance of any dog might have had a fatal effect upon his diseased heart. I fancy that he really did see something of the kind upon that last night in the yew alley. I feared that some disaster might occur, for I was very fond of the old man, and I knew that his heart was weak."

"How did you know that?"

"My friend Mortimer told me."

"You think, then, that some dog pursued Sir Charles, and that he died of fright in consequence?"

"Have you any better explanation?"

"I have not come to any conclusion."

"Has Mr. Sherlock Holmes?"

The words took away my breath for an instant but a glance at the placid face and steadfast eyes of my companion showed that no surprise was intended.

"It is useless for us to pretend that we do not know you, Dr. Watson," said he. "The records of your detective have reached us here, and you could not celebrate him without being known yourself. When Mortimer told me your name he could not deny your identity. If you are here, then it follows that Mr. Sherlock Holmes is interesting himself in the matter, and I am naturally curious to know what view he may take."

"I am afraid that I cannot answer that question."

"May I ask if he is going to honour us with a visit himself?"

"He cannot leave town at present. He has other cases which engage his attention."

"What a pity! He might throw some light on that which is so dark to us. But as to your own researches, if there is any possible way in which I can be of service to you I trust that you will command me. If I had any indication of the nature of your suspicions or how you propose to investigate the case, I might perhaps even now give you some aid or advice."

"I assure you that I am simply here upon a visit to my friend, Sir Henry, and that I need no help of any kind."

"Excellent!" said Stapleton. "You are perfectly right to be wary and discreet. I am justly reproved for what I feel was an unjustifiable intrusion, and I promise you that I will not mention the matter

l'apparition d'un chien quelconque devait produire un effet désastreux sur son cœur, mortellement atteint. J'imagine qu'il a réellement vu quelque chose de ce genre dans sa dernière promenade, le long de l'allée des Ifs. J'appréhendais sans cesse un malheur, car j'aimais beaucoup sir Charles et je lui savais le cœur très malade.

— Comment l'aviez-vous appris?

— Par mon ami, le docteur Mortimer.

— Alors vous croyez qu'un chien a poursuivi sir Charles et que la peur a occasionné sa mort?

— Pouvez-vous me fournir une meilleure explication?

— Il ne m'appartient pas de conclure.

— Quelle est l'opinion de M. Sherlock Holmes?»

Pendant quelques secondes, cette question me coupa la parole. Mais un regard sur la figure placide et sur les yeux assurés de mon compagnon me montra qu'elle ne cachait aucune arrière-pensée

«Nous essayerions vainement de prétendre que nous ne vous connaissons pas, docteur Watson, continua Stapleton. Les hauts faits de votre ami le détective sont parvenus jusqu'à nous et vous ne pouviez les célébrer sans vous rendre vous-même populaire. Lorsque Mortimer vous a nommé, j'ai aussitôt établi votre identité. Vous êtes ici parce que M. Sherlock Holmes s'intéresse à l'affaire, et je suis bien excusable de chercher à connaître son opinion.

— Je regrette de n'être pas en mesure de répondre à cette question.

— Puis-je au moins vous demander s'il nous honorera d'une visite?

— D'autres enquêtes le retiennent à la ville en ce moment.

— Quel malheur! Il jetterait un peu de lumière sur tout ce qui reste si obscur pour nous. Quant à vos recherches personnelles, si vous jugez que je vous sois de quelque utilité, j'espère que vous n'hésiterez pas à user de moi. Si vous m'indiquiez seulement la nature de vos soupçons ou de quel côté vous allez pousser vos investigations, il me serait possible de vous donner dès maintenant un avis ou une aide.

— Je vous affirme que je suis simplement en visite chez mon ami sir Henry et que je n'ai besoin d'aide d'aucune sorte.

— Parfait! dit Stapleton. Vous avez raison de vous montrer prudent et circonspect. Je regrette de vous avoir adressé cette question indiscrète, et je vous promets de m'abstenir dorénavant de la plus again."

We had come to a point where a narrow grassy path struck off from the road and wound away across the moor.

A steep, boulder-sprinkled hill lay upon the right which had in bygone days been cut into a granite quarry. The face which was turned towards us formed a dark cliff, with ferns and brambles growing in its niches.

From over a distant rise there floated a grey plume of smoke.

"A moderate walk along this moor-path brings us to Merripit House," said he. "Perhaps you will spare an hour that I may have the pleasure of introducing you to my sister."

My first thought was that I should be by Sir Henry's side.

But then I remembered the pile of papers and bills with which his study table was littered. It was certain that I could not help with those.

And Holmes had expressly said that I should study the neighbours upon the moor.

I accepted Stapleton's invitation, and we turned together down the path.

"It is a wonderful place, the moor," said he, looking round over the undulating downs, long green rollers, with crests of jagged granite foaming up into fantastic surges. "You never tire of the moor. You cannot think the wonderful secrets which it contains. It is so vast, and so barren, and so mysterious."

"You know it well, then?"

"I have only been here two years. The residents would call me a newcomer. We came shortly after Sir Charles settled. But my tastes led me to explore every part of the country round, and I should think that there are few men who know it better than I do."

"Is it hard to know?"

"Very hard. You see, for example, this great plain to the north here with the queer hills breaking out of it. Do you observe anything remarkable about that?"

"It would be a rare place for a gallop."

"You would naturally think so and the thought has cost several their lives before now. You notice those bright green spots scattered thickly over it?"

"Yes, they seem more fertile than the rest."

légère allusion à ce sujet.»

Nous étions arrivés à un endroit où un étroit sentier tapissé de mousse se branchait sur la route pour traverser ensuite la lande.

Sur la droite, un monticule escarpé, caillouteux, avait dû être exploité autrefois comme carrière de granit. Le versant qui nous faisait face était taillé à pic; dans les anfractuosités de la roche, poussaient des fougères et des ronces.

Dans le lointain, un panache de fumée montait perpendiculairement dans le ciel.

«Quelques minutes de marche dans ce sentier perdu nous conduiront à Merripit house, dit Stapleton. Voulez-vous me consacrer une heure?... Je vous présenterai à ma sœur.»

Mon premier mouvement fut de refuser. Mon devoir me commandait de retourner auprès de sir Henry.

Mais je me souvins de l'amas de papiers qui recouvrait sa table et je me dis que je ne lui étais d'aucun secours pour les examiner.

D'ailleurs Holmes ne m'avait-il pas recommandé d'étudier tous les habitants de la lande?

J'acceptai donc l'invitation de Stapleton et nous nous engageâmes dans le petit chemin.

«Quel endroit merveilleux que la lande! dit mon compagnon, en jetant un regard circulaire sur les ondulations de la montagne qui ressemblaient à de gigantesques vagues de granit. On ne se lasse jamais du spectacle qu'elle offre à l'œil de l'observateur. Vous ne pouvez imaginer quels secrets étonnants cache cette solitude!... Elle est si vaste, si dénudée, si mystérieuse!

— Vous la connaissez donc bien?

— Je ne suis ici que depuis deux ans. Les gens du pays me considèrent comme un nouveau venu... Nous nous y installâmes peu de temps après l'arrivée de sir Charles... Mes goûts me portèrent à explorer la contrée jusque dans ses plus petits recoins... Je ne pense pas qu'il existe quelqu'un qui la connaisse mieux que moi.

— Est-ce donc si difficile?

— Très difficile. Voyez-vous, par exemple, cette grande plaine, là-bas, vers le nord, avec ces proéminences bizarres? Qu'y trouvez-vous de remarquable?

— On y piquerait un fameux galop.

— Naturellement, vous deviez me répondre cela... Que de vies humaines cette erreur n'a-t-elle pas déjà coûté? Apercevez-vous ces places vertes disséminées à sa surface?

— Le sol paraît y être plus fertile.»

Stapleton laughed.

"That is the great Grimpen Mire," said he. "A false step yonder means death to man or beast. Only yesterday I saw one of the moor ponies wander into it. He never came out. I saw his head for quite a long time craning out of the bog-hole, but it sucked him down at last. Even in dry seasons it is a danger to cross it, but after these autumn rains it is an awful place. And yet I can find my way to the very heart of it and return alive. By George, there is another of those miserable ponies!"

Stapleton se mit à rire.

«C'est la grande fondrière de Grimpen, fit-il. Là-bas, un faux pas conduit à une mort certaine — homme ou bète. Pas plus tard qu'hier, j'ai vu s'y engager un des chevaux qui errent sur la lande. Il n'en est plus ressorti… Pendant un moment, sa tête s'est agitée au-dessus de la vase, puis le bourbier l'a aspiré! On ne la traverse pas sans danger dans la saison sèche; mais après la saison d'automne, l'endroit est terriblement dangereux. Et cependant je puis m'y promener en tous sens et en sortir sans encombre. Tenez! voilà encore un de ces malheureux chevaux!»

Something brown was rolling and tossing among the green sedges. Then a long, agonised, writhing neck shot upward and a dreadful cry echoed over the moor.

Une forme brune allait et venait au milieu des ajoncs. Tout à coup, une encolure se dressa, en même temps qu'un hennissement lugubre réveilla tous les échos de la lande.

It turned me cold with horror, but my companion's nerves seemed to be stronger than mine.

Je me sentis frissonner de terreur; mais les nerfs de mon compagnon me parurent beaucoup moins impressionnables que les miens.

"It's gone!" said he. "The mire has him. Two in two days, and many more, perhaps, for they get in the way of going there in the dry weather and never know the difference until the mire has them in its clutches. It's a bad place, the great Grimpen Mire."

"And you say you can penetrate it?"

«C'est fini! me dit-il. La fondrière s'en est emparée… Cela fait deux en deux jours!… Et ils seront suivis de bien d'autres. Pendant la sécheresse, ils ont l'habitude d'aller brouter de ce côté, et, lorsqu'ils s'aperçoivent que le sol est devenu moins consistant, la fondrière les a déjà saisis.

— Et vous dites que vous pouvez vous y aventurer?

"Yes, there are one or two paths which a very active man can take. I have found them out."

— Oui. Il existe un ou deux sentiers dans lesquels un homme courageux peut se risquer… Je les ai découverts.

"But why should you wish to go into so horrible a place?"

— Quel désir vous poussait donc à pénétrer dans un lieu si terrible?

"Well, you see the hills beyond? They are really islands cut off on all sides by the impassable mire, which has crawled round them in the course of years. That is where the rare plants and the butterflies are, if you have the wit to reach them."

"I shall try my luck some day."

He looked at me with a surprised face.

"For God's sake put such an idea out of your mind," said he. "Your blood would be upon my head. I assure you that there would not be the least chance of your coming back alive. It is only by remembering certain complex landmarks that I am able to do it."

— Regardez ces monticules — au delà! Ils représentent de vrais îlots de verdure découpés dans l'immensité de la fondrière. C'est là qu'on rencontre les plantes rares et les papillons peu communs… Si le cœur vous dit d'aller les y chercher?…

— Quelque jour j'essayerai.»

Stapleton me regarda avec étonnement:

«Au nom du ciel, s'écria-t-il, abandonnez ce funeste projet! Je vous affirme que vous n'avez pas la plus petite chance de vous tirer de là vivant. Je n'y parviens qu'en me servant de points de repère très compliqués.

"Halloa!" I cried. "What is that?"

A long, low moan, indescribably sad, swept over the moor. It filled the whole air, and yet it was impossible to say whence it came.

From a dull murmur it swelled into a deep roar, and then sank back into a melancholy, throbbing

— Hein? fis-je… Qu'y a-t-il encore?»

Un long gémissement, indiciblement triste, courut mur la lande. Bien qu'il eût ébranlé l'air, il était impossible de préciser d'où il venait.

Commencé sur une modulation sourde, semblable à un murmure, il se changea en un profond murmur once again. Stapleton looked at me with a curious expression in his face.

"Queer place, the moor!" said he.

"But what is it?"

"The peasants say it is the Hound of the Baskervilles calling for its prey. I've heard it once or twice before, but never quite so loud."

I looked round, with a chill of fear in my heart, at the huge swelling plain, mottled with the green patches of rushes. Nothing stirred over the vast expanse save a pair of ravens, which croaked loudly from a tor behind us.

"You are an educated man. You don't believe such nonsense as that?" said I. "What do you think is the cause of so strange a sound?"

"Bogs make queer noises sometimes. It's the mud settling, or the water rising, or something."

"No, no, that was a living voice."

"Well, perhaps it was. Did you ever hear a bittern booming?"

"No, I never did."

"It's a very rare bird—practically extinct—in England now, but all things are possible upon the moor. Yes, I should not be surprised to learn that what we have heard is the cry of the last of the bitterns."

"It's the weirdest, strangest thing that ever I heard in my life."

"Yes, it's rather an uncanny place altogether. Look at the hillside yonder. What do you make of those?"

The whole steep slope was covered with grey circular rings of stone, a score of them at least.

"What are they? Sheep-pens?"

"No, they are the homes of our worthy ancestors. Prehistoric man lived thickly on the moor, and as no one in particular has lived there since, we find all his little arrangements exactly as he left them. These are his wigwams with the roofs off. You can even see his hearth and his couch if you have the curiosity to go inside.

"But it is quite a town. When was it inhabited?"

"Neolithic man—no date."

"What did he do?"

rugissement, pour finir en un nouveau murmure, mélancolique, poignant.

«Hé! curieux endroit, la lande! répéta Stapleton.

— Qu'était-ce donc?

— Les paysans prétendent que c'est le chien de Baskerville qui hurle pour attirer sa proie. Je l'ai déjà entendu une ou deux fois, mais jamais aussi distinctement.»

Avec un tressaillement de crainte au fond du cœur, je regardai cette vaste étendue de plaine, mouchetée de larges taches vertes formées par les ajoncs. Sauf deux corbeaux qui croassaient lugubrement sur la cime d'un pic, une immobilité de mort régnait partout.

«Vous êtes un homme instruit, dis-je, vous ne pouvez croire à de pareilles balivernes! À quelle cause attribuez-vous ce bruit étrange?

— Les fondrières rendent parfois des sons bizarres, inexplicables... La boue se tasse... l'eau sourd ou quelque chose...

— Non, non, répondis-je; c'était une voix humaine.

— Peut-être bien, répondit Stapleton. Avez-vous jamais entendu s'envoler un butor?

— Non, jamais.

— C'est un oiseau très rare — à peu près complètement disparu de l'Angleterre — mais, dans la lande, rien n'est impossible. Oui, je ne serais pas étonné d'apprendre que c'est le cri du dernier butor qui vient de frapper nos oreilles.

— Quel bruit étrange!...

— Ce pays est plein de surprises. Regardez le flanc de la colline... Que croyez-vous apercevoir?»

Je vis une vingtaine de tas de pierres grises amoncelées circulairement.

«Je ne sais pas... Des abris de bergers?

— Non. Nos dignes ancêtres habitaient là. L'homme préhistorique vivait sur la lande et comme, depuis cette époque, personne ne l'a imité, nous y retrouvons encore presque intacts les vestiges de son passage. Ceci vous représente des wigwams recouverts de leur toiture. Si la curiosité vous prenait de les visiter, vous y verriez un foyer, une couchette...

— On dirait une petite ville. À quelle époque était-elle peuplée?

— L'homme néolithique,... la date nous manque.

— Que faisait-il?

"He grazed his cattle on these slopes, and he learned to dig for tin when the bronze sword began to supersede the stone axe. Look at the great trench in the opposite hill. That is his mark. Yes, you will find some very singular points about the moor, Dr. Watson. Oh, excuse me an instant! It is surely Cyclopides."

— Il menait paître son troupeau sur les pentes et, lorsque les armes de bronze remplacèrent les haches de pierre, il fouillait les entrailles de la terre à la recherche du zinc. Voyez cette grande tranchée sur la colline opposée… Voilà la preuve de ce que j'avance. Ah! vous rencontrerez de bien curieux sujets d'étude sur la lande! Excusez-moi un instant, docteur Watson,… c'est sûrement un cyclopelte!…»

A small fly or moth had fluttered across our path, and in an instant Stapleton was rushing with extraordinary energy and speed in pursuit of it.

Un petit insecte avait traversé le chemin et Stapleton s'était aussitôt élancé à sa poursuite.

To my dismay the creature flew straight for the great mire, and my acquaintance never paused for an instant, bounding from tuft to tuft behind it, his green net waving in the air. His grey clothes and jerky, zigzag, irregular progress made him not unlike some huge moth himself.

À mon grand désappointement, la bestiole vola droit vers la fondrière, et ma nouvelle connaissance, bondissant de touffe en touffe, courait après elle, son grand filet vert se balançant dans l'air. Ses vêtements gris, sa démarche irrégulière, sautillante, saccadée, le faisaient ressembler lui-même à une gigantesque phalène.

I was standing watching his pursuit with a mixture of admiration for his extraordinary activity and fear lest he should lose his footing in the treacherous mire, when I heard the sound of steps and, turning round, found a woman near me upon the path.

Je m'étais arrêté pour suivre sa chasse, et j'éprouvais un mélange d'admiration pour son extraordinaire agilité et de crainte pour le danger auquel il s'exposait dans cette perfide fondrière. Un bruit de pas me fit retourner; une femme s'avançait vers moi dans le chemin.

She had come from the direction in which the plume of smoke indicated the position of Merripit House, but the dip of the moor had hid her until she was quite close.

Elle venait du côté où le panache de fumée dénonçait l'emplacement de Merripit house; mais la courbure de la lande l'avait cachée à mes yeux jusqu'au moment où elle se trouva près de moi.

I could not doubt that this was the Miss Stapleton of whom I had been told, since ladies of any sort must be few upon the moor, and I remembered that I had heard someone describe her as being a beauty.

Je reconnus en elle miss Stapleton dont on m'avait parlé. Cela me fut aisé, car, indépendamment du petit nombre de femmes qui vivent sur la lande, on me l'avait dépeinte comme une personne d'une réelle beauté.

The woman who approached me was certainly that, and of a most uncommon type. There could not have been a greater contrast between brother and sister, for Stapleton was neutral tinted, with light hair and grey eyes, while she was darker than any brunette whom I have seen in England—slim, elegant, and tall.

La femme qui s'approchait de moi répondait au portrait qu'on m'avait tracé de la sœur du naturaliste. Impossible de concevoir un plus grand contraste entre un frère et une sœur. Stapleton était quelconque, avec ses cheveux blonds et ses yeux gris, tandis que la jeune fille avait ce teint chaud des brunes — si rare en Angleterre.

She had a proud, finely cut face, so regular that it might have seemed impassive were it not for the sensitive mouth and the beautiful dark, eager eyes. With her perfect figure and elegant dress she was, indeed, a strange apparition upon a lonely moorland path.

Son visage un peu altier, mais finement modelé, aurait paru impassible dans sa régularité, sans l'expression sensuelle de la bouche et la vivacité de deux yeux noirs largement fendus. Sa taille parfaite, moulée dans une robe de coupe élégante, la faisait ressembler, sur ce chemin désert, à une étrange apparition.

Her eyes were on her brother as I turned, and then she quickened her pace towards me.

Au moment où je me retournais, elle regardait son frère. Alors elle hâta le pas.

I had raised my hat and was about to make some explanatory remark when her own words

J'avais ôté mon chapeau et j'allais prononcer quelques mots d'explication, lorsque ses paroles turned all my thoughts into a new channel.

"Go back!" she said. "Go straight back to London, instantly."

I could only stare at her in stupid surprise. Her eyes blazed at me, and she tapped the ground impatiently with her foot.

"Why should I go back?" I asked.

"I cannot explain."

She spoke in a low, eager voice, with a curious lisp in her utterance.

"But for God's sake do what I ask you. Go back and never set foot upon the moor again."

"But I have only just come."

"Man, man!" she cried. "Can you not tell when a warning is for your own good? Go back to London! Start tonight! Get away from this place at all costs! Hush, my brother is coming! Not a word of what I have said. Would you mind getting that orchid for me among the mare's-tails yonder? We are very rich in orchids on the moor, though, of course, you are rather late to see the beauties of the place."

Stapleton had abandoned the chase and came back to us breathing hard and flushed with his exertions.

"Halloa, Beryl!" said he, and it seemed to me that the tone of his greeting was not altogether a cordial one.

"Well, Jack, you are very hot."

"Yes, I was chasing a Cyclopides. He is very rare and seldom found in the late autumn. What a pity that I should have missed him!"

He spoke unconcernedly, but his small light eyes glanced incessantly from the girl to me.

"You have introduced yourselves, I can see."

"Yes. I was telling Sir Henry that it was rather late for him to see the true beauties of the moor."

"Why, who do you think this is?"

"I imagine that it must be Sir Henry Baskerville."

"No, no," said I. "Only a humble commoner, but his friend. My name is Dr. Watson."

A flush of vexation passed over her expressive face.

"We have been talking at cross purposes," said she.

"Why, you had not very much time for talk,"

imprimèrent une autre direction à mes pensées.

«Allez-vous-en! s'écria-t-elle. Retournez vite à Londres.»

Si grande fut ma surprise, que j'en demeurai stupide. En me regardant, ses yeux brillaient et son pied frappait le sol avec impatience.

«Pourquoi m'en aller? demandai-je.

— Je ne puis vous le dire.»

Elle parlait d'une voix basse, précipitée, avec un léger grasseyement dans sa prononciation.

Elle reprit:

«Pour l'amour de Dieu, faites ce que je vous recommande. Retournez vite et ne remettez jamais plus les pieds sur la lande!

— Mais j'arrive à peine.

— Pourquoi ne tenir aucun compte d'un avertissement dicté par votre seul intérêt?... Retournez à Londres!... Partez ce soir même... Fuyez ces lieux à tout prix!... Prenez garde! Voici mon frère,... pas un mot de ce que je vous ai dit... Soyez donc assez aimable pour me cueillir cette orchidée, là-bas... La lande est très riche en orchidées... vous en jugerez par vous-même, bien que vous soyez venu à une saison trop avancée pour jouir de toutes les beautés de la nature.»

Stapleton avait renoncé à sa poursuite et retournait vers nous, essoufflé, et le teint coloré par la course.

«Eh bien, Béryl?» dit-il. Il me sembla que le ton de cette interpellation manquait de cordialité.

«Vous avez bien chaud, Jack.

— Oui; je poursuivais un cyclopelte. Ils sont très rares, surtout à la fin de l'automne. Quel malheur de n'avoir pu l'attraper!»

Il parlait avec un air dégagé, mais ses petits yeux gris allaient sans cesse de la jeune fille à moi.

«Je vois que les présentations sont faites, continua-t-il.

— Oui. Je disais à sir Henry qu'il était un peu tard pour admirer les beautés de la lande.

— À qui penses-tu donc parler?

— À sir Henry Baskerville.

— Non, non, me récriai-je vivement,... pas à sir Henry, mais à un simple bourgeois, son ami... Je me nomme le docteur Watson.»

Une expression de contrariété passa sur le visage de miss Stapleton.

«Nous avons joué aux propos interrompus, dit-elle.

— Vous n'avez pas eu le temps d'échanger

her brother remarked with the same questioning eyes.

"I talked as if Dr. Watson were a resident instead of being merely a visitor," said she.

"It cannot much matter to him whether it is early or late for the orchids. But you will come on, will you not, and see Merripit House?"

A short walk brought us to it, a bleak moorland house, once the farm of some grazier in the old prosperous days, but now put into repair and turned into a modern dwelling.

An orchard surrounded it, but the trees, as is usual upon the moor, were stunted and nipped, and the effect of the whole place was mean and melancholy.

We were admitted by a strange, wizened, rusty-coated old manservant, who seemed in keeping with the house.

Inside, however, there were large rooms furnished with an elegance in which I seemed to recognize the taste of the lady.

As I looked from their windows at the interminable granite-flecked moor rolling unbroken to the farthest horizon I could not but marvel at what could have brought this highly educated man and this beautiful woman to live in such a place.

"Queer spot to choose, is it not?" said he as if in answer to my thought. "And yet we manage to make ourselves fairly happy, do we not, Beryl?"

"Quite happy," said she, but there was no ring of conviction in her words.

"I had a school," said Stapleton. "It was in the north country. The work to a man of my temperament was mechanical and uninteresting, but the privilege of living with youth, of helping to mould those young minds, and of impressing them with one's own character and ideals was very dear to me. However, the fates were against us. A serious epidemic broke out in the school and three of the boys died. It never recovered from the blow, and much of my capital was irretrievably swallowed up. And yet, if it were not for the loss of the charming companionship of the boys, I could rejoice over my own misfortune, for, with my strong tastes for botany and zoology, I find an unlimited field of work here, and my sister is as devoted to Nature as I am. All this, Dr. Watson, has been brought upon your head by your expression as you surveyed the

beaucoup de paroles? demanda son frère, avec son même regard interrogateur.

— J'ai causé avec le docteur Watson, comme si, au lieu d'un simple visiteur, il eût été un habitant permanent de la lande.

— Que peut lui importer que la saison soit trop avancée pour les orchidées!... Nous ferez-vous le plaisir de nous accompagner jusqu'à Merripit house?» ajouta le naturaliste, en se tournant vers moi.

Quelques instants après, nous arrivions à une modeste maison ayant autrefois servi d'habitation à un herbager de la lande, mais que l'on avait réparée depuis et modernisée.

Un verger l'entourait. Les arbres, comme tous ceux de la lande, étaient rabougris et pelés. L'aspect de ce lieu remplissait l'âme d'une vague tristesse.

Nous fûmes reçus par un vieux bonhomme qui paraissait monter la garde autour de la maison.

À l'intérieur, les pièces étaient spacieuses et meublées avec une élégance qui trahissait le bon goût de la maîtresse de la maison.

Tandis que, par la fenêtre entr'ouverte, je jetais un coup d'œil sur le paysage sauvage qui se déroulait devant moi, je me demandais quelle raison avait amené dans ce pays perdu cet homme d'un esprit cultivé et cette superbe créature.

«Singulier endroit pour y planter sa tente, n'est-ce pas? fit Stapleton, répondant ainsi à ma pensée. Et cependant nous nous sommes arrangés pour y être heureux, pas, Béryl?

— Très heureux, répliqua la jeune fille, dont le ton me parut toutefois manquer de conviction.

— Je dirigeais jadis une école, continua Stapleton, dans le nord de l'Angleterre... Pour un homme de mon tempérament, la besogne était trop machinale et trop dépourvue d'intérêt. Mais j'aimais à vivre ainsi au milieu de la jeunesse, à façonner ces jeunes intelligences à ma guise et à leur inculquer mes idées et mes préférences. La malchance s'en mêla: une épidémie se déclara dans le village et trois enfants moururent. Mon établissement ne se releva jamais de ce coup et la majeure partie de mes ressources se trouva engloutie. Si je ne regrettais la charmante compagnie de mes écoliers, je me réjouirais de cet incident. Avec mon amour immodéré pour la botanique et la zoologie, je rencontrerais difficilement un champ plus ouvert à nos recherches, car ma sœur est aussi éprise que moi des choses de la nature. Ceci, docteur Watson, moor out of our window."

"It certainly did cross my mind that it might be a little dull—less for you, perhaps, than for your sister."

"No, no, I am never dull," said she quickly.

"We have books, we have our studies, and we have interesting neighbours. Dr. Mortimer is a most learned man in his own line. Poor Sir Charles was also an admirable companion. We knew him well and miss him more than I can tell. Do you think that I should intrude if I were to call this afternoon and make the acquaintance of Sir Henry?"

"I am sure that he would be delighted."

"Then perhaps you would mention that I propose to do so. We may in our humble way do something to make things more easy for him until he becomes accustomed to his new surroundings. Will you come upstairs, Dr. Watson, and inspect my collection of Lepidoptera? I think it is the most complete one in the south-west of England. By the time that you have looked through them lunch will be almost ready."

But I was eager to get back to my charge. The melancholy of the moor, the death of the unfortunate pony, the weird sound which had been associated with the grim legend of the Baskervilles, all these things tinged my thoughts with sadness. Then on the top of these more or less vague impressions there had come the definite and distinct warning of Miss Stapleton, delivered with such intense earnestness that I could not doubt that some grave and deep reason lay behind it.

I resisted all pressure to stay for lunch, and I set off at once upon my return journey, taking the grass-grown path by which we had come.

It seems, however, that there must have been some short cut for those who knew it, for before I had reached the road I was astounded to see Miss Stapleton sitting upon a rock by the side of the track.

Her face was beautifully flushed with her exertions and she held her hand to her side.

"I have run all the way in order to cut you off, Dr. Watson," said she. "I had not even time to put on my hat. I must not stop, or my brother may miss me. I wanted to say to you how sorry I am about the stupid mistake I made in thinking that

répond à une question que j'ai lue sur votre visage, pendant que vous regardiez sur la lande.

— Je me disais, en effet, que ce séjour devait être bien triste, sinon pour vous, du moins pour votre sœur.

— Non, non, dit vivement miss Stapleton; je ne connais pas la tristesse.

— Nous avons nos études, nos livres et de bons voisins, paraphrasa mon hôte. Le docteur Mortimer est un véritable savant... Puis nous possédions dans ce pauvre sir Charles un délicieux compagnon. Nous l'appréciions beaucoup, et nous ressentons plus que je ne puis le dire le vide causé par sa mort... Serais-je indiscret en me présentant cet après-midi au château pour rendre visite à sir Henry?

— Je suis sûr que vous lui ferez le plus grand plaisir.

— Alors prévenez-le de ma venue. Nous nous emploierons de tout notre pouvoir pour qu'il s'habitue ici... Désirez-vous, docteur Watson, visiter ma collection de lépidoptères? Je ne crois pas qu'il en existe de plus complète dans tout le sud de l'Angleterre. Pendant que vous l'admirerez on nous préparera un lunch.»

J'avais hâte de reprendre auprès de sir Henry mes fonctions de garde du corps. D'ailleurs, la solitude de la lande, la mort du malheureux cheval aspiré par la fondrière, le bruit étrange que le public associait à l'horrible légende des Baskerville, tout cela m'étreignait le cœur. J'ajouterai encore l'impression produite par l'avis de miss Stapleton, avis si précis et si net que je ne pouvais l'attribuer qu'à quelque grave raison.

Je résistai donc à toutes les instances de mon hôte et je repris, par le même étroit sentier, le chemin du château.

Mais il devait exister un raccourci connu des habitants du pays, car, avant que j'eusse rejoint la grande route, je fus très étonné de voir miss Stapleton, assise sur un quartier de roche, au croisement de deux voies.

Elle avait marché très vite, et la précipitation de la course avait empourpré ses joues.

«J'ai couru de toutes mes forces afin de vous devancer, me dit-elle. Je n'ai même pas pris le temps de mettre mon chapeau... Je ne m'arrête pas... Mon frère s'apercevrait de mon absence. Je voulais vous dire combien je déplorais la stupide erreur you were Sir Henry. Please forget the words I said, which have no application whatever to you."

"But I can't forget them, Miss Stapleton," said I. "I am Sir Henry's friend, and his welfare is a very close concern of mine. Tell me why it was that you were so eager that Sir Henry should return to London."

"A woman's whim, Dr. Watson. When you know me better you will understand that I cannot always give reasons for what I say or do."

"No, no. I remember the thrill in your voice. I remember the look in your eyes. Please, please, be frank with me, Miss Stapleton, for ever since I have been here I have been conscious of shadows all round me. Life has become like that great Grimpen Mire, with little green patches everywhere into which one may sink and with no guide to point the track. Tell me then what it was that you meant, and I will promise to convey your warning to Sir Henry."

An expression of irresolution passed for an instant over her face, but her eyes had hardened again when she answered me.

"You make too much of it, Dr. Watson," said she. "My brother and I were very much shocked by the death of Sir Charles. We knew him very intimately, for his favourite walk was over the moor to our house. He was deeply impressed with the curse which hung over the family, and when this tragedy came I naturally felt that there must be some grounds for the fears which he had expressed. I was distressed therefore when another member of the family came down to live here, and I felt that he should be warned of the danger which he will run. That was all which I intended to convey.

"But what is the danger?"

"You know the story of the hound?"

"I do not believe in such nonsense."

"But I do. If you have any influence with Sir Henry, take him away from a place which has always been fatal to his family. The world is wide. Why should he wish to live at the place of danger?"

"Because it is the place of danger. That is Sir Henry's nature. I fear that unless you can give me some more definite information than this it would

que j'ai commise en vous confondant avec sir Henry. Oubliez mes paroles, elles ne vous concernent en rien.

— Comment les oublierais-je, miss Stapleton, répliquai-je. Je suis l'ami de sir Henry, et le souci de sa sécurité m'incombe tout particulièrement. Apprenez-moi pourquoi vous souhaitiez si ardemment qu'il retournât à Londres.

— Caprice de femme, docteur Watson! Lorsque vous me connaîtrez davantage, vous comprendrez que je ne puisse pas toujours fournir l'explication de mes paroles ou de mes actes.

— Non, non... Je me rappelle le frémissement de votre voix, l'expression de votre regard... Je vous en prie, je vous en supplie, soyez franche, miss Stapleton! Depuis que j'ai posé le pied sur ce pays, je me sens environné de mystères. La vie sur la lande ressemble à la fondrière de Grimpen: elle est parsemée d'îlots de verdure auprès desquels l'abîme vous guette, et aucun guide ne s'offre à vous éloigner du danger. Que vouliez-vous dire? Apprenez-le-moi et je vous promets de communiquer votre avertissement à sir Henry.»

Pendant une minute, un combat se livra dans l'âme de la jeune fille. Toutefois, ses traits avaient repris leur expression résolue, lorsqu'elle me répondit:

«Vous prêtez à mes paroles plus d'importance qu'elles n'en comportent. La mort de sir Charles nous a très vivement impressionnés, mon frère et moi. Nous étions très liés... Sa promenade favorite consistait à se rendre chez nous par la lande. Cette espèce de sort qui pesait sur sa famille hantait son cerveau, et, lorsque se produisit le tragique événement, je crus ses craintes fondées jusqu'à un certain point. Quand on annonça qu'un nouveau membre de la famille Baskerville allait habiter le château, mes appréhensions se réveillèrent et j'ai pensé bien faire en le prévenant du danger qu'il courait. Voilà le mobile auquel j'ai obéi.

— Mais quel est ce danger?

— Vous connaissez bien l'histoire du chien?

— Je n'ajoute aucune foi à de pareilles absurdités.

— J'en ajoute, moi. Si vous possédez quelque influence sur sir Henry, emmenez-le loin de ce pays qui a déjà été si fatal à sa famille. Le monde est grand... Pourquoi s'obstinerait-il à vivre au milieu du péril?

— Précisément parce qu'il y a du péril. Sir Henry est ainsi fait. Je crains qu'à moins d'un avis plus motivé que celui que vous m'avez donné il ne be impossible to get him to move."

"I cannot say anything definite, for I do not know anything definite."

"I would ask you one more question, Miss Stapleton. If you meant no more than this when you first spoke to me, why should you not wish your brother to overhear what you said? There is nothing to which he, or anyone else, could object."

"My brother is very anxious to have the Hall inhabited, for he thinks it is for the good of the poor folk upon the moor. He would be very angry if he knew that I have said anything which might induce Sir Henry to go away. But I have done my duty now and I will say no more. I must go back, or he will miss me and suspect that I have seen you. Good-bye!"

She turned and had disappeared in a few minutes among the scattered boulders, while I, with my soul full of vague fears, pursued my way to Baskerville Hall.

me soit impossible de le déterminer à partir.

— Je ne puis vous dire autre chose,... je ne sais rien de précis.

— Me permettez-vous de vous adresser une dernière question, miss Stapleton? Quand vous m'avez parlé tout à l'heure, puisqu'il vous était impossible de m'en apprendre davantage, pourquoi redoutiez-vous tant que votre frère ne vous entendît. Il n'y avait rien dans vos paroles que ni lui — ni personne d'ailleurs — ne pût écouter.

— Mon frère désire que le château soit habité; il estime que le bonheur des pauvres gens de la lande l'exige. Tout avis poussant sir Henry à s'éloigner l'aurait mécontenté... J'ai accompli maintenant mon devoir et je n'ajouterai plus un mot. Je retourne vite à la maison pour que mon frère ne se doute pas que avons causé ensemble. Adieu.»

Miss Stapleton reprit le chemin par lequel elle était venue, tandis que, le cœur oppressé de vagues alarmes, je continuais ma route vers le château.

CHAPTER 8. FIRST REPORT OF DR. WATSON

From this point onward I will follow the course of events by transcribing my own letters to Mr. Sherlock Holmes which lie before me on the table. One page is missing, but otherwise they are exactly as written and show my feelings and suspicions of the moment more accurately than my memory, clear as it is upon these tragic events, can possibly do.

Baskerville Hall, October 13th.

MY DEAR HOLMES,

My previous letters and telegrams have kept you pretty well up to date as to all that has occurred in this most God-forsaken corner of the world.

The longer one stays here the more does the spirit of the moor sink into one's soul, its vastness, and also its grim charm.

When you are once out upon its bosom you have left all traces of modern England behind you, but, on the other hand, you are conscious everywhere of the homes and the work of the prehistoric people. On all sides of you as you walk are the houses of these forgotten folk, with their graves and the huge monoliths which are supposed to have marked their temples.

As you look at their grey stone huts against the scarred hillsides you leave your own age behind you, and if you were to see a skin-clad, hairy man crawl out from the low door fitting a flint-tipped arrow on to the string of his bow, you would feel that his presence there was more natural than your own.

The strange thing is that they should have lived so thickly on what must always have been most unfruitful soil. I am no antiquarian, but I could imagine that they were some unwarlike and har-

CHAPITRE 8. PREMIER RAPPORT DU DOCTEUR WATSON

J'ai sous les yeux, éparses sur ma table, les lettres que j'écrivais à Sherlock Holmes au fur et à mesure que se déroulèrent les événements. Une page manque; mais, sauf cette lacune, elles sont l'expression exacte de la vérité. De plus, elles montrent mes impressions et mes craintes d'alors plus fidèlement que ne pourrait le faire ma mémoire, quelque ineffaçable souvenir qu'elle ait gardé de ces heures tragiques.

Je vais donc reproduire ces lettres afin de relater les faits selon leur enchaînement.

Château de Baskerville, 13 octobre.

«Mon cher Holmes,

«Mes dépêches et mes lettres précédentes vous ont à peu près tenu au courant de tout ce qui s'est passé jusqu'à ce jour dans ce coin du monde, certainement oublié de Dieu.

«Plus on vit ici, plus l'influence de la lande pénètre l'âme du sentiment de son immensité, mais aussi de son charme effrayant.

«Dès qu'on a foulé ce sol, on perd la notion de l'Angleterre moderne. On heurte à chaque pas les vestiges laissés par les hommes des temps préhistoriques. Où qu'on dirige sa promenade, on rencontre les demeures de cette race éteinte, ses tombeaux et les énormes monolithes qui marquent, à ce que l'on suppose, l'emplacement de ses temples.

«Si celui qui examine ces huttes de pierres grisâtres adossées au flanc raviné des collines apercevait un homme, la barbe et les cheveux incultes, le corps recouvert d'une peau de bête, sortant de l'une d'elles et assujettissant sur la corde de son arc une flèche terminée par un silex aigu, celui-là se croirait transporté à un autre âge et jurerait que la présence en ces lieux de cet être, depuis longtemps disparu, est plus naturelle que la sienne propre.

«On se demande avec stupeur comment des êtres humains ont pu vivre en aussi grand nombre sur cette terre toujours réputée stérile. Je ne connais rien des choses de l'antiquité, mais je présume qu'il ried race who were forced to accept that which none other would occupy.

All this, however, is foreign to the mission on which you sent me and will probably be very uninteresting to your severely practical mind. I can still remember your complete indifference as to whether the sun moved round the earth or the earth round the sun.

Let me, therefore, return to the facts concerning Sir Henry Baskerville.

If you have not had any report within the last few days it is because up to today there was nothing of importance to relate.

Then a very surprising circumstance occurred, which I shall tell you in due course. But, first of all, I must keep you in touch with some of the other factors in the situation.

One of these, concerning which I have said little, is the escaped convict upon the moor. There is strong reason now to believe that he has got right away, which is a considerable relief to the lonely householders of this district.

A fortnight has passed since his flight, during which he has not been seen and nothing has been heard of him. It is surely inconceivable that he could have held out upon the moor during all that time.

Of course, so far as his concealment goes there is no difficulty at all. Any one of these stone huts would give him a hiding-place. But there is nothing to eat unless he were to catch and slaughter one of the moor sheep. We think, therefore, that he has gone, and the outlying farmers sleep the better in consequence.

We are four able-bodied men in this household, so that we could take good care of ourselves, but I confess that I have had uneasy moments when I have thought of the Stapletons.

They live miles from any help. There are one maid, an old manservant, the sister, and the brother, the latter not a very strong man. They would be helpless in the hands of a desperate fellow like this Notting Hill criminal if he could once effect an entrance.

Both Sir Henry and I were concerned at their situation, and it was suggested that Perkins the groom should go over to sleep there, but Stapleton would not hear of it.

The fact is that our friend, the baronet, begins to display a considerable interest in our fair neigh-

a existé des races pacifiques et opprimées qui ont dû se contenter des territoires dédaignés par les autres peuples plus conquérants.

«Tout ceci est étranger à la mission que vous m'avez confiée et n'intéressera que médiocrement votre esprit si merveilleusement pratique. Je me rappelle encore votre superbe indifférence à propos du mouvement terrestre. Que vous importe celui des deux, de la terre ou du soleil, qui tourne autour de l'autre!

«Je reviens aux faits concernant sir Henry Baskerville.

«Depuis ces derniers jours, je ne vous ai adressé aucun rapport, parce que, jusqu'à cette heure, je n'avais rien de marquant à vous signaler.

«Mais il vient de se produire un fait important que je dois vous raconter. Néanmoins, avant de le faire, je veux vous présenter certains facteurs du problème que nous avons à résoudre.

«L'un d'entre eux est ce prisonnier évadé, errant sur la lande, et dont je vous ai succinctement entretenu. Il y a toutes sortes de bonnes raisons de croire qu'il a quitté le pays — pour la plus grande tranquillité des habitants du district.

«Une semaine s'est écoulée depuis son évasion et on ne l'a pas plus vu qu'on n'a entendu parler de lui. Il serait inconcevable qu'il eût pu tenir la lande pendant tout ce temps.

«Certes, quelques-unes de ces huttes de pierre lui auraient aisément servi de cachette; mais de quoi se serait-il nourri dans ce pays où, à moins de tuer les moutons qui paissent l'herbe rase des collines, il n'y a rien à manger.

«Nous pensons donc qu'il s'est enfui, et les hôtes des fermes écartées goûtent de nouveau un paisible sommeil.

«Ici, nous sommes quatre hommes capables de nous défendre; il n'en est pas de même chez les Stapleton et j'avoue qu'en pensant à leur isolement, je me sens inquiet pour eux.

«Le frère, la sœur, un vieux serviteur et une domestique vivent éloignés de tout secours. Ils se trouveraient sans défense, si un gaillard décidé à tout, comme ce criminel de Notting Hill, parvenait à s'introduire dans leur maison.

«Sir Henry et moi, nous préoccupant de cette situation, nous avions décidé que Perkins, le cocher, irait coucher chez Stapleton; mais ce dernier s'y est opposé.

«Notre ami le baronnet témoigne un intérêt considérable à notre jolie voisine. Cela n'a rien bour. It is not to be wondered at, for time hangs heavily in this lonely spot to an active man like him, and she is a very fascinating and beautiful woman. There is something tropical and exotic about her which forms a singular contrast to her cool and unemotional brother.

d'étonnant, dans cette contrée déserte où les heures pèsent si lourdement sur un homme aussi actif que sir Henry... Puis miss Béryl Stapleton est bien attirante! Il y a en elle quelque chose d'exotique, de tropical, qui forme un singulier contraste avec son frère, si froid, si impassible.

Yet he also gives the idea of hidden fires. He has certainly a very marked influence over her, for I have seen her continually glance at him as she talked as if seeking approbation for what she said. I trust that he is kind to her. There is a dry glitter in his eyes and a firm set of his thin lips, which goes with a positive and possibly a harsh nature. You would find him an interesting study.

«Cependant Stapleton évoque l'idée de ces feux qui couvent sous les cendres. Il exerce une très réelle influence sur sa sœur, car j'ai remarqué qu'en parlant elle cherchait constamment son regard pour y lire une approbation. L'éclat métallique des prunelles de cet homme et ses lèvres minces, d'un dessin si ferme, dénotent une nature autoritaire. Vous le trouveriez digne de toute votre attention.

He came over to call upon Baskerville on that first day, and the very next morning he took us both to show us the spot where the legend of the wicked Hugo is supposed to have had its origin.

L'après-midi du jour où j'avais rencontré Stapleton, il vint à Baskerville, et, le lendemain matin, il nous conduisit à l'endroit où l'on suppose que se passèrent, d'après la légende, les faits relatifs à ce misérable Hugo Baskerville.

It was an excursion of some miles across the moor to a place which is so dismal that it might have suggested the story.

«Nous marchâmes pendant quelques milles sur la lande jusqu'à un site tellement sinistre d'aspect, qu'il n'en fallait pas davantage pour accréditer cette légende.

We found a short valley between rugged tors which led to an open, grassy space flecked over with the white cotton grass.

«Une étroite vallée, enserrée entre deux pics rocheux, conduisait à un espace gazonné sur lequel avaient poussé des fleurettes des champs.

In the middle of it rose two great stones, worn and sharpened at the upper end until they looked like the huge corroding fangs of some monstrous beast.

«Au milieu, se dressaient deux grandes pierres usées et comme affilées à leurs extrémités, au point de ressembler aux monstrueuses canines d'un animal fabuleux.

In every way it corresponded with the scene of the old tragedy.

«Rien dans ce décor ne détonnait avec la scène du drame de jadis.

Sir Henry was much interested and asked Stapleton more than once whether he did really believe in the possibility of the interference of the supernatural in the affairs of men. He spoke lightly, but it was evident that he was very much in earnest.

«Très intéressé, sir Henry demanda plusieurs fois à Stapleton s'il croyait véritablement aux interventions surnaturelles dans les affaires des hommes. Il parlait sur un ton badin, mais il était évident qu'il outrait son langage.

Stapleton was guarded in his replies, but it was easy to see that he said less than he might, and that he would not express his whole opinion out of consideration for the feelings of the baronet. He told us of similar cases, where families had suffered from some evil influence, and he left us with the impression that he shared the popular view upon the matter.

«Stapleton se montra circonspect dans ses réponses; mais il était non moins évident que, par égard pour l'état d'esprit du baronnet, il dissimulait une partie de sa pensée. Il nous cita le cas de plusieurs familles ayant souffert d'influences malignes, et il nous laissa sous l'impression qu'il partageait la croyance populaire en la matière.

On our way back we stayed for lunch at Merripit House, and it was there that Sir Henry made the acquaintance of Miss Stapleton.

«En revenant, nous nous arrêtâmes à Merripit house pour y déjeuner. Ce fut là que sir Henry fit la connaissance de miss Stapleton.

From the first moment that he saw her he appeared to be strongly attracted by her, and I am much mistaken if the feeling was not mutual.

«Dès cette première rencontre, la jeune fille me parut avoir profondément impressionné l'esprit de notre ami, et je me tromperais fort si ce sentiment

He took us to show us the spot.
Il nous conduisit à l'endroit.

He referred to her again and again on our walk home, and since then hardly a day has passed that we have not seen something of the brother and sister.

They dine here tonight, and there is some talk of our going to them next week.

One would imagine that such a match would be very welcome to Stapleton, and yet I have more than once caught a look of the strongest disapprobation in his face when Sir Henry has been paying some attention to his sister. He is much attached to her, no doubt, and would lead a lonely life without her, but it would seem the height of selfishness if he were to stand in the way of her making so brilliant a marriage.

Yet I am certain that he does not wish their intimacy to ripen into love, and I have several times observed that he has taken pains to prevent them from being tête-à-tête.

By the way, your instructions to me never to allow Sir Henry to go out alone will become very much more onerous if a love affair were to be added to our other difficulties. My popularity would soon suffer if I were to carry out your orders to the letter.

The other day—Thursday, to be more exact—Dr. Mortimer lunched with us. He has been excavating a barrow at Long Down and has got a prehistoric skull which fills him with great joy. Never was there such a single-minded enthusiast as he!

The Stapletons came in afterwards, and the good doctor took us all to the yew alley at Sir Henry's request to show us exactly how everything occurred upon that fatal night.

It is a long, dismal walk, the yew alley, between two high walls of clipped hedge, with a narrow band of grass upon either side. At the far end is an old tumble-down summer-house.

Halfway down is the moor-gate, where the old gentleman left his cigar-ash. It is a white wooden gate with a latch. Beyond it lies the wide moor.

I remembered your theory of the affair and tried to picture all that had occurred.

ne fut pas réciproque.

«Pendant que nous rentrions au château, le baronnet me parla sans cesse de notre voisine et, depuis lors, il ne s'est pas écoulé de jour que nous n'ayons vu quelqu'un, du frère ou de la sœur.

«Ils ont dîné hier ici et l'on a causé vaguement d'une visite que nous leur ferions la semaine prochaine.

«Vous comprenez qu'une semblable union ravirait Stapleton. Cependant, lorsque sir Henry devenait trop empressé auprès de la sœur, j'ai surpris maintes fois dans les yeux du frère un regard non équivoque de désapprobation. Il doit être partagé entre l'affection qu'il a pour elle et la crainte de l'existence solitaire qu'il mènerait après son départ. Toutefois, ce serait le comble de l'égoïsme que de s'opposer à un aussi brillant mariage.

«J'ai la conviction que Stapleton ne souhaite pas que cette intimité se change en amour, et j'ai souvent remarqué qu'il se donnait beaucoup de mal pour empêcher leurs tête-à-tête.

«Soit dit en passant, la recommandation que vous m'avez faite de ne jamais laisser sir Henry sortir seul deviendrait bien difficile à suivre, si une intrigue d'amour venait s'ajouter à nos autres embarras. Mes bons rapports avec sir Henry se ressentiraient certainement de l'exécution trop rigoureuse de vos ordres.

«L'autre jour — mardi, pour préciser — le docteur Mortimer a déjeuné avec nous. Il avait pratiqué des fouilles dans un tumulus, à Long Down, et y avait trouvé un crâne de l'époque préhistorique qui l'avait rempli de joie. Je ne connais pas de maniaque qui lui soit comparable!

«Les Stapleton arrivèrent peu après le docteur, et Mortimer, sur la demande de sir Henry, nous conduisit tous à l'allée des Ifs pour, nous expliquer comment l'événement avait dû se produire, la fatale nuit.

«Quelle lugubre promenade que cette allée des Ifs! Imaginez un chemin bordé de chaque côté par la muraille épaisse et sombre d'une haie taillée aux ciseaux avec, à droite et à gauche, une étroite bande de gazon. L'extrémité de l'allée opposée au château aboutit à une serre à moitié démolie.

«Au milieu de cette allée, une porte s'ouvre sur la lande. C'est à cet endroit que, par deux fois, sir Charles a secoué les cendres de son cigare. Cette porte, de bois peint en blanc, ne ferme qu'au loquet. Au delà s'étend l'immensité de la lande.

«Je me souviens de votre théorie sur l'affaire et j'essayai de reconstituer la scène.

The yew alley.
L'allée des Ifs.

As the old man stood there he saw something coming across the moor, something which terrified him so that he lost his wits and ran and ran until he died of sheer horror and exhaustion.

There was the long, gloomy tunnel down which he fled.

And from what?

A sheep-dog of the moor? Or a spectral hound, black, silent, and monstrous?

Was there a human agency in the matter?

Did the pale, watchful Barrymore know more than he cared to say?

It was all dim and vague, but always there is the dark shadow of crime behind it.

One other neighbour I have met since I wrote last. This is Mr. Frankland, of Lafter Hall, who lives some four miles to the south of us.

He is an elderly man, red-faced, white-haired, and choleric. His passion is for the British law, and he has spent a large fortune in litigation. He fights for the mere pleasure of fighting and is equally ready to take up either side of a question, so that it is no wonder that he has found it a costly amusement.

Sometimes he will shut up a right of way and defy the parish to make him open it. At others he will with his own hands tear down some other man's gate and declare that a path has existed there from time immemorial, defying the owner to prosecute him for trespass.

He is learned in old manorial and communal rights, and he applies his knowledge sometimes in favour of the villagers of Fernworthy and sometimes against them, so that he is periodically either carried in triumph down the village street or else burned in effigy, according to his latest exploit.

He is said to have about seven lawsuits upon his hands at present, which will probably swallow up the remainder of his fortune and so draw his sting and leave him harmless for the future.

Apart from the law he seems a kindly, good-natured person, and I only mention him because you were particular that I should send some description of the people who surround us.

He is curiously employed at present, for, being an amateur astronomer, he has an excellent telescope, with which he lies upon the roof of his own house and sweeps the moor all day in the hope of catching a glimpse of the escaped convict.

«Tandis que le vieux gentilhomme s'était arrêté, il avait vu arriver du dehors quelque chose qui le terrifia tellement qu'il en perdit l'esprit et qu'il courut, qu'il courut, jusqu'à ce qu'il tomba foudroyé par la peur et par l'épuisement.

«Voilà le long couloir de verdure par lequel il a fui.

«Que fuyait-il?

«Un chien de berger? ou bien un chien noir, silencieux, monstrueux, fantastique?

«S'agissait-il, au contraire, d'un guet-apens qui ne relevait en rien de l'ordre surnaturel?

«Le pâle et vigilant Barrymore en savait-il plus long qu'il ne voulait en dire?

«Tout cela était vague, sombre — plus sombre surtout à cause du crime que je soupçonnais.

«Depuis ma dernière lettre, j'ai fait la connaissance d'un autre voisin, M. Frankland, de Lafter Hall, qui habite à quatre milles de nous, vers le sud.

«C'est un homme âgé, rouge de teint, blanc de cheveux et colérique. La législation anglaise le passionne et il a dissipé en procès une grande fortune. Il plaide pour le seul plaisir de plaider. On le trouve toujours disposé à soutenir l'une ou l'autre face d'une question; aussi ne doit-on pas s'étonner que cet amusement lui ait coûté fort cher.

«Un jour, il supprime un droit de passage et défie la commune de l'obliger à le rétablir. Le lendemain, il démolit de ses propres mains la clôture d'un voisin et déclare la servitude prescrite depuis un temps immémorial, défiant cette fois le propriétaire de le poursuivre pour violation de propriété.

«Il est ferré sur les droits seigneuriaux et communaux et il applique ses connaissances juridiques, tantôt en faveur des paysans de Fenworthy et tantôt contre eux, de telle sorte que, périodiquement et selon sa plus récente interprétation de la loi, on le porte en triomphe dans le village ou on l'y brûle en effigie.

«On prétend qu'il soutient en ce moment sept procès, ce qui absorbera probablement le restant de sa fortune et lui enlèvera toute envie de plaider dans l'avenir.

«Cette bizarrerie de caractère mise à part, je le crois un bon et brave homme, et je ne vous en parle que pour satisfaire votre désir de connaître tous ceux qui nous entourent.

«Pour l'instant, il a une autre marotte. En sa qualité d'astronome amateur, il possède un excellent télescope qu'il a installé sur son toit et à l'aide duquel il passe son temps à interroger la lande, afin de découvrir le prisonnier échappé de

If he would confine his energies to this all would be well, but there are rumours that he intends to prosecute Dr. Mortimer for opening a grave without the consent of the next of kin because he dug up the Neolithic skull in the barrow on Long Down. He helps to keep our lives from being monotonous and gives a little comic relief where it is badly needed.

And now, having brought you up to date in the escaped convict, the Stapletons, Dr. Mortimer, and Frankland, of Lafter Hall, let me end on that which is most important and tell you more about the Barrymores, and especially about the surprising development of last night.

First of all about the test telegram, which you sent from London in order to make sure that Barrymore was really here.

I have already explained that the testimony of the postmaster shows that the test was worthless and that we have no proof one way or the other.

I told Sir Henry how the matter stood, and he at once, in his downright fashion, had Barrymore up and asked him whether he had received the telegram himself.

Barrymore said that he had.

"Did the boy deliver it into your own hands?" asked Sir Henry.

Barrymore looked surprised, and considered for a little time.

"No," said he, "I was in the box-room at the time, and my wife brought it up to me."

"Did you answer it yourself?"

"No; I told my wife what to answer and she went down to write it."

In the evening he recurred to the subject of his own accord.

"I could not quite understand the object of your questions this morning, Sir Henry," said he. "I trust that they do not mean that I have done anything to forfeit your confidence?"

Sir Henry had to assure him that it was not so and pacify him by giving him a considerable part of his old wardrobe, the London outfit having now all arrived.

Mrs. Barrymore is of interest to me. She is a heavy, solid person, very limited, intensely respectable, and inclined to be puritanical. You could hardly conceive a less emotional subject.

Yet I have told you how, on the first night here,

Princetown.

«S'il employait seulement son activité à ce but louable; tout serait pour le mieux; mais la rumeur publique fait circuler le bruit qu'il a l'intention de poursuivre le docteur Mortimer pour avoir ouvert un tombeau sans l'autorisation des parents du défunt — il s'agit du crâne de l'âge néolithique retiré du tumulus de Long Down. En un mot, il rompt la monotonie de notre existence et apporte une note gaie dans ce milieu, qui en a réellement besoin.

«Maintenant que je vous ai entretenu du prisonnier évadé, des Stapleton, du docteur Mortimer, de Frankland, laissez-moi finir par un fait très important: il concerne les Barrymore.

«Vous vous souvenez du télégramme envoyé de Londres pour nous assurer que Barrymore se trouvait bien ici.

«Je vous ai déjà informé que le témoignage du directeur de la poste de Grimpen n'était concluant ni dans un sens ni dans l'autre.

«Je dis à sir Henry ce qu'il en était. Immédiatement il appela Barrymore et lui demanda s'il avait reçu lui-même le télégramme.

«Barrymore répondit affirmativement.

«— Le petit télégraphiste vous l'a-t-il remis en mains propres?» interrogea sir Henry.

«Barrymore parut étonné et réfléchit quelques instants:

«— Non, fit-il; j'étais au grenier à ce moment-là; ma femme me l'y a monté.

«— Est-ce vous qui avez envoyé la réponse?

«— Non. J'ai dit à ma femme ce qu'il fallait répondre et elle est redescendue pour écrire.»

«Dans la soirée, le valet de chambre revint de lui-même sur ce sujet:

«— Je cherche vraiment, sir Henry, à comprendre l'objet de vos questions, dit-il. J'espère qu'elles ne tendent pas à établir que j'ai fait quoi que ce soit pour perdre votre confiance.»

«Sir Henry affirma qu'il n'en était rien. Il acheva de le tranquilliser en lui donnant presque toute son ancienne garde-robe.

«Mme Barrymore m'intéresse au plus haut degré. C'est une femme un peu corpulente, bornée, excessivement respectable et de mœurs puritaines. Vous imagineriez difficilement une nature plus glaciale.

«Je vous ai raconté comment je l'entendis san-

I heard her sobbing bitterly, and since then I have more than once observed traces of tears upon her face. Some deep sorrow gnaws ever at her heart.

Sometimes I wonder if she has a guilty memory which haunts her, and sometimes I suspect Barrymore of being a domestic tyrant.

I have always felt that there was something singular and questionable in this man's character, but the adventure of last night brings all my suspicions to a head.

And yet it may seem a small matter in itself.

You are aware that I am not a very sound sleeper, and since I have been on guard in this house my slumbers have been lighter than ever.

Last night, about two in the morning, I was aroused by a stealthy step passing my room.

I rose, opened my door, and peeped out.

A long black shadow was trailing down the corridor.

It was thrown by a man who walked softly down the passage with a candle held in his hand.

He was in shirt and trousers, with no covering to his feet. I could merely see the outline, but his height told me that it was Barrymore.

He walked very slowly and circumspectly, and there was something indescribably guilty and furtive in his whole appearance.

I have told you that the corridor is broken by the balcony which runs round the hall, but that it is resumed upon the farther side.

I waited until he had passed out of sight and then I followed him.

When I came round the balcony he had reached the end of the farther corridor, and I could see from the glimmer of light through an open door that he had entered one of the rooms.

Now, all these rooms are unfurnished and unoccupied so that his expedition became more mysterious than ever.

The light shone steadily as if he were standing motionless. I crept down the passage as noiselessly as I could and peeped round the corner of the door.

Barrymore was crouching at the window with the candle held against the glass. His profile was half turned towards me, and his face seemed to

gloter, la nuit de mon arrivée au château. Depuis, j'ai surpris maintes fois des traces de larmes sur son visage. Quelque profond chagrin lui ronge le cœur.

«Est-ce le souvenir d'une faute qui la hante? Ou bien Barrymore jouerait-il les tyrans domestiques?

«J'ai toujours pressenti qu'il y avait quelque chose d'anormal et de louche dans les manières de cet homme. L'aventure de la nuit dernière a fortifié mes soupçons.

«Et cependant elle semble de bien petite importance par elle-même!

«Vous savez si, en temps ordinaire, mon sommeil est léger… Il est plus léger encore, depuis que vous m'avez placé de garde auprès de sir Henry.

«Or, la nuit dernière, vers deux heures du matin, je fus réveillé par un bruit de pas glissant furtivement dans le corridor.

«Je me levai et j'ouvris ma porte pour risquer un œil.

«Une ombre noire allongée — celle d'un homme tenant une bougie à la main — traînait sur le tapis.

«L'homme était en bras de chemise et pieds nus.

«Je ne voyais que les contours de son ombre; mais, à ses dimensions, je reconnus qu'elle ne pouvait appartenir qu'à Barrymore.

«Il marchait lentement, avec précaution. Il y avait dans son allure quelque chose d'indéfinissable — de criminel et de craintif à la fois.

«Je vous ai écrit que le balcon qui court autour du hall coupe en deux le corridor et que ce dernier se prolonge à droite et à gauche jusqu'à chaque extrémité du château.

«J'attendis que Barrymore eût disparu, puis je le suivis.

«Lorsque j'arrivai au tournant du balcon, il avait atteint le fond du corridor et, à une clarté qui passait par l'entre-bâillement d'une porte, je vis qu'il était entré dans une chambre.

«Toutes ces chambres sont nues et inoccupées; son expédition n'en devenait que plus incompréhensible pour moi.

«En étouffant le bruit de mes pas, je me glissai le long du passage et j'avançai ma tête par l'ouverture de la porte.

«Barrymore était blotti dans le coin de la fenêtre, sa bougie tout près de la vitre. Son profil, à demi tourné vers moi, me permit de constater l'exbe rigid with expectation as he stared out into the blackness of the moor.

For some minutes he stood watching intently. Then he gave a deep groan and with an impatient gesture he put out the light.

Instantly I made my way back to my room, and very shortly came the stealthy steps passing once more upon their return journey.

Long afterwards when I had fallen into a light sleep I heard a key turn somewhere in a lock, but I could not tell whence the sound came.

What it all means I cannot guess, but there is some secret business going on in this house of gloom which sooner or later we shall get to the bottom of.

I do not trouble you with my theories, for you asked me to furnish you only with facts. I have had a long talk with Sir Henry this morning, and we have made a plan of campaign founded upon my observations of last night.

I will not speak about it just now, but it should make my next report interesting reading.

pression d'attente impatiente peinte sur son visage, tandis qu'il scrutait les ténèbres de la lande.

«Pendant quelques minutes, son regard eut une fixité étonnante. Puis il poussa un profond soupir, et, avec un geste de mauvaise humeur, il éteignit sa bougie.

«Toujours aussi furtivement, je regagnai ma chambre et, bientôt après, j'entendis Barrymore retourner également chez lui.

«Une heure s'écoula. Alors je perçus vaguement, dans un demi-sommeil, le grincement d'une clef dans une serrure; mais je ne pus distinguer d'où venait ce bruit.

«Comment deviner ce que cela signifie? Il se passe certainement dans cette maison des choses mystérieuses que nous finirons bien par découvrir, un jour ou l'autre.

«Je ne vous importunerai pas de mes théories, puisque vous ne réclamez de moi que des faits. Mais, ce matin, j'ai eu une longue conversation avec sir Henry, et nous avons dressé un plan de campagne basé sur ma découverte de la nuit précédente.

«Je ne vous en entretiendrai pas aujourd'hui; il fera l'objet de mon prochain rapport, dont la lecture ne manquera pas de vous intéresser.»

CHAPTER 9. THE LIGHT UPON THE MOOR [SECOND REPORT OF DR. WATSON]

Baskerville Hall, Oct. 15th.

MY DEAR HOLMES,

If I was compelled to leave you without much news during the early days of my mission you must acknowledge that I am making up for lost time, and that events are now crowding thick and fast upon us. In my last report I ended upon my top note with Barrymore at the window, and now I have quite a budget already which will, unless I am much mistaken, considerably surprise you.

Things have taken a turn which I could not have anticipated. In some ways they have within the last forty-eight hours become much clearer and in some ways they have become more complicated.

But I will tell you all and you shall judge for yourself.

Before breakfast on the morning following my adventure I went down the corridor and examined the room in which Barrymore had been on the night before.

The western window through which he had stared so intently has, I noticed, one peculiarity above all other windows in the house—it commands the nearest outlook on to the moor. There is an opening between two trees which enables one from this point of view to look right down upon it, while from all the other windows it is only a distant glimpse which can be obtained.

It follows, therefore, that Barrymore, since only this window would serve the purpose, must have been looking out for something or somebody upon the moor. The night was very dark, so that I can hardly imagine how he could have hoped to see anyone.

It had struck me that it was possible that some love intrigue was on foot. That would have accounted for his stealthy movements and also for

CHAPITRE 9. LA LUMIÈRE SUR LA LANDE [DEUXIÈME RAPPORT DU DOCTEUR WATSON]

Baskerville, 15 octobre.

«Mon cher Holmes,

«Si, pendant quelques jours, je vous ai laissé sans nouvelles, vous conviendrez que je répare aujourd'hui le temps perdu. Les événements se précipitent autour de nous.

«Dans mon dernier rapport, je terminais en vous narrant la promenade nocturne de Barrymore. Aujourd'hui, voici une abondante moisson de renseignements qui vous surprendront grandement — ou bien je me tromperais fort.

«Les choses ont pris une tournure que je ne pouvais prévoir. Pendant les quarante-huit heures qui viennent de s'écouler, il est survenu quelques éclaircissements qui, si j'ose m'exprimer ainsi, ont, d'un autre côté, rendu la situation plus compliquée.

«Je vais tout vous conter; vous jugerez vous-même.

«Le lendemain de mon aventure, j'allai examiner avant le déjeuner la chambre dans laquelle Barrymore avait pénétré la nuit précédente.

«Je remarquai que la fenêtre par laquelle notre homme regardait si attentivement la lande avait une particularité, celle de donner le plus près sur la campagne. Par une échappée ménagée entre deux rangées d'arbres, une personne placée dans la situation occupée par le valet de chambre, pouvait découvrir un assez vaste horizon, alors que, des autres croisées, elle n'en aurait aperçu qu'un coin très restreint.

«Il résultait de cette constatation que Barrymore avait choisi cette fenêtre dans le dessein de voir quelque chose ou quelqu'un sur la lande. Mais, comme la nuit était obscure, on ne pouvait supposer qu'il eût l'intention de voir quelqu'un.

«Je pensai tout d'abord à une intrigue d'amour. Cela expliquait et ses pas furtifs et les pleurs de sa femme.

the uneasiness of his wife.

The man is a striking-looking fellow, very well equipped to steal the heart of a country girl, so that this theory seemed to have something to support it.

«Barrymore est un fort beau garçon, bien fait pour séduire une fille de la campagne. Cette supposition paraissait donc très vraisemblable.

That opening of the door which I had heard after I had returned to my room might mean that he had gone out to keep some clandestine appointment.

De plus, la porte, ouverte après mon retour dans ma chambre, indiquait qu'il était sorti pour courir à quelque rendez-vous clandestin.

So I reasoned with myself in the morning, and I tell you the direction of my suspicions, however much the result may have shown that they were unfounded.

«Le lendemain matin, je raisonnais donc ainsi et je vous communique l'orientation de mes soupçons, bien que la suite ait prouvé combien peu ils étaient fondés.

But whatever the true explanation of Barrymore's movements might be, I felt that the responsibility of keeping them to myself until I could explain them was more than I could bear. I had an interview with the baronet in his study after breakfast, and I told him all that I had seen. He was less surprised than I had expected.

«La conduite de Barrymore pouvait s'expliquer le plus naturellement du monde; cependant je ne crus pas devoir taire ma découverte à sir Henry. J'eus un entretien avec le baronnet et je lui fis part de tout ce que j'avais vu.

"I knew that Barrymore walked about nights, and I had a mind to speak to him about it," said he. "Two or three times I have heard his steps in the passage, coming and going, just about the hour you name."

«— Je savais que Barrymore se promenait toutes les nuits, me dit-il, et je voulais le questionner à ce sujet. Deux ou trois fois, à la même heure que vous, je l'ai entendu aller et venir dans le corridor.

"Perhaps then he pays a visit every night to that particular window," I suggested.

«— Peut-être va-t-il toutes les nuits à cette fenêtre, insinuai-je.

"Perhaps he does. If so, we should be able to shadow him and see what it is that he is after. I wonder what your friend Holmes would do if he were here."

«— Peut-être. Guettons-le; nous aurons vite appris la raison de ces promenades. Je me demande ce que ferait votre ami Holmes, s'il se trouvait ici.

"I believe that he would do exactly what you now suggest," said I. "He would follow Barrymore and see what he did."

«— Il s'arrêterait certainement au parti que vous proposez, répondis-je; il suivrait Barrymore.

"Then we shall do it together."

«— Alors, nous le suivrons aussi.

"But surely he would hear us."

«— Ne nous entendra-t-il pas?

"The man is rather deaf, and in any case we must take our chance of that. We'll sit up in my room tonight and wait until he passes."

«— Non; il est un peu sourd… En tout cas, il faut que nous tentions l'aventure. Cette nuit, nous veillerons dans ma chambre et nous attendrons qu'il ait passé.»

Sir Henry rubbed his hands with pleasure, and it was evident that he hailed the adventure as a relief to his somewhat quiet life upon the moor.

«Sir Henry se frottait les mains de plaisir. Évidemment, il se réjouissait de cette perspective qui apportait un changement dans la monotonie de son existence.

The baronet has been in communication with the architect who prepared the plans for Sir Charles, and with a contractor from London, so that we may expect great changes to begin here soon.

«Le baronnet s'est mis en rapports avec l'architecte qui avait dressé pour sir Charles les plans de la réfection du château. Il a traité avec un entrepreneur de Londres, et les réparations vont bientôt commencer.

There have been decorators and furnishers up from Plymouth, and it is evident that our friend has large ideas and means to spare no pains or ex-

«Il a commandé des décorateurs et des tapissiers de Plymouth et, sans nul doute, notre jeune ami ne veut rien négliger pour tenir l'ancien rang pense to restore the grandeur of his family.

When the house is renovated and refurnished, all that he will need will be a wife to make it complete.

Between ourselves there are pretty clear signs that this will not be wanting if the lady is willing, for I have seldom seen a man more infatuated with a woman than he is with our beautiful neighbour, Miss Stapleton. And yet the course of true love does not run quite as smoothly as one would under the circumstances expect.

Today, for example, its surface was broken by a very unexpected ripple, which has caused our friend considerable perplexity and annoyance.

After the conversation which I have quoted about Barrymore, Sir Henry put on his hat and prepared to go out. As a matter of course I did the same.

"What, are you coming, Watson?" he asked, looking at me in a curious way.

"That depends on whether you are going on the moor," said I.

"Yes, I am."

"Well, you know what my instructions are. I am sorry to intrude, but you heard how earnestly Holmes insisted that I should not leave you, and especially that you should not go alone upon the moor."

Sir Henry put his hand upon my shoulder with a pleasant smile.

"My dear fellow," said he, "Holmes, with all his wisdom, did not foresee some things which have happened since I have been on the moor. You understand me? I am sure that you are the last man in the world who would wish to be a spoil-sport. I must go out alone."

It put me in a most awkward position. I was at a loss what to say or what to do, and before I had made up my mind he picked up his cane and was gone.

But when I came to think the matter over my conscience reproached me bitterly for having on any pretext allowed him to go out of my sight.

I imagined what my feelings would be if I had to return to you and to confess that some misfortune had occurred through my disregard for your instructions.

I assure you my cheeks flushed at the very

de sa famille.

«Lorsque la maison sera réparée et remeublée, il n'y manquera plus que la présence d'une femme.

«Entre nous, il existe des indices caractéristiques de la prompte exécution de ce projet — pour peu que la dame y consente. En effet, j'ai rarement rencontré un homme plus emballé sur une femme que ne l'est sir Henry sur notre belle voisine, miss Stapleton. Cependant je crains bien que leur voyage sur le fleuve du Tendre ne soit très mouvementé.

«Aujourd'hui, par exemple, la surface de l'onde chère aux amoureux a été ridée par un coup de vent inattendu, qui a causé un vif mécompte à notre ami.

«Lorsque notre conversation sur Barrymore eut pris fin, sir Henry mit son chapeau et se disposa à sortir. Naturellement, j'en fis autant.

«— Où allez-vous, Watson? me demanda-t-il en me regardant avec curiosité.

«— Cela dépend... Devez-vous traverser la lande?

«— Oui.

«— Alors vous connaissez mes instructions. Je regrette de vous importuner de ma personne, mais vous n'ignorez pas qu'Holmes m'a recommandé avec instance de ne pas vous perdre de vue, surtout quand vous iriez sur la lande.»

«Sir Henry posa en riant sa main sur mon épaule.

«— Mon cher ami, fit-il, malgré toute sa perspicacité, Holmes n'a pas prévu certaines choses qui se sont passées depuis mon arrivée ici. Vous me comprenez?... Je jurerais bien que vous êtes le dernier homme qui consentirait à jouer auprès de moi le rôle de trouble-fête. Il faut que je sorte seul.»

«Ces paroles me plaçaient dans une situation embarrassante. Je ne savais trop que dire ni que faire et, avant que mon irrésolution cessât, sir Henry avait enlevé sa canne du portemanteau et s'était éloigné.

«À la réflexion, ma conscience me reprocha amèrement de n'avoir pas exigé, sous un prétexte quelconque, que le baronnet me gardât auprès de lui.

«Je me représentais la posture que j'aurais vis-à-vis de vous, si je retournais à Baker street vous avouer que ma désobéissance à vos ordres avait causé un malheur.

«Je vous assure qu'à cette pensée, le sang me

thought.

It might not even now be too late to overtake him, so I set off at once in the direction of Merripit House.

I hurried along the road at the top of my speed without seeing anything of Sir Henry, until I came to the point where the moor path branches off.

There, fearing that perhaps I had come in the wrong direction after all, I mounted a hill from which I could command a view—the same hill which is cut into the dark quarry. Thence I saw him at once.

He was on the moor path about a quarter of a mile off, and a lady was by his side who could only be Miss Stapleton.

It was clear that there was already an understanding between them and that they had met by appointment.

They were walking slowly along in deep conversation, and I saw her making quick little movements of her hands as if she were very earnest in what she was saying, while he listened intently, and once or twice shook his head in strong dissent.

I stood among the rocks watching them, very much puzzled as to what I should do next.

To follow them and break into their intimate conversation seemed to be an outrage, and yet my clear duty was never for an instant to let him out of my sight.

To act the spy upon a friend was a hateful task. Still, I could see no better course than to observe him from the hill, and to clear my conscience by confessing to him afterwards what I had done. It is true that if any sudden danger had threatened him I was too far away to be of use, and yet I am sure that you will agree with me that the position was very difficult, and that there was nothing more which I could do.

Our friend, Sir Henry, and the lady had halted on the path and were standing deeply absorbed in their conversation, when I was suddenly aware that I was not the only witness of their interview.

A wisp of green floating in the air caught my eye, and another glance showed me that it was carried on a stick by a man who was moving among the broken ground.

It was Stapleton with his butterfly-net.

He was very much closer to the pair than I was, and he appeared to be moving in their direction.

brûla les joues.

«Je me dis que je pouvais encore rattraper mon promeneur et je partis immédiatement dans la direction de Merripit house.

«Je courus de toute la vitesse de mes jambes jusqu'au point où la route bifurque sur la lande. Sir Henry demeurait invisible.

«Alors, craignant d'avoir suivi une mauvaise direction, j'escaladai une colline — celle que l'on avait exploitée comme carrière de granit — du haut de laquelle ma vue embrassait presque tout le pays.

«Immédiatement, j'aperçus le baronnet à cinq cents mètres devant moi. Il s'était engagé dans le petit sentier. Une femme, qui ne pouvait être que miss Stapleton, marchait à côté de lui.

«Certainement un accord existait déjà entre eux et je surprenais un rendez-vous convenu.

«Ils allaient, lentement, absorbés par leur conversation. Je vis miss Stapleton faire de rapides mouvements avec sa main, comme pour souligner ce qu'elle disait, tandis que sir Henry l'écoutait attentivement et secouait parfois négativement la tête.

«Je me dissimulai derrière un rocher, curieux de voir comment tout cela finirait.

«Me jeter au travers de leur entretien, c'eût été commettre une impertinence dont je me sentais incapable. Mais, d'autre part, ma consigne m'ordonnait de marcher dans les pas de sir Henry.

«Espionner un ami est un acte odieux. Cependant je me résolus à l'observer du haut de ma cachette et de lui confesser plus tard ma faute. J'étais certain qu'il conviendrait avec moi de la difficulté de ma situation et qu'il approuverait le parti que j'avais pris, bien que, si un danger soudain l'eût menacé, je me fusse trouvé trop éloigné pour le secourir promptement.

«Sir Henry et sa compagne, perdus dans leur absorbante conversation, s'étaient arrêtés au milieu du sentier. Tout à coup j'eus la sensation de n'être pas le seul témoin de leur entrevue.

«Quelque chose de vert, flottant dans l'air, attira mon attention. Un nouveau regard me montra ce quelque chose fixé à l'extrémité d'un bâton porté par un homme qui enjambait les quartiers de roches.

«Je reconnus Stapleton et son filet.

«La distance qui le séparait du couple était moins grande que celle qui m'en séparait moi-

At this instant Sir Henry suddenly drew Miss Stapleton to his side. His arm was round her, but it seemed to me that she was straining away from him with her face averted. He stooped his head to hers, and she raised one hand as if in protest.

Next moment I saw them spring apart and turn hurriedly round.

Stapleton was the cause of the interruption. He was running wildly towards them, his absurd net dangling behind him. He gesticulated and almost danced with excitement in front of the lovers.

What the scene meant I could not imagine, but it seemed to me that Stapleton was abusing Sir Henry, who offered explanations, which became more angry as the other refused to accept them.

The lady stood by in haughty silence.

Finally Stapleton turned upon his heel and beckoned in a peremptory way to his sister, who, after an irresolute glance at Sir Henry, walked off by the side of her brother.

The naturalist's angry gestures showed that the lady was included in his displeasure. The baronet stood for a minute looking after them, and then he walked slowly back the way that he had come, his head hanging, the very picture of dejection.

What all this meant I could not imagine, but I was deeply ashamed to have witnessed so intimate a scene without my friend's knowledge.

I ran down the hill therefore and met the baronet at the bottom. His face was flushed with anger and his brows were wrinkled, like one who is at his wit's ends what to do.

"Halloa, Watson! Where have you dropped from?" said he. "You don't mean to say that you came after me in spite of all?"

I explained everything to him: how I had found it impossible to remain behind, how I had followed him, and how I had witnessed all that had occurred. For an instant his eyes blazed at me, but my frankness disarmed his anger, and he broke at last into a rather rueful laugh.

"You would have thought the middle of that prairie a fairly safe place for a man to be private," said he, "but, by thunder, the whole countryside seems to have been out to see me do my wooing—and a mighty poor wooing at that! Where had you

même, et il paraissait se diriger du côté des deux jeunes gens.

«À ce moment, sir Henry attira miss Stapleton vers lui. Il avait passé son bras autour de la taille de Béryl, qui se recula, en détournant son visage. Il se pencha vers elle; mais elle étendit la main pour se protéger.

«Une seconde après, je les vis s'éloigner précipitamment l'un de l'autre et faire demi-tour.

«Stapleton avait provoqué cette brusque séparation. Il accourait au-devant d'eux, son ridicule filet se balançant sur son épaule. Il gesticulait comme un possédé et sa surexcitation était telle qu'il dansait presque en face des amoureux.

«Je ne pouvais imaginer ce qui se passait. Toutefois, je crus deviner que Stapleton gourmandait sir Henry; que ce dernier présentait des explications et que sa colère croissait à mesure que l'autre refusait de les accepter.

«La dame gardait un silence hautain.

«Finalement Stapleton tourna sur ses talons et fit de la main un signe péremptoire à sa sœur. Celle-ci, après un regard plein d'hésitation adressé à Sir Henry, se décida à marcher aux côtés de son frère.

«Les gestes de colère du naturaliste indiquaient que la jeune fille n'échappait pas à son mécontentement. Après les avoir considérés l'un et l'autre pendant l'espace d'une minute, le baronnet, la tête basse et l'air abattu, reprit lentement le chemin par lequel il était venu.

«Je ne pouvais deviner ce que tout cela signifiait, mais je me sentais honteux d'avoir assisté à cette scène, à l'insu de mon ami.

«Je dégringolai vivement la colline pour aller à la rencontre de sir Henry. Son visage était pourpre de colère et ses sourcils froncés, comme ceux d'un homme poussé à bout.

«— Allô! Watson, d'où sortez-vous? me dit-il. J'aime à croire que vous ne m'avez pas suivi?»

«Je lui expliquai tout: comment j'avais jugé impossible de le laisser s'engager seul sur la lande et comment j'avais assisté à ce qui venait d'arriver. Pendant un moment, ses yeux flambèrent; mais ma franchise le désarma et il eut un triste sourire.

«— On aurait pensé, reprit-il, que cette solitude offrirait un abri sûr!... Ah! ouiche, tout le pays semble s'y être réuni pour me voir faire ma cour — et quelle misérable cour! Où aviez-vous loué un fauteuil?

engaged a seat?"

"I was on that hill."

"Quite in the back row, eh? But her brother was well up to the front. Did you see him come out on us?"

"Yes, I did."

"Did he ever strike you as being crazy—this brother of hers?"

"I can't say that he ever did."

"I dare say not. I always thought him sane enough until today, but you can take it from me that either he or I ought to be in a straitjacket. What's the matter with me, anyhow? You've lived near me for some weeks, Watson. Tell me straight, now! Is there anything that would prevent me from making a good husband to a woman that I loved?"

"I should say not."

"He can't object to my worldly position, so it must be myself that he has this down on. What has he against me? I never hurt man or woman in my life that I know of. And yet he would not so much as let me touch the tips of her fingers."

"Did he say so?"

"That, and a deal more. I tell you, Watson, I've only known her these few weeks, but from the first I just felt that she was made for me, and she, too—she was happy when she was with me, and that I'll swear. There's a light in a woman's eyes that speaks louder than words. But he has never let us get together and it was only today for the first time that I saw a chance of having a few words with her alone.

She was glad to meet me, but when she did it was not love that she would talk about, and she wouldn't have let me talk about it either if she could have stopped it.

She kept coming back to it that this was a place of danger, and that she would never be happy until I had left it.

I told her that since I had seen her I was in no hurry to leave it, and that if she really wanted me to go, the only way to work it was for her to arrange to go with me.

With that I offered in as many words to marry her, but before she could answer, down came this brother of hers, running at us with a face on him like a madman. He was just white with rage, and

«— Sur la colline.

«— Au dernier rang! Son frère, à elle, était assis aux premières loges!... L'avez-vous aperçu s'approcher de nous?

«— Oui.

«— Aviez-vous jamais remarqué qu'il fût toqué?

«— Non.

«— Moi non plus. Jusqu'à ce jour, je le jugeais sain d'esprit... Mais, à cette heure, je vous affirme que l'un de nous deux mérite une camisole de force. À propos de quoi en a-t-il après moi?... Voilà déjà plusieurs semaines, Watson, que nous vivons côte à côte... Parlez-moi franchement... Y a-t-il un empêchement à ce que je sois un bon mari pour une femme que j'aimerais?

«— Je n'en vois pas.

«— Stapleton ne peut arguer de ma situation mondaine... C'est donc ma personne qu'il méprise!... Qu'a-t-il contre moi? Je n'ai jamais fait de tort à personne, que je sache! Et cependant il ne m'autorise pas à toucher le bout des doigts de sa sœur.

«— Non?

«— Si, et bien plus encore. Écoutez, Watson... Je ne connais miss Stapleton que depuis quelques semaines, mais, le jour où je l'ai rencontrée pour la première fois, j'ai senti que Dieu l'avait faite pour moi — et elle pareillement. Elle était heureuse de se trouver près de moi, je le jurerais! Il passe dans les yeux des femmes des lueurs qui sont plus éloquentes que des paroles... Son frère ne nous permettait pas de rester seuls ensemble et, aujourd'hui seulement, j'ai saisi l'occasion de causer avec elle sans témoins.

«Notre rencontre l'a comblée de joie... mais ce n'était pas d'amour qu'elle désirait m'entretenir, et, si elle avait pu m'en empêcher, elle n'aurait pas souffert que je lui en eusse parlé.

«Elle a commencé à insister sur le danger que je cours ici et sur l'inquiétude dans laquelle elle vivrait, si je ne quittais pas Baskerville.

«Je lui ai répondu que, depuis que je la connaissais, je n'étais plus pressé de partir et que, si réellement elle souhaitait mon départ, le meilleur moyen d'en venir à ses fins était de s'arranger pour m'accompagner.

«Je lui proposai de l'épouser, mais, avant qu'elle eût pu me répondre, son espèce de frère arrivait sur nous avec des façons d'énergumène. Ses joues blêmissaient de rage et, dans ses yeux, de sinistres those light eyes of his were blazing with fury.

What was I doing with the lady? How dared I offer her attentions which were distasteful to her? Did I think that because I was a baronet I could do what I liked?

If he had not been her brother I should have known better how to answer him. As it was I told him that my feelings towards his sister were such as I was not ashamed of, and that I hoped that she might honour me by becoming my wife.

That seemed to make the matter no better, so then I lost my temper too, and I answered him rather more hotly than I should perhaps, considering that she was standing by. So it ended by his going off with her, as you saw, and here am I as badly puzzled a man as any in this county. Just tell me what it all means, Watson, and I'll owe you more than ever I can hope to pay."

I tried one or two explanations, but, indeed, I was completely puzzled myself.

Our friend's title, his fortune, his age, his character, and his appearance are all in his favour, and I know nothing against him unless it be this dark fate which runs in his family.

That his advances should be rejected so brusquely without any reference to the lady's own wishes and that the lady should accept the situation without protest is very amazing. However, our conjectures were set at rest by a visit from Stapleton himself that very afternoon.

He had come to offer apologies for his rudeness of the morning, and after a long private interview with Sir Henry in his study the upshot of their conversation was that the breach is quite healed, and that we are to dine at Merripit House next Friday as a sign of it.

"I don't say now that he isn't a crazy man," said Sir Henry; "I can't forget the look in his eyes when he ran at me this morning, but I must allow that no man could make a more handsome apology than he has done."

"Did he give any explanation of his conduct?"

"His sister is everything in his life, he says. That is natural enough, and I am glad that he should understand her value. They have always been together, and according to his account he has been a very lonely man with only her as a companion, so that the thought of losing her was really terrible to him. He had not understood, he said, that

éclairs de folie s'allumaient.

«Que faisais-je avec madame?... Comment avais-je l'audace de lui rendre des hommages qui lui étaient odieux?... Mon titre de baronnet autorisait-il donc une conduite aussi cavalière?

«Si Stapleton n'avait pas été le frère de Béryl, j'aurais mieux su que lui répondre. En tout cas, je lui ai dit quels sentiments m'inspirait sa sœur et que j'espérais qu'elle me ferait l'honneur de devenir ma femme.

«Au lieu de se calmer, ce discours l'irrita encore davantage. À mon tour, je m'emportai et je ripostai un peu plus aigrement que je ne l'aurais dû, Béryl étant présente à notre altercation. Leur départ précipité a terminé cette scène pénible et vous voyez en moi l'homme le plus bouleversé de tout le comté.»

«Je risquai une ou deux explications; mais j'étais en réalité tout aussi troublé que sir Henry.

«Le titre de notre ami, sa fortune, son âge, ses manières, son physique, tout militait en sa faveur. On ne pouvait rien lui reprocher — rien que le fatal destin qui s'acharnait sur sa famille.

«Pourquoi repousser brusquement ses avances, sans même prendre l'avis de la personne qui en était l'objet? Et pourquoi miss Stapleton avait-elle obéi à son frère, sans protester autrement que par son effarement?

«Dans l'après-midi, une visite du naturaliste fit cesser nos conjectures. Il venait s'excuser de sa conduite grossière. Après un long entretien avec sir Henry, dans le cabinet de ce dernier, tout malentendu fut dissipé, et l'on convint que, pour fêter cette réconciliation, nous irions dîner le vendredi suivant à Merripit house.

«— Cette démarche de Stapleton ne modifie pas mon appréciation sur lui, me dit sir Henry... Je le considère toujours comme un peu toqué... Je ne puis oublier l'expression de son regard, quand il courut sur moi ce matin. Cependant je dois reconnaître qu'il s'est excusé de fort bonne grâce.

«— Vous a-t-il donné une explication de sa conduite?

«— Oui. Il prétend qu'il a reporté sur sa sœur toutes ses affections. Cela est très naturel et je me réjouis de ces sentiments à son égard... Il m'a dit qu'ils avaient toujours vécu ensemble, menant une existence de cénobites, et que la pensée de la perdre lui était intolérable. Il a ensuite ajouté qu'il ne s'était pas tout d'abord aperçu de mon attache-

I was becoming attached to her, but when he saw with his own eyes that it was really so, and that she might be taken away from him, it gave him such a shock that for a time he was not responsible for what he said or did.

ment pour miss Stapleton, mais que, lorsqu'il avait vu de ses propres yeux l'impression produite sur moi par sa sœur et qu'il avait compris qu'un jour viendrait peut-être où il serait forcé de se séparer d'elle, il avait ressenti un tel choc que, pendant une minute, il ne fut plus conscient de ses paroles ou de ses actes.

He was very sorry for all that had passed, and he recognized how foolish and how selfish it was that he should imagine that he could hold a beautiful woman like his sister to himself for her whole life. If she had to leave him he had rather it was to a neighbour like myself than to anyone else.

«Il se confondit en excuses et reconnut de quelle folie et de quel égoïsme il se rendait coupable, en voulant retenir éternellement autour de lui une aussi belle personne que sa sœur. Il conclut en convenant que, si elle devait le quitter, il valait mieux que ce fût pour épouser un voisin tel que moi.

«— Vraiment?

But in any case it was a blow to him and it would take him some time before he could prepare himself to meet it. He would withdraw all opposition upon his part if I would promise for three months to let the matter rest and to be content with cultivating the lady's friendship during that time without claiming her love. This I promised, and so the matter rests."

«— Il s'appesantit sur la rudesse du coup et sur le temps qu'il lui faudrait pour s'y accoutumer. Il s'engagea à ne plus s'opposer à mes projets, si je lui promettais de n'en plus parler de trois mois et si, pendant ce temps, je me contentais de l'amitié de miss Béryl, sans lui demander son amour. Je promis tout ce qu'il désirait et cela clôtura le débat.»

So there is one of our small mysteries cleared up.

«Voilà donc un de nos petits mystères éclairci.

It is something to have touched bottom anywhere in this bog in which we are floundering. We know now why Stapleton looked with disfavour upon his sister's suitor—even when that suitor was so eligible a one as Sir Henry.

«Nous savons maintenant pourquoi Stapleton regardait avec défaveur l'amoureux de sa sœur — même lorsque cet amoureux est un parti aussi enviable que sir Henry.

And now I pass on to another thread which I have extricated out of the tangled skein, the mystery of the sobs in the night, of the tear-stained face of Mrs. Barrymore, of the secret journey of the butler to the western lattice window.

«Passons maintenant à un autre fil que j'ai débrouillé dans cet écheveau pourtant si emmêlé. Je veux parler des gémissements nocturnes, du visage éploré de Mme Barrymore et des pérégrinations clandestines de son mari.

Congratulate me, my dear Holmes, and tell me that I have not disappointed you as an agent—that you do not regret the confidence which you showed in me when you sent me down. All these things have by one night's work been thoroughly cleared.

«Félicitez-moi, mon cher Holmes… Dites-moi que je n'ai pas déçu l'espoir que vous aviez placé dans mes qualités de détective, et que vous ne regrettez pas le témoignage de confiance dont vous m'avez honoré en m'envoyant ici. Il ne m'a fallu qu'une nuit pour tirer tout cela au clair!

I have said "by one night's work," but, in truth, it was by two nights' work, for on the first we drew entirely blank.

«En disant une nuit, j'exagère. Deux nuits m'ont été nécessaires, car, la première, nous avons fait chou blanc.

I sat up with Sir Henry in his rooms until nearly three o'clock in the morning, but no sound of any sort did we hear except the chiming clock upon the stairs.

«Nous étions restés dans la chambre de sir Henry à fumer des cigarettes jusqu'à trois heures du matin. Sauf le carillon de l'horloge du hall, aucun bruit ne frappa nos oreilles.

It was a most melancholy vigil and ended by each of us falling asleep in our chairs.

«Ce fut une veillée peu réjouissante, qui se termina par notre assoupissement dans les bras de nos fauteuils respectifs.

Fortunately we were not discouraged, and we determined to try again.

«Nous ne nous découragêames pas pour cela, et nous convînmes de recommencer.

The next night we lowered the lamp and sat smoking cigarettes without making the least sound.

It was incredible how slowly the hours crawled by, and yet we were helped through it by the same sort of patient interest which the hunter must feel as he watches the trap into which he hopes the game may wander.

One struck, and two, and we had almost for the second time given it up in despair when in an instant we both sat bolt upright in our chairs with all our weary senses keenly on the alert once more.

We had heard the creak of a step in the passage.

Very stealthily we heard it pass along until it died away in the distance. Then the baronet gently opened his door and we set out in pursuit.

Already our man had gone round the gallery and the corridor was all in darkness. Softly we stole along until we had come into the other wing.

We were just in time to catch a glimpse of the tall, black-bearded figure, his shoulders rounded as he tiptoed down the passage.

Then he passed through the same door as before, and the light of the candle framed it in the darkness and shot one single yellow beam across the gloom of the corridor.

We shuffled cautiously towards it, trying every plank before we dared to put our whole weight upon it.

We had taken the precaution of leaving our boots behind us, but, even so, the old boards snapped and creaked beneath our tread.

Sometimes it seemed impossible that he should fail to hear our approach.

However, the man is fortunately rather deaf, and he was entirely preoccupied in that which he was doing.

When at last we reached the door and peeped through we found him crouching at the window, candle in hand, his white, intent face pressed against the pane, exactly as I had seen him two nights before.

We had arranged no plan of campaign, but the baronet is a man to whom the most direct way is always the most natural.

He walked into the room, and as he did so Barrymore sprang up from the window with a sharp

«La nuit suivante, nous baissâmes la lampe et, la cigarette aux lèvres, nous nous tînmes cois.

«Ah! combien les heures s'écoulèrent lentement! Cependant nous avions pour nous soutenir l'ardeur du chasseur qui surveille le piège dans lequel il espère voir tomber la bête de chasse.

«Une heure sonna... puis deux heures. Pour la seconde fois, nous allions nous séparer bredouilles, lorsque d'un même mouvement nous nous levâmes de nos sièges.

«Un pas glissait furtivement le long du corridor.

«Quand il se fut évanoui dans le lointain, le baronnet, très doucement, ouvrit la porte et nous sortîmes de la chambre.

«Notre homme avait déjà dépassé le balcon du hall. Le corridor était plongé dans les ténèbres. Nous le parcourûmes jusqu'à l'autre aile du château.

«Nous arrivâmes assez tôt pour apercevoir la silhouette d'un homme barbu, de haute taille, qui marchait sur la pointe des pieds, en courbant les épaules.

«Il poussa la même porte que l'avant-veille. La lueur de la bougie en dessina lumineusement l'encadrement et piqua d'un rayon de clarté jaune l'obscurité du corridor.

«Avec des précautions infinies, nous nous dirigeâmes de ce côté, tâtant du pied chaque lame du parquet avant de lui confier le poids de notre corps.

«Nous avions au préalable enlevé nos bottines; mais le plancher vermoulu fléchissait et criait sous nos pas.

«Parfois il nous semblait impossible que Barrymore ne nous entendît pas.

«Fort heureusement, il est sourd, et la préoccupation de ne pas faire de bruit l'absorbait entièrement.

«Nous atteignîmes enfin la porte derrière laquelle il avait disparu et nous jetâmes un coup d'œil dans la chambre. Barrymore, une bougie à la main, était presque collé contre la fenêtre et regardait attentivement à travers les carreaux — dans la même position que les nuits précédentes.

«Nous n'étions convenus de rien. Mais le caractère résolu du baronnet le porte naturellement à aller droit au but.

«Il pénétra dans la chambre. Au bruit, Barrymore se retira vivement de la fenêtre et nous aphiss of his breath and stood, livid and trembling, before us. His dark eyes, glaring out of the white mask of his face, were full of horror and astonishment as he gazed from Sir Henry to me.

"What are you doing here, Barrymore?"

"Nothing, sir."

His agitation was so great that he could hardly speak, and the shadows sprang up and down from the shaking of his candle.

"It was the window, sir. I go round at night to see that they are fastened."

"On the second floor?"

"Yes, sir, all the windows."

"Look here, Barrymore," said Sir Henry sternly, "we have made up our minds to have the truth out of you, so it will save you trouble to tell it sooner rather than later. Come, now! No lies! What were you doing at that window?"

The fellow looked at us in a helpless way, and he wrung his hands together like one who is in the last extremity of doubt and misery.

"I was doing no harm, sir. I was holding a candle to the window."

"And why were you holding a candle to the window?"

"Don't ask me, Sir Henry—don't ask me! I give you my word, sir, that it is not my secret, and that I cannot tell it. If it concerned no one but myself I would not try to keep it from you."

A sudden idea occurred to me, and I took the candle from the trembling hand of the butler.

"He must have been holding it as a signal," said I. "Let us see if there is any answer."

I held it as he had done, and stared out into the darkness of the night.

Vaguely I could discern the black bank of the trees and the lighter expanse of the moor, for the moon was behind the clouds.

And then I gave a cry of exultation, for a tiny pinpoint of yellow light had suddenly transfixed the dark veil, and glowed steadily in the centre of the black square framed by the window.

"There it is!" I cried.

"No, no, sir, it is nothing—nothing at all!" the butler broke in; "I assure you, sir—"

parut, tremblant, livide, haletant. Ses yeux noirs, rendus plus brillants par la pâleur exsangue de la face avaient, en nous regardant, sir Henry et moi, une expression d'étonnement et d'effroi.

«— Que faites-vous là, Barrymore? demanda le baronnet.

«— Rien, monsieur.»

«Sa frayeur était si grande qu'il pouvait à peine parler, et le tremblement de sa main agitait à tel point la bougie que les ombres dansaient sur la muraille.

«— C'est la fenêtre, reprit-il... Je fais une ronde, toutes les nuits, pour m'assurer qu'elles sont bien fermées.

«— Au second étage?

«— Oui, monsieur,... toutes les fenêtres.

«Écoutez-moi, Barrymore! dit sir Henry sévèrement. Nous sommes décidés à vous arracher la vérité... Cela vous évitera des ennuis dans l'avenir. Allons, pas de mensonges! Que faisiez-vous à cette fenêtre?»

«Le pauvre diable nous adressa un regard désespéré et croisa ses mains dans un geste de muette supplication.

«— Je ne faisais rien de mal, monsieur... Je tenais une bougie contre cette fenêtre.

«— Dans quel but?

«— Ne me le demandez pas, sir Henry!... ne me le demandez pas!... Je vous jure que ce secret ne m'appartient pas et que je ne puis vous le dire. S'il n'intéressait que moi seul, je vous le confierais sans hésiter.»

«Une pensée soudaine me traversa l'esprit et je pris la bougie des mains tremblantes du valet de chambre.

«— Ce doit être un signal, dis-je au baronnet. Voyons si l'on y répondra.»

«J'imitai la manœuvre de Barrymore et, regardant au dehors, j'essayai de percer les ténèbres de la nuit.

«De gros nuages voilaient la lune.Je distinguai vaguement la ligne sombre formée par la cimes des arbres, et, au delà, une vaste étendue plus éclairée: la lande.

«Tout à coup un cri de joie m'échappa. Un point lumineux avait surgi dans le lointain.

«— Le voilà! m'écriai-je.

«— Non, monsieur... Non, ce n'est rien! répliqua le valet de chambre... Je vous assure...

"Move your light across the window, Watson!" cried the baronet. "See, the other moves also! Now, you rascal, do you deny that it is a signal? Come, speak up! Who is your confederate out yonder, and what is this conspiracy that is going on?"

The man's face became openly defiant.

"It is my business, and not yours. I will not tell."

"Then you leave my employment right away."

"Very good, sir. If I must I must."

"And you go in disgrace. By thunder, you may well be ashamed of yourself. Your family has lived with mine for over a hundred years under this roof, and here I find you deep in some dark plot against me."

"No, no, sir; no, not against you!" It was a woman's voice, and Mrs. Barrymore, paler and more horror-struck than her husband, was standing at the door.

Her bulky figure in a shawl and skirt might have been comic were it not for the intensity of feeling upon her face.

"We have to go, Eliza. This is the end of it. You can pack our things," said the butler.

"Oh, John, John, have I brought you to this? It is my doing, Sir Henry—all mine. He has done nothing except for my sake and because I asked him."

"Speak out, then! What does it mean?"

"My unhappy brother is starving on the moor. We cannot let him perish at our very gates. The light is a signal to him that food is ready for him, and his light out yonder is to show the spot to which to bring it."

"Then your brother is—"

"The escaped convict, sir—Selden, the criminal."

"That's the truth, sir," said Barrymore. "I said that it was not my secret and that I could not tell it to you. But now you have heard it, and you will see that if there was a plot it was not against you."

This, then, was the explanation of the stealthy expeditions at night and the light at the window.

Sir Henry and I both stared at the woman in amazement. Was it possible that this stolidly respectable person was of the same blood as one of

«— Promenez votre bougie devant la fenêtre, Watson, me dit le baronnet. Tenez, l'autre lumière remue également. Maintenant, coquin, nierez-vous que c'était un signal? Parlez! Quel est là-bas votre complice et contre qui conspirez-vous?»

«Le visage de Barrymore exprima aussitôt une défiance manifeste:

«— C'est mon affaire et non la vôtre!... Vous ne saurez rien!...

«— Alors quittez mon service... immédiatement!

«— Très bien, monsieur.

«— Je vous chasse! Vous devriez être honteux de votre conduite... Votre famille a vécu pendant plusieurs siècles sous le même toit que la mienne et je vous trouve mêlé à quelque complot tramé contre moi!...

«— Non, monsieur,... non, pas contre vous», fit une voix de femme. Nous nous retournâmes, et, sur le seuil de la chambre, nous aperçûmes Mme Barrymore, plus pâle et plus terrifiée que son mari.

«Enveloppée dans un châle, en jupons, cet accoutrement l'aurait rendue grotesque, n'avait été l'intensité des sentiments imprimés sur son visage.

«— Il nous faut partir, Élisa, lui dit Barrymore. C'en est fait... Prépare nos paquets.

«— Oh! Jean, Jean, répondit-elle, je suis la cause de ton renvoi... Il n'y a que moi seule de coupable!... Il n'a fait que ce que je lui ai demandé...

«— Parlez, alors! commanda sir Henry. Que voulez-vous dire?

«— Mon malheureux frère meurt de faim sur la lande. Nous ne pouvons le laisser périr si près de nous... Au moyen de cette bougie, nous lui annonçons que nous lui avons préparé des vivres, et la lueur que vous avez aperçue là-bas nous indique l'endroit où nous devons les lui apporter.

«— Votre frère est?...

«— Le prisonnier évadé de Princetown... Selden l'assassin.

«— Voilà la vérité, monsieur, fit Barrymore. Je vous ai dit que ce secret ne m'appartenait pas et qu'il m'était impossible de vous l'apprendre. Vous le connaissez maintenant, et vous voyez que, s'il y a un complot, il n'est pas dirigé contre vous.»

«Ainsi se trouvent expliqués les expéditions nocturnes de Barrymore et les échanges de signaux entre le château et la lande.

«Sir Henry et moi, nous regardions avec stupéfaction Mme Barrymore. Cette personne d'aspect si respectable était donc du même sang que l'un the most notorious criminals in the country?

"Yes, sir, my name was Selden, and he is my younger brother. We humoured him too much when he was a lad and gave him his own way in everything until he came to think that the world was made for his pleasure, and that he could do what he liked in it. Then as he grew older he met wicked companions, and the devil entered into him until he broke my mother's heart and dragged our name in the dirt.

From crime to crime he sank lower and lower until it is only the mercy of God which has snatched him from the scaffold; but to me, sir, he was always the little curly-headed boy that I had nursed and played with as an elder sister would.

That was why he broke prison, sir. He knew that I was here and that we could not refuse to help him.

When he dragged himself here one night, weary and starving, with the warders hard at his heels, what could we do?

We took him in and fed him and cared for him.

Then you returned, sir, and my brother thought he would be safer on the moor than anywhere else until the hue and cry was over, so he lay in hiding there.

But every second night we made sure if he was still there by putting a light in the window, and if there was an answer my husband took out some bread and meat to him.

Every day we hoped that he was gone, but as long as he was there we could not desert him.

That is the whole truth, as I am an honest Christian woman and you will see that if there is blame in the matter it does not lie with my husband but with me, for whose sake he has done all that he has."

The woman's words came with an intense earnestness which carried conviction with them.

"Is this true, Barrymore?"

"Yes, Sir Henry. Every word of it."

"Well, I cannot blame you for standing by your own wife. Forget what I have said. Go to your room, you two, and we shall talk further about this matter in the morning."

When they were gone we looked out of the window again.

Sir Henry had flung it open, and the cold night

des plus célèbres criminels de l'Angleterre?

«— Oui, monsieur, reprit-elle, je m'appelle Selden, et il est mon frère. Nous l'avons trop gâté dans son enfance… Il a fini par croire que le monde n'avait été créé que pour son plaisir et qu'il était libre d'y faire ce que bon lui semblait … Devenu grand, il fréquenta de mauvais compagnons, et le chagrin causé par son inconduite hâta la mort de notre pauvre mère.

«De crime en crime, il descendit toujours plus bas, et il ne dut qu'à la miséricorde divine d'échapper à l'échafaud. Mais pour moi, mon bon monsieur, il est toujours resté le petit enfant aux cheveux bouclés que j'avais soigné, avec lequel j'avais joué autrefois, en sœur aînée aimante et dévouée.

«Il connaît ces sentiments, et c'est ce qui l'a déterminé à s'évader de prison. Il est venu me retrouver, certain d'avance que je ne refuserais pas de l'aider.

«Une nuit, il arriva ici, exténué de fatigue et de faim, traqué par la police; que devions-nous faire?

«Nous le recueillîmes, nous le nourrîmes et nous prîmes soin de lui.

«Lorsqu'on annonça votre venue ici, mon frère pensa qu'il serait plus en sûreté sur la lande que partout ailleurs. Il attend dans sa cachette que l'oubli se fasse autour de son nom.

«Toutes les deux nuits, nous plaçons une bougie devant la fenêtre pour nous assurer de sa présence; s'il nous répond par le même signal, mon mari va lui porter des vivres.

«Nous espérons toujours qu'il pourra fuir; mais tant qu'il sera là, nous ne l'abandonnerons pas.

«Voilà, monsieur, aussi vrai que je suis une honnête femme, la vérité tout entière. Vous conviendrez que, si quelqu'un mérite un blâme ce n'est pas mon mari, mais moi seule, pour l'amour de qui il a tout fait.»

«Mme Barrymore parlait avec un air de sincérité qui entraînait la conviction.

«— Est-ce vrai, Barrymore? demanda le baronnet.

«— Oui, sir Henry,… absolument.

«— Je ne puis vous blâmer d'avoir assisté votre femme. Oubliez ce que j'ai dit. Rentrez chez vous; nous causerons de tout cela demain matin.»

«Lorsque les deux époux furent sortis, nous regardâmes encore par la fenêtre.

«Sir Henry l'avait ouverte toute grande. Le vent

wind beat in upon our faces.

Far away in the black distance there still glowed that one tiny point of yellow light.

"I wonder he dares," said Sir Henry.

"It may be so placed as to be only visible from here."

"Very likely. How far do you think it is?"

"Out by the Cleft Tor, I think."

"Not more than a mile or two off."

"Hardly that."

"Well, it cannot be far if Barrymore had to carry out the food to it. And he is waiting, this villain, beside that candle. By thunder, Watson, I am going out to take that man!"

The same thought had crossed my own mind. It was not as if the Barrymores had taken us into their confidence. Their secret had been forced from them.

The man was a danger to the community, an unmitigated scoundrel for whom there was neither pity nor excuse. We were only doing our duty in taking this chance of putting him back where he could do no harm.

With his brutal and violent nature, others would have to pay the price if we held our hands.

Any night, for example, our neighbours the Stapletons might be attacked by him, and it may have been the thought of this which made Sir Henry so keen upon the adventure.

"I will come," said I.

"Then get your revolver and put on your boots. The sooner we start the better, as the fellow may put out his light and be off."

In five minutes we were outside the door, starting upon our expedition.

We hurried through the dark shrubbery, amid the dull moaning of the autumn wind and the rustle of the falling leaves.

The night air was heavy with the smell of damp and decay.

Now and again the moon peeped out for an instant, but clouds were driving over the face of the sky, and just as we came out on the moor a thin rain began to fall.

The light still burned steadily in front.

glacial de la nuit nous cinglait le visage.

«Au loin, le point lumineux brillait toujours.

«— Je me demande comment Selden ose allumer cette bougie, dit sir Henry.

«— Peut-être la dispose-t-il de façon à ne la rendre visible que du château.

«— Très vraisemblablement. À combien évaluez-vous la distance qui nous sépare d'elle?

«— Heu! Elle doit être près du Cleft-Tor.

«— À un mille ou deux?

«— À peine.

«— C'est juste... Puisque Barrymore doit y porter des provisions, elle ne peut se trouver à une trop grande distance... Et dire que ce misérable attend à côté de sa bougie! Vraiment, Watson, j'ai envie de sortir et d'arrêter cet homme!»

«Un désir semblable avait traversé mon esprit. Je ne l'aurais certainement pas eu, si les Barrymore s'étaient spontanément confiés à nous. Mais nous avions dû leur arracher leur secret.

«Et puis cet homme ne constituait-il pas un danger permanent pour la société? N'était-il pas un scélérat endurci, indigne de pitié? En somme, nous ne faisions que notre devoir en essayant de le replonger dans le cachot où il serait inoffensif.

«Si nous n'exécutions pas ce projet, qui sait si d'autres ne payeraient pas de leur vie le prix de notre indifférence!...

«Qui sait, par exemple, si, quelque nuit, il ne s'attaquerait pas à nos voisins, les Stapleton! Je soupçonne sir Henry d'avoir obéi à cette pensée, en se montrant si décidé à tenter dette aventure.

«— Je vous accompagne, lui dis-je.

«— Alors prenez votre revolver et chaussez vos bottines. Plus tôt nous partirons, mieux cela vaudra... le drôle n'aurait qu'à souffler sa bougie et qu'à filer...»

«Cinq minutes plus tard, nous étions dehors, en route pour notre expédition.

«Nous marchions à travers les taillis, au milieu du triste sifflement du vent d'automne et du bruissement des feuilles mortes.

«L'air de la nuit était chargé d'humidité et la terre dégageait l'acre senteur des plantes en décomposition.

«De temps en temps, la lune pointait entre deux nuages; mais bientôt les nuées se rejoignaient et recouvraient toute la surface du ciel. Au moment où nous mettions le pied sur la lande, une pluie menue commença à tomber.

«Devant nous, la lueur jaune brillait toujours.

"Are you armed?" I asked.

"I have a hunting-crop."

"We must close in on him rapidly, for he is said to be a desperate fellow. We shall take him by surprise and have him at our mercy before he can resist."

"I say, Watson," said the baronet, "what would Holmes say to this? How about that hour of darkness in which the power of evil is exalted?"

As if in answer to his words there rose suddenly out of the vast gloom of the moor that strange cry which I had already heard upon the borders of the great Grimpen Mire.

It came with the wind through the silence of the night, a long, deep mutter, then a rising howl, and then the sad moan in which it died away. Again and again it sounded, the whole air throbbing with it, strident, wild, and menacing.

The baronet caught my sleeve and his face glimmered white through the darkness.

"My God, what's that, Watson?"

"I don't know. It's a sound they have on the moor. I heard it once before."

It died away, and an absolute silence closed in upon us. We stood straining our ears, but nothing came.

"Watson," said the baronet, "it was the cry of a hound."

My blood ran cold in my veins, for there was a break in his voice which told of the sudden horror which had seized him.

"What do they call this sound?" he asked.

"Who?"

"The folk on the countryside."

"Oh, they are ignorant people. Why should you mind what they call it?"

"Tell me, Watson. What do they say of it?"

I hesitated but could not escape the question.

"They say it is the cry of the Hound of the Baskervilles."

He groaned and was silent for a few moments.

"A hound it was," he said at last, "but it seemed to come from miles away, over yonder, I think."

"It was hard to say whence it came."

"It rose and fell with the wind. Isn't that the direction of the great Grimpen Mire?"

«— Êtes-vous armé? dis-je tout bas à sir Henry.

«— J'ai un fusil de chasse à répétition.

«— Il faudra surprendre Selden et nous emparer de lui, avant qu'il soit en état de nous résister, repris-je; il paraît que c'est un garçon déterminé.

«— Dites donc, Watson, que penserait M. Sherlock Holmes de nous voir ainsi sur la lande, «à l'heure où l'esprit du mal chemine»?

«Comme en réponse à ces paroles, il s'éleva dans la vaste solitude de la lande ce cri étrange que j'avais déjà entendu sur les bords de la grande fondrière de Grimpen.

«Porté par le vent dans le silence de la nuit, arriva jusqu'à nous ce long murmure, bientôt suivi d'un hurlement sonore et terminé par une sorte de lugubre gémissement. Il retentit à plusieurs reprises, strident, sauvage, menaçant, ébranlant l'atmosphère entière.

«Le baronnet me saisit le bras et, malgré l'obscurité, je le vis blêmir.

«— Mon Dieu! Watson, qu'y a-t-il?

«— Je l'ignore. C'est un bruit de la lande… Je l'ai déjà entendu une fois.»

«Le cri ne se renouvela pas et un silence de mort s'abattit sur nous. Nous prêtâmes attentivement l'oreille, mais en vain.

«— Watson, me dit le baronnet, c'était le hurlement d'un chien.»

«Mon sang se glaça dans mes veines. Pendant que sir Henry parlait, un tremblement secouait sa voix et montrait toute la soudaine terreur qui s'était emparée de lui.

«— Comment appellent-ils ce bruit? ajouta-t-il.

«— Qui: ils?

«— Les gens du pays.

«— Ce sont des paysans ignorants… Que vous importe le nom par lequel ils le désignent.

«— Dites-le-moi toujours, Watson?»

«J'hésitai. Cependant, je ne pus éluder la question.

«— Ils prétendent que c'est le hurlement du chien des Baskerville.»

«Sir Henry soupira et resta un moment silencieux.

«— Un chien, soit! fit-il enfin. En tout cas, il me semble que le son venait de là-bas, à plusieurs milles de distance.

«— Il est difficile d'en indiquer la direction.

«— Il s'élevait et diminuait selon le vent. N'est-ce pas du côté de la grande fondrière de Grimpen?

"Yes, it is."

"Well, it was up there. Come now, Watson, didn't you think yourself that it was the cry of a hound? I am not a child. You need not fear to speak the truth."

"Stapleton was with me when I heard it last. He said that it might be the calling of a strange bird."

"No, no, it was a hound. My God, can there be some truth in all these stories? Is it possible that I am really in danger from so dark a cause? You don't believe it, do you, Watson?"

"No, no."

"And yet it was one thing to laugh about it in London, and it is another to stand out here in the darkness of the moor and to hear such a cry as that. And my uncle! There was the footprint of the hound beside him as he lay. It all fits together. I don't think that I am a coward, Watson, but that sound seemed to freeze my very blood. Feel my hand!"

It was as cold as a block of marble.

"You'll be all right tomorrow."

"I don't think I'll get that cry out of my head. What do you advise that we do now?"

"Shall we turn back?"

"No, by thunder; we have come out to get our man, and we will do it. We after the convict, and a hell-hound, as likely as not, after us. Come on! We'll see it through if all the fiends of the pit were loose upon the moor."

We stumbled slowly along in the darkness, with the black loom of the craggy hills around us, and the yellow speck of light burning steadily in front.

There is nothing so deceptive as the distance of a light upon a pitch-dark night, and sometimes the glimmer seemed to be far away upon the horizon and sometimes it might have been within a few yards of us.

But at last we could see whence it came, and then we knew that we were indeed very close. A guttering candle was stuck in a crevice of the rocks which flanked it on each side so as to keep the wind from it and also to prevent it from being visible, save in the direction of Baskerville Hall.

A boulder of granite concealed our approach, and crouching behind it we gazed over it at the signal light.

«— Oui.

«— Ne croyez-vous pas aussi que c'était un hurlement de chien? Je ne suis plus un enfant… N'appréhendez pas de me dire la vérité.

«Lorsque je l'entendis pour la première fois, Stapleton m'accompagnait. Il m'affirma que ce pouvait être l'appel d'un oiseau de passage.

Non, non… c'était bien un chien… Mon Dieu! y aurait-il quelque chose de vrai dans toutes ces histoires? Suis-je réellement menacé d'un danger de provenance mystérieuse? Vous ne croyez pas, n'est-ce pas, Watson?

«— Non… certainement non.

«— Autre chose est de plaisanter de cela, à Londres, ou d'entendre un cri pareil, ici, sur la lande… Et mon oncle? N'a-t-on pas remarqué près de son cadavre l'empreinte d'une patte de chien? Tout cela se tient. Je ne me crois pas poltron, Watson; mais ce bruit a figé mon sang. Tâtez mes mains!

«— Il n'y paraîtra plus demain, dis-je à sir Henry en manière d'encouragement.

«— J'ai peur de ne pouvoir chasser ce cri de ma pensée… Que conseillez-vous de faire maintenant?

«— Retournons au château.

«— Jamais de la vie! Nous sommes venus pour arrêter Selden, nous l'arrêterons. Le prisonnier nous aura à ses trousses, et nous, un chien-fantôme aux nôtres!… En avant! Nous verrons bien si le diable a lâché sur la lande tous les démons de l'enfer.»

«Toujours guidés par la petite lueur qui scintillait devant nous, nous reprîmes notre marche, en trébuchant à chaque pas dans les broussailles.

«Par une nuit noire comme une gueule de four, on se trompe facilement dans l'évaluation de la distance à laquelle on croit apercevoir une lumière. Elle nous paraissait parfois très éloignée, tandis qu'à certains moments nous l'aurions crue seulement à quelques mètres de nous.

«Nous la découvrîmes enfin. En la collant avec sa propre cire, on avait fiché une bougie dans une crevasse de rochers. Cette précaution avait le double avantage de la préserver du vent et de ne la rendre visible que du château.

«Un bloc de granit dissimulait notre présence. Accroupis derrière cet abri, nous avançâmes la tête pour examiner ce phare minuscule.

Over the rocks was thrust out an evil yellow face.
Sur les rochers se profilait la silhouette d'un homme.

It was strange to see this single candle burning there in the middle of the moor, with no sign of life near it—just the one straight yellow flame and the gleam of the rock on each side of it.

"What shall we do now?" whispered Sir Henry.

"Wait here. He must be near his light. Let us see if we can get a glimpse of him."

The words were hardly out of my mouth when we both saw him.

Over the rocks, in the crevice of which the candle burned, there was thrust out an evil yellow face, a terrible animal face, all seamed and scored with vile passions.

Foul with mire, with a bristling beard, and hung with matted hair, it might well have belonged to one of those old savages who dwelt in the burrows on the hillsides.

The light beneath him was reflected in his small, cunning eyes which peered fiercely to right and left through the darkness like a crafty and savage animal who has heard the steps of the hunters.

Something had evidently aroused his suspicions. It may have been that Barrymore had some private signal which we had neglected to give, or the fellow may have had some other reason for thinking that all was not well, but I could read his fears upon his wicked face.

Any instant he might dash out the light and vanish in the darkness.

I sprang forward therefore, and Sir Henry did the same.

At the same moment the convict screamed out a curse at us and hurled a rock which splintered up against the boulder which had sheltered us.

I caught one glimpse of his short, squat, strongly built figure as he sprang to his feet and turned to run.

At the same moment by a lucky chance the moon broke through the clouds. We rushed over the brow of the hill, and there was our man running with great speed down the other side, springing over the stones in his way with the activity of a mountain goat.

A lucky long shot of my revolver might have crippled him, but I had brought it only to defend myself if attacked and not to shoot an unarmed man who was running away.

We were both swift runners and in fairly good

«Cette simple bougie, brûlant au milieu de la lande sans autre signe de vie autour d'elle, était un bizarre spectacle.

«— Que faire? murmura sir Henry à mon oreille.

«— Attendre, répondis-je sur le même ton. Notre homme doit se tenir à proximité de sa lumière. Tâchons de l'apercevoir.»

«À peine avais-je achevé ces mots que mon désir fut réalisé.

«Sur les rochers qui surplombaient la crevasse où brûlait la bougie, se profilait la silhouette d'un homme dont la figure bestiale décelait toutes les plus basses passions.

«Souillé de boue, avec sa barbe inculte et ses longs cheveux emmêlés, on aurait pu le prendre pour un de ces êtres primitifs, ensevelis depuis des siècles dans les sarcophages de la montagne.

«La clarté de la bougie montait jusqu'à lui et se jouait dans ses yeux, petits, astucieux, qui scrutaient fiévreusement à droite et à gauche l'épaisseur des ténèbres, comme ceux d'une bête sauvage qui a éventé la présence des chasseurs.

«Quelque chose avait évidemment éveillé ses soupçons. Peut-être avions-nous omis un signal convenu entre Barrymore et lui. Ou bien le drôle avait-il des raisons de croire qu'un danger le menaçait... Toujours est-il que je lisais ses craintes sur son horrible visage.

«À chaque instant il pouvait sortir du cercle lumineux qui l'entourait et disparaître dans la nuit.

«Je bondis en avant suivi de sir Henry.

«Au même moment, le prisonnier proféra un épouvantable blasphème et fit rouler sur nous un quartier de roche, qui se brisa sur le bloc de granit derrière lequel nous nous abritions.

«Pendant l'espace d'un éclair, je le vis très distinctement, tandis qu'il se levait pour fuir; il était de petite taille, trapu et très solidement charpenté.

«Par un heureux hasard, la lune vint à déchirer son voile de nuages. Nous escaladâmes le monticule. Parvenus au sommet, nous distinguâmes Selden qui en descendait précipitamment la pente escarpée, en faisant voler les cailloux de tous côtés, tel un chamois.

«J'aurais pu l'abattre d'un coup de revolver; mais je n'avais emporté cette arme que pour me défendre en cas d'attaque, et non pas pour tirer sur un fuyard sans défense.

«Nous étions, sir Henry et moi, d'excellents

training, but we soon found that we had no chance of overtaking him.

We saw him for a long time in the moonlight until he was only a small speck moving swiftly among the boulders upon the side of a distant hill.

We ran and ran until we were completely blown, but the space between us grew ever wider. Finally we stopped and sat panting on two rocks, while we watched him disappearing in the distance.

And it was at this moment that there occurred a most strange and unexpected thing.

We had risen from our rocks and were turning to go home, having abandoned the hopeless chase.

The moon was low upon the right, and the jagged pinnacle of a granite tor stood up against the lower curve of its silver disc.

There, outlined as black as an ebony statue on that shining background, I saw the figure of a man upon the tor.

Do not think that it was a delusion, Holmes. I assure you that I have never in my life seen anything more clearly.

As far as I could judge, the figure was that of a tall, thin man. He stood with his legs a little separated, his arms folded, his head bowed, as if he were brooding over that enormous wilderness of peat and granite which lay before him.

He might have been the very spirit of that terrible place.

It was not the convict. This man was far from the place where the latter had disappeared. Besides, he was a much taller man.

With a cry of surprise I pointed him out to the baronet, but in the instant during which I had turned to grasp his arm the man was gone.

There was the sharp pinnacle of granite still cutting the lower edge of the moon, but its peak bore no trace of that silent and motionless figure.

I wished to go in that direction and to search the tor, but it was some distance away.

The baronet's nerves were still quivering from that cry, which recalled the dark story of his family, and he was not in the mood for fresh adventures.

He had not seen this lonely man upon the tor and could not feel the thrill which his strange

coureurs parfaitement entraînés. Seulement nous nous rendîmes bien vite compte que nous ne rattraperions pas notre homme.

«Longtemps, à la clarté de la lune, nous le suivîmes jusqu'à ce qu'il ne fût plus qu'un point imperceptible, glissant rapidement à travers les rochers qui hérissaient une colline éloignée.

«Nous courûmes jusqu'à perte d'haleine; mais l'espace entre lui et nous s'élargissait de plus en plus. Finalement nous nous arrêtâmes, exténués, pour nous asseoir et le regarder disparaître au loin.

«Ce fut à ce moment que survint la chose du monde la plus extraordinaire et la plus inattendue.

«Nous venions de nous relever, et nous nous disposions à reprendre le chemin du château, abandonnant cette inutile poursuite.

«Vers notre droite, la lune s'abaissait sur l'horizon. Déjà la cime d'un pic avait mordu la partie inférieure de son disque argenté.

«Alors, là, sur ce pic, se dessina, noir comme une statue d'ébène sur ce fond éclatant de lumière, le profil d'un homme.

«Ne croyez pas, mon cher Holmes, que j'aie été le jouet d'une illusion. Je vous assure que, de ma vie, je n'ai rien vu de plus distinct.

«Autant qu'il m'a été possible d'en juger, cet homme m'a paru grand et mince. Il se tenait debout, les jambes un peu écartées, les bras croisés, la tête basse, dans l'attitude de quelqu'un méditant sur l'immensité qui se déroule devant lui.

«On aurait pu le prendre pour le génie de ce terrible lieu.

«Ce n'était pas Selden, car cet homme se trouvait très loin de l'endroit où le prisonnier avait disparu à nos yeux. D'ailleurs, il paraissait beaucoup plus grand que le frère de Mme Barrymore.

«J'étouffai un cri de surprise, et j'allais le montrer au baronnet, lorsqu'il s'éclipsa pendant le temps que je me mis à saisir le bras de mon ami.

«La crête de la colline avait entamé plus profondément le disque de la lune; mais, sur le pic, il ne restait plus de trace de cette muette apparition.

«Je voulus me diriger de ce côté et fouiller cette partie de la lande; j'y renonçai, elle était trop distante de nous.

«Les nerfs du baronnet vibraient encore sous le cri qui lui rappelait la sombre histoire de sa famille. Je ne le sentais pas d'humeur à tenter de nouvelles aventures.

«Sir Henry n'avait pas vu l'homme du pic; il ne pouvait partager le frisson que son étrange pré-

I saw the figure of a man upon the tor.
J'ai vu la figure d'un homme.

presence and his commanding attitude had given to me.

"A warder, no doubt," said he. "The moor has been thick with them since this fellow escaped."

Well, perhaps his explanation may be the right one, but I should like to have some further proof of it.

Today we mean to communicate to the Princetown people where they should look for their missing man, but it is hard lines that we have not actually had the triumph of bringing him back as our own prisoner.

Such are the adventures of last night, and you must acknowledge, my dear Holmes, that I have done you very well in the matter of a report. Much of what I tell you is no doubt quite irrelevant, but still I feel that it is best that I should let you have all the facts and leave you to select for yourself those which will be of most service to you in helping you to your conclusions.

We are certainly making some progress.

So far as the Barrymores go we have found the motive of their actions, and that has cleared up the situation very much.

But the moor with its mysteries and its strange inhabitants remains as inscrutable as ever.

Perhaps in my next I may be able to throw some light upon this also.

Best of all would it be if you could come down to us. In any case you will hear from me again in the course of the next few days.

sence et sa majestueuse attitude avaient fait passer dans tout mon être.

«— Quelque sentinelle! dit-il,... depuis l'évasion de Selden, la lande en est couverte.»

«Malgré la vraisemblance de cette explication, je ne suis pas convaincu. J'irai aux preuves.

«Aujourd'hui nous écrivons au directeur de la prison de Princetown pour lui indiquer les parages où se cache le contumace. Mais quel malheur que nous n'ayons pu nous emparer de lui et le ramener triomphalement à son cachot!

«Telles sont, mon cher Holmes, les aventures de la dernière nuit. Vous ne vous plaindrez pas de l'étendue de mon rapport. Certes, il contient force détails qui ne touchent que de très loin à l'affaire. Toutefois, il me semble qu'il vaut mieux que vous soyez tenu au courant de tout; vous trierez vous-même les renseignements utiles qui vous aideront à asseoir votre opinion.

«Avouez que nous avons fait quelques pas en avant.

«En ce qui concerne les Barrymore, nous avons découvert le mobile de leurs actions et, de ce côté, le terrain est déblayé.

«Seule la lande avec ses mystères et ses étranges habitants, demeure toujours plus insondable que jamais.

«Peut-être, dans ma prochaine lettre, pourrai-je vous fournir quelques éclaircissements sur ce qui s'y passe.

«Le mieux serait que vous vinssiez au plus tôt, En tout cas, vous recevrez d'autres nouvelles sous peu de jours.»

CHAPTER 10. EXTRACT FROM THE DIARY OF DR. WATSON

So far I have been able to quote from the reports which I have forwarded during these early days to Sherlock Holmes. Now, however, I have arrived at a point in my narrative where I am compelled to abandon this method and to trust once more to my recollections, aided by the diary which I kept at the time. A few extracts from the latter will carry me on to those scenes which are indelibly fixed in every detail upon my memory.

I proceed, then, from the morning which followed our abortive chase of the convict and our other strange experiences upon the moor.

October 16th.—A dull and foggy day with a drizzle of rain.

The house is banked in with rolling clouds, which rise now and then to show the dreary curves of the moor, with thin, silver veins upon the sides of the hills, and the distant boulders gleaming where the light strikes upon their wet faces.

It is melancholy outside and in.

The baronet is in a black reaction after the excitements of the night.

I am conscious myself of a weight at my heart and a feeling of impending danger—ever present danger, which is the more terrible because I am unable to define it.

And have I not cause for such a feeling? Consider the long sequence of incidents which have all pointed to some sinister influence which is at work around us. There is the death of the last occupant of the Hall, fulfilling so exactly the conditions of the family legend, and there are the repeated reports from peasants of the appearance of a strange creature upon the moor. Twice I have with my own ears heard the sound which resembled the distant baying of a hound.

It is incredible, impossible, that it should really be outside the ordinary laws of nature. A spectral hound which leaves material footmarks and fills the air with its howling is surely not to be thought of.

CHAPITRE 10. EXTRAITS DU JOURNAL DE WATSON

Jusqu'ici j'ai cité certains passages des rapports que j'adressais presque journellement à Sherlock Holmes. Aujourd'hui, j'en suis arrivé à un point de mon récit où je me vois forcé d'abandonner ce procédé et d'avoir recours à mes souvenirs personnels, aidé en cela par le journal que j'ai tenu à cette époque. Quelques extraits me remettront en mémoire les détails de ces scènes fixées dans mon esprit d'une manière indélébile.

Je reprends donc au matin qui suivit notre vaine poursuite de Selden et nos autres aventures sur la lande.

«16 octobre. — Journée triste, brumeuse; il bruine presque sans relâche.

«D'épais nuages enveloppent le château; parfois ils se déchirent et laissent entrevoir les ondulations de la lande striée de minces filets d'argent, ruisselets occasionnellement créés par la pluie dévalant sur le flanc raviné des collines.

«Tout est mélancolie — au dehors comme au dedans.

«Le baronnet subit maintenant le contre-coup des émotions trop vives de la nuit précédente.

«Moi-même, je me sens oppressé. Il me semble qu'un péril nous menace — péril sans cesse présent et d'autant plus terrible que je ne puis le préciser.

«N'ai-je pas raison de craindre? Cette longue série d'incidents ne dénote-t-elle pas une influence maligne s'exerçant autour de nous? C'est d'abord la fin tragique du dernier commensal du château de Baskerville qui meurt de la même mort que son ancêtre Hugo. Puis viennent les affirmations des paysans relatives à la présence sur la lande d'un animal extraordinaire. N'ai-je pas entendu deux fois de mes propres oreilles, un bruit qui ressemblait à l'aboiement lointain d'un chien?

«Mais il est incroyable, inadmissible, que ce bruit soit dû à une cause surnaturelle. Comment un chien-fantôme marquerait-il sur le sol l'empreinte de ses pas et remplirait-il l'air de ses hurlements?

Stapleton may fall in with such a superstition, and Mortimer also, but if I have one quality upon earth it is common sense, and nothing will persuade me to believe in such a thing.

«Stapleton peut avoir de ces superstitions; Mortimer également. Mais moi? Je me flatte de posséder une qualité inappréciable: le sens commun — et rien ne me fera croire à de pareilles absurdités.

To do so would be to descend to the level of these poor peasants, who are not content with a mere fiend dog but must needs describe him with hell-fire shooting from his mouth and eyes.

Ma crédulité me rabaisserait au niveau de ces paysans ignares qui ne se contentent pas d'affirmer l'existence d'un animal fantastique, mais qui le dépeignent comme lançant du feu par la gueule et par les yeux.

Holmes would not listen to such fancies, and I am his agent.

«Holmes n'ajouterait aucune foi à ces inventions — et je suis son agent.

But facts are facts, and I have twice heard this crying upon the moor.

«Mais, d'autre part, les faits sont les faits, et, à deux reprises différentes, j'ai entendu ces cris sur la lande.

Suppose that there were really some huge hound loose upon it; that would go far to explain everything.

«Supposons pour un instant qu'un animal prodigieux, d'une espèce inconnue, erre la nuit dans la campagne. Sa présence ne suffirait-elle pas à tout expliquer?

But where could such a hound lie concealed, where did it get its food, where did it come from, how was it that no one saw it by day?

«Alors, où ce chien se cacherait-il? Où prendrait-il sa nourriture? D'où viendrait-il et pourquoi ne l'aurait-on jamais aperçu à la clarté du jour?

It must be confessed that the natural explanation offers almost as many difficulties as the other.

«On doit avouer qu'une explication naturelle de ces faits offre presque autant de difficulté que l'admission d'une intervention surnaturelle.

And always, apart from the hound, there is the fact of the human agency in London, the man in the cab, and the letter which warned Sir Henry against the moor.

«En dehors du chien, il reste toujours le fait matériel de l'homme aperçu dans le cab et de la lettre qui mettait sir Henry en garde contre les dangers de la lande.

This at least was real, but it might have been the work of a protecting friend as easily as of an enemy.

«Ceci, au moins, appartient bien au domaine de la réalité; mais ce peut être l'œuvre d'un ami aussi bien que celle d'un ennemi.

Where is that friend or enemy now? Has he remained in London, or has he followed us down here? Could he—could he be the stranger whom I saw upon the tor?

«À cette heure, où se trouvait cet ami ou cet ennemi? N'a-t-il pas quitté Londres ou nous a-t-il accompagnés jusqu'ici? Serait-ce... Oui, serait-ce l'inconnu que j'ai entrevu sur le pic?

It is true that I have had only the one glance at him, and yet there are some things to which I am ready to swear. He is no one whom I have seen down here, and I have now met all the neighbours. The figure was far taller than that of Stapleton, far thinner than that of Frankland.

«Je reconnais que je ne l'ai vu que l'espace d'une minute, et cependant je suis prêt à jurer certaines choses le concernant. D'abord, il ne ressemble à aucune des personnes que j'ai rencontrées dans le pays, et je connais maintenant tous nos voisins. Cet homme était plus grand que Stapleton et plus mince que Frankland.

Barrymore it might possibly have been, but we had left him behind us, and I am certain that he could not have followed us.

«Il se rapprocherait davantage de l'aspect de Barrymore. Mais le valet de chambre était resté au château, derrière nous, et je suis sûr qu'il ne pouvait nous avoir suivis.

A stranger then is still dogging us, just as a stranger dogged us in London. We have never shaken him off. If I could lay my hands upon that man, then at last we might find ourselves at the

«Alors un inconnu nous espionne ici, de même qu'un inconnu nous espionnait à Londres. Si je mets jamais la main sur cet homme, nous toucherons au terme de nos embarras.

end of all our difficulties.

To this one purpose I must now devote all my energies.

My first impulse was to tell Sir Henry all my plans. My second and wisest one is to play my own game and speak as little as possible to anyone.

He is silent and distrait. His nerves have been strangely shaken by that sound upon the moor. I will say nothing to add to his anxieties, but I will take my own steps to attain my own end.

We had a small scene this morning after breakfast.

Barrymore asked leave to speak with Sir Henry, and they were closeted in his study some little time.

Sitting in the billiard-room I more than once heard the sound of voices raised, and I had a pretty good idea what the point was which was under discussion.

After a time the baronet opened his door and called for me.

"Barrymore considers that he has a grievance," he said. "He thinks that it was unfair on our part to hunt his brother-in-law down when he, of his own free will, had told us the secret."

The butler was standing very pale but very collected before us.

"I may have spoken too warmly, sir," said he, "and if I have, I am sure that I beg your pardon. At the same time, I was very much surprised when I heard you two gentlemen come back this morning and learned that you had been chasing Selden. The poor fellow has enough to fight against without my putting more upon his track."

"If you had told us of your own free will it would have been a different thing," said the baronet, "you only told us, or rather your wife only told us, when it was forced from you and you could not help yourself."

"I didn't think you would have taken advantage of it, Sir Henry—indeed I didn't."

"The man is a public danger. There are lonely houses scattered over the moor, and he is a fellow who would stick at nothing. You only want to get a glimpse of his face to see that. Look at Mr. Stapleton's house, for example, with no one but himself to defend it. There's no safety for anyone until he is

«Tous mes efforts vont tendre vers ce seul but.

«Mon premier mouvement fut de confier mes projets à sir Henry. Mon second — beaucoup plus sage me poussa à jouer la partie tout seul et à parler le moins possible de ce que je comptais entreprendre.

«Le baronnet est préoccupé. Ce bruit perçu sur la lande a ébranlé ses nerfs. Je ne viendrai pas augmenter ses angoisses; mais je vais prendre toutes mes mesures pour réussir.

«Ce matin, il s'est passé au château une petite scène qui mérite d'être racontée.

«Barrymore demanda à sir Henry la faveur d'un entretien. Ils allèrent s'enfermer quelque temps dans la bibliothèque.

«Je demeurai dans la salle de billard d'où j'entendis plusieurs fois un bruit de voix montées à un diapason assez aigu. Je me doutais bien de ce qui faisait l'objet de leur discussion.

«Enfin, le baronnet ouvrit la porte et m'appela:

«— Barrymore, me dit-il, estime qu'il a un grief contre nous. Il pense qu'il était peu délicat de notre part de nous mettre à la recherche de son beau-frère, alors qu'il nous avait parlé en confidence de sa présence sur la lande.»

«Le valet de chambre se tenait devant nous, très pâle, mais aussi très calme.

«— Peut-être, répondit-il, ai-je eu le tort de m'emporter… S'il en est ainsi, veuillez me pardonner, sir Henry. Tout de même j'ai été fort surpris d'apprendre ce matin que vous aviez donné la chasse à Selden. Le pauvre garçon a déjà bien assez de monde à ses trousses, sans que j'en grossisse le nombre par mon fait.

«— Si vous aviez parlé spontanément, reprit le baronnet, la chose serait toute différente. Mais vous n'êtes entré — ou mieux votre femme n'est entrée dans la voie des aveux, que contrainte par nous et lorsqu'il vous était difficile à tous deux de faire autrement.

«— Je ne m'attendais pas, sir Henry, à ce que vous vous prévaudriez de notre confiance… non, je ne m'y attendais pas!

«— Cet homme constitue un danger public. Il existe, disséminées sur la lande, des maisons isolées… et c'est un misérable que rien n'arrêterait. Il n'y a qu'à le regarder pour s'en convaincre. Prenez, par exemple, l'intérieur de M. Stapleton… Le naturaliste est l'unique défenseur de son foyer. Non, la under lock and key."

"He'll break into no house, sir. I give you my solemn word upon that. But he will never trouble anyone in this country again. I assure you, Sir Henry, that in a very few days the necessary arrangements will have been made and he will be on his way to South America. For God's sake, sir, I beg of you not to let the police know that he is still on the moor. They have given up the chase there, and he can lie quiet until the ship is ready for him. You can't tell on him without getting my wife and me into trouble. I beg you, sir, to say nothing to the police."

"What do you say, Watson?"

I shrugged my shoulders.

"If he were safely out of the country it would relieve the tax-payer of a burden."

"But how about the chance of his holding someone up before he goes?"

"He would not do anything so mad, sir. We have provided him with all that he can want. To commit a crime would be to show where he was hiding."

"That is true," said Sir Henry. "Well, Barrymore—"

"God bless you, sir, and thank you from my heart! It would have killed my poor wife had he been taken again."

"I guess we are aiding and abetting a felony, Watson? But, after what we have heard I don't feel as if I could give the man up, so there is an end of it. All right, Barrymore, you can go."

With a few broken words of gratitude the man turned, but he hesitated and then came back.

"You've been so kind to us, sir, that I should like to do the best I can for you in return. I know something, Sir Henry, and perhaps I should have said it before, but it was long after the inquest that I found it out. I've never breathed a word about it yet to mortal man. It's about poor Sir Charles's death."

The baronet and I were both upon our feet.

sécurité ne règnera dans les environs que lorsque Selden sera bel et bien sous les verrous.

«— Selden ne s'introduira dans aucune maison, monsieur, je vous en donne solennellement ma parole d'honneur. D'ailleurs, il débarrassera bientôt le pays de sa présence. Je vous assure, sir Henry, qu'avant peu de jours toutes les démarches seront terminées pour qu'il s'embarque à destination de l'Amérique du Sud. Au nom du ciel, je vous supplie de ne pas le dénoncer à la justice... On a renoncé à le rechercher; qu'il vive, tranquille, les quelques jours qui le séparent encore de son départ! Appeler de nouveau sur lui l'attention de la police, c'est nous causer de graves ennuis, à ma femme et à moi... Je vous en prie, monsieur, ne dites rien.

«— Quel est votre avis, Watson?» me demanda sir Henry.

«Je haussai les épaules:

«— S'il allait se faire pendre ailleurs, répondis-je, ce serait une charge de moins pour les contribuables.

«— Oui; mais en attendant, comment l'empêcher de commettre des méfaits? répliqua mon jeune ami.

«— Ne craignez pas cela de lui, insista Barrymore. Nous lui avons procuré tout ce dont il pouvait avoir besoin. Et puis, commettre un crime équivaudrait à révéler l'endroit où il se cache.

«— C'est vrai, convint sir Henry... Soit! Barrymore, nous ne dirons rien.

«— Dieu vous bénisse, monsieur, et je vous remercie du fond du cœur. Si l'on avait repris son frère ma pauvre femme en serait morte.»

«Le baronnet parut regretter aussitôt sa promesse, car, en s'adressant à moi, il reprit:

«— En somme, nous protégeons et nous encourageons un criminel... Enfin, après les paroles de Barrymore, je ne me sens plus le courage de livrer cet homme... Allons, ne parlons plus de cela... Vous pouvez vous retirer.»

«Avec toutes sortes de protestations de gratitude, le domestique se disposait à sortir. Tout à coup il hésita et revint sur ses pas.

«— Vous vous êtes montré si bon pour moi, dit-il en s'adressant à sir Henry, que je tiens à vous en témoigner ma reconnaissance. Je sais une chose que j'aurais déjà racontée, si je ne l'avais apprise postérieurement à la clôture de l'enquête. Je n'en ai encore soufflé mot à personne... C'est à propos de la mort de ce pauvre sir Charles.»

«À ces mots, nous nous dressâmes, le baronnet

"Do you know how he died?"

"No, sir, I don't know that."

"What then?"

"I know why he was at the gate at that hour. It was to meet a woman."

"To meet a woman! He?"

"Yes, sir."

"And the woman's name?"

"I can't give you the name, sir, but I can give you the initials. Her initials were L. L."

"How do you know this, Barrymore?"

"Well, Sir Henry, your uncle had a letter that morning. He had usually a great many letters, for he was a public man and well known for his kind heart, so that everyone who was in trouble was glad to turn to him. But that morning, as it chanced, there was only this one letter, so I took the more notice of it. It was from Coombe Tracey, and it was addressed in a woman's hand."

"Well?"

"Well, sir, I thought no more of the matter, and never would have done had it not been for my wife. Only a few weeks ago she was cleaning out Sir Charles's study—it had never been touched since his death—and she found the ashes of a burned letter in the back of the grate. The greater part of it was charred to pieces, but one little slip, the end of a page, hung together, and the writing could still be read, though it was grey on a black ground. It seemed to us to be a postscript at the end of the letter and it said: 'Please, please, as you are a gentleman, burn this letter, and be at the gate by ten o clock. Beneath it were signed the initials L. L."

"Have you got that slip?"

"No, sir, it crumbled all to bits after we moved it."

"Had Sir Charles received any other letters in the same writing?"

"Well, sir, I took no particular notice of his letters. I should not have noticed this one, only it happened to come alone."

"And you have no idea who L. L. is?"

"No, sir. No more than you have. But I expect if we could lay our hands upon that lady we should know more about Sir Charles's death."

et moi.

«— Savez-vous comment il est mort?

«— Non, monsieur; il ne s'agit pas de cela.

«— De quoi, alors?

«— De la raison pour laquelle sir Charles se trouvait à la porte de la lande. Il attendait une femme.

«— Il attendait une femme! Lui?

«— Oui, monsieur.

«— Le nom de cette femme?

«— J'ignore son nom, mais je puis vous donner ses initiales.

«— Quelles sont-elles?

«— L. L.

«— Comment les connaissez-vous?

«— Voici. Le matin de sa mort, votre oncle avait reçu une lettre. Il en recevait journellement un grand nombre... Il avait le cœur généreux et tous ceux qui se trouvaient dans le besoin ne manquaient pas de s'adresser à lui. Par extraordinaire, ce matin là, le courrier n'apporta qu'une lettre... Je la remarquai davantage... Elle venait de Coombe Tracey... Une femme en avait écrit la suscription.

«— Après?

«— Je n'y pensai plus, et, sans ma femme, je ne m'en serais certainement plus souvenu. Seulement, il y a quelques jours, en nettoyant le cabinet de sir Charles — on n'y avait pas touché depuis le jour de sa mort. Élisa trouva au fond de la cheminée les cendres d'une lettre qu'on avait brûlée. Auparavant on l'avait déchirée en menus morceaux. Cependant, sur une petite bande de papier — une fin de page on pouvait encore lire l'écriture qui se détachait en gris sur le vélin calciné. Il nous sembla que c'était un post-scriptum. Nous lûmes: «Je vous en prie, je vous en supplie, vous êtes un homme d'honneur, brûlez cette lettre et venez ce soir, à dix heures, à la porte de la lande». On avait signé des deux initiales L. L.

«— Avez-vous conservé cette bande de papier?

«— Non, monsieur; dès que nous la touchâmes, elle tomba en poussière.

«— Sir Charles avait-il reçu d'autres lettres de cette même écriture?

«— Je ne prenais pas garde à ses lettres. Je n'aurais prêté aucune attention à celle-là, si d'autres l'avaient accompagnée.

«— Vous ne soupçonnez pas qui peut être L. L.?

«— Non, monsieur,... pas plus que vous-même. Je crois que si nous parvenions à percer l'anonymat de cette dame, nous en saurions plus

"I cannot understand, Barrymore, how you came to conceal this important information."

"Well, sir, it was immediately after that our own trouble came to us. And then again, sir, we were both of us very fond of Sir Charles, as we well might be considering all that he has done for us. To rake this up couldn't help our poor master, and it's well to go carefully when there's a lady in the case. Even the best of us—"

"You thought it might injure his reputation?"

"Well, sir, I thought no good could come of it. But now you have been kind to us, and I feel as if it would be treating you unfairly not to tell you all that I know about the matter."

"Very good, Barrymore; you can go."

When the butler had left us Sir Henry turned to me.

"Well, Watson, what do you think of this new light?"

"It seems to leave the darkness rather blacker than before."

"So I think. But if we can only trace L. L. it should clear up the whole business. We have gained that much. We know that there is someone who has the facts if we can only find her. What do you think we should do?"

"Let Holmes know all about it at once. It will give him the clue for which he has been seeking. I am much mistaken if it does not bring him down."

I went at once to my room and drew up my report of the morning's conversation for Holmes. It was evident to me that he had been very busy of late, for the notes which I had from Baker Street were few and short, with no comments upon the information which I had supplied and hardly any reference to my mission.

No doubt his blackmailing case is absorbing all his faculties. And yet this new factor must surely arrest his attention and renew his interest. I wish that he were here.

October 17th.—All day today the rain poured down, rustling on the ivy and dripping from the eaves.

long sur la mort de sir Charles.

«— Je ne m'explique pas, Barrymore, pourquoi vous avez caché un détail de cette importance.

«— Que voulez-vous, monsieur?... Le malheur nous avait frappés, nous aussi... Selden, mon beau-frère!... Et puis nous aimions beaucoup sir Charles,... il nous avait fait tant de bien!... Raconter ce détail n'aurait pas ressuscité notre pauvre maître; nous nous sommes tus par égard pour lui... Dame! il faut toujours se montrer prudent, lorsque la réputation d'une femme est en jeu. Le meilleur d'entre nous...

«— En quoi la mémoire de mon oncle aurait-elle souffert?

«— En tout cas, je ne pensais pas que cette révélation dût la servir. Mais maintenant j'aurais mal reconnu votre bonté, si je ne vous avais pas dit tout ce que je savais sur ce sujet.

«— Très bien, Barrymore; vous pouvez vous retirer.»

«Lorsque le valet de chambre fut sorti, sir Henry se retourna vers moi.

«— Eh bien, Watson, votre opinion sur ce fait nouveau?

«— Je crois qu'il plonge l'affaire dans des ténèbres plus épaisses qu'auparavant.

«— C'est également mon avis. Ah! si nous découvrions qui est cette L. L., tout se trouverait singulièrement éclairci. Nous avons fait néanmoins un grand pas. Nous savons qu'il existe une femme qui, si nous la retrouvons, devra nous expliquer ce nouvel incident. Quel est votre avis?

«— Communiquer d'abord ceci à Sherlock Holmes, nous tenons peut-être la clef du mystère qu'il cherche encore à cette heure.»

Je montai dans ma chambre et je rédigeai immédiatement pour Sherlock Holmes la relation de cette intéressante conversation. Mon ami devait être fort occupé à Londres, car les notes que je recevais de Baker street étaient rares, courtes, sans commentaires sur les renseignements transmis par moi, et ne contenaient que de brèves recommandations au sujet de ma mission.

Probablement, le cas de chantage soumis à Holmes absorbait tous ses instants. Cependant je pensai que ce nouveau facteur introduit dans l'affaire de Baskerville appellerait sûrement son attention et raviverait son intérêt. Je souhaitais du fond du cœur qu'il fût près de moi.

«17 octobre. — La pluie n'a cessé de tomber toute la journée, fouettant les vitres et les feuilles du lierre qui tapisse le château.

I thought of the convict out upon the bleak, cold, shelterless moor. Poor devil! Whatever his crimes, he has suffered something to atone for them.

And then I thought of that other one—the face in the cab, the figure against the moon. Was he also out in that deluged—the unseen watcher, the man of darkness?

In the evening I put on my waterproof and I walked far upon the sodden moor, full of dark imaginings, the rain beating upon my face and the wind whistling about my ears. God help those who wander into the great mire now, for even the firm uplands are becoming a morass.

I found the black tor upon which I had seen the solitary watcher, and from its craggy summit I looked out myself across the melancholy downs.

Rain squalls drifted across their russet face, and the heavy, slate-coloured clouds hung low over the landscape, trailing in grey wreaths down the sides of the fantastic hills.

In the distant hollow on the left, half hidden by the mist, the two thin towers of Baskerville Hall rose above the trees. They were the only signs of human life which I could see, save only those prehistoric huts which lay thickly upon the slopes of the hills.

Nowhere was there any trace of that lonely man whom I had seen on the same spot two nights before.

As I walked back I was overtaken by Dr. Mortimer driving in his dog-cart over a rough moorland track which led from the outlying farmhouse of Foulmire.

He has been very attentive to us, and hardly a day has passed that he has not called at the Hall to see how we were getting on.

He insisted upon my climbing into his dog-cart, and he gave me a lift homeward.

«Malgré moi, je songeais au prisonnier évadé qui errait sans abri sur la lande morne et glaciale. Le pauvre diable! Quels que soient ses crimes, il faut lui tenir compte de ce qu'il a souffert.

«Ce souvenir en évoque d'autres: celui de l'homme entrevu à travers la glace du cab et la silhouette qui se profila sur le ciel, au sommet du pic. Était-il également dehors, sous ce déluge, cet ami des ténèbres, ce veilleur inconnu?

«Vers le soir, je passai mon manteau en caoutchouc et je sortis sur la lande. La pluie me battait le visage; le vent sifflait à mes oreilles. J'étais en proie aux plus sombres pensées. Que Dieu vienne en aide à ceux qui s'engagent à cette heure sur la fondrière de Grimpen, car la terre ferme n'est déjà plus qu'un immense marécage!

«Je gravis le pic Noir, celui sur lequel j'avais aperçu le veilleur solitaire, et du haut de sa cime rocheuse, je contemplai à mon tour la plaine dénudée qui s'étendait à mes pieds.

«Les rafales de pluie s'écrasaient sur la surface rouge de la terre et les nuages, lourds, aux teintes d'ardoise, formaient comme de grises couronnes aux sommets des collines fantastiques.

«À gauche, dans un bas-fond à moitié caché par les embruns, les deux tourelles du château de Baskerville se dressaient au-dessus des arbres du parc. Elles représentaient, avec les huttes préhistoriques qui se pressaient sur le flanc des coteaux, les seuls indices de vie humaine que je pusse apercevoir.

«Je ne découvris aucune trace de l'homme entrevu, deux nuits auparavant, à l'endroit même où je me trouvais.

«En revenant à Baskerville par un petit sentier, je rencontrai Mortimer en dog-cart.

«Le docteur s'était montré plein d'attentions pour nous. Il ne se passait pas de jour qu'il ne vînt au château s'informer de ce que nous devenions.

«Mortimer insista pour me faire monter dans sa voiture, il voulait me reconduire un bout de che-

I found him much troubled over the disappearance of his little spaniel. It had wandered on to the moor and had never come back.

I gave him such consolation as I might, but I thought of the pony on the Grimpen Mire, and I do not fancy that he will see his little dog again.

"By the way, Mortimer," said I as we jolted along the rough road, "I suppose there are few people living within driving distance of this whom you do not know?"

"Hardly any, I think."

"Can you, then, tell me the name of any woman whose initials are L. L.?"

He thought for a few minutes.

"No," said he. "There are a few gipsies and labouring folk for whom I can't answer, but among the farmers or gentry there is no one whose initials are those. Wait a bit though," he added after a pause. "There is Laura Lyons—her initials are L. L.—but she lives in Coombe Tracey."

"Who is she?" I asked.

"She is Frankland's daughter."

"What! Old Frankland the crank?"

"Exactly. She married an artist named Lyons, who came sketching on the moor. He proved to be a blackguard and deserted her. The fault from what I hear may not have been entirely on one side. Her father refused to have anything to do with her because she had married without his consent and perhaps for one or two other reasons as well. So, between the old sinner and the young one the girl has had a pretty bad time."

"How does she live?"

"I fancy old Frankland allows her a pittance, but it cannot be more, for his own affairs are considerably involved. Whatever she may have deserved one could not allow her to go hopelessly to the bad. Her story got about, and several of the people here did something to enable her to earn an honest living. Stapleton did for one, and Sir Charles for another. I gave a trifle myself. It was to set her up in a typewriting business."

He wanted to know the object of my inquiries,

min.

«Il me fit part de la préoccupation que lui causait la perte de son caniche. Le chien s'était échappé sur la lande et, depuis lors, son maître ne l'avait plus revu.

«Je prodiguai à ce bon docteur toutes sortes de consolations, mais je revis dans mon esprit le cheval disparaissant dans la fondrière de Grimpen, et je me dis que notre ami ne retrouverait plus son fidèle compagnon.

«— À propos, Mortimer, lui dis-je, tandis que la voiture nous cahotait, je présume que vous connaissez toutes les personnes qui habitent ici, dans un rayon de plusieurs milles.

«— Vous avez raison.

«— Dans ce cas, pourriez-vous m'apprendre quelle est la femme dont le nom et le prénom commencent tous les deux par la lettre L?»

«Le docteur réfléchit pendant un instant.

«— Non, fit-il. Il existe bien quelques laboureurs et quelques bohémiens dont j'ignore le nom; mais, parmi les femmes de bourgeois ou de fermiers, je n'en vois pas qui aient ces initiales. Attendez un peu! reprit-il après une pause… Il y a Laura Lyons,… ses initiales sont bien L. L;… seulement elle demeure à Coombe Tracey.

«— Qui est-elle? demandai-je.

«— C'est la fille de Frankland,

«— Quoi! de ce vieux toqué de Frankland?

«— Parfaitement, elle a épousé un artiste, nommé Lyons, qui venait prendre des croquis sur la lande. Il s'est conduit envers elle comme un goujat,… il l'a abandonnée. S'il faut en croire la rumeur publique, il n'avait pas tous les torts. Quant à Frankland, il ne veut plus entendre parler de sa fille, sous prétexte qu'elle s'est mariée malgré lui — et peut-être aussi pour deux ou trois autres raisons. En tout cas, abandonnée de son mari et de son père, la jeune femme n'a pas beaucoup d'agrément.

«— De quoi vit-elle?

«— Je crois que Frankland lui envoie quelques subsides… bien maigres probablement, car ses affaires sont peu prospères. Quels que soient les torts de Laura, on ne pouvait la laisser dans cette affreuse misère. Son histoire a transpiré, et plusieurs de nos amis ont fait leur possible pour l'aider à gagner honnêtement sa vie. Stapleton, sir Charles et moi-même, nous y avons contribué dans la mesure de nos moyens. Nous voulions la placer à la tête d'une entreprise de dactylographie.»

«Mortimer essaya de connaître le pourquoi de

but I managed to satisfy his curiosity without telling him too much, for there is no reason why we should take anyone into our confidence.

ces questions. Je m'arrangeai de façon à satisfaire sa curiosité, sans toutefois lui en dire trop long, car je ne jugeais pas utile de lui confier mes projets.

Tomorrow morning I shall find my way to Coombe Tracey, and if I can see this Mrs. Laura Lyons, of equivocal reputation, a long step will have been made towards clearing one incident in this chain of mysteries.

«Je me promis d'aller le lendemain matin à Coombe Tracey. J'espérais que, si je parvenais à joindre cette Laura Lyons, de si équivoque réputation, j'aurais fait un grand pas vers l'éclaircissement de tous ces mystères enchevêtrés les uns dans les autres.

I am certainly developing the wisdom of the serpent, for when Mortimer pressed his questions to an inconvenient extent I asked him casually to what type Frankland's skull belonged, and so heard nothing but craniology for the rest of our drive. I have not lived for years with Sherlock Holmes for nothing.

«Au cours de ma conversation avec Mortimer, je dus user de l'astuce du serpent. À un moment, le docteur me pressa de questions embarrassantes; je m'en tirai en lui demandant d'un air fort innocent à quelle catégorie appartenait le crâne de Frankland. À partir de cet instant, nous ne parlâmes plus que de phrénologie. — Je ne pouvais avoir passé inutilement de si longues années auprès de Sherlock Holmes!

I have only one other incident to record upon this tempestuous and melancholy day. This was my conversation with Barrymore just now, which gives me one more strong card which I can play in due time.

«À noter encore pour ce jour-là une conversation avec Barrymore, qui m'a fourni un atout que je compte bien jouer au moment opportun.

Mortimer had stayed to dinner, and he and the baronet played écarté afterwards.

«Nous avions retenu Mortimer à dîner. Le soir, le baronnet et lui se livrèrent à d'interminables parties d'écarté.

The butler brought me my coffee into the library, and I took the chance to ask him a few questions.

«Barrymore m'avait servi le café dans la bibliothèque, et je profitai de ce que nous étions seuls pour lui poser quelques questions.

"Well," said I, "has this precious relation of yours departed, or is he still lurking out yonder?"

«— Votre cher beau-frère est-il parti, lui dis-je, ou bien vagabonde-t-il toujours sur la lande?

"I don't know, sir. I hope to heaven that he has gone, for he has brought nothing but trouble here! I've not heard of him since I left out food for him last, and that was three days ago."

«— Je l'ignore, monsieur. J'aime à croire que nous en sommes enfin débarrassés, car il ne nous a jamais procuré que des ennuis. Je lui ai porté des provisions pour la dernière fois, il y a trois jours; depuis, il ne nous a pas donné signe de vie.

"Did you see him then?"

«— Ce jour-là, l'avez-vous vu?

"No, sir, but the food was gone when next I went that way."

«— Non, monsieur. Mais, le lendemain, les provisions avaient disparu.

"Then he was certainly there?"

«— Donc, il était encore là.

"So you would think, sir, unless it was the other man who took it."

«— Oui… à moins que ce ne soit l'autre qui les ait prises.»

I sat with my coffee-cup halfway to my lips and stared at Barrymore.

«La tasse que je portais à mes lèvres s'arrêta à mi-chemin de son parcours et je regardai Barrymore avec étonnement.

"You know that there is another man then?"

«— Vous saviez qu'un autre homme se cachait sur la lande!

"Yes, sir; there is another man upon the moor."

«— Oui, monsieur.

"Have you seen him?"

«— L'avez-vous aperçu?

"No, sir."

«— Non, monsieur.

"How do you know of him then?"

«— Alors comment l'avez-vous appris?

"Selden told me of him, sir, a week ago or more.

«— Selden m'en a parlé… cet homme se cache

He's in hiding, too, but he's not a convict as far as I can make out. I don't like it, Dr. Watson—I tell you straight, sir, that I don't like it."

He spoke with a sudden passion of earnestness.

"Now, listen to me, Barrymore! I have no interest in this matter but that of your master. I have come here with no object except to help him. Tell me, frankly, what it is that you don't like."

Barrymore hesitated for a moment, as if he regretted his outburst or found it difficult to express his own feelings in words.

"It's all these goings-on, sir," he cried at last, waving his hand towards the rain-lashed window which faced the moor.

"There's foul play somewhere, and there's black villainy brewing, to that I'll swear! Very glad I should be, sir, to see Sir Henry on his way back to London again!"

"But what is it that alarms you?"

"Look at Sir Charles's death! That was bad enough, for all that the coroner said. Look at the noises on the moor at night. There's not a man would cross it after sundown if he was paid for it. Look at this stranger hiding out yonder, and watching and waiting! What's he waiting for? What does it mean? It means no good to anyone of the name of Baskerville, and very glad I shall be to be quit of it all on the day that Sir Henry's new servants are ready to take over the Hall."

"But about this stranger," said I. "Can you tell me anything about him? What did Selden say? Did he find out where he hid, or what he was doing?"

"He saw him once or twice, but he is a deep one and gives nothing away. At first he thought that he was the police, but soon he found that he had some lay of his own. A kind of gentleman he was, as far as he could see, but what he was doing he could not make out."

"And where did he say that he lived?"

"Among the old houses on the hillside—the

également; mais, d'après ce que je suppose, ce n'est pas un convict… Tout cela me semble louche, docteur Watson,… je vous le dis en vérité, cela me semble très louche.»

«Barrymore avait prononcé ces paroles avec un grand accent de sincérité.

«— Écoutez-moi, répliquai-je. Je n'ai d'autre souci que l'intérêt de votre maître et ma présence à Baskerville n'a d'autre but que de lui prêter mon concours. Dites-moi bien franchement ce qui vous paraît louche.»

«Barrymore hésita un instant; regrettait-il déjà sa confidence et éprouvait-il de la difficulté à expliquer ses propres sentiments?

«Enfin, il agita ses mains vers la fenêtre fouettée par la pluie, et, désignant la lande dans un geste de colère, il s'écria:

«— Ce sont tous les potins qui courent!… Il y a quelque anguille sous roche… On prépare quelque scélératesse; ça, j'en jurerais! Je ne me sentirai heureux que lorsque sir Henry sera reparti pour Londres.

«— Quelle est la cause de vos alarmes?

«— Souvenez-vous de la mort de sir Charles!… Le juge d'instruction nous a dit qu'elle était singulière… Rappelez-vous les bruits de la lande pendant la nuit! Une fois le soleil couché, aucun homme, même à prix d'argent, n'oserait s'y aventurer… Et puis cet étranger qui se cache là-bas, guettant, attendant! Qu'attend-il? Que signifie tout cela? Certainement rien de bon pour celui qui porte le nom de Baskerville. Je ne serai vraiment soulagé d'un grand poids que le jour où les nouveaux serviteurs de sir Henry prendront leur service au château.

«— Parlons de cet inconnu, fis-je, en ramenant la conversation sur le seul sujet qui m'intéressât, Pouvez-vous m'apprendre quelque chose sur son compte? Que vous a raconté Selden? Sait-il pourquoi cet homme se cache? Quelles sont ses intentions?…

«— Mon beau-frère l'a aperçu une ou deux fois; mais, comme il est peu communicatif, il ne s'est pas montré prodigue de renseignements. Tout d'abord Selden a cru que cet inconnu appartenait à la police; mais, comme il cherchait également la solitude, mon beau-frère a vite reconnu son erreur. D'après ce que Selden a pu en juger, ce nouvel habitant de la lande aurait les allures d'un gentleman. Que fait-il là?… Mon parent l'ignore.

«— Où vit-il?

«— Sur le versant de la colline, au milieu de

stone huts where the old folk used to live."

ces huttes de pierres habitées autrefois par nos ancêtres.

"But how about his food?"

«— Comment se procure-t-il de la nourriture?

"Selden found out that he has got a lad who works for him and brings all he needs. I dare say he goes to Coombe Tracey for what he wants."

«— Un jeune garçon prend soin de lui et lui apporte tout ce dont il a besoin. Selden croit que le gamin va s'approvisionner à Coombe Tracey.

"Very good, Barrymore. We may talk further of this some other time."

«— Fort bien, Barrymore, répondis-je. Nous reprendrons plus tard cette conversation.»

When the butler had gone I walked over to the black window, and I looked through a blurred pane at the driving clouds and at the tossing outline of the wind-swept trees.

«Le valet de chambre sorti, je m'approchai de la fenêtre. Dehors, il faisait noir. À travers les vitres recouvertes de buée, je contemplai les nuages que le vent chassait dans le ciel et la cime des arbres qui se courbait sous la bourrasque.

It is a wild night indoors, and what must it be in a stone hut upon the moor.

«La nuit, déjà dure pour les gens calfeutrés dans une maison confortable, devait être terrible pour ceux qui n'avaient d'autre abri sur la lande qu'une hutte de pierre!

What passion of hatred can it be which leads a man to lurk in such a place at such a time! And what deep and earnest purpose can he have which calls for such a trial!

«Fallait-il qu'elle fût profonde, la haine qui poussait un homme à errer à une pareille heure et dans un tel endroit! Seul un mobile bien puissant pouvait justifier une semblable séquestration du monde!

There, in that hut upon the moor, seems to lie the very centre of that problem which has vexed me so sorely.

«Ainsi donc, dans une hutte de la lande, se trouvait la solution du problème que je brûlais du désir de résoudre.

I swear that another day shall not have passed before I have done all that man can do to reach the heart of the mystery.

«Je jurai que vingt-quatre heures ne s'écouleraient pas sans que j'eusse tenté tout ce qu'il est humainement possible de faire pour aller jusqu'au tréfonds même de ce mystère.»

CHAPTER 11. THE MAN ON THE TOR

The extract from my private diary which forms the last chapter has brought my narrative up to the eighteenth of October, a time when these strange events began to move swiftly towards their terrible conclusion.

The incidents of the next few days are indelibly graven upon my recollection, and I can tell them without reference to the notes made at the time.

I start them from the day which succeeded that upon which I had established two facts of great importance, the one that Mrs. Laura Lyons of Coombe Tracey had written to Sir Charles Baskerville and made an appointment with him at the very place and hour that he met his death, the other that the lurking man upon the moor was to be found among the stone huts upon the hillside.

With these two facts in my possession I felt that either my intelligence or my courage must be deficient if I could not throw some further light upon these dark places.

I had no opportunity to tell the baronet what I had learned about Mrs. Lyons upon the evening before, for Dr. Mortimer remained with him at cards until it was very late.

At breakfast, however, I informed him about my discovery and asked him whether he would care to accompany me to Coombe Tracey.

At first he was very eager to come, but on second thoughts it seemed to both of us that if I went alone the results might be better. The more formal we made the visit the less information we might obtain.

I left Sir Henry behind, therefore, not without some prickings of conscience, and drove off upon my new quest.

When I reached Coombe Tracey I told Perkins to put up the horses, and I made inquiries for the lady whom I had come to interrogate.

I had no difficulty in finding her rooms, which were central and well appointed.

A maid showed me in without ceremony, and as I entered the sitting-room a lady, who was sit-

CHAPITRE 11. L'HOMME DU PIC NOIR

L'extrait de mon journal particulier qui forme le chapitre précédent m'a conduit jusqu'au 18 octobre, date à laquelle commença à se précipiter la conclusion de ces étranges événements.

Tous les incidents des jours suivants sont gravés dans ma mémoire d'une façon indélébile, et je puis les conter par le menu sans recourir aux notes prises à cette époque.

Je recommence donc mon récit au lendemain du jour où j'avais établi deux faits d'une importante gravité: le premier, que Mme Laura Lyons, de Coombe Tracey, avait écrit à sir Charles Baskerville et pris rendez-vous avec lui pour le lieu et l'heure mêmes où il avait trouvé la mort; le second, que l'inconnu de la lande se terrait dans les huttes de pierre, sur le versant de la colline.

Ces deux points acquis, je compris néanmoins que mon intelligence ou mon courage ne suffiraient pas pour mener à bien mon entreprise, si je ne parvenais à jeter un supplément de lumière sur ceux encore obscurs.

La veille, le docteur Mortimer et sir Henry avaient joué aux cartes jusqu'à une heure avancée de la nuit, et je n'avais pas eu l'occasion d'entretenir le baronnet de ce que j'avais appris sur Mme Laura Lyons.

Pendant le déjeuner, je lui fis part de ma découverte, et je lui demandai s'il lui plairait de m'accompagner à Coombe Tracey.

Tout d'abord, il se montra enchanté de cette petite excursion; puis, après mûre réflexion, il nous parut préférable à tous deux que je la fisse seul. Plus la visite serait cérémonieuse, plus il nous serait difficile d'obtenir des renseignements.

Je quittai sir Henry — non sans quelques remords — et je courus vers cette nouvelle piste.

En arrivant à Coombe Tracey, j'ordonnai à Perkins de dételer les chevaux, et je m'enquis de la dame que je venais interroger.

Je la trouvai sans peine: elle habitait au centre de la petite localité.

La bonne m'introduisit dans le salon, sans m'annoncer. Une femme, assise devant une mating before a Remington typewriter, sprang up with a pleasant smile of welcome.

Her face fell, however, when she saw that I was a stranger, and she sat down again and asked me the object of my visit.

The first impression left by Mrs. Lyons was one of extreme beauty. Her eyes and hair were of the same rich hazel colour, and her cheeks, though considerably freckled, were flushed with the exquisite bloom of the brunette, the dainty pink which lurks at the heart of the sulphur rose.

Admiration was, I repeat, the first impression. But the second was criticism. There was something subtly wrong with the face, some coarseness of expression, some hardness, perhaps, of eye, some looseness of lip which marred its perfect beauty. But these, of course, are afterthoughts.

At the moment I was simply conscious that I was in the presence of a very handsome woman, and that she was asking me the reasons for my visit.

I had not quite understood until that instant how delicate my mission was.

"I have the pleasure," said I, "of knowing your father."

It was a clumsy introduction, and the lady made me feel it.

"There is nothing in common between my father and me," she said. "I owe him nothing, and his friends are not mine. If it were not for the late Sir Charles Baskerville and some other kind hearts I might have starved for all that my father cared."

"It was about the late Sir Charles Baskerville that I have come here to see you."

The freckles started out on the lady's face.

"What can I tell you about him?" she asked, and her fingers played nervously over the stops of her typewriter.

"You knew him, did you not?"

"I have already said that I owe a great deal to his kindness. If I am able to support myself it is largely due to the interest which he took in my unhappy situation."

"Did you correspond with him?"

The lady looked quickly up with an angry gleam in her hazel eyes.

"What is the object of these questions?" she

chine à écrire, se leva et s'avança vers moi avec un sourire de bienvenue.

Quand elle se trouva en face d'un étranger, ce sourire s'évanouit; elle se rassit et s'informa de l'objet de ma visite.

À première vue, Mme Laura Lyons produisait l'impression d'une très jolie femme. Ses yeux et ses cheveux avaient cette chaude coloration de la noisette; ses joues, quoique marquées de quelques taches de rousseur, possédaient l'éclat exquis des brunes avec, aux pommettes, ce léger vermillon qui brille au cœur de la rose thé.

La première impression, je le répète, engendrait l'admiration. La critique ne naissait qu'à un second examen. Le visage avait quelque chose de défectueux — une expression vulgaire, peut-être une dureté de l'œil ou un relâchement de la lèvre en altéraient la parfaite beauté. Mais la remarque de ces défectuosités ne venait qu'après une étude plus approfondie des traits.

Sur le moment, je n'éprouvai que la sensation d'être en présence d'une très jolie femme, qui me demandait le motif de ma visite.

Jusqu'alors, je ne m'étais nullement douté de la délicatesse de ma démarche.

«J'ai le plaisir, dis-je, de connaître monsieur votre père.»

Ce préambule était maladroit, la dame me le fit aussitôt comprendre.

«Il n'existe rien de commun entre mon père et moi, répliqua-t-elle, et ses amis ne sont pas les miens. Si je n'avais eu que mon père, à cette heure je serais morte de faim. Fort heureusement, sir Charles Baskerville et quelques autres âmes généreuses…

— Je suis précisément venu vous voir à propos de Sir Charles Baskerville, interrompis-je.»

À ces mots, les taches de rousseur devinrent plus apparentes sur les joues de Mme Lyons.

«Que puis-je vous dire sur lui? demanda-t-elle, tandis que ses doigts jouaient nerveusement sur les touches de sa machine à écrire.

— Vous le connaissiez, n'est-ce pas?

— Je vous ai déjà dit que je lui étais redevable de grands services. Si je puis me suffire à moi-même, je le dois surtout à l'intérêt que lui avait inspiré ma triste situation.

— Lui écriviez-vous?»

La dame releva vivement la tête; un éclair de colère passa dans ses beaux yeux veloutés.

«Dans quel but toutes ces questions? interroasked sharply.

"The object is to avoid a public scandal. It is better that I should ask them here than that the matter should pass outside our control."

She was silent and her face was still very pale. At last she looked up with something reckless and defiant in her manner.

"Well, I'll answer," she said. "What are your questions?"

"Did you correspond with Sir Charles?"

"I certainly wrote to him once or twice to acknowledge his delicacy and his generosity."

"Have you the dates of those letters?"

"No."

"Have you ever met him?"

"Yes, once or twice, when he came into Coombe Tracey. He was a very retiring man, and he preferred to do good by stealth."

"But if you saw him so seldom and wrote so seldom, how did he know enough about your affairs to be able to help you, as you say that he has done?"

She met my difficulty with the utmost readiness.

"There were several gentlemen who knew my sad history and united to help me. One was Mr. Stapleton, a neighbour and intimate friend of Sir Charles's. He was exceedingly kind, and it was through him that Sir Charles learned about my affairs."

I knew already that Sir Charles Baskerville had made Stapleton his almoner upon several occasions, so the lady's statement bore the impress of truth upon it.

"Did you ever write to Sir Charles asking him to meet you?" I continued.

Mrs. Lyons flushed with anger again.

"Really, sir, this is a very extraordinary question."

"I am sorry, madam, but I must repeat it."

"Then I answer, certainly not."

"Not on the very day of Sir Charles's death?"

The flush had faded in an instant, and a deathly face was before me.

Her dry lips could not speak the "No" which I saw rather than heard.

"Surely your memory deceives you," said I. "I

gea-t-elle sèchement.

— Dans quel but? répétai-je... Pour éviter un scandale public... Il vaut mieux que je vous adresse ces questions, ici, dans l'intimité, sans que l'affaire qui m'amène franchisse cette enceinte.»

Mme Lyons garda le silence et ses joues devinrent excessivement pâles. Puis en me jetant un regard de défi:

«Soit! dit-elle, je vous répondrai. Que désirez-vous savoir?

— Correspondiez-vous avec sir Charles?

— Oui; je lui ai écrit une ou deux fois pour le remercier de sa délicate générosité.

— Vous rappelez-vous les dates de vos lettres?

— Non.

— Vous êtes-vous rencontrés?

— Oui; une ou deux fois... quand il est venu à Coombe Tracey. C'était un homme très simple, qui faisait le bien sans ostentation.

— Puisque vous l'avez peu vu et que vous ne lui avez écrit que fort rarement, comment pouvait-il connaître assez vos besoins pour vous aider ainsi qu'il l'a fait, d'après vos propres aveux?»

Mme Lyons rétorqua cette objection avec une extrême promptitude:

«Plusieurs personnes connaissant mon dénuement s'étaient associées pour me secourir. L'une d'elles était M. Stapleton, voisin et ami intime de sir Charles Baskerville. Excessivement bon, il consentit à parler de moi à sir Charles.»

Je savais déjà que, dans plusieurs circonstances, le vieux gentilhomme s'était servi de l'intermédiaire de Stapleton pour distribuer ses aumônes. Le récit de la dame paraissait donc très vraisemblable.

Je continuai: «Avez-vous écrit à sir Charles pour lui donner un rendez-vous?»

La colère empourpra de nouveau les joues de Mme Lyons:

«Vraiment, monsieur, répondit-elle, vous me posez là une question bien extraordinaire.

— Je le regrette, madame, mais je dois la renouveler.

— Je vous répondrai: certainement non!

— Pas même le jour de la mort de sir Charles?»

La rougeur du visage de Mme Laura Lyons fit place à une pâleur cadavérique.

Ses lèvres desséchées s'entr'ouvrirent à peine pour laisser tomber un «non», que je vis, plutôt que je ne l'entendis.

— Votre mémoire vous trahit sûrement, dis-je.

could even quote a passage of your letter. It ran 'Please, please, as you are a gentleman, burn this letter, and be at the gate by ten o'clock.'"

I thought that she had fainted, but she recovered herself by a supreme effort.

"Is there no such thing as a gentleman?" she gasped.

"You do Sir Charles an injustice. He did burn the letter. But sometimes a letter may be legible even when burned. You acknowledge now that you wrote it?"

"Yes, I did write it," she cried, pouring out her soul in a torrent of words.

"I did write it. Why should I deny it? I have no reason to be ashamed of it. I wished him to help me. I believed that if I had an interview I could gain his help, so I asked him to meet me."

"But why at such an hour?"

"Because I had only just learned that he was going to London next day and might be away for months. There were reasons why I could not get there earlier."

"But why a rendezvous in the garden instead of a visit to the house?"

"Do you think a woman could go alone at that hour to a bachelor's house?"

"Well, what happened when you did get there?"

"I never went."

"Mrs. Lyons!"

"No, I swear it to you on all I hold sacred. I never went. Something intervened to prevent my going."

"What was that?"

"That is a private matter. I cannot tell it."

"You acknowledge then that you made an appointment with Sir Charles at the very hour and place at which he met his death, but you deny that you kept the appointment."

"That is the truth."

Again and again I cross-questioned her, but I could never get past that point.

"Mrs. Lyons," said I as I rose from this long and inconclusive interview, "you are taking a very great responsibility and putting yourself in a very false position by not making an absolutely clean breast of all that you know. If I have to call in the aid of the police you will find how seriously you are compromised. If your position is innocent, why did you in the first instance deny having written to Sir

Je puis vous citer un passage de votre lettre. Le voici: «Je vous en prie, je vous en supplie, vous êtes un homme d'honneur, brûlez cette lettre et soyez ce soir, à dix heures, à la porte de la lande».

Je crus que Mme Lyons allait s'évanouir; mais, par un suprême effort de volonté, elle se ressaisit.

«Je croyais un galant homme incapable d'une telle action! bégaya-t-elle.

— Vous êtes injuste pour sir Charles... Il a brûlé votre lettre. Mais quelquefois une lettre, même carbonisée, reste encore lisible... Reconnaissez-vous l'avoir écrite?

— Oui, je l'ai écrite!» s'écria-t-elle. Et, répandant son âme dans un torrent de mots, elle ajouta:

«Oui, je l'ai écrite! Pourquoi le nierais-je? Je n'ai pas à en rougir!... Je désirais qu'il me secourût et j'espérais l'y amener, s'il consentait à m'écouter. Voilà pourquoi je lui ai demandé une entrevue.

— Pourquoi avoir choisi cette heure tardive?

— Parce que j'avais appris le matin que sir Charles partait le lendemain pour Londres et que son absence se prolongerait pendant plusieurs mois.

— Mais pourquoi lui donner rendez-vous dans le jardin plutôt que dans le château?

— Pensez-vous qu'il soit convenable qu'une femme seule aille, à cette heure-là, chez un célibataire?

— Qu'arriva-t-il au cours de votre entrevue?

— Je ne suis pas allée à Baskerville.

— Madame Lyons!

— Je vous le jure sur tout ce que j'ai de plus sacré!... Non, je ne suis pas allée à Baskerville... Un événement imprévu m'en a empêchée.

— Quel est-il?

— Il est d'ordre tout intime. Je ne puis vous le dire.

— Alors vous reconnaissez avoir donné rendez-vous à sir Charles à l'heure et à l'endroit où il a trouvé la mort, mais vous niez être venue à ce rendez-vous?

— Je vous ai dit la vérité.»

À maintes reprises, j'interrogeai Mme Lyons sur ce fait; ses réponses ne varièrent pas.

«Madame, lui dis-je en me levant pour clore cette longue et inutile visite, par votre manque de confiance et de franchise, vous assumez une lourde responsabilité et vous vous placez dans une situation très fausse. Si vous me forcez à requérir l'intervention de la justice, vous verrez à quel point vous serez sérieusement compromise! Si vous n'avez pas trempé dans ce tragique événe-

Charles upon that date?"

"Because I feared that some false conclusion might be drawn from it and that I might find myself involved in a scandal."

"And why were you so pressing that Sir Charles should destroy your letter?"

"If you have read the letter you will know."

"I did not say that I had read all the letter."

"You quoted some of it."

"I quoted the postscript. The letter had, as I said, been burned and it was not all legible. I ask you once again why it was that you were so pressing that Sir Charles should destroy this letter which he received on the day of his death."

"The matter is a very private one."

"The more reason why you should avoid a public investigation."

"I will tell you, then. If you have heard anything of my unhappy history you will know that I made a rash marriage and had reason to regret it."

"I have heard so much."

"My life has been one incessant persecution from a husband whom I abhor. The law is upon his side, and every day I am faced by the possibility that he may force me to live with him. At the time that I wrote this letter to Sir Charles I had learned that there was a prospect of my regaining my freedom if certain expenses could be met. It meant everything to me—peace of mind, happiness, self-respect—everything. I knew Sir Charles's generosity, and I thought that if he heard the story from my own lips he would help me."

"Then how is it that you did not go?"

"Because I received help in the interval from another source."

"Why then, did you not write to Sir Charles and explain this?"

"So I should have done had I not seen his death in the paper next morning."

The woman's story hung coherently together, and all my questions were unable to shake it. I could only check it by finding if she had, indeed, instituted divorce proceedings against her husband at or about the time of the tragedy.

It was unlikely that she would dare to say that she had not been to Baskerville Hall if she real-

ment, pourquoi avez-vous nié tout d'abord la lettre envoyée par vous à sir Charles à cette date?

— Je craignais qu'on ne tirât de ce fait une conclusion erronée et que je ne fusse ainsi mêlée à un scandale.

— Pourquoi avez-vous tant insisté pour que sir Charles brûlât votre lettre?

— Vous devez le savoir, puisque vous l'avez lue.

— Je ne prétends pas avoir lu cette lettre,

— Vous m'en avez cité un passage.

— Le post-scriptum seulement. Ainsi que je vous l'ai dit, la lettre avait été brûlée et cette partie demeurait seule lisible. Je vous demande encore une fois pourquoi vous insistiez si fort pour que sir Charles brûlât cette lettre, reçue quelques heures avant sa mort?

— Ceci est également d'ordre intime.

— Raison de plus pour éviter une enquête publique.

— Eh bien, je vais vous l'apprendre. Si vous connaissez un peu ma malheureuse histoire, vous devez savoir que j'ai fait un mariage ridicule et que je le déplore pour plusieurs raisons.

— Je le sais.

— Par ses persécutions quotidiennes, mon mari — que je déteste — m'avait rendu la vie commune odieuse. Mais il a la loi pour lui et je suis tous les jours exposée à ce qu'il m'oblige à réintégrer le foyer conjugal. À l'époque où j'écrivis cette lettre à sir Charles, j'avais appris que je pourrais reconquérir mon indépendance, moyennant certains frais qu'il fallait consigner. Il s'agissait de tout ce qui m'est le plus cher au monde — tranquillité d'esprit, bonheur, respect de moi-même — de tout! Je connaissais sir Charles, et je me disais que, s'il entendait mon histoire de ma propre bouche, il ne repousserait pas mes prières.

— Alors pourquoi n'êtes-vous pas allée le retrouver?

— Dans l'intervalle, j'avais reçu du secours d'un autre côté.

— Pourquoi ne pas écrire une seconde fois à sir Charles pour lui expliquer tout cela?

— Je l'eusse certainement fait si les journaux du lendemain matin n'avaient pas annoncé sa mort.»

Le récit de Mme Lyons était vraisemblable et cohérent. Pour en contrôler la véracité, il ne me restait plus qu'à vérifier si, vers cette époque, elle avait introduit une action en divorce contre son mari.

D'autre part, il me paraissait inadmissible qu'elle osât affirmer ne pas être allée à Baskerville, ly had been, for a trap would be necessary to take her there, and could not have returned to Coombe Tracey until the early hours of the morning. Such an excursion could not be kept secret.

The probability was, therefore, that she was telling the truth, or, at least, a part of the truth.

si elle s'y était réellement rendue; elle aurait dû s'y faire porter en voiture et ne rentrer à Coombe Tracey qu'aux premières heures du matin. Or, comment tenir ce voyage secret?

Selon toute probabilité, Mme Lyons m'avait confessé toute la vérité — ou tout au moins une partie de la vérité.

I came away baffled and disheartened.

Once again I had reached that dead wall which seemed to be built across every path by which I tried to get at the object of my mission.

Je m'en retournai confus et découragé.

Ainsi donc, une fois encore, je me heurtais à un obstacle qui me barrait la voie au bout de laquelle j'espérais trouver la clef du mystère que j'avais mission de découvrir.

And yet the more I thought of the lady's face and of her manner the more I felt that something was being held back from me.

Why should she turn so pale?

Why should she fight against every admission until it was forced from her?

Why should she have been so reticent at the time of the tragedy?

Surely the explanation of all this could not be as innocent as she would have me believe.

Et cependant, plus je songeais au visage et à l'attitude de Mme Lyons, plus j'avais le pressentiment qu'elle me cachait quelque chose.

Pourquoi était-elle devenue si pâle?

Pourquoi avais-je dû lutter pour lui arracher certaines explications?

Pourquoi enfin avait-elle gardé le silence au moment du drame?

Et ses explications mêmes ne la rendaient pas aussi innocente à mes yeux qu'elle aurait voulu le paraître?

For the moment I could proceed no farther in that direction, but must turn back to that other clue which was to be sought for among the stone huts upon the moor.

And that was a most vague direction. I realised it as I drove back and noted how hill after hill showed traces of the ancient people.

Pour l'instant, je résolus de ne pas pousser plus loin mes investigations du côté de Mme Lyons et de chercher, au contraire, la solution du problème parmi les huttes de pierre de la lande.

Le renseignement fourni par Barrymore était très vague. Je m'en convainquis pendant mon retour au château, à la vue de cette succession de collines qui portaient toutes les traces de l'habitation des anciens hommes.

Barrymore's only indication had been that the stranger lived in one of these abandoned huts, and many hundreds of them are scattered throughout the length and breadth of the moor.

But I had my own experience for a guide since it had shown me the man himself standing upon the summit of the Black Tor. That, then, should be the centre of my search.

From there I should explore every hut upon the moor until I lighted upon the right one. If this man were inside it I should find out from his own lips, at the point of my revolver if necessary, who he was and why he had dogged us so long.

La seule indication précise consistait à affecter à l'inconnu une de ces antiques demeures de pierre. Or, j'en comptais plus de cent disséminées un peu partout sur la lande.

Cependant, depuis que j'avais vu l'homme juché sur le sommet du pic Noir, j'avais un point de repère pour me guider. Je me promis de concentrer mes recherches autour de ce point.

De là-haut, je pouvais explorer successivement toutes les huttes, jusqu'à ce que j'eusse découvert la bonne. Si j'y rencontrais mon inconnu, je saurais bien, mon revolver aidant, lui arracher son secret. Il faudra qu'il m'apprenne qui il est et pourquoi il nous espionne depuis si longtemps!

He might slip away from us in the crowd of Regent Street, but it would puzzle him to do so upon the lonely moor.

On the other hand, if I should find the hut and its tenant should not be within it I must remain there, however long the vigil, until he returned.

Il nous avait échappé au milieu de la foule de Regent street; dans cette contrée déserte, la même manœuvre serait plus difficile.

Si, au contraire, la hutte était vide, je m'y installerais aussi longtemps qu'il le faudrait pour attendre le retour de son hôte.

Holmes had missed him in London. It would indeed be a triumph for me if I could run him to earth where my master had failed.

Luck had been against us again and again in this inquiry, but now at last it came to my aid.

And the messenger of good fortune was none other than Mr. Frankland, who was standing, grey-whiskered and red-faced, outside the gate of his garden, which opened on to the highroad along which I travelled.

"Good-day, Dr. Watson," cried he with unwonted good humour, "you must really give your horses a rest and come in to have a glass of wine and to congratulate me."

My feelings towards him were very far from being friendly after what I had heard of his treatment of his daughter, but I was anxious to send Perkins and the wagonette home, and the opportunity was a good one.

I alighted and sent a message to Sir Henry that I should walk over in time for dinner.

Then I followed Frankland into his dining-room.

"It is a great day for me, sir—one of the red-letter days of my life," he cried with many chuckles. "I have brought off a double event. I mean to teach them in these parts that law is law, and that there is a man here who does not fear to invoke it. I have established a right of way through the centre of old Middleton's park, slap across it, sir, within a hundred yards of his own front door. What do you think of that? We'll teach these magnates that they cannot ride roughshod over the rights of the commoners, confound them! And I've closed the wood where the Fernworthy folk used to picnic. These infernal people seem to think that there are no rights of property, and that they can swarm where they like with their papers and their bottles. Both cases decided, Dr. Watson, and both in my favour. I haven't had such a day since I had Sir John Morland for trespass because he shot in his own warren."

"How on earth did you do that?"

"Look it up in the books, sir. It will repay reading—Frankland v. Morland, Court of Queen's Bench. It cost me £200, but I got my verdict."

"Did it do you any good?"

Holmes l'avait manqué à Londres... Quel triomphe pour moi si je réussissais là où mon maître avait échoué!

Dans cette enquête, la malchance s'était acharnée contre nous. Mais tout à coup la fortune tourna et commença à me sourire.

Le messager de bonheur se présenta sous les traits de M. Frankland qui, la figure rubiconde encadrée par ses favoris grisonnants, se tenait sur le pas de la porte de son jardin. La grande route que je suivais passait devant cette porte.

«Bonjour, docteur Watson! s'écria-t-il avec une bonne humeur inaccoutumée. Vos chevaux ont besoin de repos... Entrez donc vous rafraîchir... Vous me féliciterez.»

Depuis que je connaissais la conduite de Frankland envers sa fille, je n'éprouvais plus aucune sympathie pour lui. Mais comme je souhaitais un prétexte pour renvoyer Perkins et la voiture au château, l'occasion me parut excellente.

Je mis pied à terre et je fis dire à sir Henry par le cocher que je rentrerais pour l'heure du dîner.

Puis je pénétrai dans la maison de Frankland.

«C'est un grand jour pour moi, fit cet original, un de ces jours qu'on marque avec un caillou blanc. J'ai remporté aujourd'hui un double succès. Je. voulais apprendre aux gens de ce pays que la loi est la loi et qu'il existe un homme qui ne craint pas de l'invoquer. J'avais revendiqué un droit de passage au beau milieu du parc du vieux Middleton, monsieur, sur un espace de cent mètres et devant la porte de la maison. Qu'en pensez-vous?... Ils verront bien, ces grands seigneurs, qu'ils ne nous écraseront pas toujours sous le sabot ferré de leurs chevaux!... Ensuite, j'avais entouré de clôtures le bois où les habitants de Fenworthy ont coutume d'aller en pique-nique. Les maroufles croient vraiment qu'on a abrogé les lois qui protègent la propriété et qu'ils peuvent déposer partout leurs papiers graisseux et leurs tessons de bouteilles! Ces deux procès ont été jugés, docteur Watson, et j'ai obtenu gain de cause dans les deux affaires. Je n'avais plus remporté de succès pareil depuis le jour où j'avais fait condamner sir John Morland parce qu'il tirait des lapins sur sa propre garenne.

— Comment diable vous y êtes-vous pris?

— Feuilletez les recueils de jurisprudence... Vous y lirez: «Frankland c. Morland, Cour du Banc de la Reine...» Ça m'a coûté cinq mille francs, mais j'ai eu mon jugement!

— Quel profit en avez-vous tiré?

"None, sir, none. I am proud to say that I had no interest in the matter. I act entirely from a sense of public duty. I have no doubt, for example, that the Fernworthy people will burn me in effigy tonight. I told the police last time they did it that they should stop these disgraceful exhibitions. The County Constabulary is in a scandalous state, sir, and it has not afforded me the protection to which I am entitled. The case of Frankland v. Regina will bring the matter before the attention of the public. I told them that they would have occasion to regret their treatment of me, and already my words have come true."

"How so?" I asked.

The old man put on a very knowing expression. "Because I could tell them what they are dying to know; but nothing would induce me to help the rascals in any way."

I had been casting round for some excuse by which I could get away from his gossip, but now I began to wish to hear more of it.

I had seen enough of the contrary nature of the old sinner to understand that any strong sign of interest would be the surest way to stop his confidences.

"Some poaching case, no doubt?" said I with an indifferent manner.

"Ha, ha, my boy, a very much more important matter than that! What about the convict on the moor?"

I stared.

"You don't mean that you know where he is?" said I.

"I may not know exactly where he is, but I am quite sure that I could help the police to lay their hands on him. Has it never struck you that the way to catch that man was to find out where he got his food and so trace it to him?"

He certainly seemed to be getting uncomfortably near the truth.

"No doubt," said I; "but how do you know that he is anywhere upon the moor?"

"I know it because I have seen with my own eyes the messenger who takes him his food."

My heart sank for Barrymore. It was a serious thing to be in the power of this spiteful old busybody.

But his next remark took a weight from my mind.

"You'll be surprised to hear that his food is tak-

— Aucun, monsieur, aucun… Je suis fier de dire que je n'avais aucun intérêt dans l'affaire… Je remplis mon devoir de citoyen… Par exemple, je ne doute pas que les gens de Fenworthy ne me brûlent ce soir en effigie. La dernière fois qu'ils se sont livrés à ce petit divertissement, j'avais averti la police qu'elle eût à intervenir… La police du comté est déplorablement conduite, monsieur; elle ne m'a pas accordé la protection à laquelle j'avais droit! Le procès Frankland c. la Reine portera la cause devant le public… J'ai prévenu les agents qu'ils se repentiront de leur attitude envers moi — et déjà ma prédiction se réalise.

— Comment? demandai-je.

— Je pourrais leur apprendre ce qu'ils meurent d'envie de connaître; mais, pour rien au monde, je n'aiderais des coquins de cette espèce.»

Depuis un moment, je cherchais un prétexte pour échapper aux bavardages de ce vieux fou. En entendant ces paroles, je voulus en savoir davantage.

Je connaissais suffisamment le caractère de Frankland pour être certain que le moindre signe d'intérêt arrêterait immédiatement ses confidences.

Quelque délit de braconnage sans doute? dis-je d'un air indifférent.

— Ah! ouiche!… La chose est bien plus importante… Que pensez-vous du contumace qui erre sur la lande?»

Je le regardai, stupéfait.

«Insinueriez-vous que vous savez où il est?

— J'ignore l'endroit précis où il se cache; mais je pourrais tout de même procurer à la police le moyen de lui mettre la main au collet. Que faudrait-il pour s'emparer de lui? Découvrir le lieu où il vient chercher sa nourriture et, de là, le suivre à la trace.»

Certainement Frankland touchait à la vérité.

«Vous avez raison, répondis-je. Mais comment avez deviné qu'il habitait la lande?

— J'ai vu, de mes yeux vu, le commissionnaire qui lui apporte ses provisions.»

Je tremblai pour Barrymore, car c'était chose dangereuse que de se trouver à la merci de cet incorrigible bavard.

La phrase qui suivit me rassura.

«C'est un jeune garçon qui lui sert de pour-en to him by a child. I see him every day through my telescope upon the roof. He passes along the same path at the same hour, and to whom should he be going except to the convict?"

Here was luck indeed! And yet I suppressed all appearance of interest.

A child! Barrymore had said that our unknown was supplied by a boy. It was on his track, and not upon the convict's, that Frankland had stumbled. If I could get his knowledge it might save me a long and weary hunt.

But incredulity and indifference were evidently my strongest cards.

"I should say that it was much more likely that it was the son of one of the moorland shepherds taking out his father's dinner."

The least appearance of opposition struck fire out of the old autocrat. His eyes looked malignantly at me, and his grey whiskers bristled like those of an angry cat.

"Indeed, sir!" said he, pointing out over the wide-stretching moor. "Do you see that Black Tor over yonder?"

"Well, do you see the low hill beyond with the thornbush upon it? It is the stoniest part of the whole moor. Is that a place where a shepherd would be likely to take his station? Your suggestion, sir, is a most absurd one."

I meekly answered that I had spoken without knowing all the facts. My submission pleased him and led him to further confidences.

"You may be sure, sir, that I have very good grounds before I come to an opinion. I have seen the boy again and again with his bundle. Every day, and sometimes twice a day, I have been able—but wait a moment, Dr. Watson. Do my eyes deceive me, or is there at the present moment something moving upon that hillside?"

It was several miles off, but I could distinctly see a small dark dot against the dull green and grey.

"Come, sir, come!" cried Frankland, rushing upstairs. "You will see with your own eyes and judge for yourself."

The telescope, a formidable instrument mounted upon a tripod, stood upon the flat leads of the

voyeur, ajouta Frankland. À l'aide du télescope que j'ai installé sur mon toit, je l'aperçois tous les jours, parcourant à la même heure le même chemin. Qui irait-il retrouver, sinon le prisonnier évadé?»

Ce renseignement marquait le retour de la bonne fortune. Et cependant je ne l'accueillis par aucun témoignage d'intérêt.

Un enfant!... Barrymore n'avait-il pas affirmé qu'un enfant ravitaillait l'inconnu? Alors Frankland se trouvait sur la piste de mon inconnu, et non pas sur celle de Selden! Que de longues et pénibles recherches n'éviterais-je pas s'il consentait à partager ce secret avec moi!

Il me fallait jouer serré, feindre l'incrédulité et l'indifférence.

«Il est plus probable, repris-je, que c'est le fils de quelque berger de la lande qui porte le dîner de son père.»

La moindre velléité de contradiction mettait le vieil entêté hors de lui. Il me lança un mauvais regard et ses favoris gris se hérissèrent comme les poils d'un chat sauvage.

«Un fils de fermier!... Vraiment? fit-il en désignant de la main la lande solitaire que nous apercevions à travers la croisée. Voyez-vous le pic Noir, là-bas?»

Je fis un signe affirmatif.

«Voyez-vous plus loin, reprit-il, cette colline peu élevée couronnée de buissons? C'est la partie la plus pierreuse de la lande... Un berger voudrait-il y établir son parc?... Tenez, votre supposition est tout bonnement absurde!»

Je répondis humblement que j'avais parlé dans l'ignorance de tous ces détails. Mon humilité désarma Frankland, qui continua ses confidences.

«Je vous assure que j'ai de bonnes raisons de croire que je ne me trompe pas. Maintes fois, j'ai vu ce jeune garçon, chargé de son paquet, parcourir le même chemin. Chaque jour, et souvent deux fois par jour, j'ai pu... Mais attendez donc, docteur Watson! Mes yeux me trompent-ils? N'y a-t-il pas quelque chose qui se meut sur le versant de la colline?»

Plusieurs milles nous séparaient du point indiqué. Cependant je distinguai une forme se dessinant en noir sur les teintes vertes et grises du paysage.

«Venez, monsieur, venez! s'écria Frankland, en se précipitant vers l'escalier. Vous verrez par vous-même et vous jugerez.»

Un énorme télescope, monté sur un trépied, encombrait le faîte de la maison. Avidement, Franhouse. Frankland clapped his eye to it and gave a cry of satisfaction.

"Quick, Dr. Watson, quick, before he passes over the hill!"

There he was, sure enough, a small urchin with a little bundle upon his shoulder, toiling slowly up the hill. When he reached the crest I saw the ragged uncouth figure outlined for an instant against the cold blue sky. He looked round him with a furtive and stealthy air, as one who dreads pursuit. Then he vanished over the hill.

kland y appliqua son œil et poussa un cri de satisfaction.

«Vite, docteur Watson, vite, avant qu'il ait disparu!»

À mon tour, je collai mon œil à la lentille, et j'aperçus un jeune garçon qui, un paquet sur l'épaule, grimpait la colline. Arrivé au sommet, sa silhouette se profila sur l'azur du ciel. Il regarda autour de lui, de l'air inquiet de ceux qui redoutent d'être poursuivis; puis il s'éclipsa derrière l'autre versant.

"Well! Am I right?"

"Certainly, there is a boy who seems to have some secret errand."

"And what the errand is even a county constable could guess. But not one word shall they have from me, and I bind you to secrecy also, Dr. Watson. Not a word! You understand!"

"Just as you wish."

"They have treated me shamefully—shamefully. When the facts come out in Frankland v. Regina I venture to think that a thrill of indignation will run through the country. Nothing would induce me to help the police in any way. For all they cared it might have been me, instead of my effigy, which these rascals burned at the stake. Surely you are not going! You will help me to empty the decanter in honour of this great occasion!"

But I resisted all his solicitations and succeeded in dissuading him from his announced intention of walking home with me.

I kept the road as long as his eye was on me, and then I struck off across the moor and made for the stony hill over which the boy had disappeared.

Everything was working in my favour, and I swore that it should not be through lack of energy or perseverance that I should miss the chance which fortune had thrown in my way.

The sun was already sinking when I reached the summit of the hill, and the long slopes beneath me were all golden-green on one side and grey

«Eh bien, ai-je raison? demanda Frankland.

— J'en conviens. Voilà un garçon qui me paraît engagé dans une expédition secrète.

— Un agent de police lui-même ne se tromperait pas sur la nature de l'expédition. Mais je ne leur communiquerai rien et je vous requiers, docteur Watson, d'imiter mon silence. Pas un mot!... Vous comprenez?

— Je vous le promets.

— La police s'est indignement conduite envers moi... indignement! Quand le procès Frankland contre la Reine dévoilera l'ensemble des faits, un frisson d'indignation secouera tout le comté. Rien ne pourrait me décider à seconder la police... la police qui aurait été ravie si, au lieu de mon effigie, on avait brûlé ma modeste personne! Vous vous tairez, n'est-ce pas?... Acceptez donc de vider un flacon en l'honneur de mes récentes victoires!»

Je résistai à toutes les sollicitations de Frankland et j'eus toutes les peines du monde à le dissuader de m'accompagner au château.

Je suivis la grande route jusqu'au moment où Frankland devait me perdre de vue; puis je me dirigeai vers la colline derrière laquelle le jeune garçon avait disparu.

Les choses prenaient une tournure favorable et je jurai d'employer toute mon énergie et toute ma persévérance à profiter des chances que le hasard mettait à ma disposition.

Le soleil était à son déclin lorsque je parvins au sommet de la colline. Les longues pentes qui dévalaient vers la plaine revêtaient, du côté de l'occishadow on the other.

dent, des teintes dorées, tandis que, de l'autre côté, l'ombre croissante les colorait d'un gris sombre.

A haze lay low upon the farthest sky-line, out of which jutted the fantastic shapes of Belliver and Vixen Tor. Over the wide expanse there was no sound and no movement.

Le brouillard, au-dessus duquel le Belliver et le pic du Renard faisaient encore saillie, montait lentement sur l'horizon. Aucun bruit ne troublait le silence de la lande.

One great grey bird, a gull or curlew, soared aloft in the blue heaven. He and I seemed to be the only living things between the huge arch of the sky and the desert beneath it.

Un grand oiseau gris — une mouette ou un courlis — planait dans le ciel bleu. Lui et moi, nous semblions être les deux seules créatures vivantes s'agitant entre l'arc immense du firmament et le désert qui se développait au-dessous.

The barren scene, the sense of loneliness, and the mystery and urgency of my task all struck a chill into my heart.

Ce paysage aride, cette impression de solitude, ce mystère, ainsi que les dangers de l'heure présente, tout cela me glaçait le cœur.

The boy was nowhere to be seen. But down beneath me in a cleft of the hills there was a circle of the old stone huts, and in the middle of them there was one which retained sufficient roof to act as a screen against the weather.

Le gamin entrevu à travers le télescope de Frankland restait invisible. Mais, en bas, dans la déchirure de la colline, se dressaient de nombreuses huttes de pierre dont l'agglomération affectait la forme d'un immense cercle. Il en était une qui conservait encore une toiture suffisante pour abriter quelqu'un contre les intempéries des saisons.

My heart leaped within me as I saw it. This must be the burrow where the stranger lurked. At last my foot was on the threshold of his hiding place—his secret was within my grasp.

À cette vue, mon cœur battit à tout rompre. Mon inconnu gîtait certainement là! Je touchais à sa cachette — son secret était à portée de ma main!

As I approached the hut, walking as warily as Stapleton would do when with poised net he drew near the settled butterfly, I satisfied myself that the place had indeed been used as a habitation. A vague pathway among the boulders led to the dilapidated opening which served as a door.

Avec autant de précaution que Stapleton s'approchant, le filet levé, d'un papillon posé sur une fleur, je fis quelques pas en avant. Un sentier, à peine frayé à travers les blocs de rochers, conduisait à une ouverture béante qui tenait lieu de porte.

All was silent within. The unknown might be lurking there, or he might be prowling on the moor.

À l'intérieur, tout était silencieux. De deux choses l'une: l'inconnu s'y trouvait blotti ou bien il rôdait sur la lande.

My nerves tingled with the sense of adventure.

Mes nerfs vibraient sous la solennité du moment.

Throwing aside my cigarette, I closed my hand upon the butt of my revolver and, walking swiftly up to the door, I looked in. The place was empty.

Jetant ma cigarette, je saisis la crosse de mon revolver, et, courant précipitamment vers la porte, je regardai dans la hutte. Elle était vide.

But there were ample signs that I had not come upon a false scent. This was certainly where the man lived. Some blankets rolled in a waterproof lay upon that very stone slab upon which Neolithic man had once slumbered. The ashes of a fire were heaped in a rude grate. Beside it lay some cooking utensils and a bucket half-full of water.

Une rapide inspection me montra qu'elle était habitée. Je vis des couvertures, doublées de toile cirée, étendues sur la large dalle de pierre où les hommes néolithiques avaient coutume de reposer. Des cendres s'amoncelaient dans un foyer rudimentaire. On avait placé dans un coin quelques ustensiles de cuisine et une jarre pleine d'eau.

A litter of empty tins showed that the place had been occupied for some time, and I saw, as my eyes became accustomed to the checkered light, a pannikin and a half-full bottle of spirits standing in the corner.

De vieilles boîtes de conserves mises en tas indiquaient que le lieu était occupé depuis assez longtemps, et, dès que mes yeux furent habitués à cette demi-obscurité, je distinguai une miche de pain et une bouteille de cognac entamées.

In the middle of the hut a flat stone served the purpose of a table, and upon this stood a small cloth bundle—the same, no doubt, which I had seen through the telescope upon the shoulder of the boy. It contained a loaf of bread, a tinned tongue, and two tins of preserved peaches.

As I set it down again, after having examined it, my heart leaped to see that beneath it there lay a sheet of paper with writing upon it. I raised it, and this was what I read, roughly scrawled in pencil:

"Dr. Watson has gone to Coombe Tracey."

For a minute I stood there with the paper in my hands thinking out the meaning of this curt message.

It was I, then, and not Sir Henry, who was being dogged by this secret man. He had not followed me himself, but he had set an agent—the boy, perhaps—upon my track, and this was his report.

Possibly I had taken no step since I had been upon the moor which had not been observed and reported.

Always there was this feeling of an unseen force, a fine net drawn round us with infinite skill and delicacy, holding us so lightly that it was only at some supreme moment that one realised that one was indeed entangled in its meshes.

If there was one report there might be others, so I looked round the hut in search of them. There was no trace, however, of anything of the kind, nor could I discover any sign which might indicate the character or intentions of the man who lived in this singular place, save that he must be of Spartan habits and cared little for the comforts of life.

When I thought of the heavy rains and looked at the gaping roof I understood how strong and immutable must be the purpose which had kept him in that inhospitable abode.

Was he our malignant enemy, or was he by chance our guardian angel?

I swore that I would not leave the hut until I knew.

Outside the sun was sinking low and the west was blazing with scarlet and gold. Its reflection was shot back in ruddy patches by the distant pools which lay amid the great Grimpen Mire. There were the two towers of Baskerville Hall, and there a distant blur of smoke which marked the village of Grimpen. Between the two, behind the hill, was

Au centre de la hutte, une grande pierre plate remplaçait la table absente. On y avait posé un paquet enveloppé d'étoffe — le même sans doute qu'une heure auparavant le gamin portait sur ses épaules. Il contenait un morceau de pain frais, de la langue fumée et deux petits pots de confiture.

Lorsque je le replaçai sur la pierre, après l'avoir examiné, je tressaillis à la vue d'une feuille de papier sur laquelle une main inexpérimentée avait, d'une grosse écriture, griffonné ces mots:

«Le docteur Watson est allé à Coombe Tracey.»

Pendant une minute, je demeurai immobile, ce papier à la main, me demandant ce que signifiait ce laconique message.

C'était donc moi — et non pas sir Henry — qu'espionnait l'inconnu! N'osant pas me suivre lui-même, il avait lancé quelqu'un à mes trousses — le gamin, sans doute — et j'avais son rapport sous les yeux!

Peut-être, depuis mon arrivée sur la lande, n'avais-je pas fait un pas ou dit un mot qui n'eût été observé et rapporté!

Je ressentis alors le poids d'une force invisible, d'un filet tendu autour de nous avec une adresse si surprenante et nous enserrant si légèrement, qu'il ne fallait rien moins qu'une circonstance solennelle pour deviner qu'on était enveloppé dans ses mailles.

D'autres rapports avaient dû précéder celui-ci. Je les cherchai partout. Je n'en trouvai de traces nulle part — pas plus d'ailleurs que d'indices révélateurs de la personnalité et des intentions de l'homme qui vivait dans cette retraite. De mon examen de la hutte, je ne pouvais déduire que deux choses: sa sobriété spartiate et son mépris du confort de la vie.

Songeant à la pluie torrentielle des jours précédents et regardant les pierres disjointes qui formaient son toit, je compris combien fort et inébranlable devait être le dessein qui le retenait sous un semblable abri.

Cet homme était-il un ennemi implacable ou un ange gardien?

Je me promis de ne pas quitter la hutte sans l'avoir appris.

Au dehors, le soleil empourprait l'horizon sous le flot de ses derniers rayons. Ses reflets teintaient de rouge les flaques marécageuses de la grande fondrière. Dans le lointain, pointaient les deux tours du château de Baskerville et, plus loin, un panache de fumée montant dans l'espace marquait l'emplacement du village de Grimpen. Entre the house of the Stapletons.

les deux, derrière la colline, s'élevait la maison de Stapleton.

All was sweet and mellow and peaceful in the golden evening light, and yet as I looked at them my soul shared none of the peace of Nature but quivered at the vagueness and the terror of that interview which every instant was bringing nearer.

Tout était calme, doux, paisible, dans ce glorieux crépuscule. Et cependant, tout en l'admirant, mon âme ne partageait pas la paix de la nature. J'éprouvais comme une vague terreur à la pensée de l'entrevue que chaque minute rendait plus prochaine.

With tingling nerves but a fixed purpose, I sat in the dark recess of the hut and waited with sombre patience for the coming of its tenant.

Les nerfs tendus, mais le cœur très résolu, je m'assis dans le coin le plus obscur de la hutte et j'attendis avec une impatience fébrile l'arrivée de son hôte.

And then at last I heard him.

Je l'entendis enfin venir.

Far away came the sharp clink of a boot striking upon a stone.

Je perçus le bruit d'un talon de botte sonnant sur les cailloux du chemin.

Then another and yet another, coming nearer and nearer.

Les pas se rapprochaient de plus en plus.

I shrank back into the darkest corner and cocked the pistol in my pocket, determined not to discover myself until I had an opportunity of seeing something of the stranger.

Je me blottis dans mon coin et j'armai mon revolver, déterminé à ne me montrer qu'au moment où l'inconnu aurait pénétré dans la hutte.

There was a long pause which showed that he had stopped.

Une longue pause m'apprit qu'il s'était arrêté.

Then once more the footsteps approached and a shadow fell across the opening of the hut.

Puis les pas se rapprochèrent encore et une ombre se dessina dans l'encadrement de la porte.

"It is a lovely evening, my dear Watson," said a well-known voice. "I really think that you will be more comfortable outside than in."

«Quelle belle soirée, mon cher Watson! me dit une voix bien connue. Je crois vraiment que nous serons mieux dehors que dedans».

CHAPTER 12. DEATH ON THE MOOR

For a moment or two I sat breathless, hardly able to believe my ears. Then my senses and my voice came back to me, while a crushing weight of responsibility seemed in an instant to be lifted from my soul. That cold, incisive, ironical voice could belong to but one man in all the world.

"Holmes!" I cried—"Holmes!"

"Come out," said he, "and please be careful with the revolver."

I stooped under the rude lintel, and there he sat upon a stone outside, his grey eyes dancing with amusement as they fell upon my astonished features. He was thin and worn, but clear and alert, his keen face bronzed by the sun and roughened by the wind. In his tweed suit and cloth cap he looked like any other tourist upon the moor, and he had contrived, with that catlike love of personal cleanliness which was one of his characteristics, that his chin should be as smooth and his linen as perfect as if he were in Baker Street.

"I never was more glad to see anyone in my life," said I as I wrung him by the hand.

"Or more astonished, eh?"

"Well, I must confess to it."

"The surprise was not all on one side, I assure you. I had no idea that you had found my occasional retreat, still less that you were inside it, until I was within twenty paces of the door."

"My footprint, I presume?"

"No, Watson, I fear that I could not undertake to recognize your footprint amid all the footprints of the world. If you seriously desire to deceive me you must change your tobacconist; for when

CHAPITRE 12. MORT SUR LA LANDE

Pendant une ou deux minutes, la surprise me suffoqua; j'eus toutes les peines du monde à en croire mes oreilles. Cependant je me ressaisis et, en même temps que je reprenais ma respiration, je sentis mon âme soulagée du poids de la terrible responsabilité qui l'oppressait. Cette parole froide, incisive, ironique, ne pouvait appartenir qu'à un seul homme.

«Holmes! m'écriai-je.... Holmes!

— Venez! me dit-il... et ne faites pas d'imprudence avec votre revolver.»

Je me courbai pour passer sous le linteau de la porte, et, près de la hutte, j'aperçus mon ami, assis sur une pierre. À la vue de mon visage étonné, ses yeux gris papillotèrent de joie.

Holmes paraissait amaigri, fatigué, mais toujours aussi vif et aussi alerte. Dans son complet de cheviotte, avec son chapeau de drap sur la tête, on l'aurait pris pour un simple touriste visitant la lande. Soigneux de sa personne comme un chat de sa fourrure — c'est une de ses caractéristiques — il s'était arrangé pour avoir son menton aussi finement rasé et son linge aussi irréprochable que s'il fût sorti de son cabinet de toilette de Baker street.

«Je n'ai jamais été plus heureux de voir quelqu'un, fis-je, en lui secouant les mains.

— Ni plus étonné, hein?

— Je l'avoue.

— Croyez bien que ma surprise a égalé la vôtre. Comment supposer que vous auriez retrouvé ma retraite momentanée.... Jusqu'à vingt mètres d'ici, je ne me serais pas douté que vous occupiez la hutte.

— Vous avez reconnu l'empreinte de mes pas?

— Non, Watson. Je ne me livrerais pas à une recherche aussi ardue. Seulement, si vous désirez vous cacher de moi, je vous conseille de changer de marchand de tabac. Lorsque je trouve un bout

I see the stub of a cigarette marked Bradley, Oxford Street, I know that my friend Watson is in the neighbourhood. You will see it there beside the path. You threw it down, no doubt, at that supreme moment when you charged into the empty hut."

"Exactly."

"I thought as much—and knowing your admirable tenacity I was convinced that you were sitting in ambush, a weapon within reach, waiting for the tenant to return. So you actually thought that I was the criminal?"

"I did not know who you were, but I was determined to find out."

"Excellent, Watson! And how did you localise me? You saw me, perhaps, on the night of the convict hunt, when I was so imprudent as to allow the moon to rise behind me?"

"Yes, I saw you then."

"And have no doubt searched all the huts until you came to this one?"

"No, your boy had been observed, and that gave me a guide where to look."

"The old gentleman with the telescope, no doubt. I could not make it out when first I saw the light flashing upon the lens."

He rose and peeped into the hut.

"Ha, I see that Cartwright has brought up some supplies. What's this paper? So you have been to Coombe Tracey, have you?"

"Yes."

"To see Mrs. Laura Lyons?"

"Exactly."

"Well done! Our researches have evidently been running on parallel lines, and when we unite our results I expect we shall have a fairly full knowledge of the case."

"Well, I am glad from my heart that you are here, for indeed the responsibility and the mystery were both becoming too much for my nerves. But how in the name of wonder did you come here, and what have you been doing? I thought that you were in Baker Street working out that case of blackmailing."

"That was what I wished you to think."

"Then you use me, and yet do not trust me!" I cried with some bitterness. "I think that I have deserved better at your hands, Holmes."

"My dear fellow, you have been invaluable to

de cigarette portant la marque de Bradley, Oxford Dirent, je devine que mon ami Watson n'est pas loin. Regardez, en voilà une à peu près intacte dans le sentier. Vous l'avez jetée, sans doute, au moment de faire irruption dans la hutte vide?

— Oui.

— Je l'aurais parié!... Et, connaissant votre admirable ténacité, j'étais certain de vous y trouver embusqué, une arme à portée de votre main, attendant ainsi le retour de celui qui l'habite. Vous pensiez donc qu'elle servait de refuge à un criminel?

— J'ignorais le nom de son hôte de passage, mais j'étais déterminé à découvrir son identité.

— Très bien, Watson. Mais comment aviez-vous appris la présence d'un étranger sur la lande? Peut-être m'avez-vous vu, la nuit où vous avez donné la chasse au convict — cette nuit où je fus assez imprudent pour m'exposer à la clarté de la lune?

— En effet, je vous ai vu, cette nuit-là.

— Alors, vous avez fouillé toutes les huttes, jusqu'à ce que vous soyez arrivé à celle-ci?

— Non; j'ai guetté votre jeune commissionnaire et j'ai su où venir tout droit.

— Je comprends... le vieux bonhomme au télescope!... J'aurais dû m'en méfier lorsque, pour la première fois, je vis ses lentilles étinceler aux feux du soleil.»

Holmes se leva et jeta un coup d'œil dans l'intérieur de la hutte.

«Ah! reprit-il, Cartwright m'a ravitaillé... Tiens, un papier!... Vous êtes donc allé à Coombe Tracey?

— Oui.

— Voir Mme Laura Lyons?

— Parfaitement.

— Bonne idée! Nos enquêtes suivaient une route parallèle, et, à l'heure où nous combinerons nos renseignements respectifs, nous ne serons pas loin d'avoir fait la lumière.

— Si vous saviez, mon cher Holmes, combien je suis heureux de vous retrouver ici!... Ce mystère, cette responsabilité pesaient trop lourdement sur mes pauvres nerfs. Mais pourquoi diable êtes-vous venu à Dartmoor et qu'y faisiez-vous? Je vous croyais toujours à Baker street, occupé à débrouiller cette affaire de chantage.

— J'avais intérêt à ne pas vous détromper.

— Ainsi; vous vous moquez de moi et, qui plus est, vous me refusez votre confiance! fis-je avec quelque amertume. Je méritais mieux que cela, Holmes.

— Mon cher ami, dans ce cas, comme dans

me in this as in many other cases, and I beg that you will forgive me if I have seemed to play a trick upon you. In truth, it was partly for your own sake that I did it, and it was my appreciation of the danger which you ran which led me to come down and examine the matter for myself. Had I been with Sir Henry and you it is confident that my point of view would have been the same as yours, and my presence would have warned our very formidable opponents to be on their guard. As it is, I have been able to get about as I could not possibly have done had I been living in the Hall, and I remain an unknown factor in the business, ready to throw in all my weight at a critical moment."

"But why keep me in the dark?"

"For you to know could not have helped us and might possibly have led to my discovery. You would have wished to tell me something, or in your kindness you would have brought me out some comfort or other, and so an unnecessary risk would be run. I brought Cartwright down with me—you remember the little chap at the express office—and he has seen after my simple wants: a loaf of bread and a clean collar. What does man want more? He has given me an extra pair of eyes upon a very active pair of feet, and both have been invaluable."

"Then my reports have all been wasted!"—My voice trembled as I recalled the pains and the pride with which I had composed them.

Holmes took a bundle of papers from his pocket.

"Here are your reports, my dear fellow, and very well thumbed, I assure you. I made excellent arrangements, and they are only delayed one day upon their way. I must compliment you exceedingly upon the zeal and the intelligence which you have shown over an extraordinarily difficult case."

I was still rather raw over the deception which had been practised upon me, but the warmth of Holmes's praise drove my anger from my mind. I felt also in my heart that he was right in what he said and that it was really best for our purpose that I should not have known that he was upon the moor.

"That's better," said he, seeing the shadow rise from my face. "And now tell me the result of your visit to Mrs. Laura Lyons—it was not difficult for me to guess that it was to see her that you had gone, for I am already aware that she is the one person in Coombe Tracey who might be of service

beaucoup d'autres, votre concours m'a été très utile, et je vous prie de me pardonner ce semblant de méfiance. En vérité, je ne me suis caché de vous que par souci de votre propre sécurité, et, seul, le sentiment du danger que vous couriez m'a poussé à venir examiner par moi-même la situation. Auprès de sir Henry et de vous, j'aurais partagé votre manière de voir et ma présence aurait mis en garde nos redoutables adversaires. Notre séparation, au contraire, m'a permis d'atteindre un résultat que je n'aurais pas osé espérer, si j'avais vécu au château. Je reste un facteur inconnu, prêt à se lancer dans la bagarre au moment opportun.

— Pourquoi ne pas me prévenir?

— Cela ne nous aurait été d'aucune utilité et aurait peut-être amené ma découverte. Vous auriez eu à me parler; avec le cœur compatissant que je vous connais, vous m'auriez apporté des provisions de toutes sortes, que sais-je?... Enfin nous aurions couru un risque inutile. Cartwright — le gamin de l'Express Office, vous vous rappelez? — m'avait accompagné; il a pourvu à mes besoins peu compliqués: une miche de pain et un col propre. Que faut-il de plus? Ensuite, il représentait une paire d'yeux supplémentaires, surmontant deux pieds excessivement agiles. J'ai tiré grand profit des uns et des autres.

— Mes rapports ont donc été perdus!» m'écriai-je. Au souvenir de la peine et de l'orgueil éprouvés en les rédigeant, ma voix tremblait.

Holmes tira de sa poche un paquet de papiers.

«Les voilà, vos rapports, dit-il,... lus et relus, je vous l'assure. J'avais pris toutes mes précautions pour qu'on me les réexpédiât sans retard de Baker street. Je tiens à vous féliciter du zèle et de l'intelligence que vous avez déployés dans une affaire aussi difficile.»

Je gardais encore rancune à Holmes du tour qu'il m'avait joué, mais la spontanéité et la chaleur de ses louanges dissipèrent bien vite mon ressentiment. Dans mon for intérieur, je convenais qu'il avait raison et qu'il était préférable, pour la réussite de nos projets, que sa présence sur la lande demeurât ignorée.

«Je vous aime mieux ainsi, dit mon ami, en voyant s'éclaircir mon visage rembruni. Et maintenant, racontez-moi votre visite à Mme Laura Lyons... J'ai deviné sans peine que vous alliez là-bas pour causer avec elle... Je suis convaincu qu'elle seule, à Coombe Tracey, peut nous rendre to us in the matter. In fact, if you had not gone today it is exceedingly probable that I should have gone tomorrow."

The sun had set and dusk was settling over the moor. The air had turned chill and we withdrew into the hut for warmth. There, sitting together in the twilight, I told Holmes of my conversation with the lady. So interested was he that I had to repeat some of it twice before he was satisfied.

"This is most important," said he when I had concluded. "It fills up a gap which I had been unable to bridge in this most complex affair. You are aware, perhaps, that a close intimacy exists between this lady and the man Stapleton?"

"I did not know of a close intimacy."

"There can be no doubt about the matter. They meet, they write, there is a complete understanding between them. Now, this puts a very powerful weapon into our hands. If I could only use it to detach his wife—"

"His wife?"

"I am giving you some information now, in return for all that you have given me. The lady who has passed here as Miss Stapleton is in reality his wife."

"Good heavens, Holmes! Are you sure of what you say? How could he have permitted Sir Henry to fall in love with her?"

"Sir Henry's falling in love could do no harm to anyone except Sir Henry. He took particular care that Sir Henry did not make love to her, as you have yourself observed. I repeat that the lady is his wife and not his sister."

"But why this elaborate deception?"

"Because he foresaw that she would be very much more useful to him in the character of a free woman."

All my unspoken instincts, my vague suspicions, suddenly took shape and centred upon the naturalist. In that impassive colourless man, with his straw hat and his butterfly-net, I seemed to see something terrible—a creature of infinite patience and craft, with a smiling face and a murderous heart.

"It is he, then, who is our enemy—it is he who dogged us in London?"

"So I read the riddle."

"And the warning—it must have come from her!"

quelques services. Si vous n'aviez pas tenté cette démarche aujourd'hui, moi, je l'aurais faite demain.»

Le soleil s'était couché. Peu à peu l'obscurité envahissait la lande. Le vent ayant fraîchi, nous entrâmes dans la hutte pour y chercher un abri. Là, assis dans la pénombre, je narrai à Holmes ma conversation avec la fille de Frankland; le récit l'intéressa à tel point que je dus le recommencer.

«Tout ceci est fort important, me dit Sherlock, lorsque j'eus terminé. Vous avez éliminé du problème une inconnue que j'étais incapable de dégager: peut-être savez-vous qu'il existe une grande intimité entre Mme Lyons et Stapleton?

— Je l'ignorais.

— Si, une très grande intimité. Ils se rencontrent. Ils s'écrivent; il y a entre eux une entente parfaite. C'est une arme puissante entre nos mains... Si je pouvais seulement l'utiliser pour détacher sa femme de lui...

— Sa femme? interrompis-je.

— Oui, sa femme. Je vous donne des renseignements en échange des vôtres. La dame qui passe ici pour Mlle Stapleton est en réalité la femme du naturaliste.

— Grands dieux, Holmes! Êtes-vous sûr de ce que vous dites? Comment aurait-il permis que le baronnet en devînt amoureux?

— L'amour de sir Henry ne devait nuire qu'à lui-même. Stapleton — vous en avez été témoin vous-même — ne veillait qu'à une chose: empêcher sir Henry de courtiser sa femme. Je vous répète que la dame n'est pas mademoiselle, mais bien madame Stapleton.

— Pourquoi ce mensonge?

— Son mari prévoyait qu'elle servirait mieux ses projets, si le baronnet se croyait en face d'une jeune fille à marier.»

Tous mes secrets pressentiments, tous mes vagues soupçons prirent un corps et se concentrèrent sur le naturaliste. Dans cet homme impassible, terne, avec son chapeau de paille et son filet à papillons, je découvrais maintenant quelque chose de terrible — un être infiniment patient, diaboliquement rusé, qui dissimulait une âme de meurtrier sous un visage souriant.

«Alors c'est lui qui nous a espionnés à Londres? demandai-je à Holmes. Notre ennemi, le voilà donc?

— Oui. J'explique ainsi l'énigme.

— Et la lettre d'avis? Elle émanait de sa femme?

"Exactly."

The shape of some monstrous villainy, half seen, half guessed, loomed through the darkness which had girt me so long.

"But are you sure of this, Holmes? How do you know that the woman is his wife?"

"Because he so far forgot himself as to tell you a true piece of autobiography upon the occasion when he first met you, and I dare say he has many a time regretted it since. He was once a schoolmaster in the north of England. Now, there is no one more easy to trace than a schoolmaster. There are scholastic agencies by which one may identify any man who has been in the profession. A little investigation showed me that a school had come to grief under atrocious circumstances, and that the man who had owned it—the name was different—had disappeared with his wife. The descriptions agreed. When I learned that the missing man was devoted to entomology the identification was complete."

The darkness was rising, but much was still hidden by the shadows.

"If this woman is in truth his wife, where does Mrs. Laura Lyons come in?" I asked.

"That is one of the points upon which your own researches have shed a light. Your interview with the lady has cleared the situation very much. I did not know about a projected divorce between herself and her husband. In that case, regarding Stapleton as an unmarried man, she counted no doubt upon becoming his wife."

"And when she is undeceived?"

"Why, then we may find the lady of service. It must be our first duty to see her—both of us—tomorrow. Don't you think, Watson, that you are away from your charge rather long? Your place should be at Baskerville Hall."

The last red streaks had faded away in the west and night had settled upon the moor. A few faint stars were gleaming in a violet sky.

"One last question, Holmes," I said as I rose. "Surely there is no need of secrecy between you and me. What is the meaning of it all? What is he after?"

Holmes's voice sank as he answered:

"It is murder, Watson—refined, cold-blooded,

— Parfaitement.»

Des ténèbres qui nous environnaient, je voyais poindre une monstrueuse infamie.

«Ne vous trompez-vous pas, Holmes? insistai-je. Comment avez-vous découvert qu'ils étaient mariés?

— La première fois que Stapleton vous rencontra, il eut le tort de vous confier une partie de sa véritable biographie. Depuis, il a dû regretter bien souvent ce moment de franchise... J'appris par vous qu'il avait ouvert autrefois une école dans le nord de l'Angleterre. Rien n'est plus aisé que de retrouver les traces d'un magister. Il existe des agences à l'aide desquelles on peut identifier tout homme ayant exercé cette profession. Quelques recherches me montrèrent qu'on avait supprimé une école dans d'assez vilaines circonstances... Son propriétaire — le nom différait — avait disparu ainsi que sa femme. Les signalements concordaient. Lorsque je sus que l'homme s'adonnait à l'entomologie, je ne conservai plus de doutes sur son identité.»

Le nuage se déchirait insensiblement; toutefois beaucoup de points restaient encore dans l'ombre.

Je questionnai de nouveau Sherlock Holmes.

«Si cette femme est vraiment Mme Stapleton, dis-je, que vient faire ici Mme Laura Lyons?

— Vos enquêtes ont élucidé ce point. Votre entrevue avec cette jeune femme a considérablement déblayé la situation... J'ignorais l'existence d'un projet de divorce entre son mari et elle. Si les tribunaux prononçaient la séparation, elle espérait que Stapleton, qu'elle croyait célibataire, l'épouserait.

— Qu'adviendra-t-il, lorsqu'elle connaîtra la vérité?

— Elle nous sera un précieux allié. Demain nous irons la voir ensemble... Mais ne pensez-vous pas, Watson, que vous avez abandonné votre poste depuis bien longtemps? Votre place, mon ami, est au château de Baskerville.»

Les dernières lueurs du crépuscule venaient de s'éteindre dans la direction de l'occident, et la nuit était descendue sur la lande. Quelques étoiles clignotaient sur la surface violacée du ciel.

«Une dernière question, Holmes! fis-je, en me levant. Il ne peut y avoir de secrets entre vous et moi... Que signifie tout ceci? Où Stapleton veut-il en arriver?»

Sherlock baissa la voix pour me répondre.

«À un meurtre, Watson,... à un meurtre londeliberate murder. Do not ask me for particulars. My nets are closing upon him, even as his are upon Sir Henry, and with your help he is already almost at my mercy. There is but one danger which can threaten us. It is that he should strike before we are ready to do so. Another day—two at the most—and I have my case complete, but until then guard your charge as closely as ever a fond mother watched her ailing child. Your mission today has justified itself, and yet I could almost wish that you had not left his side. Hark!"

A terrible scream—a prolonged yell of horror and anguish—burst out of the silence of the moor. That frightful cry turned the blood to ice in my veins.

"Oh, my God!" I gasped. "What is it? What does it mean?"

Holmes had sprung to his feet, and I saw his dark, athletic outline at the door of the hut, his shoulders stooping, his head thrust forward, his face peering into the darkness.

"Hush!" he whispered. "Hush!"

The cry had been loud on account of its vehemence, but it had pealed out from somewhere far off on the shadowy plain. Now it burst upon our ears, nearer, louder, more urgent than before.

"Where is it?" Holmes whispered; and I knew from the thrill of his voice that he, the man of iron, was shaken to the soul. "Where is it, Watson?"

"There, I think." I pointed into the darkness.

"No, there!"

Again the agonised cry swept through the silent night, louder and much nearer than ever.

And a new sound mingled with it, a deep, muttered rumble, musical and yet menacing, rising and falling like the low, constant murmur of the sea.

"The hound!" cried Holmes. "Come, Watson, come! Great heavens, if we are too late!"

He had started running swiftly over the moor, and I had followed at his heels.

But now from somewhere among the broken ground immediately in front of us there came one last despairing yell, and then a dull, heavy thud. We halted and listened.

Not another sound broke the heavy silence of the windless night.

guement prémédité, froidement exécuté avec d'odieux raffinements. Ne me demandez pas de détails. Mes filets se resserrent autour du meurtrier — autant que les siens autour de sir Henry — et, grâce à votre appui, je le sens déjà à ma merci. Un seul danger nous menace: c'est qu'il frappe avant que nous soyons prêts à frapper nous-mêmes. Encore un jour — deux au plus — et j'aurai réuni toutes mes preuves. Jusque-là veillez sur le baronnet avec la sollicitude d'une tendre mère pour son enfant malade. Votre sortie d'aujourd'hui s'imposait, et cependant je souhaiterais que vous n'eussiez pas quitté sir Henry... Écoutez!»

Un cri perçant, cri d'horreur et d'angoisse, éclata dans le silence de la lande et nous glaça le sang.

«Oh! mon Dieu! balbutiai-je. Que se passe-t-il? Pourquoi ce cri?»

Holmes s'était dressé vivement. Sa silhouette athlétique se profilait dans l'encadrement de la porte, les épaules voûtées, la tête penchée en avant, ses yeux fouillant l'épaisseur des ténèbres.

«Silence! dit-il tout bas... Silence!»

Ce cri n'était parvenu jusqu'à nous qu'en raison de sa violence. Tout d'abord il avait surgi des profondeurs lointaines de la lande. Maintenant il se rapprochait, plus fort et plus pressant que jamais.

«Où est-ce? reprit Holmes, en sourdine. Où est-ce, Watson?»

Au tremblement de sa voix, je reconnus que cet homme d'airain était remué jusqu'au fond de l'âme.

J'indiquai un point dans la nuit.

«Là, répondis-je.

— Non, là», rectifia Holmes.

Une fois encore, ce cri, toujours plus proche et plus strident, passa sur la lande.

Il s'y mêlait un nouveau son, un grondement profond, rythmé quoique menaçant, qui s'élevait et s'abaissait, semblable au murmure continu de la mer.

«Le chien! s'écria Holmes. Venez, Watson, venez vite! Pourvu que nous n'arrivions pas trop tard!»

Mon ami partit comme une flèche; je courais sur ses talons.

D'un endroit quelconque de ce sol tourmenté, en avant de nous, monta un dernier appel désespéré, suivi du bruit sourd que fait un corps en s'abattant comme une masse.

Nul autre bruit ne troubla plus le calme de cette nuit sans vent.

I saw Holmes put his hand to his forehead like a man distracted. He stamped his feet upon the ground.

"He has beaten us, Watson. We are too late."

"No, no, surely not!"

"Fool that I was to hold my hand. And you, Watson, see what comes of abandoning your charge! But, by Heaven, if the worst has happened we'll avenge him!"

Blindly we ran through the gloom, blundering against boulders, forcing our way through gorse bushes, panting up hills and rushing down slopes, heading always in the direction whence those dreadful sounds had come.

At every rise Holmes looked eagerly round him, but the shadows were thick upon the moor, and nothing moved upon its dreary face.

"Can you see anything?"

"Nothing."

"But, hark, what is that?"

A low moan had fallen upon our ears. There it was again upon our left! On that side a ridge of rocks ended in a sheer cliff which overlooked a stone-strewn slope. On its jagged face was spread-eagled some dark, irregular object. As we ran towards it the vague outline hardened into a definite shape.

It was a prostrate man face downward upon the ground, the head doubled under him at a horrible angle, the shoulders rounded and the body hunched together as if in the act of throwing a somersault. So grotesque was the attitude that I could not for the instant realise that that moan had been the passing of his soul. Not a whisper, not a rustle, rose now from the dark figure over which we stooped.

Holmes laid his hand upon him and held it up again with an exclamation of horror. The gleam of the match which he struck shone upon his clotted fingers and upon the ghastly pool which widened slowly from the crushed skull of the victim.

Je vis Holmes porter la main à son front, comme un homme affolé. Il frappait du pied avec impatience.

«Ce Stapleton nous a vaincus, dit-il. Nous arriverons trop tard.

— Non, non! répondis-je,… sûrement non!

— J'ai été assez insensé pour ne pas lui mettre la main au collet!… Et vous, Watson, voyez ce que nous coûte votre sortie du château! Mais par Dieu! si sir Henry est mort, nous le vengerons!»

En aveugles, nous marchions dans l'obscurité, trébuchant contre les quartiers de roches, escaladant les collines, dégringolant les pentes, dans la direction des appels déchirants que nous avions entendus.

Du haut de chaque sommet, Holmes regardait avidement autour de lui; mais l'ombre était épaisse sur la lande et rien ne bougeait sur cette immense solitude.

Holmes me demanda:

«Apercevez-vous quelque chose, Watson?

— Non, rien.

— Écoutez!

Sur notre gauche, on avait poussé un faible gémissement. De ce côté, une ligne de rochers formait une sorte de falaise, surplombant un escarpement parsemé de grosses pierres. Au bas, nous distinguâmes vaguement quelque chose de noir et d'informe.

La face contre terre, un homme gisait sur le sol, la tête repliée sous lui, suivant un angle horrible à voir, les épaules remontées et le corps en boule, dans le mouvement de quelqu'un qui va exécuter un saut périlleux. L'attitude était si grotesque que, sur le moment, je ne pus admettre que le gémissement qui avait appelé notre attention fût un râle d'agonie. Pas une plainte, pas un souffle ne sortait de cette masse noire sur laquelle nous étions penchés.

Holmes promena sa main sur ce corps inerte, mais il la retira aussitôt avec une exclamation d'horreur. Je frottai une allumette et je vis que ses doigts étaient ensanglantés… Un filet de sang suintait du crâne de la victime.

And it shone upon something else which turned our hearts sick and faint within us—the body of Sir Henry Baskerville!

There was no chance of either of us forgetting that peculiar ruddy tweed suit—the very one which he had worn on the first morning that we had seen him in Baker Street.

We caught the one clear glimpse of it, and then the match flickered and went out, even as the hope had gone out of our souls.

Holmes groaned, and his face glimmered white through the darkness.

"The brute! The brute!" I cried with clenched hands. "Oh Holmes, I shall never forgive myself for having left him to his fate."

"I am more to blame than you, Watson. In order to have my case well rounded and complete, I have thrown away the life of my client. It is the greatest blow which has befallen me in my career. But how could I know—how could I know—that he would risk his life alone upon the moor in the face of all my warnings?"

"That we should have heard his screams—my God, those screams!—and yet have been unable to save him! Where is this brute of a hound which drove him to his death? It may be lurking among these rocks at this instant. And Stapleton, where is he? He shall answer for this deed."

"He shall. I will see to that. Uncle and nephew have been murdered—the one frightened to death by the very sight of a beast which he thought to be supernatural, the other driven to his end in his wild flight to escape from it. But now we have to prove the connection between the man and the beast. Save from what we heard, we cannot even swear to the existence of the latter, since Sir Henry has evidently died from the fall. But, by heavens, cunning as he is, the fellow shall be in my power before another day is past!"

We stood with bitter hearts on either side of the mangled body, overwhelmed by this sudden and irrevocable disaster which had brought all our long and weary labours to so piteous an end.

Then as the moon rose we climbed to the top of the rocks over which our poor friend had fallen, and from the summit we gazed out over the shadowy moor, half silver and half gloom.

Far away, miles off, in the direction of Grimp-

L'allumette nous permit de voir autre chose encore: le corps de sir Henry Baskerville. — Nous faillîmes nous évanouir.

Nous ne pouvions pas ne pas reconnaître ce burlesque complet de cheviotte rougeâtre — celui que le baronnet portait le matin où il se présenta pour la première fois à Baker street.

Nous l'aperçûmes l'espace d'une seconde, au moment où l'allumette jeta une dernière clarté avant de s'éteindre — de même que s'éteignait en nos âmes notre suprême lueur d'espoir.

Holmes soupira profondément, et, malgré l'obscurité, je le vis pâlir.

«La brute! Oh! la brute! m'écriai-je, les mains crispées. Je ne me pardonnerai jamais d'avoir causé ce malheur.

— Je suis tout autant à blâmer que vous, Watson... Pour satisfaire mon amour-propre professionnel, pour réunir un faisceau de preuves irréfutables, j'ai laissé tuer mon client!... C'est le plus gros échec de toute ma carrière... Mais comment pouvais-je prévoir que, malgré mes avis réitérés, sir Henry s'aventurerait seul sur la lande!... Oui, comment pouvais-je le prévoir?

— Dire que nous avons entendu ses appels — et quels appels, mon Dieu! — et qu'il nous a été impossible de le sauver! Où est ce chien qui l'a tué? Il doit errer parmi ces roches... Et Stapleton? Où se cache-t-il? Il le payera cher, ce meurtre!

— Oui, mais ce soin me regarde, répondit Holmes avec énergie. L'oncle et le neveu sont morts, le premier, de la frayeur ressentie à la vue d'un animal qu'il croyait surnaturel; le second, d'une chute faite en voulant échapper à la bête. Il ne nous reste plus qu'à prouver la complicité de l'homme et du chien. Malheureusement, nous ne pouvons affirmer l'existence de ce dernier que pour l'avoir entendu aboyer, car sir Henry est évidemment mort à la suite de sa chute. Mais, quelque rusé que soit Stapleton, je jure bien que je le tiendrai en mon pouvoir avant la nuit prochaine.»

Le cœur serré, abattus par l'épouvantable accident qui terminait si brusquement notre longue et ingrate mission, nous nous tenions chacun d'un côté de ce cadavre.

La lune se levait. Nous gravîmes le sommet des roches du haut desquels cet infortuné sir Henry était tombé et, de ce point culminant, nous promenâmes nos regards sur la lande, irrégulièrement illuminée par les pâles rayons de l'astre de la nuit.

Dans le lointain, à plusieurs milles de distance,

en, a single steady yellow light was shining. It could only come from the lonely abode of the Stapletons. With a bitter curse I shook my fist at it as I gazed.

"Why should we not seize him at once?"

"Our case is not complete. The fellow is wary and cunning to the last degree. It is not what we know, but what we can prove. If we make one false move the villain may escape us yet."

"What can we do?"

"There will be plenty for us to do tomorrow. Tonight we can only perform the last offices to our poor friend."

Together we made our way down the precipitous slope and approached the body, black and clear against the silvered stones. The agony of those contorted limbs struck me with a spasm of pain and blurred my eyes with tears.

"We must send for help, Holmes! We cannot carry him all the way to the Hall. Good heavens, are you mad?"

He had uttered a cry and bent over the body. Now he was dancing and laughing and wringing my hand. Could this be my stern, self-contained friend? These were hidden fires, indeed!

"A beard! A beard! The man has a beard!"

"A beard?"

"It is not the baronet—it is—why, it is my neighbour, the convict!"

With feverish haste we had turned the body over, and that dripping beard was pointing up to the cold, clear moon.

There could be no doubt about the beetling forehead, the sunken animal eyes. It was indeed the same face which had glared upon me in the light of the candle from over the rock—the face of Selden, the criminal.

Then in an instant it was all clear to me. I remembered how the baronet had told me that he had handed his old wardrobe to Barrymore. Barrymore had passed it on in order to help Selden in his escape. Boots, shirt, cap—it was all Sir Henry's.

The tragedy was still black enough, but this man had at least deserved death by the laws of his country.

I told Holmes how the matter stood, my heart bubbling over with thankfulness and joy.

brillait, dans la direction de Grimpen, une petite lumière jaune. Elle ne pouvait venir que de la demeure isolée de Stapleton. Je me tournai vers elle et, montrant le poing dans un geste de menace:

«Pourquoi n'avons-nous pas arrêté cet homme? dis-je à Sherlock Holmes.

— Les preuves suffisantes nous manquent. Le coquin est habile et rusé au suprême degré. En justice, il ne faut pas se contenter de savoir, il faut encore prouver. À la première fausse manœuvre, le drôle nous aurait échappé certainement.

— Alors qu'allons-nous faire?

— La journée de demain sera bien remplie. Pour cette nuit, bornons-nous à rendre les derniers devoirs à notre pauvre ami.»

Nous nous rapprochâmes du cadavre de sir Henry. J'eus un accès de douleur à la vue de ces membres tordus par les dernières convulsions de l'agonie, et mes yeux se remplirent de larmes.

Holmes avait poussé un cri et s'était penché sur le cadavre. Il riait, il dansait, en se frottant les mains. Était-ce bien là mon compagnon, si flegmatique, si maître de lui?

«Une barbe! une barbe! s'écria-t-il. Cet homme a une barbe!

— Une barbe? répétai-je, de plus en plus étonné.

— Ce n'est pas le baronnet… c'est… oui, c'est mon voisin le convict!»

Fiévreusement, nous retournâmes le cadavre en le plaçant sur le dos. Une barbe, raidie par le sang coagulé, dressa sa pointe vers le ciel.

Impossible de se méprendre sur ce front proéminent ni sur ces yeux caves. Je reconnus le visage aperçu quelques jours auparavant au-dessus de la bougie placée dans une anfractuosité de roche — le visage de Selden l'assassin.

La lumière se fit aussitôt dans mon esprit. Je me souvins que le baronnet avait donné ses vieux effets à Barrymore. Celui-ci les avait remis à son beau-frère pour l'aider à fuir. Bottines, chemise, chapeau, tout avait appartenu à sir Henry.

Certes, cet homme avait trouvé la mort dans des circonstances particulièrement tragiques, mais les juges ne l'avaient-ils pas déjà condamné?

Le cœur transporté d'allégresse, je racontai à Holmes que le baronnet avait fait cadeau de sa vieille garde-robe à son valet de chambre.

"Then the clothes have been the poor devil's death," said he. "It is clear enough that the hound has been laid on from some article of Sir Henry's—the boot which was abstracted in the hotel, in all probability—and so ran this man down. There is one very singular thing, however: How came Selden, in the darkness, to know that the hound was on his trail?"

"He heard him."

"To hear a hound upon the moor would not work a hard man like this convict into such a paroxysm of terror that he would risk recapture by screaming wildly for help. By his cries he must have run a long way after he knew the animal was on his track. How did he know?"

"A greater mystery to me is why this hound, presuming that all our conjectures are correct—"

"I presume nothing."

"Well, then, why this hound should be loose tonight. I suppose that it does not always run loose upon the moor. Stapleton would not let it go unless he had reason to think that Sir Henry would be there."

"My difficulty is the more formidable of the two, for I think that we shall very shortly get an explanation of yours, while mine may remain forever a mystery. The question now is, what shall we do with this poor wretch's body? We cannot leave it here to the foxes and the ravens."

"I suggest that we put it in one of the huts until we can communicate with the police."

"Exactly. I have no doubt that you and I could carry it so far. Halloa, Watson, what's this? It's the man himself, by all that's wonderful and audacious! Not a word to show your suspicions—not a word, or my plans crumble to the ground."

A figure was approaching us over the moor, and I saw the dull red glow of a cigar. The moon shone upon him, and I could distinguish the dapper shape and jaunty walk of the naturalist.

He stopped when he saw us, and then came on again.

"Why, Dr. Watson, that's not you, is it? You are the last man that I should have expected to see out on the moor at this time of night. But, dear me, what's this? Somebody hurt? Not—don't tell me that it is our friend Sir Henry!"

«Ces vêtements ont occasionné la mort de ce pauvre diable, me répondit Sherlock. Pour dresser son chien, Stapleton s'est servi d'un objet soustrait à sir Henry — probablement de la bottine volée à l'hôtel — et la bête a poursuivi Selden. Une chose cependant me paraît inexplicable. Comment, dans les ténèbres, le convict a-t-il su que le chien lui donnait la chasse?

— Il l'a entendu probablement.

— Parce qu'un chien aboie sur la lande, un homme de la rudesse de Selden ne s'expose pas, en criant comme un forcené, au risque d'une arrestation. Il devait être arrivé au paroxysme de la terreur. D'ailleurs, de la durée de ses appels, je puis conclure qu'il a couru longtemps devant le chien et à une assez grande distance de lui. Comment savait-il que l'animal avait pris sa piste?

— En supposant que nos conjectures soient vraies, je trouve plus inexplicable encore…

— Je ne suppose rien, interrompit Sherlock Holmes.

— Alors, ripostai-je, pourquoi aurait-on lâché ce chien sur la lande, cette nuit? Je ne présume pas qu'on le laisse continuellement vagabonder. Stapleton l'aura mis en liberté parce qu'il avait de bonnes misons de croire que sir Henry sortirait ce soir.

— Il est plus difficile de répondre à mes points d'interrogation qu'aux vôtres. Nous serons bientôt fixés sur ce qui vous préoccupe, tandis que les questions que je me pose demeureront éternellement un mystère pour nous… En attendant, nous voilà bien embarrassés de ce cadavre. Nous ne pouvons l'abandonner en pâture aux vautours et aux renards.

— Je propose de le placer dans une de ces huttes, jusqu'à ce que nous ayons prévenu la police.

— Accepté, dit Holmes. À nous deux, nous l'y porterons facilement… Mais qui vient là, Watson?… C'est Stapleton lui-même! Quelle audace! Pas un mot qui donne l'éveil… pas un mot, sinon toutes mes combinaisons s'effondreront.»

Sur la lande, une forme indécise s'avançait vers nous; je distinguais le cercle rouge d'un cigare allumé. Sous la lumière incertaine de la lune, je reconnus la démarche saccadée du naturaliste.

À notre vue, il s'arrêta; puis, presque aussitôt, il continua son chemin.

«Hé quoi, docteur Watson, vous ici? fit-il. Vous êtes le dernier homme que je comptais rencontrer à cette heure sur la lande. Mais que vois-je? Un blessé! Ce n'est pas?… Dites-moi vite que ce n'est pas sir Henry!»

He hurried past me and stooped over the dead man. I heard a sharp intake of his breath and the cigar fell from his fingers.

"Who—who's this?" he stammered.

"It is Selden, the man who escaped from Princetown."

Stapleton turned a ghastly face upon us, but by a supreme effort he had overcome his amazement and his disappointment. He looked sharply from Holmes to me.

"Dear me! What a very shocking affair! How did he die?"

"He appears to have broken his neck by falling over these rocks. My friend and I were strolling on the moor when we heard a cry."

"I heard a cry also. That was what brought me out. I was uneasy about Sir Henry."

"Why about Sir Henry in particular?" I could not help asking.

"Because I had suggested that he should come over. When he did not come I was surprised, and I naturally became alarmed for his safety when I heard cries upon the moor. By the way"—his eyes darted again from my face to Holmes's—"did you hear anything else besides a cry?"

"No," said Holmes; "did you?"

"No."

"What do you mean, then?"

"Oh, you know the stories that the peasants tell about a phantom hound, and so on. It is said to be heard at night upon the moor. I was wondering if there were any evidence of such a sound tonight."

"We heard nothing of the kind," said I.

"And what is your theory of this poor fellow's death?"

"I have no doubt that anxiety and exposure

Il passa rapidement devant moi et se baissa pour regarder le cadavre. Je l'entendis aspirer l'air profondément; en même temps son cigare s'échappa de ses doigts.

«Quel est cet homme? bégaya-t-il.

— Selden, le prisonnier évadé de la prison de Princetown.»

Stapleton tourna vers nous un visage hagard. Par un suprême effort, il refoula au fond de son être son désappointement et sa stupeur. Ses regards se portaient alternativement sur Holmes et sur moi.

«Quelle déplorable aventure!» reprit-il enfin.

Et s'adressant plus particulièrement à moi, il ajouta: «De quoi est-il mort?

— Nous croyons, répondis-je, qu'il se sera cassé la tête en tombant de ces rochers. Nous nous promenions sur la lande mon ami et moi, lorsque nous avons entendu des cris.

— Moi aussi… Je ne suis même accouru que pour cela. J'avais des inquiétudes au sujet de sir Henry.»

Je ne pus m'empêcher de demander: «Pourquoi plutôt au sujet de sir Henry que de toute autre personne?

— Je l'avais invité à passer la soirée chez nous. J'étais fort surpris qu'il ne fût pas venu et, naturellement, en entendant crier, j'ai redouté quelque malheur… Auriez-vous par hasard entendu autre chose?»

Bien que Stapleton eût prononcé négligemment cette dernière phrase il nous couvait des yeux tout en parlant.

«Non,… n'est-ce pas, Watson? répliqua Holmes. Non.

— Mais pourquoi cette question? interrogea mon ami d'un air innocent.

— Vous connaissez les sottes histoires que racontent les paysans sur un chien-fantôme… On prétend qu'il hurle parfois la nuit sur la lande… Je me demandais si, par hasard, cet étrange bruit n'aurait pas retenti ce soir.

— Pas que je sache, répondis-je.

— Quel est votre avis sur l'accident survenu à ce pauvre diable? continua Stapleton.

— Les transes perpétuelles dans lesquelles il

have driven him off his head. He has rushed about the moor in a crazy state and eventually fallen over here and broken his neck."

"That seems the most reasonable theory," said Stapleton, and he gave a sigh which I took to indicate his relief. "What do you think about it, Mr. Sherlock Holmes?"

My friend bowed his compliments.

"You are quick at identification," said he.

"We have been expecting you in these parts since Dr. Watson came down. You are in time to see a tragedy."

"Yes, indeed. I have no doubt that my friend's explanation will cover the facts. I will take an unpleasant remembrance back to London with me tomorrow."

"Oh, you return tomorrow?"

"That is my intention."

"I hope your visit has cast some light upon those occurrences which have puzzled us?"

Holmes shrugged his shoulders.

"One cannot always have the success for which one hopes. An investigator needs facts and not legends or rumours. It has not been a satisfactory case."

My friend spoke in his frankest and most unconcerned manner. Stapleton still looked hard at him. Then he turned to me.

"I would suggest carrying this poor fellow to my house, but it would give my sister such a fright that I do not feel justified in doing it. I think that if we put something over his face he will be safe until morning."

And so it was arranged. Resisting Stapleton's offer of hospitality, Holmes and I set off to Baskerville Hall, leaving the naturalist to return alone. Looking back we saw the figure moving slowly away over the broad moor, and behind him that one black smudge on the silvered slope which showed where the man was lying who had come so horribly to his end.

"We're at close grips at last," said Holmes as we walked together across the moor. "What a nerve the fellow has! How he pulled himself together in the face of what must have been a paralyzing shock when he found that the wrong man had fallen a victim to his plot. I told you in London, Watson,

vivait et les privations auxquelles l'exposait son genre de vie ont probablement ébranlé sa raison. Dans un accès de folie, il s'est mis à courir sur le plateau et, en tombant du haut de ces roches, il se sera fracturé le crâne.

— Cela me paraît très vraisemblable, approuva Stapleton, avec un soupir qui témoignait d'un soulagement interne. Et vous, monsieur Holmes, quel est votre avis?»

Mon ami esquissa un vague salut.

«Je trouve, dit-il, que vous acceptez bien facilement les solutions.

— Depuis la venue du docteur Watson, reprit le naturaliste, nous vous attendions tous les jours... Vous arrivez pour assister à un drame.

— Oui. Demain, en retournant à Londres, j'emporterai avec moi un pénible souvenir.

— Vous repartez demain?

— J'en ai l'intention.

— Je souhaite que votre visite ait fait un peu de lumière sur ces événements qui troublent la contrée.»

Holmes haussa les épaules;

«On ne cueille pas toujours autant de lauriers que l'on croit, fit-il. Pour dégager la vérité, il faut des faits et non des légendes ou des rumeurs. J'ai complètement échoué dans ma mission.»

Mon ami parlait sur un ton de franchise et d'indifférence parfaitement joué. Cependant Stapleton ne le perdait pas des yeux. Il se retourna vers moi, en disant:

«Je voudrais bien transporter chez moi le cadavre de ce malheureux, mais je crains d'effrayer ma sœur. Recouvrons-lui le visage... Il restera ainsi sans danger jusqu'à demain matin.»

Nous fîmes ce que conseillait Stapleton. Puis, malgré son insistance pour nous emmener à Merripit house, Holmes et moi nous reprîmes le chemin de Baskerville, laissant le naturaliste rentrer seul chez lui. En nous retournant nous vîmes sa silhouette s'éloigner lentement à travers l'immensité de la lande.

«Nous touchons au moment critique, me dit Sherlock, tandis que nous marchions silencieusement. Cet homme est joliment fort! Au lieu de sir Henry, c'est Selden qui tombe victime de ses machinations... Avez-vous remarqué comment il a supporté ce coup, qui en aurait paralysé bien and I tell you now again, that we have never had a foeman more worthy of our steel."

"I am sorry that he has seen you."

"And so was I at first. But there was no getting out of it."

"What effect do you think it will have upon his plans now that he knows you are here?"

"It may cause him to be more cautious, or it may drive him to desperate measures at once. Like most clever criminals, he may be too confident in his own cleverness and imagine that he has completely deceived us."

"Why should we not arrest him at once?"

"My dear Watson, you were born to be a man of action. Your instinct is always to do something energetic. But supposing, for argument's sake, that we had him arrested tonight, what on earth the better off should we be for that? We could prove nothing against him. There's the devilish cunning of it! If he were acting through a human agent we could get some evidence, but if we were to drag this great dog to the light of day it would not help us in putting a rope round the neck of its master."

"Surely we have a case."

"Not a shadow of one—only surmise and conjecture. We should be laughed out of court if we came with such a story and such evidence."

"There is Sir Charles's death."

"Found dead without a mark upon him. You and I know that he died of sheer fright, and we know also what frightened him, but how are we to get twelve stolid jurymen to know it? What signs are there of a hound? Where are the marks of its fangs? Of course we know that a hound does not bite a dead body and that Sir Charles was dead before ever the brute overtook him. But we have to prove all this, and we are not in a position to do it."

"Well, then, tonight?"

"We are not much better off tonight. Again, there was no direct connection between the hound and the man's death. We never saw the hound. We heard it, but we could not prove that it was running upon this man's trail. There is a complete absence of motive. No, my dear fellow; we must reconcile ourselves to the fact that we have no case at present, and that it is worth our while to run any risk in order to establish one."

d'autres. Je vous l'ai dit à Londres, Watson, et je vous le répète ici, nous n'avons jamais eu à combattre d'ennemi plus digne de nous.

— Je regrette qu'il vous ait vu.

— Je le regrettais aussi, tout d'abord. Mais il n'y avait pas moyen d'éviter cette rencontre.

— Pensez-vous que votre présence au château modifie ses plans? demandai-je.

— Elle peut le rendre plus prudent ou, au contraire, le pousser à la témérité. Comme la plupart des criminels habiles, il est capable de trop compter sur son habileté et de croire qu'il nous a dupés.

— Pourquoi ne l'avons-nous pas arrêté?

— Mon cher Watson, vous êtes un homme d'action, vous! Votre tempérament vous porte aux actes d'énergie. Mais supposons, par exemple, que nous l'ayons arrêté tout à l'heure, qu'en serait-il résulté de bon pour nous? Quelles preuves fournirions-nous contre lui? C'est en cela qu'il est rusé comme un démon. Si nous tenions un complice qui fût en mesure de déposer devant les juges, passe encore! J'admets même que nous nous emparions de ce chien... Il ne constituerait pas une preuve suffisante pour qu'on nouât une corde autour du cou de son maître.

— Il y a la mort de sir Charles.

— L'examen de son cadavre n'a révélé aucune trace de blessure. Vous et moi, nous savons qu'une frayeur l'a tué et nous connaissons la cause de cette frayeur. Mais comment faire pénétrer cette certitude dans le cœur de douze jurés imbéciles? Comment prouver l'intervention du chien? Où est la marque de ses crocs? D'ailleurs, un chien ne mord jamais un cadavre, et sir Charles était trépassé, lorsque l'animal l'atteignit. Nous devrions établir tout cela, vous dis-je, et nous sommes loin de pouvoir le faire.

— Et le drame de cette nuit?

— Il ne nous a rien apporté de concluant. Quelle relation directe existe-t-il entre le chien et la mort de Selden? Avons-nous vu la bête?

— Non; mais nous l'avons entendue.

— Je vous l'accorde. Prouvez-moi qu'elle poursuivait le convict... Pour quelle raison, cette poursuite? Moi, je n'en trouve pas... Non, mon cher Watson, il faut nous résigner à la pensée que nous ne pouvons formuler aucune accusation précise et nous efforcer de recueillir des preuves indiscutables.

"And how do you propose to do so?"

"I have great hopes of what Mrs. Laura Lyons may do for us when the position of affairs is made clear to her. And I have my own plan as well. Sufficient for tomorrow is the evil thereof; but I hope before the day is past to have the upper hand at last."

I could draw nothing further from him, and he walked, lost in thought, as far as the Baskerville gates.

"Are you coming up?"

"Yes; I see no reason for further concealment. But one last word, Watson. Say nothing of the hound to Sir Henry. Let him think that Selden's death was as Stapleton would have us believe. He will have a better nerve for the ordeal which he will have to undergo tomorrow, when he is engaged, if I remember your report aright, to dine with these people."

"And so am I."

"Then you must excuse yourself and he must go alone. That will be easily arranged. And now, if we are too late for dinner, I think that we are both ready for our suppers."

— Comment y arriver?

— Par Mme Laura Lyons. Lorsque nous l'aurons renseignée sur le compte de Stapleton, elle nous sera d'un grand secours. J'ai mes plans, moi aussi!... Attendons-nous à de graves événements pour la journée de demain... Toutefois, avant vingt-quatre heures, j'espère bien avoir définitivement le dessus.»

Holmes borna là ses confidences. Il continua à marcher, perdu dans ses réflexions, jusqu'à la porte du château de Baskerville.

«Entrez-vous? lui demandai-je,

— Pourquoi pas? Je n'ai plus de raisons de me cacher... Encore un mot, Watson. Ne parlez pas du chien à sir Henry... Qu'il pense de la mort de Selden ce que Stapleton voulait que nous crussions nous-mêmes! Il n'en sera que plus dispos pour l'épreuve qu'il subira demain. Vous m'avez dit qu'il est invité à dîner à Merripit house?

— Je le suis également.

— Vous vous excuserez... Sir Henry doit seul accepter l'invitation. Nous inventerons un bon prétexte à votre absence. Et maintenant allons prier le baronnet de nous donner à souper.»

CHAPTER 13. FIXING THE NETS

Sir Henry was more pleased than surprised to see Sherlock Holmes, for he had for some days been expecting that recent events would bring him down from London. He did raise his eyebrows, however, when he found that my friend had neither any luggage nor any explanations for its absence.

Between us we soon supplied his wants, and then over a belated supper we explained to the baronet as much of our experience as it seemed desirable that he should know.

But first I had the unpleasant duty of breaking the news to Barrymore and his wife. To him it may have been an unmitigated relief, but she wept bitterly in her apron. To all the world he was the man of violence, half animal and half demon; but to her he always remained the little wilful boy of her own girlhood, the child who had clung to her hand. Evil indeed is the man who has not one woman to mourn him.

"I've been moping in the house all day since Watson went off in the morning," said the baronet. "I guess I should have some credit, for I have kept my promise. If I hadn't sworn not to go about alone I might have had a more lively evening, for I had a message from Stapleton asking me over there."

"I have no doubt that you would have had a more lively evening," said Holmes drily. "By the way, I don't suppose you appreciate that we have been mourning over you as having broken your neck?"

Sir Henry opened his eyes.

"How was that?"

"This poor wretch was dressed in your clothes. I fear your servant who gave them to him may get into trouble with the police."

"That is unlikely. There was no mark on any of them, as far as I know."

"That's lucky for him—in fact, it's lucky for all of you, since you are all on the wrong side of the law in this matter. I am not sure that as a con-

CHAPITRE 13. FILETS TENDUS

En raison des derniers événements, sir Henry attendait depuis quelques jours l'arrivée de Sherlock Holmes. Aussi se montra-t-il plus satisfait que surpris de le voir. Toutefois il ouvrit de grands yeux en s'apercevant que mon ami n'avait pas de bagages et ne lui donnait aucune explication sur cette absence de valise.

Nous procurâmes à Sherlock tout ce dont il pouvait avoir besoin et, après un dîner servi bien longtemps après l'heure accoutumée, nous apprîmes au baronnet ce qu'il nous importait qu'il connût de mon aventure.

Auparavant, j'avais eu la corvée de raconter à Barrymore et à sa femme la mort de Selden. Cette nouvelle causa au valet de chambre un soulagement sans égal; mais Mme Barrymore porta son tablier à ses yeux et pleura amèrement. Pour tout le monde, le convict était un être violent, moitié brute et moitié démon; pour elle, il demeurait toujours l'enfant volontaire qui s'attachait à ses jupes, à l'époque où elle était jeune fille.

«J'ai erré tristement dans la maison depuis le départ matinal de Watson, dit le baronnet. Je mérite des compliments pour la façon dont j'ai tenu ma promesse. Si je ne vous avais pas juré de ne pas sortir seul, j'aurais pu passer une meilleure soirée… Les Stapleton m'avaient prié d'aller dîner chez eux.

— Je suis certain que vous auriez passé une meilleure soirée, répondit Holmes sèchement. En tout cas, vous n'avez pas l'air de vous douter que nous avons pleuré votre mort.»

Sir Henry releva la tête.

«Comment cela? demanda-t-il.

— Ce pauvre diable de Selden portait des vêtements qui vous avaient appartenu. Je crains fort que votre domestique, de qui il les tenait, n'ait maille à partir avec la police.

— C'est impossible. Autant qu'il m'en souvienne, ces vêtements n'étaient pas marqués à mon chiffre.

— Tant mieux pour Barrymore… et pour vous aussi, car, tous, dans cette affaire, vous avez agi contre les prescriptions de la loi. Je me demande scientious detective my first duty is not to arrest the whole household. Watson's reports are most incriminating documents."

"But how about the case?" asked the baronet. "Have you made anything out of the tangle? I don't know that Watson and I are much the wiser since we came down."

"I think that I shall be in a position to make the situation rather more clear to you before long. It has been an exceedingly difficult and most complicated business. There are several points upon which we still want light—but it is coming all the same."

"We've had one experience, as Watson has no doubt told you. We heard the hound on the moor, so I can swear that it is not all empty superstition. I had something to do with dogs when I was out West, and I know one when I hear one. If you can muzzle that one and put him on a chain I'll be ready to swear you are the greatest detective of all time."

"I think I will muzzle him and chain him all right if you will give me your help."

"Whatever you tell me to do I will do."

"Very good; and I will ask you also to do it blindly, without always asking the reason."

"Just as you like."

"If you will do this I think the chances are that our little problem will soon be solved. I have no doubt—"

He stopped suddenly and stared fixedly up over my head into the air.

The lamp beat upon his face, and so intent was it and so still that it might have been that of a clear-cut classical statue, a personification of alertness and expectation.

"What is it?" we both cried.

I could see as he looked down that he was repressing some internal emotion. His features were still composed, but his eyes shone with amused exultation.

"Excuse the admiration of a connoisseur," said he as he waved his hand towards the line of portraits which covered the opposite wall. "Watson

même si, en ma qualité de détective consciencieux, mon premier devoir ne serait pas d'arrêter toute la maisonnée… Les rapports de Watson vous accablent…

— Faites!» dit le baronnet en riant.

Puis, redevenant sérieux, il ajouta:

«Quoi de neuf, à propos de votre affaire? Avez-vous un peu débrouillé l'écheveau? Je ne crois pas que, depuis votre arrivée ici, nous ayons fait un pas en avant, Watson et moi.

— Avant qu'il soit longtemps, j'espère avoir déblayé le terrain et rendu votre situation sensiblement plus claire. Tout cela est très difficile, très compliqué. Il existe encore quelques points sur lesquels la lumière est nécessaire… Mais elle est en marche, la lumière!

— Watson vous a certainement appris que nous avions acquis une certitude, reprit le baronnet. Nous avons entendu le chien hurler sur la lande, et je jurerais bien que la légende accréditée dans le pays n'est pas une vaine superstition. Autrefois, quand je vivais en Amérique, dans le Far-West, j'ai eu des chiens et je ne puis me méprendre sur leurs hurlements. Si vous parvenez à museler celui-là, je vous proclamerai partout le plus grand détective des temps modernes.

— Je crois que je le musellerai et que je l'enchaînerai facilement, à la condition que vous consentiez à m'aider.

— Je ferai tout ce que vous me commanderez.

— Parfait… Je vous demande en outre de m'obéir aveuglément, sans vous enquérir des raisons qui me guident.

— Je m'y engage.

— Si vous tenez cette promesse, nous avons les plus grandes chances de résoudre bientôt le problème qui vous intéresse. Je n'ai aucun doute…»

Sherlock Holmes s'arrêta soudain pour regarder en l'air, au-dessus de ma tête.

La lumière de la lampe tombait d'aplomb sur son visage, qui avait pris une expression si attentive, si immobile, qu'il ressemblait à une tête de statue personnifiant l'étonnement et la réflexion.

«Qu'y a-t-il?» criâmes-nous, le baronnet et moi.

Lorsque les yeux de Sherlock se reportèrent sur nous, je vis qu'il réprimait une violente émotion intérieure.

«Excusez l'admiration d'un connaisseur, dit-il à sir Henry, en étendant la main vers la série de portraits qui couvraient le mur. Watson me dénie won't allow that I know anything of art but that is mere jealousy because our views upon the subject differ. Now, these are a really very fine series of portraits."

"Well, I'm glad to hear you say so," said Sir Henry, glancing with some surprise at my friend. "I don't pretend to know much about these things, and I'd be a better judge of a horse or a steer than of a picture. I didn't know that you found time for such things."

"I know what is good when I see it, and I see it now. That's a Kneller, I'll swear, that lady in the blue silk over yonder, and the stout gentleman with the wig ought to be a Reynolds. They are all family portraits, I presume?"

"Every one."

"Do you know the names?"

"Barrymore has been coaching me in them, and I think I can say my lessons fairly well."

"Who is the gentleman with the telescope?"

"That is Rear-Admiral Baskerville, who served under Rodney in the West Indies. The man with the blue coat and the roll of paper is Sir William Baskerville, who was Chairman of Committees of the House of Commons under Pitt."

"And this Cavalier opposite to me—the one with the black velvet and the lace?"

"Ah, you have a right to know about him. That is the cause of all the mischief, the wicked Hugo, who started the Hound of the Baskervilles. We're not likely to forget him."

I gazed with interest and some surprise upon the portrait.

"Dear me!" said Holmes, "he seems a quiet, meek-mannered man enough, but I dare say that there was a lurking devil in his eyes. I had pictured him as a more robust and ruffianly person."

"There's no doubt about the authenticity, for the name and the date, 1647, are on the back of the canvas."

Holmes said little more, but the picture of the old roysterer seemed to have a fascination for him, and his eyes were continually fixed upon it during supper.

It was not until later, when Sir Henry had gone to his room, that I was able to follow the trend of his thoughts.

He led me back into the banqueting-hall, his bedroom candle in his hand, and he held it up against the time-stained portrait on the wall.

toute compétence en matière d'art, par pure jalousie, parce que nous ne sommes pas de la même école. Vous avez là une fort belle collection de portraits.

— Je suis heureux de vous les entendre vanter, fit sir Henry, avec surprise. Je ne connais pas grand'chose à tout cela, et je ne puis mieux juger un cheval qu'un tableau. Je ne croyais pas que vous eussiez le temps de vous occuper de ces bagatelles.

— Je sais apprécier le beau, quand je l'ai sous les yeux. Tenez, ceci est un Kneller... Je parierais que cette dame en soie bleue, là-bas, ainsi que ce gros gentilhomme en perruque, doivent être des Reynolds. Des portraits de famille, je suppose?

— Tous.

— Savez-vous le nom de ces ancêtres?

— Barrymore m'en a rebattu les oreilles, et je crois que je puis réciter ma leçon.

— Quel est ce gentilhomme avec un télescope?

— Il s'appelait le vice-amiral de Baskerville et servit aux Indes sous Rodney. Celui qui a cet habit bleu et ce rouleau de papiers à la main fut sir William Baskerville, président des commissions de la Chambre des communes, sous Pitt.

— Et ce cavalier, en face de moi,... celui qui porte un habit de velours noir garni de dentelles?

— Il mérite qu'on vous le présente, car il est la cause de tous nos malheurs. Il se nomme Hugo, Hugo le maudit, celui pour qui l'enfer a vomi le chien des Baskerville. Nous ne sommes pas près de l'oublier.»

Intéressé et surpris, j'examinai le portrait.

«Vraiment! dit Holmes. Il a l'air d'un homme simple et paisible, mais cependant on devine dans ses yeux une pensée de mal qui sommeille. Je me le figurais plus robuste et d'aspect plus brutal.

— L'authenticité du portrait n'est pas douteuse; le nom et la date — 1647 — se trouvent au dos de la toile.»

Pendant le dîner, Holmes parla peu. Le portrait du vieux libertin exerçait sur lui une sorte de fascination, et ses yeux ne s'en détachèrent pas.

Ce ne fut que plus tard, à l'heure où sir Henry se retira dans sa chambre, que mon ami me communiqua ses pensées.

Nous redescendîmes dans la salle à manger, et, là, son bougeoir à la main, Holmes attira mon attention sur la vieille peinture que le temps avait recouverte de sa patine.

"Do you see anything there?"

I looked at the broad plumed hat, the curling love-locks, the white lace collar, and the straight, severe face which was framed between them. It was not a brutal countenance, but it was prim, hard, and stern, with a firm-set, thin-lipped mouth, and a coldly intolerant eye.

"Is it like anyone you know?"

"There is something of Sir Henry about the jaw."

"Just a suggestion, perhaps. But wait an instant!"

He stood upon a chair, and, holding up the light in his left hand, he curved his right arm over the broad hat and round the long ringlets.

"Good heavens!" I cried in amazement.

The face of Stapleton had sprung out of the canvas.

"Ha, you see it now. My eyes have been trained to examine faces and not their trimmings. It is the first quality of a criminal investigator that he should see through a disguise."

"But this is marvellous. It might be his portrait."

"Yes, it is an interesting instance of a throwback, which appears to be both physical and spiritual. A study of family portraits is enough to convert a man to the doctrine of reincarnation. The fellow is a Baskerville—that is evident."

"With designs upon the succession."

"Exactly. This chance of the picture has supplied us with one of our most obvious missing links. We have him, Watson, we have him, and I dare swear that before tomorrow night he will be fluttering in our net as helpless as one of his own butterflies. A pin, a cork, and a card, and we add him to the Baker Street collection!"

He burst into one of his rare fits of laughter as he turned away from the picture. I have not heard him laugh often, and it has always boded ill to somebody.

I was up betimes in the morning, but Holmes was afoot earlier still, for I saw him as I dressed, coming up the drive.

«Apercevez-vous quelque chose?» me demanda Sherlock.

J'examinai ce visage long et sévère, encadré par un grand chapeau à plumes, une abondante chevelure bouclée et une collerette de dentelles blanches. La physionomie, point bestiale, avait toutefois un air faux et mauvais, avec sa bouche en coup de sabre, ourlée de lèvres minces, et ses yeux insupportablement fixes.

«Ressemble-t-il à quelqu'un que vous connaissiez? me demanda Sherlock Holmes.

— Il a quelque chose des maxillaires de sir Henry, répondis-je.

— Un phénomène de suggestion, probablement. Attendez un instant!»

Holmes monta sur une chaise et, élevant son bougeoir qu'il tenait de la main gauche, il arrondit son bras sur le portrait, de façon à cacher le large chapeau à plumes et les boucles de cheveux.

«Grand Dieu!» m'écriai-je étonné.

Le visage de Stapleton venait de surgir de la toile.

«Voyez-vous, maintenant? fit Holmes. Mes yeux sont exercés à détailler les traits des visages et non pas les accessoires. La première qualité de ceux qui se vouent à la recherche des criminels consiste à savoir percer les déguisements.

— C'est merveilleux. On dirait le portrait de Stapleton.

— Oui. Nous nous trouvons en présence d'un cas intéressant d'atavisme — aussi bien au physique qu'au moral. Il suffit d'étudier des portraits de famille pour se convertir à la théorie de la réincarnation. Ce Stapleton est un Baskerville — la chose me paraît hors de doute.

— Un Baskerville — avec des vues sur la succession, repartis-je.

— Exactement. L'examen de ce portrait nous a procuré le plus intéressant des chaînons qui nous manquaient… Nous le tenons, Watson, nous le tenons! Je jure qu'avant demain soir, il se débattra dans nos filets aussi désespérément que ses propres papillons. Une épingle, un bouchon, une étiquette, et nous l'ajouterons à notre collection de Baker street!…»

En s'éloignant du portrait, Holmes fut pris d'un de ces accès de rire peu fréquents chez lui. Je l'ai rarement entendu rire; mais sa gaieté a toujours été fatale à quelqu'un.

Le lendemain matin, je me levai de bonne heure. Holmes avait été plus matinal que moi, puisque, de ma fenêtre, je l'aperçus dans la grande

"Yes, we should have a full day today," he remarked, and he rubbed his hands with the joy of action. "The nets are all in place, and the drag is about to begin. We'll know before the day is out whether we have caught our big, lean-jawed pike, or whether he has got through the meshes."

"Have you been on the moor already?"

"I have sent a report from Grimpen to Princetown as to the death of Selden. I think I can promise that none of you will be troubled in the matter. And I have also communicated with my faithful Cartwright, who would certainly have pined away at the door of my hut, as a dog does at his master's grave, if I had not set his mind at rest about my safety."

"What is the next move?"

"To see Sir Henry. Ah, here he is!"

"Good-morning, Holmes," said the baronet. "You look like a general who is planning a battle with his chief of the staff."

"That is the exact situation. Watson was asking for orders."

"And so do I."

"Very good. You are engaged, as I understand, to dine with our friends the Stapletons tonight."

"I hope that you will come also. They are very hospitable people, and I am sure that they would be very glad to see you."

"I fear that Watson and I must go to London."

"To London?"

"Yes, I think that we should be more useful there at the present juncture."

The baronet's face perceptibly lengthened.

"I hoped that you were going to see me through this business. The Hall and the moor are not very pleasant places when one is alone."

"My dear fellow, you must trust me implicitly and do exactly what I tell you. You can tell your friends that we should have been happy to have come with you, but that urgent business required us to be in town. We hope very soon to return to Devonshire. Will you remember to give them that message?"

"If you insist upon it."

"There is no alternative, I assure you."

I saw by the baronet's clouded brow that he was

allée du parc.

«Nous aurons aujourd'hui une journée bien remplie», fit-il, en se frottant les mains, à la pensée de l'action prochaine. «Les filets sont tendus et la «traîne» va commencer. Avant la fin du jour, nous saurons si nous avons ramené le gros brochet que nous guettons ou s'il a passé à travers les mailles.

— Êtes-vous allé déjà sur la lande?

— De Grimpen, j'ai envoyé à la prison de Princetown un rapport sur la mort de Selden. Je ne pense pas m'avancer trop, en promettant que personne de vous ne sera inquiété à ce sujet. J'ai écrit aussi à mon fidèle Cartwright. Le pauvre garçon se serait lamenté sur la porte de ma hutte, comme un chien sur le tombeau de son maître, si je n'avais eu la précaution de le rassurer sur mon sort.

— Et maintenant, qu'allons-nous faire en premier lieu?

— Causer avec sir Henry... Justement, le voici.

— Bonjour, Holmes, dit le baronnet. Vous ressemblez à un général en chef dressant un plan avec son chef d'état-major.

— Votre comparaison est exacte... Watson me demandait les ordres.

— Je vous en demande aussi pour moi.

— Très bien. Vous êtes invité à dîner ce soir chez les Stapleton?

— Oui; vous y viendrez également. Ce sont des gens très accueillants... Ils seront très heureux de vous voir.

— Je crains que nous ne soyons obligés, Watson et moi, d'aller à Londres aujourd'hui.

— À Londres?

— Oui; j'ai le pressentiment que, dans les présentes conjonctures, notre présence là-bas est indispensable.»

La figure du baronnet s'allongea considérablement.

«J'espérais que vous étiez venus ici pour m'assister. Quand on est seul, le séjour du château et de la lande manque de gaieté.

— Mon cher ami, répliqua Holmes, vous devez vous fier aveuglément à moi et exécuter fidèlement mes ordres. Vous direz aux Stapleton que nous aurions été très heureux de vous accompagner, mais que des affaires urgentes nous ont rappelés à Londres. Vous ajouterez que nous comptons revenir bientôt dans le Devonshire. Voulez-vous ne pas oublier de faire cette commission à vos amis?

— Si vous y tenez.

— Certainement... C'est très important.»

Je vis au front rembruni de sir Henry que notre

deeply hurt by what he regarded as our desertion.

"When do you desire to go?" he asked coldly.

"Immediately after breakfast. We will drive in to Coombe Tracey, but Watson will leave his things as a pledge that he will come back to you. Watson, you will send a note to Stapleton to tell him that you regret that you cannot come."

"I have a good mind to go to London with you," said the baronet. "Why should I stay here alone?"

"Because it is your post of duty. Because you gave me your word that you would do as you were told, and I tell you to stay."

"All right, then, I'll stay."

"One more direction! I wish you to drive to Merripit House. Send back your trap, however, and let them know that you intend to walk home."

"To walk across the moor?"

"Yes."

"But that is the very thing which you have so often cautioned me not to do."

"This time you may do it with safety. If I had not every confidence in your nerve and courage I would not suggest it, but it is essential that you should do it."

"Then I will do it."

"And as you value your life do not go across the moor in any direction save along the straight path which leads from Merripit House to the Grimpen Road, and is your natural way home."

"I will do just what you say."

"Very good. I should be glad to get away as soon after breakfast as possible, so as to reach London in the afternoon."

I was much astounded by this programme, though I remembered that Holmes had said to Stapleton on the night before that his visit would terminate next day. It had not crossed my mind however, that he would wish me to go with him, nor could I understand how we could both be absent at a moment which he himself declared to be critical.

There was nothing for it, however, but implic-

désertion — il qualifiait ainsi intérieurement notre départ — l'affectait péniblement.

«Quand désirez-vous partir? interrogea-t-il, d'un ton sec.

— Aussitôt après déjeuner… Nous irons en voiture à Coombe-Tracey… Afin de vous prouver que son absence sera de courte durée, Watson laissera ici tous ses bagages.»

Et, se retournant vers moi, Holmes continua:

«Watson, envoyez donc un mot aux Stapleton pour leur dire que vous regrettez de ne pouvoir accepter leur invitation.

— J'ai bien envie de vous suivre à Londres, fit le baronnet. Pourquoi resterais-je seul ici?

— Parce que le devoir vous y retient… Parce que vous m'avez engagé votre parole d'exécuter tous mes ordres, et que je vous commande de demeurer ici.

— Très bien alors,… je resterai…

— Encore une recommandation, reprit Sherlock. Je veux que vous alliez en voiture à Merripit house et qu'ensuite vous renvoyiez votre cocher, en disant aux Stapleton que vous rentrerez à pied au château.

— À pied… À travers la lande?

— Oui.

— Mais c'est précisément la chose que vous m'avez le plus expressément défendue!

— Aujourd'hui vous pouvez faire cette promenade en toute sécurité. Si je n'avais la plus entière confiance dans la solidité de vos nerfs et la fermeté de votre courage, je ne vous y autoriserais pas… Il est essentiel que les choses se passent ainsi.

— Je vous obéirai.

— Si vous tenez à votre existence, ne suivez, sur la lande, d'autre route que celle qui conduit de Merripit house au village de Grimpen… C'est d'ailleurs votre chemin tout naturel pour retourner au château.

— Je ferai ce que vous me commandez.

— À la bonne heure, approuva Holmes. Je partirai le plus tôt possible, après déjeuner, de façon à arriver à Londres dans le courant de l'après-midi.

Ce programme ne manquait pas de me surprendre, bien que, la nuit précédente, Holmes eût dit à Stapleton que son séjour à Baskerville ne se prolongerait pas au delà du lendemain. Il ne m'était jamais venu à l'idée que Sherlock pût m'emmener avec lui — pas plus que je ne comprenais que nous fussions absents l'un et l'autre, à un moment que mon ami lui-même qualifiait de très critique.

Il n'y avait qu'à obéir en silence. Nous prîmes

it obedience; so we bade good-bye to our rueful friend, and a couple of hours afterwards we were at the station of Coombe Tracey and had dispatched the trap upon its return journey. A small boy was waiting upon the platform.

"Any orders, sir?"

"You will take this train to town, Cartwright. The moment you arrive you will send a wire to Sir Henry Baskerville, in my name, to say that if he finds the pocketbook which I have dropped he is to send it by registered post to Baker Street."

"Yes, sir."

"And ask at the station office if there is a message for me."

The boy returned with a telegram, which Holmes handed to me.

It ran:

Wire received. Coming down with unsigned warrant. Arrive five-forty. Lestrade.

"That is in answer to mine of this morning. He is the best of the professionals, I think, and we may need his assistance. Now, Watson, I think that we cannot employ our time better than by calling upon your acquaintance, Mrs. Laura Lyons."

His plan of campaign was beginning to be evident. He would use the baronet in order to convince the Stapletons that we were really gone, while we should actually return at the instant when we were likely to be needed. That telegram from London, if mentioned by Sir Henry to the Stapletons, must remove the last suspicions from their minds.

Already I seemed to see our nets drawing closer around that lean-jawed pike.

Mrs. Laura Lyons was in her office, and Sherlock Holmes opened his interview with a frankness and directness which considerably amazed her.

"I am investigating the circumstances which attended the death of the late Sir Charles Baskerville," said he. "My friend here, Dr. Watson, has informed me of what you have communicated, and also of what you have withheld in connection with

congé de notre pauvre sir Henry et, une couple d'heures plus tard, nous arrivions à la gare de Coombe Tracey. La voiture repartit pour le château et nous passâmes sur le quai où nous attendait un jeune garçon.

«Avez-vous des ordres à me donner, monsieur? demanda-t-il à Sherlock Holmes.

— Oui, Cartwright. Vous prendrez le train pour Londres… Aussitôt en ville, vous expédierez en mon nom à sir Henry un télégramme pour le prier de m'envoyer à Baker street, sous pli recommandé, le portefeuille que j'ai laissé tomber dans le salon.

— Oui, monsieur.

— Allez donc voir maintenant au télégraphe si l'on n'a pas un message pour moi.»

Cartwright revint avec une dépêche. Holmes me la tendit.

Elle était ainsi conçue:

«Selon votre désir, j'arrive avec un mandat d'arrêt en blanc. Serai à Grimpen à cinq heures quarante.

«Lestrade.»

«Ceci, me dit Holmes, répond à un de mes télégrammes de ce matin. Ce Lestrade est le plus habile détective de Scotland Yard, et nous pouvons avoir besoin d'aide… Tâchons, Watson, d'utiliser notre temps. Nous n'en trouverons pas de meilleur emploi qu'en allant rendre visite à votre connaissance, Mme Laura Lyons.»

Le plan de campagne de Sherlock Holmes commençait à devenir évident. Par le baronnet, il voulait convaincre les Stapleton de notre départ, alors que nous devions reprendre clandestinement le chemin de Grimpen, pour nous trouver là au moment où notre présence serait nécessaire. Le télégramme, expédié de Londres par Cartwright, achèverait de dissiper les soupçons des Stapleton, si sir Henry leur en parlait.

Je voyais déjà les filets se resserrer davantage autour du brochet que nous désirions capturer.

Mme Laura Lyons nous reçut dans son bureau. Sherlock Holmes ouvrit le feu avec une franchise et une précision qui la déconcertèrent un peu.

«Je suis en train de rechercher, dit-il, les circonstances qui ont accompagné la mort de feu Charles Baskerville. Mon ami le docteur Watson m'a fait part de ce que vous lui aviez raconté et aussi de ce que vous lui aviez caché à ce sujet.

that matter."

"What have I withheld?" she asked defiantly.

"You have confessed that you asked Sir Charles to be at the gate at ten o'clock. We know that that was the place and hour of his death. You have withheld what the connection is between these events."

"There is no connection."

"In that case the coincidence must indeed be an extraordinary one. But I think that we shall succeed in establishing a connection, after all. I wish to be perfectly frank with you, Mrs. Lyons. We regard this case as one of murder, and the evidence may implicate not only your friend Mr. Stapleton but his wife as well."

The lady sprang from her chair.

"His wife!" she cried.

"The fact is no longer a secret. The person who has passed for his sister is really his wife."

Mrs. Lyons had resumed her seat. Her hands were grasping the arms of her chair, and I saw that the pink nails had turned white with the pressure of her grip.

"His wife!" she said again. "His wife! He is not a married man."

Sherlock Holmes shrugged his shoulders.

"Prove it to me! Prove it to me! And if you can do so—!"

The fierce flash of her eyes said more than any words.

"I have come prepared to do so," said Holmes, drawing several papers from his pocket. "Here is a photograph of the couple taken in York four years ago. It is indorsed 'Mr. and Mrs. Vandeleur,' but you will have no difficulty in recognizing him, and her also, if you know her by sight. Here are three written descriptions by trustworthy witnesses of Mr. and Mrs. Vandeleur, who at that time kept St. Oliver's private school. Read them and see if you can doubt the identity of these people."

She glanced at them, and then looked up at us with the set, rigid face of a desperate woman.

"Mr. Holmes," she said, "this man had offered me marriage on condition that I could get a divorce from my husband. He has lied to me, the villain, in every conceivable way. Not one word of

— Qu'ai-je caché? demanda Mme Lyons, devenue subitement défiante.

— Vous avouez avoir prié sir Charles de venir à la porte du parc, à dix heures du soir. Nous savons que le vieux gentilhomme a trouvé la mort à cette heure et à cet endroit. Pourquoi avez-vous passé sous silence la relation qui existe entre ces différents événements?

— Il n'existe entre eux aucune relation.

— Permettez-moi de vous faire remarquer qu'en tout cas, la coïncidence est au moins extraordinaire. J'estime cependant que nous parviendrons à établir cette relation. Je veux agir franchement avec vous, madame Lyons. Un meurtre a été commis, nous en sommes certains, et l'enquête peut impliquer non seulement votre ami M. Stapleton, mais encore sa femme.»

Laura Lyons quitta brusquement son fauteuil.

«Sa femme! s'écria-t-elle.

— C'est aujourd'hui le secret de Polichinelle. Celle que l'on croyait sa sœur est bien réellement sa femme.»

Mme Lyons se rassit. Ses mains s'étaient à tel point crispées sur les bras du fauteuil que ses ongles — roses quelques minutes auparavant — avaient blanchi sous la violence de l'étreinte.

«Sa femme! répéta-t-elle. Sa femme! Il était donc marié?»

Sherlock Holmes se contenta de hausser les épaules.

«Prouvez-le-moi!... Prouvez-le-moi, reprit-elle... Et si vous m'apportez cette-preuve...»

L'éclair qui passa alors dans ses yeux en dit plus long que tous les discours.

«Je suis venu dans cette intention, continua Holmes, en tirant plusieurs papiers de sa poche. Voici d'abord une photographie du couple prise à York, il y a plusieurs années. Lisez la mention écrite au dos: «M. et Mme Vandeleur...» Vous le reconnaîtrez sans peine, — et elle aussi, si vous l'avez vue. Voilà trois signalements de M. et Mme Vandeleur, signés par des témoins dignes de foi. Le ménage tenait à cette époque l'école de Saint-Olivier. Lisez ces attestations et voyez si vous pouvez douter de l'identité de ces gens.»

Mme Lyons prit les documents, les parcourut et tourna ensuite vers nous un visage consterné.

«Monsieur Holmes, dit-elle, cet homme m'a proposé de m'épouser, si je divorçais d'avec mon mari. Il m'a menti, le lâche, d'une inconcevable façon. Il ne m'a jamais dit un mot de vérité... Et truth has he ever told me. And why—why? I imagined that all was for my own sake. But now I see that I was never anything but a tool in his hands. Why should I preserve faith with him who never kept any with me? Why should I try to shield him from the consequences of his own wicked acts? Ask me what you like, and there is nothing which I shall hold back. One thing I swear to you, and that is that when I wrote the letter I never dreamed of any harm to the old gentleman, who had been my kindest friend."

"I entirely believe you, madam," said Sherlock Holmes. "The recital of these events must be very painful to you, and perhaps it will make it easier if I tell you what occurred, and you can check me if I make any material mistake. The sending of this letter was suggested to you by Stapleton?"

"He dictated it."

"I presume that the reason he gave was that you would receive help from Sir Charles for the legal expenses connected with your divorce?"

"Exactly."

"And then after you had sent the letter he dissuaded you from keeping the appointment?"

"He told me that it would hurt his self-respect that any other man should find the money for such an object, and that though he was a poor man himself he would devote his last penny to removing the obstacles which divided us."

"He appears to be a very consistent character. And then you heard nothing until you read the reports of the death in the paper?"

"No."

"And he made you swear to say nothing about your appointment with Sir Charles?"

"He did. He said that the death was a very mysterious one, and that I should certainly be suspected if the facts came out. He frightened me into remaining silent."

"Quite so. But you had your suspicions?"

She hesitated and looked down.

"I knew him," she said. "But if he had kept faith with me I should always have done so with him."

"I think that on the whole you have had a for-

pourquoi?… pourquoi? Je croyais qu'il n'agissait que dans mon seul intérêt. Mais maintenant je me rends compte que je n'étais qu'un instrument entre ses mains… Pourquoi me montrerais-je généreuse envers celui qui m'a si indignement trompée? Pourquoi tenterais-je de le soustraire aux conséquences de ses actes déloyaux? Interrogez-moi! Demandez-moi ce que vous voulez savoir, je vous répondrai sans ambages… Je vous jure qu'au moment d'écrire à sir Charles Baskerville, je n'aurais même pas osé rêver qu'il arriverait malheur à ce vieillard que je considérais comme le meilleur de mes amis.

— Je vous crois absolument, madame, dit Sherlock Holmes. Je comprends que le récit de ces événements vous soit très pénible et peut-être vaudrait-il mieux qu'il vînt de moi… Reprenez-moi si je commets quelque erreur matérielle… L'envoi de cette lettre vous fut suggéré par Stapleton?

— Il me l'a dictée.

— Je présume qu'il fit miroiter à vos yeux le secours que sir Charles vous enverrait pour faire face aux dépenses nécessitées par votre instance en divorce.

— Très exact.

— Puis, après le départ de votre lettre, il vous dissuada d'aller au rendez-vous?

— Il me dit qu'il se sentirait froissé si un autre homme me remettait de l'argent pour une semblable destination. Il ajouta que, quoique pauvre, il dépenserait volontiers jusqu'à son dernier sou pour abattre l'obstacle qui nous séparait.

— Ah! il se montrait d'une logique irréfutable, dit Holmes… Ensuite, vous n'avez plus entendu parler de rien jusqu'au moment où vous avez lu dans les journaux les détails de la mort de sir Charles?

— Non.

— Je suppose qu'il vous fit jurer de ne révéler à personne votre rendez-vous avec le vieux baronnet.

— En effet. Il prétexta que cette mort était environnée de mystères, et que, si je parlais de ma lettre, on me soupçonnerait certainement. Il m'effraya pour obtenir mon silence.

— Évidemment. Cependant vous eûtes des doutes?»

Mme Lyons hésita et baissa la tête.

«Je le connaissais, reprit-elle. Toutefois, s'il s'était conduit autrement à mon égard, jamais je ne l'aurais trahi.

— À mon avis, vous l'avez échappé belle, dit

tunate escape," said Sherlock Holmes. "You have had him in your power and he knew it, and yet you are alive. You have been walking for some months very near to the edge of a precipice. We must wish you good-morning now, Mrs. Lyons, and it is probable that you will very shortly hear from us again."

"Our case becomes rounded off, and difficulty after difficulty thins away in front of us," said Holmes as we stood waiting for the arrival of the express from town. "I shall soon be in the position of being able to put into a single connected narrative one of the most singular and sensational crimes of modern times. Students of criminology will remember the analogous incidents in Godno, in Little Russia, in the year '66, and of course there are the Anderson murders in North Carolina, but this case possesses some features which are entirely its own. Even now we have no clear case against this very wily man. But I shall be very much surprised if it is not clear enough before we go to bed this night."

The London express came roaring into the station, and a small, wiry bulldog of a man had sprung from a first-class carriage. We all three shook hands, and I saw at once from the reverential way in which Lestrade gazed at my companion that he had learned a good deal since the days when they had first worked together. I could well remember the scorn which the theories of the reasoner used then to excite in the practical man.

"Anything good?" he asked.

"The biggest thing for years," said Holmes. "We have two hours before we need think of starting. I think we might employ it in getting some dinner and then, Lestrade, we will take the London fog out of your throat by giving you a breath of the pure night air of Dartmoor. Never been there? Ah, well, I don't suppose you will forget your first visit."

Sherlock Holmes. Vous le teniez en votre pouvoir, il le savait et vous vivez encore! Pendant plusieurs mois, vous avez côtoyé un précipice... Maintenant, madame, il ne nous reste plus qu'à prendre congé de vous. Avant peu, vous entendrez parler de nous.»

Nous allâmes à la gare attendre l'arrivée du train de Londres. Sur le quai, Holmes me dit:

«Tout s'éclaircit et, peu à peu, les difficultés s'aplanissent autour de nous. Bientôt, je pourrai raconter d'une façon cohérente le crime le plus singulier et le plus sensationnel de notre époque. Ceux qui se livrent à l'étude de la criminalité se souviendront alors d'événements analogues survenus à Grodno, dans la Petite-Russie, en 1866. Il y a aussi les meurtres d'Anderson commis dans la Caroline du Nord... Mais cette affaire présente des particularités qui lui sont propres. Ainsi, à cette heure encore, la culpabilité de ce Stapleton n'est pas matériellement établie. Seulement j'espère bien y être arrivé ce soir, avant de me mettre au lit.»

L'express de Londres pénétrait en gare. Un petit homme, trapu, musclé, sauta d'un wagon de première classe. Nous échangeâmes avec lui une poignée de main et je devinai, à la façon respectueuse dont Lestrade regarda mon compagnon, qu'il avait appris beaucoup de choses depuis le jour où nous avions «travaillé» ensemble pour la première fois. Je me souvenais du profond mépris avec lequel le praticien accueillit alors les raisonnements d'un théoricien tel que Sherlock Holmes.

«Un cas sérieux? interrogea Lestrade.

— Le fait le plus extraordinaire qui se soit produit depuis nombre d'années, répondit Holmes. Nous avons devant nous deux heures avant de songer à nous mettre en route... Dînons! Puis, mon cher Lestrade, vous chasserez le brouillard de Londres en aspirant à pleins poumons la fraîche brise vespérale de Dartmoor... Jamais venu dans ces parages?... Non?... Eh bien, je ne pense pas que vous oubliiez de longtemps votre première visite.»

The hound of Baskervilles.
Le Chien des Baskerville.

CHAPTER 14. THE HOUND OF THE BASKERVILLES

One of Sherlock Holmes's defects—if, indeed, one may call it a defect—was that he was exceedingly loath to communicate his full plans to any other person until the instant of their fulfilment. Partly it came no doubt from his own masterful nature, which loved to dominate and surprise those who were around him. Partly also from his professional caution, which urged him never to take any chances. The result, however, was very trying for those who were acting as his agents and assistants. I had often suffered under it, but never more so than during that long drive in the darkness.

The great ordeal was in front of us; at last we were about to make our final effort, and yet Holmes had said nothing, and I could only surmise what his course of action would be.

My nerves thrilled with anticipation when at last the cold wind upon our faces and the dark, void spaces on either side of the narrow road told me that we were back upon the moor once again. Every stride of the horses and every turn of the wheels was taking us nearer to our supreme adventure.

Our conversation was hampered by the presence of the driver of the hired wagonette, so that we were forced to talk of trivial matters when our nerves were tense with emotion and anticipation.

It was a relief to me, after that unnatural restraint, when we at last passed Frankland's house and knew that we were drawing near to the Hall and to the scene of action.

We did not drive up to the door but got down near the gate of the avenue.

The wagonette was paid off and ordered to return to Coombe Tracey forthwith, while we started to walk to Merripit House.

"Are you armed, Lestrade?"

CHAPITRE 14. LE CHIEN DES BASKERVILLE

Un des défauts de Sherlock Holmes — si l'on peut appeler cela un défaut — consistait en sa répugnance à communiquer ses projets à ceux qui devaient l'aider dans leur exécution. Il préférait attendre le dernier moment. J'attribue cette retenue, partie à son caractère impérieux qui le portait à dominer et à surprendre ses amis, et partie aussi à sa méfiance professionnelle, qui le poussait à ne négliger aucune précaution. Le résultat n'en était pas moins fort désagréable pour ceux qui l'assistaient dans ses entreprises. Pour mon compte, j'en ai souvent souffert, mais jamais autant que pendant la longue course en voiture que nous fîmes, ce soir-là, dans l'obscurité.

Nous étions sur le point de tenter la suprême épreuve; nous allions enfin donner notre dernier effort, et Holmes ne nous avait encore rien dit. À peine pouvais-je soupçonner ce qu'il comptait faire.

Je frémis par anticipation, lorsque le vent glacial qui nous frappait le visage et les sombres espaces qui s'étendaient de chaque côté de l'étroite route m'apprirent que nous retournions de nouveau sur la lande. Chaque tour de roue, chaque foulée des chevaux nous rapprochaient davantage de notre ultime aventure.

La présence du conducteur s'opposait à toute espèce de conversation intéressante, et nous ne parlâmes que de choses insignifiantes, alors que nos nerfs vibraient sous le coup de l'émotion et de l'attente.

Après cette longue contrainte, je me sentis soulagé à la vue de la maison de Frankland et en reconnaissant que nous nous dirigions vers le château.

Au lieu de nous arrêter à l'entrée principale, nous poussâmes jusqu'à la porte de l'avenue.

Là, Sherlock Holmes paya le cocher, et lui ordonna de retourner sur-le-champ à Coombe Tracey. Nous nous acheminâmes vers Merripit house.

«Êtes-vous armé, Lestrade?» demanda mon ami.

The little detective smiled.

"As long as I have my trousers I have a hip-pocket, and as long as I have my hip-pocket I have something in it."

"Good! My friend and I are also ready for emergencies."

"You're mighty close about this affair, Mr. Holmes. What's the game now?"

"A waiting game."

"My word, it does not seem a very cheerful place," said the detective with a shiver, glancing round him at the gloomy slopes of the hill and at the huge lake of fog which lay over the Grimpen Mire. "I see the lights of a house ahead of us."

"That is Merripit House and the end of our journey. I must request you to walk on tiptoe and not to talk above a whisper."

We moved cautiously along the track as if we were bound for the house, but Holmes halted us when we were about two hundred yards from it.

"This will do," said he. "These rocks upon the right make an admirable screen."

"We are to wait here?"

"Yes, we shall make our little ambush here. Get into this hollow, Lestrade. You have been inside the house, have you not, Watson? Can you tell the position of the rooms? What are those latticed windows at this end?"

"I think they are the kitchen windows."

"And the one beyond, which shines so brightly?"

"That is certainly the dining-room."

"The blinds are up. You know the lie of the land best. Creep forward quietly and see what they are doing—but for heaven's sake don't let them know that they are watched!"

I tiptoed down the path and stooped behind the low wall which surrounded the stunted orchard.

Creeping in its shadow I reached a point whence I could look straight through the uncurtained window.

There were only two men in the room, Sir Henry and Stapleton. They sat with their profiles towards me on either side of the round table. Both of them were smoking cigars, and coffee and wine were in front of them.

Le petit détective sourit.

«Tant que j'aurai un pantalon, dit-il, j'y ferai coudre une poche-revolver, et aussi longtemps que j'aurai une poche-revolver, il se trouvera quelque chose dedans.

— Bien. Nous sommes également prêts pour toute éventualité, Watson et moi.

— Vous êtes peu communicatif, monsieur Holmes, reprit Lestrade. Qu'allons-nous faire?

— Attendre.

— Vrai! l'endroit ne me semble pas folâtre, fit le détective, en frissonnant à l'aspect des pentes sombres de la colline et de l'immense voile de brouillard qui recouvrait la grande fondrière de Grimpen. Je crois apercevoir devant nous les lumières d'une maison.

— C'est Merripit house, le terme de notre voyage, murmura Holmes. Je vous enjoins de marcher sur la pointe des pieds et de ne parler qu'à voix très basse.»

Nous suivîmes le sentier qui conduisait à la demeure des Stapleton; mais, à deux cents mètres d'elle, Holmes fit halte.

«Cela suffit, dit-il. Ces rochers, à droite, nous serviront d'abri.

— C'est ici que nous devons attendre? demanda Lestrade.

— Oui. Nous allons nous mettre en embuscade ici. Placez-vous dans ce creux, Lestrade. Vous, Watson, vous avez pénétré dans la maison, n'est-ce pas? Pouvez-vous m'indiquer la situation des pièces? Qu'y a-t-il derrière ces fenêtres grillées, de ce côté?

— Les cuisines probablement.

— Et plus loin, celles, qui sont si brillamment éclairées?

— La salle à manger.

— Les stores sont levés. Vous connaissez mieux le terrain… Rampez sans bruit et voyez ce qui s'y passe… Mais au nom du ciel, que Stapleton ne se doute pas qu'on le surveille.»

Sur la pointe des pieds, je m'avançai dans le sentier et je parvins au petit mur qui entourait le verger.

À la faveur de cet abri, je me glissai jusqu'à un endroit d'où je pus apercevoir l'intérieur de la pièce.

Deux hommes étaient assis en face l'un de l'autre: sir Henry et Stapleton. Je distinguais nettement leur profil. Ils fumaient. Du café et des liqueurs se trouvaient devant eux, sur la table.

Stapleton was talking with animation, but the baronet looked pale and distrait. Perhaps the thought of that lonely walk across the ill-omened moor was weighing heavily upon his mind.

As I watched them Stapleton rose and left the room, while Sir Henry filled his glass again and leaned back in his chair, puffing at his cigar.

I heard the creak of a door and the crisp sound of boots upon gravel.

The steps passed along the path on the other side of the wall under which I crouched. Looking over, I saw the naturalist pause at the door of an out-house in the corner of the orchard.

A key turned in a lock, and as he passed in there was a curious scuffling noise from within.

He was only a minute or so inside, and then I heard the key turn once more and he passed me and reentered the house.

I saw him rejoin his guest, and I crept quietly back to where my companions were waiting to tell them what I had seen.

"You say, Watson, that the lady is not there?" Holmes asked when I had finished my report.

"No."

"Where can she be, then, since there is no light in any other room except the kitchen?"

"I cannot think where she is."

I have said that over the great Grimpen Mire there hung a dense, white fog. It was drifting slowly in our direction and banked itself up like a wall on that side of us, low but thick and well defined. The moon shone on it, and it looked like a great shimmering ice-field, with the heads of the distant tors as rocks borne upon its surface.

Holmes's face was turned towards it, and he muttered impatiently as he watched its sluggish drift.

"It's moving towards us, Watson."

"Is that serious?"

"Very serious, indeed—the one thing upon earth which could have disarranged my plans. He can't be very long, now. It is already ten o'clock. Our success and even his life may depend upon his coming out before the fog is over the path."

The night was clear and fine above us. The stars

Stapleton parlait avec animation; le baronnet semblait pâle et distrait. La longue promenade nocturne qu'il devrait faire sur cette lande maudite assombrissait peut-être ses pensées.

Un instant, Stapleton se leva et sortit. Sir Henry remplit son verre, s'enfonça dans son fauteuil et souffla vers le plafond la fumée de son cigare.

J'entendis le grincement d'une porte et le craquement d'une chaussure sur le gravier.

Les pas suivaient l'allée qui borde le mur derrière lequel j'étais accroupi. Je risquai un œil et je vis le naturaliste s'arrêter à la porte d'un pavillon construit dans un coin du verger.

Une clef tourna dans la serrure et, comme Stapleton pénétrait dans le réduit, je perçus un bruit singulier, semblable au claquement d'une lanière de fouet.

Stapleton ne resta pas enfermé plus d'une minute. La clef tourna de nouveau; il repassa devant moi et rentra dans la maison.

Quand il eut rejoint son hôte, je revins doucement auprès de mes compagnons auxquels je racontai ce dont j'avais été témoin.

«Vous dites donc, Watson, que la dame n'est pas là? me demanda Holmes, lorsque j'eus terminé mon rapport.

— Non.

— Où peut-elle être, puisque, sauf celles de la cuisine, toutes les autres fenêtres sont plongées dans l'obscurité?

— Je l'ignore.»

J'ai dit qu'au-dessus de la grande fondrière de Grimpen s'étendait un voile de brouillard, épais et blanchâtre. Lentement, comme un mur mobile, bas, mais épais, il se rapprochait de nous. La lune l'éclairait, lui donnant, avec la cime des pics éloignés qui émergeaient de sa surface, l'aspect d'une gigantesque banquise.

Holmes se tourna de ce côté et laissa échapper quelques paroles d'impatience, arrachées sans doute par la marche lente — mais continue — du brouillard.

«Il va nous gagner, Watson, fit-il, en me le désignant d'un geste.

— Est-ce un contretemps fâcheux?

— Très fâcheux... La seule chose au monde qui pût déranger mes combinaisons... Sir Henry ne tardera pas à partir maintenant!... Il est déjà dix heures... Notre succès — et même sa vie à lui — dépendent de sa sortie, avant que le brouillard ait atteint ce sentier.»

Au-dessus de nos têtes, la nuit était calme et se-shone cold and bright, while a half-moon bathed the whole scene in a soft, uncertain light.

reine. Les étoiles scintillaient, pareilles à des clous d'or fixés sur la voûte céleste, et la lune baignait tout le paysage d'une lumière douce et incertaine.

Before us lay the dark bulk of the house, its serrated roof and bristling chimneys hard outlined against the silver-spangled sky. Broad bars of golden light from the lower windows stretched across the orchard and the moor. One of them was suddenly shut off. The servants had left the kitchen.

Devant nous se détachait la masse sombre de la maison dont les toits dentelés, hérissés de cheminées, se profilaient sur un ciel teinté d'argent. De larges traînées lumineuses, partant des fenêtres du rez-de-chaussée, s'allongeaient sur le verger et jusque sur la lande. L'une d'elles s'éteignit subitement. Les domestiques venaient de quitter la cuisine.

There only remained the lamp in the dining-room where the two men, the murderous host and the unconscious guest, still chatted over their cigars.

Il ne resta plus que la lampe de la salle à manger où les deux hommes, le maître de céans aux pensées sanguinaires et le convive inconscient du danger qui le menaçait, continuaient à causer en fumant leur cigare.

Every minute that white woolly plain which covered one-half of the moor was drifting closer and closer to the house.

De minute en minute, le voile opaque qui recouvrait la lande se rapprochait davantage de la demeure de Stapleton.

Already the first thin wisps of it were curling across the golden square of the lighted window. The farther wall of the orchard was already invisible, and the trees were standing out of a swirl of white vapour. As we watched it the fog-wreaths came crawling round both corners of the house and rolled slowly into one dense bank on which the upper floor and the roof floated like a strange ship upon a shadowy sea.

Déjà les légers flocons d'ouate, avant-coureurs de la brume, s'enroulaient autour du rayon de lumière projeté par la fenêtre illuminée. Le mur du verger le plus éloigné de nous devenait invisible et les arbres disparaissaient presque derrière un nuage de vapeurs blanches. Bientôt des vagues de brouillard léchèrent les deux angles de la maison et se rejoignirent, la faisant ressembler à un vaisseau-fantôme qui voguerait sur une mer silencieuse.

Holmes struck his hand passionately upon the rock in front of us and stamped his feet in his impatience.

"If he isn't out in a quarter of an hour the path will be covered. In half an hour we won't be able to see our hands in front of us."

Holmes crispa sa main sur le rocher qui nous cachait et frappa du pied dans un mouvement d'impatience.

«Si sir Henry n'est pas sorti avant un quart d'heure, dit-il, le sentier sera envahi à son tour. Dans une demi-heure, il nous sera impossible de distinguer notre main au bout de notre bras.

"Shall we move farther back upon higher ground?"

"Yes, I think it would be as well."

So as the fog-bank flowed onward we fell back before it until we were half a mile from the house, and still that dense white sea, with the moon silvering its upper edge, swept slowly and inexorably on.

"We are going too far," said Holmes. "We dare not take the chance of his being overtaken before he can reach us. At all costs we must hold our ground where we are."

He dropped on his knees and clapped his ear to the ground.

"Thank God, I think that I hear him coming."

— Si nous nous retirions jusqu'à l'endroit où le terrain se relève? insinuai-je.

— Oui, c'est préférable.»

À mesure que cette inondation de brouillard nous gagnait, nous fuyions devant elle. Maintenant six cents mètres environ nous séparaient de la maison. Et ce flot inexorable, dont la lune argentait la crête, nous repoussait toujours.

«Nous reculons trop, dit Holmes. Nous ne devons pas courir la chance que le baronnet soit terrassé avant d'arriver jusqu'à nous. Restons où nous sommes, à tout prix.»

Mon ami se baissa et appliqua son oreille contre la terre.

«Merci, mon Dieu! fit-il en se relevant,... il me semble que je l'entends venir!»

A sound of quick steps broke the silence of the moor.

Crouching among the stones we stared intently at the silver-tipped bank in front of us.

The steps grew louder, and through the fog, as through a curtain, there stepped the man whom we were awaiting.

He looked round him in surprise as he emerged into the clear, starlit night.

Then he came swiftly along the path, passed close to where we lay, and went on up the long slope behind us. As he walked he glanced continually over either shoulder, like a man who is ill at ease.

"Hist!" cried Holmes, and I heard the sharp click of a cocking pistol. "Look out! It's coming!"

There was a thin, crisp, continuous patter from somewhere in the heart of that crawling bank.

The cloud was within fifty yards of where we lay, and we glared at it, all three, uncertain what horror was about to break from the heart of it.

I was at Holmes's elbow, and I glanced for an instant at his face. It was pale and exultant, his eyes shining brightly in the moonlight. But suddenly they started forward in a rigid, fixed stare, and his lips parted in amazement.

At the same instant Lestrade gave a yell of terror and threw himself face downward upon the ground.

I sprang to my feet, my inert hand grasping my pistol, my mind paralyzed by the dreadful shape which had sprung out upon us from the shadows of the fog.

A hound it was, an enormous coal-black hound, but not such a hound as mortal eyes have ever seen.

Fire burst from its open mouth, its eyes glowed with a smouldering glare, its muzzle and hackles and dewlap were outlined in flickering flame.

Never in the delirious dream of a disordered brain could anything more savage, more appalling, more hellish be conceived than that dark form and savage face which broke upon us out of the wall of fog.

With long bounds the huge black creature was leaping down the track, following hard upon the

Un bruit de pas précipités rompit le silence de la lande.

Blottis au milieu des pierres, nous regardions avec insistance la muraille floconneuse qui nous barrait la vue de la maison.

Les pas devinrent de plus en plus distincts et, du brouillard, sortit, comme d'un rideau, l'homme que nous attendions.

Dès qu'il se retrouva dans une atmosphère plus claire, il regarda autour de lui, surpris de la limpidité de la nuit.

Rapidement, sir Henry descendit le sentier, passa tout près de l'endroit où nous étions tapis, et commença l'ascension de la colline qui se dressait derrière nous. Tout en marchant, il tournait à chaque instant la tête de côté et d'autre, comme un homme qui se sent mal à l'aise.

«Attention! cria Holmes. Gare à vous! je l'entends!»

En même temps, je perçus le bruit sec d'un pistolet qu'on arme.

Il s'élevait du sein de cette mer de brume un bruit continu, semblable à un fouaillement. Les nuées ne se trouvaient plus qu'à cinquante mètres de nous et, tous trois, nous ne les perdions pas de vue, incertains de l'horreur qu'elles allaient nous vomir.

Mon coude touchait celui d'Holmes, et, à ce moment, je levai la tête vers lui. Il était pâle, mais exultant. Ses yeux étincelaient, à la pâle clarté de la lune. Soudain, ils devinrent fixes et ses lèvres s'entr'ouvrirent d'étonnement.

En même temps, Lestrade poussa un cri de terreur et se jeta la face contre terre.

Je sautai sur mes pieds. Ma main inerte se noua sur la crosse de mon revolver; je sentis mon cerveau se paralyser devant l'effrayante apparition qui venait de surgir des profondeurs du brouillard.

C'était un chien! un énorme chien noir, tel que les yeux des mortels n'en avaient jamais contemplé auparavant.

Sa gueule soufflait du feu; ses prunelles luisaient comme des charbons ardents; autour de ses babines et de ses crocs vacillaient des flammes.

Jamais les rêves les plus insensés d'un esprit en délire n'enfantèrent rien de plus sauvage, de plus terrifiant, de plus diabolique, que cette forme noire et cette face féroce qui s'étaient frayé un passage à travers le mur de brouillard.

Avec des bonds énormes, ce fantastique animal flairait la piste de notre ami, le serrant de près.

footsteps of our friend.

So paralyzed were we by the apparition that we allowed him to pass before we had recovered our nerve.

Cette apparition nous hypnotisait à tel point, qu'elle nous avait déjà dépassés, lorsque nous revînmes à nous.

Then Holmes and I both fired together, and the creature gave a hideous howl, which showed that one at least had hit him. He did not pause, however, but bounded onward.

Holmes et moi fîmes feu simultanément. La bête hurla hideusement, ce qui nous prouva qu'au moins l'un de nous l'avait touchée. Cependant elle bondit en avant et continua sa course.

Far away on the path we saw Sir Henry looking back, his face white in the moonlight, his hands raised in horror, glaring helplessly at the frightful thing which was hunting him down.

Sir Henry s'était retourné. Nous aperçûmes son visage décomposé et ses mains étendues en signe d'horreur devant cet être sans nom qui lui donnait la chasse.

But that cry of pain from the hound had blown all our fears to the winds. If he was vulnerable he was mortal, and if we could wound him we could kill him.

Au cri de douleur du chien, toutes nos craintes s'évanouirent. Il était mortel, puisque vulnérable, et, si nous l'avions blessé, nous pouvions également le tuer.

Never have I seen a man run as Holmes ran that night. I am reckoned fleet of foot, but he outpaced me as much as I outpaced the little professional.

Je n'ai jamais vu courir un homme avec la rapidité que Sherlock Holmes déploya cette nuit-là. Je suis réputé pour ma vitesse, mais il me devança avec autant de facilité que je dépassai moi-même le petit Lestrade.

In front of us as we flew up the track we heard scream after scream from Sir Henry and the deep roar of the hound. I was in time to see the beast spring upon its victim, hurl him to the ground, and worry at his throat. But the next instant Holmes had emptied five barrels of his revolver into the creature's flank. With a last howl of agony and a vicious snap in the air, it rolled upon its back, four feet pawing furiously, and then fell limp upon its side.

Tandis que nous volions sur les traces du chien, nous entendîmes plusieurs cris répétés de sir Henry, ainsi que l'aboiement furieux de la bête. Je la vis s'élancer sur sa victime, la précipiter à terre et la saisir à la gorge. Holmes déchargea cinq fois son revolver dans les flancs du monstre. Dans un dernier hurlement d'agonie et après un dernier coup de dents lancé dans le vide, il roula sur le dos. Ses quatre pattes s'agitèrent convulsivement, puis il s'affaissa sur le côté, immobile.

I stooped, panting, and pressed my pistol to the dreadful, shimmering head, but it was useless to press the trigger. The giant hound was dead.

Je m'avançai, tremblant encore, et j'appuyai le canon de mon revolver sur cette horrible tête. Inutile de presser la détente, le chien-géant était mort — et bien mort, cette fois!

Sir Henry lay insensible where he had fallen. We tore away his collar, and Holmes breathed a prayer of gratitude when we saw that there was no sign of a wound and that the rescue had been in time.

Sir Henry s'était évanoui. Nous déchirâmes son col et Holmes murmura une prière d'action de grâces, en ne découvrant aucune trace de blessure. Dans quelques minutes, le baronnet serait revenu à lui.

Already our friend's eyelids shivered and he made a feeble effort to move.

Déjà notre jeune ami ouvrait ses yeux et essayait de se lever.

Lestrade thrust his brandy-flask between the baronet's teeth, and two frightened eyes were looking up at us.

Lestrade lui desserra les dents et lui fit avaler quelques gouttes de cognac.

"My God!" he whispered. "What was it? What, in heaven's name, was it?"

«Mon Dieu! balbutia-t-il en tournant vers nous des yeux que la frayeur troublait encore. Qu'était-ce? Au nom du ciel, dites-moi ce que c'était!

"It's dead, whatever it is," said Holmes. "We've laid the family ghost once and forever."

— Peu importe, puisqu'il est mort! dit Holmes. Nous avons tué pour une bonne fois le revenant de la famille Baskerville.»

In mere size and strength it was a terrible crea-

L'animal qui gisait à nos pieds avait des pro-

Holmes emptied five barrels of his revolver into the creature's side.
Holmes déchargea cinq fois son revolver dans les flancs du monstre.

ture which was lying stretched before us. It was not a pure bloodhound and it was not a pure mastiff; but it appeared to be a combination of the two—gaunt, savage, and as large as a small lioness. Even now in the stillness of death, the huge jaws seemed to be dripping with a bluish flame and the small, deep-set, cruel eyes were ringed with fire.

I placed my hand upon the glowing muzzle, and as I held them up my own fingers smouldered and gleamed in the darkness.

"Phosphorus," I said.

"A cunning preparation of it," said Holmes, sniffing at the dead animal. "There is no smell which might have interfered with his power of scent. We owe you a deep apology, Sir Henry, for having exposed you to this fright. I was prepared for a hound, but not for such a creature as this. And the fog gave us little time to receive him."

"You have saved my life."

"Having first endangered it. Are you strong enough to stand?"

"Give me another mouthful of that brandy and I shall be ready for anything. So! Now, if you will help me up. What do you propose to do?"

"To leave you here. You are not fit for further adventures tonight. If you will wait, one or other of us will go back with you to the Hall."

He tried to stagger to his feet; but he was still ghastly pale and trembling in every limb.

We helped him to a rock, where he sat shivering with his face buried in his hands.

"We must leave you now," said Holmes. "The rest of our work must be done, and every moment is of importance. We have our case, and now we only want our man.

"It's a thousand to one against our finding him at the house," he continued as we retraced our steps swiftly down the path. "Those shots must have told him that the game was up."

"We were some distance off, and this fog may have deadened them."

"He followed the hound to call him off—of that you may be certain. No, no, he's gone by this time!

portions qui le rendaient effrayant. Ce n'était ni un limier ni un dogue. Élancé, sauvage, aussi gros qu'une petite lionne, il était mâtiné de ces deux races. Même en ce moment, dans le repos de la mort, une flamme bleuâtre semblait suinter de son énorme gueule et un cercle de feu cernait ses yeux, petits, féroces.

«Je posai la main sur ce museau lumineux et, quant je retirai mes doigts, ils brillèrent dans les ténèbres.

— C'est du phosphore! dis-je.

— Oui… une très curieuse préparation, répliqua Holmes, en flairant l'animal. Elle ne répand aucune odeur capable de nuire à l'odorat de la bête. Nous vous devons des excuses, sir Henry, pour vous avoir exposé à une semblable frayeur. Je croyais avoir affaire à un chien et non pas à une créature de cette sorte. Et puis le brouillard nous avait laissé peu de temps pour lui faire l'accueil que nous lui réservions.

— Vous m'avez sauvé la vie.

— Après l'avoir d'abord mise en péril. Vous sentez-vous assez fort pour vous tenir debout?

— Versez-moi encore une gorgée de cognac et je serai prêt à tout… Là, merci!… Maintenant voulez-vous m'aider à me mettre sur pied… Qu'allez-vous faire?

— Vous n'êtes pas en état de tenter cette nuit de nouvelles aventures. Attendez un moment et l'un de nous retournera avec vous au château.»

Sir Henry essaya de s'affermir sur ses jambes; mais il était encore pâle comme un spectre et il tremblait de tous ses membres.

Nous le conduisîmes jusqu'à une roche sur laquelle il s'assit, tout frissonnant, la tête enfouie entre ses mains.

«Il faut que nous vous quittions, dit Holmes. Nous devons achever notre tâche et chaque minute a une importance capitale. Nous tenons notre crime, à cette heure; il ne nous manque plus que le criminel.»

Et, tandis que nous nous hâtions dans le petit sentier, mon ami ajouta:

«Il y a mille à parier contre un que nous ne trouverons plus Stapleton chez lui. Les coups de revolver lui auront appris qu'il a perdu la partie.

— Nous étions assez loin de Merripit house, hasardai-je; le brouillard aura étouffé le bruit des détonations.

— Il suivait le chien pour l'exciter,… vous pouvez en être certain… Non, non,… il est déjà

But we'll search the house and make sure."

The front door was open, so we rushed in and hurried from room to room to the amazement of a doddering old manservant, who met us in the passage.

There was no light save in the dining-room, but Holmes caught up the lamp and left no corner of the house unexplored. No sign could we see of the man whom we were chasing. On the upper floor, however, one of the bedroom doors was locked.

"There's someone in here," cried Lestrade. "I can hear a movement. Open this door!"

A faint moaning and rustling came from within.

Holmes struck the door just over the lock with the flat of his foot and it flew open. Pistol in hand, we all three rushed into the room.

But there was no sign within it of that desperate and defiant villain whom we expected to see. Instead we were faced by an object so strange and so unexpected that we stood for a moment staring at it in amazement.

The room had been fashioned into a small museum, and the walls were lined by a number of glass-topped cases full of that collection of butterflies and moths the formation of which had been the relaxation of this complex and dangerous man.

In the centre of this room there was an upright beam, which had been placed at some period as a support for the old worm-eaten baulk of timber which spanned the roof. To this post a figure was tied, so swathed and muffled in the sheets which had been used to secure it that one could not for the moment tell whether it was that of a man or a woman.

One towel passed round the throat and was secured at the back of the pillar. Another covered the lower part of the face, and over it two dark eyes—eyes full of grief and shame and a dreadful questioning—stared back at us.

In a minute we had torn off the gag, unswathed the bonds, and Mrs. Stapleton sank upon the floor in front of us. As her beautiful head fell upon her chest I saw the clear red weal of a whiplash across her neck.

"The brute!" cried Holmes. "Here, Lestrade, your brandy-bottle! Put her in the chair! She has fainted from ill-usage and exhaustion."

loin!... D'ailleurs nous fouillerons la maison pour nous en assurer.»

La porte d'entrée était ouverte. Nous nous ruâmes à l'intérieur, courant d'une chambre à l'autre, au grand étonnement d'un vieux domestique que nous rencontrâmes dans le corridor.

Seule, la salle à manger était restée éclairée. Holmes prit la lampe et explora jusqu'aux plus petits recoins. Nous ne découvrîmes aucune trace de Stapleton. Cependant, à l'étage supérieur, on avait fermé une porte à clef.

«Il y a quelqu'un! s'écria Lestrade. J'ai entendu du bruit... Ouvrez!»

Une plainte étouffée, un gémissement, partit de l'intérieur.

Holmes prit son élan et, d'un violent coup de pied appliqué à la hauteur de la serrure, fit voler la porte en éclats. Le revolver au poing, nous nous précipitâmes dans la pièce.

Nous ne vîmes rien qui ressemblât à l'affreux coquin que nous espérions y surprendre. Au contraire, nous nous arrêtâmes devant un objet si étrange, si inattendu, que nous en demeurâmes saisis pendant un moment.

Stapleton avait converti cette pièce en un petit musée. Dans des casiers vitrés, fixés au mur, cet être dangereux et complexe avait réuni ses collections de papillons et de phalènes.

Au centre, une poutre verticale soutenait l'armature de chêne vermoulu qui supportait les ardoises du toit. De cette poutre, pendait un corps si enveloppé, si emmailloté dans un drap qu'il nous fut impossible de reconnaître sur le moment si c'était celui d'un homme ou d'une femme.

Une première serviette enroulée autour du cou du pendu était fortement assujettie à la poutre par un clou. Une seconde enveloppait la partie inférieure du visage, laissant à découvert deux grands yeux noirs — pleins de surprise et de honte — qui nous regardaient avec angoisse.

Dans l'espace d'une seconde, nous eûmes tranché le bâillon, desserré les liens, et Mme Stapleton s'affaissait à nos pieds sur le parquet. Au moment où sa jolie tête retombait sur sa poitrine je distinguai sur la blancheur du cou le sillon rouge produit par une mèche de fouet.

«La brute! cria Holmes... Vite, Lestrade, votre bouteille de cognac! Asseyons-la dans un fauteuil... Elle s'est évanouie d'épuisement.»

She opened her eyes again.
"Is he safe?" she asked. "Has he escaped?"
"He cannot escape us, madam."

"No, no, I did not mean my husband. Sir Henry? Is he safe?"
"Yes."
"And the hound?"
"It is dead."
She gave a long sigh of satisfaction.

"Thank God! Thank God! Oh, this villain! See how he has treated me!"
She shot her arms out from her sleeves, and we saw with horror that they were all mottled with bruises.
"But this is nothing—nothing! It is my mind and soul that he has tortured and defiled. I could endure it all, ill-usage, solitude, a life of deception, everything, as long as I could still cling to the hope that I had his love, but now I know that in this also I have been his dupe and his tool." She broke into passionate sobbing as she spoke.

"You bear him no good will, madam," said Holmes. "Tell us then where we shall find him. If you have ever aided him in evil, help us now and so atone."

"There is but one place where he can have fled," she answered. "There is an old tin mine on an island in the heart of the mire. It was there that he kept his hound and there also he had made preparations so that he might have a refuge. That is where he would fly."

The fog-bank lay like white wool against the window. Holmes held the lamp towards it.
"See," said he. "No one could find his way into the Grimpen Mire tonight."

She laughed and clapped her hands. Her eyes and teeth gleamed with fierce merriment.
"He may find his way in, but never out," she cried. "How can he see the guiding wands tonight? We planted them together, he and I, to mark the pathway through the mire. Oh, if I could only have plucked them out today. Then indeed you would have had him at your mercy!"

It was evident to us that all pursuit was in vain until the fog had lifted. Meanwhile we left Lest-

La jeune femme entr'ouvrit les yeux.
«Est-il sauvé? s'écria-t-elle, s'est-il échappé?...
— Il ne peut nous échapper, madame, répondit froidement Sherlock Holmes.
— Non, non,... pas mon mari,... sir Henry? Est-il sain et sauf?
— Oui.
— Et le chien?
— Mort.»
Mme Stapleton poussa un long soupir de satisfaction.
«Merci, mon Dieu, merci!... Oh! le misérable!... Voyez dans quel état il m'a mise!»
Elle releva ses manches et nous montra ses bras couverts d'ecchymoses.

«Mais cela n'est rien... rien! reprit-elle, d'une voix entrecoupée de sanglots. C'est mon esprit et mon âme qu'il a torturés et souillés! J'aurais tout supporté: les mauvais traitements, la solitude, ma vie brisée, tout, si j'avais pu conserver l'espoir qu'il m'aimait encore! Aujourd'hui, mes illusions se sont envolées, et je sais que je n'ai été qu'un instrument entre ses mains.
— Vous n'éprouvez plus pour lui que du ressentiment, n'est-ce pas, madame? demanda Holmes. Désignez-nous sa retraite. Vous l'avez aidé dans le mal, venez-nous en aide maintenant; ce sera votre expiation.
— Il ne peut avoir dirigé ses pas que vers un seul endroit, répondit-elle. Au cœur même de la grande fondrière, il existe, sur un îlot de terre ferme, une ancienne mine d'étain. C'était là qu'il cachait son chien. Là, également, il s'était ménagé un refuge pour le cas où il aurait dû fuir précipitamment. Il y a couru certainement.»
Holmes prit la lampe et l'approcha de la fenêtre. Le brouillard en obscurcissait les vitres.
«Voyez, madame, dit-il. Je défie qui que ce soit de retrouver cette nuit son chemin à travers la grande fondrière de Grimpen.»
Mme Stapleton battit des mains; ses lèvres se retroussèrent dans un rictus sinistre.
«Il peut y pénétrer, mais il n'en ressortira jamais! s'écria-t-elle. Comment, par cette nuit épaisse, verrait-il les balises qui doivent le guider?... Nous les avons plantées ensemble, lui et moi, pour marquer le seul chemin praticable... Ah! s'il m'avait été permis de les arracher aujourd'hui, vous l'auriez à votre merci!»
Il était évident que, pour commencer nos recherches, nous étions condamnés à attendre que

rade in possession of the house while Holmes and I went back with the baronet to Baskerville Hall.

le brouillard se fût dissipé. Nous confiâmes à Lestrade la garde de la maison et nous reprîmes, Holmes et moi, le chemin du château de Baskerville en compagnie du baronnet.

The story of the Stapletons could no longer be withheld from him, but he took the blow bravely when he learned the truth about the woman whom he had loved.

But the shock of the night's adventures had shattered his nerves, and before morning he lay delirious in a high fever under the care of Dr. Mortimer. The two of them were destined to travel together round the world before Sir Henry had become once more the hale, hearty man that he had been before he became master of that ill-omened estate.

And now I come rapidly to the conclusion of this singular narrative, in which I have tried to make the reader share those dark fears and vague surmises which clouded our lives so long and ended in so tragic a manner.

Impossible de taire plus longtemps à sir Henry l'histoire des Stapleton... Il supporta courageusement le coup que lui porta au cœur la vérité sur la femme qu'il avait aimée.

La secousse produite sur ses nerfs par les aventures de cette nuit déterminèrent une fièvre cérébrale. Le docteur Mortimer, accouru à son chevet, déclara qu'il ne faudrait rien moins qu'un long voyage autour du monde, pour rendre à sir Henry la vigueur et la santé qu'il possédait avant de devenir propriétaire de ce néfaste domaine.

J'arrive rapidement à la conclusion de cette singulière histoire, dans laquelle je me suis efforcé de faire partager au lecteur les angoisses et les vagues soupçons qui, pendant quelques jours, avaient troublé notre existence et qui venaient de se terminer d'une si tragique façon.

On the morning after the death of the hound the fog had lifted and we were guided by Mrs. Stapleton to the point where they had found a pathway through the bog. It helped us to realise the horror of this woman's life when we saw the eagerness and joy with which she laid us on her husband's track.

We left her standing upon the thin peninsula of firm, peaty soil which tapered out into the widespread bog. From the end of it a small wand planted here and there showed where the path zigzagged from tuft to tuft of rushes among those green-scummed pits and foul quagmires which barred the way to the stranger. Rank reeds and lush, slimy water-plants sent an odour of decay and a heavy miasmatic vapour onto our faces, while a false step plunged us more than once thigh-deep into the dark, quivering mire, which shook for yards in soft undulations around our feet.

Its tenacious grip plucked at our heels as we walked, and when we sank into it it was as if some malignant hand was tugging us down into those obscene depths, so grim and purposeful was the clutch in which it held us.

Le lendemain du drame de Merripit house, le brouillard se dissipa, et Mme Stapleton nous guida vers l'endroit où son mari et elle avaient tracé un chemin à travers la fondrière. Pendant le trajet, nous pûmes mesurer, à l'empressement qu'elle mettait à nous conduire sur les traces du naturaliste, combien cette femme avait souffert.

Elle resta sur une sorte de promontoire que la terre ferme jetait dans l'intérieur du marécage. À partir de ce point, de petites balises, plantées ça et là, indiquaient le sentier qui serpentait d'une touffe d'ajoncs à l'autre, au milieu de trous tapissés d'écume verdâtre et de flaques bourbeuses qui barraient la route aux étrangers. Des roseaux desséchés et des plantes aquatiques limoneuses exhalaient des odeurs fades de choses en décomposition; une vapeur lourde, chargée de miasmes, nous montait au visage.

Au moindre faux pas, nous enfoncions jusqu'au-dessus du genou dans cette boue visqueuse, frissonnante, qui ondulait sous la pression de nos pieds jusqu'à plusieurs mètres de distance. Elle se collait à nos talons et, lorsque nous y tombions, on aurait dit qu'une main homicide nous tirait en bas, tellement était tenace l'étreinte qui nous enserrait.

Once only we saw a trace that someone had passed that perilous way before us. From amid a tuft of cotton grass which bore it up out of the

Une seule fois, nous acquîmes la preuve que Stapleton nous avait devancés dans le sentier. Dans une touffe de joncs émergeant de la vase, il nous slime some dark thing was projecting.

Holmes sank to his waist as he stepped from the path to seize it, and had we not been there to drag him out he could never have set his foot upon firm land again. He held an old black boot in the air. "Meyers, Toronto," was printed on the leather inside.

"It is worth a mud bath," said he. "It is our friend Sir Henry's missing boot."

"Thrown there by Stapleton in his flight."

"Exactly. He retained it in his hand after using it to set the hound upon the track. He fled when he knew the game was up, still clutching it. And he hurled it away at this point of his flight. We know at least that he came so far in safety."

But more than that we were never destined to know, though there was much which we might surmise. There was no chance of finding footsteps in the mire, for the rising mud oozed swiftly in upon them, but as we at last reached firmer ground beyond the morass we all looked eagerly for them. But no slightest sign of them ever met our eyes. If the earth told a true story, then Stapleton never reached that island of refuge towards which he struggled through the fog upon that last night. Somewhere in the heart of the great Grimpen Mire, down in the foul slime of the huge morass which had sucked him in, this cold and cruel-hearted man is forever buried.

Many traces we found of him in the bog-girt island where he had hid his savage ally. A huge driving-wheel and a shaft half-filled with rubbish showed the position of an abandoned mine. Beside it were the crumbling remains of the cottages of the miners, driven away no doubt by the foul reek of the surrounding swamp.

In one of these a staple and chain with a quantity of gnawed bones showed where the animal had been confined. A skeleton with a tangle of brown hair adhering to it lay among the débris.

"A dog!" said Holmes. "By Jove, a curly-haired spaniel. Poor Mortimer will never see his pet

sembla distinguer quelque chose de noir.

Du sentier, Holmes sauta sur la touffe et s'enfonça jusqu'à la ceinture. Si nous n'avions pas été là pour le retirer, il n'aurait jamais plus foulé la terre ferme. Il tenait à la main une vieille bottine. À l'intérieur, on lisait cette adresse imprimée: «Meyer, Toronto».

«Cela vaut bien un bain de boue, dit Sherlock. C'est la bottine volée à notre ami sir Henry.

— Stapleton l'aura jetée là dans sa fuite, fis-je.

— Certainement. Il l'avait conservée à la main, après s'en être servi pour mettre le chien sur la piste. Quand il a vu que tout était perdu, il s'est enfui de Merripit house, ayant toujours cette bottine, et il s'en est débarrassé ici. Cela nous montre qu'il a atteint, sain et sauf, ce point de la fondrière.»

Ce fut tout ce que nous découvrîmes de lui. D'ailleurs, comment relever des traces de pas dans le marécage où cette surface de fange mobile reprenait son uniformité après le passage d'un homme? Parvenus sur un terrain plus solide formant une espèce d'île au milieu de la fondrière, nous poursuivîmes nos recherches avec un soin minutieux. Elles furent inutiles. Si la terre ne mentait pas, jamais Stapleton n'avait dû gagner cet endroit, malgré sa lutte désespérée contre le brouillard. Quelque part dans la grande fondrière de Grimpen, cet homme au cœur froid et cruel était enseveli, aspiré par la boue visqueuse.

Dans cette île surgie du milieu de la vase, nous trouvâmes de nombreuses traces de ses visites, ainsi que du séjour de son féroce allié. Une vieille roue et une brouette à demi remplie de décombres marquaient l'emplacement d'une mine abandonnée. Tout près de là, on retrouvait encore les vestiges des cabanes de mineurs, chassés sans doute par les exhalaisons pestilentielles du marais.

Dans l'une de ces cabanes, une niche à laquelle était fixée une chaîne, puis un amas d'os, indiquaient l'endroit où Stapleton attachait son chien. Un crâne auquel adhéraient encore des poils noirs gisait au milieu des débris.

«Un chien! fit Holmes, en le retournant du pied. Par Dieu! c'était un caniche! Pauvre Morti-

again. Well, I do not know that this place contains any secret which we have not already fathomed. He could hide his hound, but he could not hush its voice, and hence came those cries which even in daylight were not pleasant to hear. On an emergency he could keep the hound in the outhouse at Merripit, but it was always a risk, and it was only on the supreme day, which he regarded as the end of all his efforts, that he dared do it. This paste in the tin is no doubt the luminous mixture with which the creature was daubed. It was suggested, of course, by the story of the family hell-hound, and by the desire to frighten old Sir Charles to death. No wonder the poor devil of a convict ran and screamed, even as our friend did, and as we ourselves might have done, when he saw such a creature bounding through the darkness of the moor upon his track. It was a cunning device, for, apart from the chance of driving your victim to his death, what peasant would venture to inquire too closely into such a creature should he get sight of it, as many have done, upon the moor? I said it in London, Watson, and I say it again now, that never yet have we helped to hunt down a more dangerous man than he who is lying yonder."

He swept his long arm towards the huge mottled expanse of green-splotched bog which stretched away until it merged into the russet slopes of the moor.

mer, il ne reverra plus son favori!… Je doute qu'il reste ici des secrets que nous n'ayons pas pénétrés… Stapleton pouvait cacher son chien, mais il ne pouvait l'empêcher d'aboyer! De là ces hurlements si terrifiants à entendre, même en plein jour. Enfermer la bête dans un des pavillons de Merripit house exposait le naturaliste aux plus grands risques et ce ne fut que le dernier jour, alors qu'il se croyait au terme de ses efforts, qu'il osa s'y décider… La pâte contenue dans cette boîte d'étain est sans doute la composition phosphorescente dont il enduisait son chien. Cette idée lui fut sûrement suggérée par l'histoire du chien des Baskerville et par le désir d'effrayer sir Charles jusqu'à le tuer. Est-il étonnant que ce pauvre diable de Selden ait couru, ait crié — ainsi que sir Henry et nous-mêmes — lorsqu'il vit bondir à sa poursuite, dans les ténèbres de la lande, une créature aussi étrange?… Il faut admirer l'ingéniosité de l'invention. En effet, indépendamment de la possibilité de tuer sa victime, cela présentait l'avantage d'éloigner du monstre tous les paysans qui, le rencontrant sur la lande — cela est arrivé à plusieurs — auraient eu l'intention de l'examiner de trop près. Je l'ai dit à Londres, Watson, et je le répète ici à cette heure, nous n'avons jamais donné la chasse à un homme plus dangereux que celui qui gît là-bas.»

En prononçant ces dernières paroles, Holmes étendit la main vers le grand espace moucheté de vert qui représentait la fondrière de Grimpen et qui s'étendait au loin jusqu'aux pentes sombres de la lande.

CHAPTER 15. A RETROSPECTION

It was the end of November, and Holmes and I sat, upon a raw and foggy night, on either side of a blazing fire in our sitting-room in Baker Street.

Since the tragic upshot of our visit to Devonshire he had been engaged in two affairs of the utmost importance, in the first of which he had exposed the atrocious conduct of Colonel Upwood in connection with the famous card scandal of the Nonpareil Club, while in the second he had defended the unfortunate Mme. Montpensier from the charge of murder which hung over her in connection with the death of her step-daughter, Mlle. Carére, the young lady who, as it will be remembered, was found six months later alive and married in New York.

My friend was in excellent spirits over the success which had attended a succession of difficult and important cases, so that I was able to induce him to discuss the details of the Baskerville mystery. I had waited patiently for the opportunity for I was aware that he would never permit cases to overlap, and that his clear and logical mind would not be drawn from its present work to dwell upon memories of the past.

Sir Henry and Dr. Mortimer were, however, in London, on their way to that long voyage which had been recommended for the restoration of his shattered nerves. They had called upon us that very afternoon, so that it was natural that the subject should come up for discussion.

"The whole course of events," said Holmes, "from the point of view of the man who called himself Stapleton was simple and direct, although to us, who had no means in the beginning of knowing the motives of his actions and could only learn part of the facts, it all appeared exceedingly complex. I have had the advantage of two conversations with Mrs. Stapleton, and the case has now been so entirely cleared up that I am not aware that there is anything which has remained a secret to us. You will find a few notes upon the matter under

CHAPITRE 15. DÉTAILS RÉTROSPECTIFS

Un soir de novembre, âpre et brumeux, nous étions assis, Holmes et moi, au coin du feu qui pétillait gaiement dans la cheminée de notre salon de Baker street.

Depuis l'issue tragique de notre visite au château de Baskerville, mon ami s'était occupé de deux affaires de la plus haute importance. Dans la première, il avait dévoilé l'abominable conduite du colonel Upwood, lors du scandale des cartes à jouer au Nonpareil Club. Dans la seconde, au contraire, il avait démontré l'innocence de Mme Montpensier, accusée d'avoir assassiné sa belle-fille, Mlle Carère, jeune fille que l'on retrouva six mois plus tard à New York, vivante et mariée.

Le succès de ces dernières entreprises, si délicates et si importantes, avait mis Holmes en belle humeur; je crus le moment venu de discuter les détails du mystère de Baskerville. J'avais patiemment attendu une occasion, car je savais qu'il n'aimait pas qu'on le troublât dans ses travaux, ni que son esprit, clair et méthodique, fût distrait de ses occupations présentes par un retour vers le passé.

Sir Henry et le docteur Mortimer, à la veille de partir pour le long voyage qui devait rendre au baronnet l'équilibre de ses nerfs rompu par les drames de la lande, se trouvaient de passage à Londres. Nos deux amis avaient passé l'après-midi avec nous et ce sujet de conversation était tout naturellement indiqué.

«En ce qui concerne l'homme qui se déguisait sous le nom de Stapleton, dit Holmes, la succession des événements était simple et compréhensible, bien qu'elle nous parût excessivement complexe, à nous qui n'avions, au début, aucune donnée sur le mobile de ses actions et qui ne pouvions connaître qu'une partie des faits. J'ai eu la bonne fortune de causer deux fois avec Mme Stapleton, et tous les points sont tellement élucidés que je crois être en mesure d'affirmer qu'il ne reste plus rien d'obscur dans cette affaire. Reportez-vous, d'ailleurs, aux the heading B in my indexed list of cases."

"Perhaps you would kindly give me a sketch of the course of events from memory."

"Certainly, though I cannot guarantee that I carry all the facts in my mind. Intense mental concentration has a curious way of blotting out what has passed. The barrister who has his case at his fingers' ends and is able to argue with an expert upon his own subject finds that a week or two of the courts will drive it all out of his head once more. So each of my cases displaces the last, and Mlle. Carére has blurred my recollection of Baskerville Hall. Tomorrow some other little problem may be submitted to my notice which will in turn dispossess the fair French lady and the infamous Upwood.

So far as the case of the hound goes, however, I will give you the course of events as nearly as I can, and you will suggest anything which I may have forgotten.

"My inquiries show beyond all question that the family portrait did not lie, and that this fellow was indeed a Baskerville. He was a son of that Rodger Baskerville, the younger brother of Sir Charles, who fled with a sinister reputation to South America, where he was said to have died unmarried. He did, as a matter of fact, marry, and had one child, this fellow, whose real name is the same as his father's.

He married Beryl Garcia, one of the beauties of Costa Rica, and, having purloined a considerable sum of public money, he changed his name to Vandeleur and fled to England, where he established a school in the east of Yorkshire. His reason for attempting this special line of business was that he had struck up an acquaintance with a consumptive tutor upon the voyage home, and that he had used this man's ability to make the undertaking a success.

Fraser, the tutor, died however, and the school which had begun well sank from disrepute into infamy. The Vandeleurs found it convenient to change their name to Stapleton, and he brought the remains of his fortune, his schemes for the future, and his taste for entomology to the south of England.

différentes notes de mon répertoire classées à la lettre B.

— Alors, demandai-je à Sherlock Holmes, expliquez-moi de mémoire comment vous êtes arrivé à dégager la vérité.

— Volontiers. Cependant je ne vous garantis pas de ne rien oublier. Une intense contention mentale produit le très curieux effet d'effacer le passé de notre esprit. Ainsi l'avocat, qui possède sa cause sur le bout du doigt et qui peut ergoter avec un témoin sur des détails infimes, s'aperçoit une ou deux semaines après sa plaidoirie, qu'il ne se souvient plus que de très peu de chose. De même, chacun des cas dont je m'occupe chasse le précédent, et Mlle Carère a remplacé dans ma mémoire sir Henry Baskerville. Demain, quelque nouveau problème soumis à mon appréciation chassera à son tour de mon souvenir la jeune Française et l'infâme colonel Upwood.

«Quant au chien des Baskerville, je suivrai de mon mieux l'ordre des événements; si je viens à me tromper, vous me reprendrez.

«Mes enquêtes démontrent irréfutablement que la ressemblance entre le portrait d'Hugo et Stapleton n'était pas menteuse et que ce dernier appartenait bien à la race des Baskerville. Il était le fils du plus jeune frère de sir Charles, de ce Roger qui partit, à la suite de plusieurs scandales, pour l'Amérique du Sud, où, prétendait-on, il mourut célibataire. Il se maria, au contraire, et eut un enfant, ce misérable Stapleton auquel nous devons restituer le nom de son père.

«Là, ce descendant des Baskerville épousa Béryl Garcia, une des beautés de Costa-Rica, et pour fuir les conséquences d'un vol considérable commis au préjudice de l'État, il changea son nom en celui de Vandeleur, vint en Angleterre et ouvrit une école dans une petite localité du Yorkshire. La connaissance d'un pauvre précepteur, poitrinaire, faite sur le bateau qui amenait le naturaliste en Angleterre, l'avait décidé à se tourner vers l'enseignement et à mettre à profit le savoir de Fraser.

«Ainsi se nommait le précepteur. Mais Fraser succomba bientôt à la maladie qui le minait, et l'école, jusqu'alors en pleine prospérité, tomba peu à peu dans le discrédit. Stapleton se vit un beau jour forcé de mettre la clef sous la porte. Une fois encore; les Vandeleur abandonnèrent leur nom, et le naturaliste transporta dans le sud de l'Angleterre les restes de sa fortune, ses projets d'avenir et son goût pour l'entomologie.

I learned at the British Museum that he was a recognized authority upon the subject, and that the name of Vandeleur has been permanently attached to a certain moth which he had, in his Yorkshire days, been the first to describe.

"We now come to that portion of his life which has proved to be of such intense interest to us. The fellow had evidently made inquiry and found that only two lives intervened between him and a valuable estate.

When he went to Devonshire his plans were, I believe, exceedingly hazy, but that he meant mischief from the first is evident from the way in which he took his wife with him in the character of his sister. The idea of using her as a decoy was clearly already in his mind, though he may not have been certain how the details of his plot were to be arranged.

He meant in the end to have the estate, and he was ready to use any tool or run any risk for that end. His first act was to establish himself as near to his ancestral home as he could, and his second was to cultivate a friendship with Sir Charles Baskerville and with the neighbours.

"The baronet himself told him about the family hound, and so prepared the way for his own death. Stapleton, as I will continue to call him, knew that the old man's heart was weak and that a shock would kill him. So much he had learned from Dr. Mortimer. He had heard also that Sir Charles was superstitious and had taken this grim legend very seriously. His ingenious mind instantly suggested a way by which the baronet could be done to death, and yet it would be hardly possible to bring home the guilt to the real murderer.

"Having conceived the idea he proceeded to carry it out with considerable finesse. An ordinary schemer would have been content to work with a savage hound.

The use of artificial means to make the creature diabolical was a flash of genius upon his part. The dog he bought in London from Ross and Mangles, the dealers in Fulham Road. It was the strongest and most savage in their possession. He brought it down by the North Devon line and walked a great distance over the moor so as to get it home without exciting any remarks.

He had already on his insect hunts learned to penetrate the Grimpen Mire, and so had found a

J'ai appris qu'au Bristish Museum, il faisait autorité en la matière, et que le nom de Vandeleur était pour toujours attaché à une certaine phalène qu'il avait décrite le premier, lors de son séjour dans le Yorkshire.

«Arrivons maintenant à la seule partie de sa vie qui nous offre vraiment de l'intérêt. Stapleton avait pris ses informations et savait que deux existences seulement le séparaient de la possession du riche domaine de Baskerville.

«Je crois qu'à son arrivée dans le Devonshire, son plan était encore mal défini. Mais, dans le fait de présenter sa femme comme sa sœur, je trouve la preuve que, dès le début, il nourrissait déjà de mauvais desseins. Il avait l'intention manifeste de se servir d'elle comme d'un appât, quoiqu'il ne sût pas encore exactement de quelle façon il tendrait sa toile.

«Il convoitait le domaine et, pour en venir à ses fins, il était prêt à employer tous les moyens, à courir tous les risques. D'abord il s'installa dans le plus immédiat voisinage de la demeure de ses ancêtres; puis il tâcha de conquérir l'amitié de sir Charles Baskerville et de ses autres voisins.

«Le baronnet lui-même se chargea de lui apprendre l'histoire du chien de la famille et prépara — ainsi les voies de sa propre mort. Stapleton — je continuerai à l'appeler de ce nom — fut mis au courant, par Mortimer, de la maladie de cœur dont souffrait le vieux gentilhomme, qu'une émotion pouvait tuer. Sir Charles, acceptant comme véridique la lugubre légende, lui apparut également sous le jour d'un être superstitieux. Aussitôt, son esprit ingénieux lui suggéra le moyen de se débarrasser du baronnet. Malgré cela, il serait difficile de justifier une accusation de meurtre contre ce coquin.

«Cette idée une fois conçue, il commença à la mettre à exécution avec une incontestable finesse. Un criminel vulgaire se serait contenté de jouer purement et simplement du chien.

«L'artifice dont il usa pour donner à-la bête un aspect diabolique fut un trait de génie de sa part. Il l'avait achetée à Londres chez Ross et Mangles, les grands marchands de Fulham street; elle était la plus grosse et la plus féroce qu'ils eussent à vendre en ce moment. Il la conduisit à Grimpen par la ligne du chemin de fer du North Decon et fit à pied, sur la lande, une grande partie de la route, afin de ne pas attirer l'attention des gens du pays.

«Au cours de ses recherches entomologiques, il avait découvert le sentier qui conduisait au cœur safe hiding-place for the creature. Here he kennelled it and waited his chance.

"But it was some time coming. The old gentleman could not be decoyed outside of his grounds at night. Several times Stapleton lurked about with his hound, but without avail. It was during these fruitless quests that he, or rather his ally, was seen by peasants, and that the legend of the demon dog received a new confirmation.

He had hoped that his wife might lure Sir Charles to his ruin, but here she proved unexpectedly independent. She would not endeavour to entangle the old gentleman in a sentimental attachment which might deliver him over to his enemy. Threats and even, I am sorry to say, blows refused to move her. She would have nothing to do with it, and for a time Stapleton was at a deadlock.

"He found a way out of his difficulties through the chance that Sir Charles, who had conceived a friendship for him, made him the minister of his charity in the case of this unfortunate woman, Mrs. Laura Lyons.

By representing himself as a single man he acquired complete influence over her, and he gave her to understand that in the event of her obtaining a divorce from her husband he would marry her.

His plans were suddenly brought to a head by his knowledge that Sir Charles was about to leave the Hall on the advice of Dr. Mortimer, with whose opinion he himself pretended to coincide. He must act at once, or his victim might get beyond his power. He therefore put pressure upon Mrs. Lyons to write this letter, imploring the old man to give her an interview on the evening before his departure for London. He then, by a specious argument, prevented her from going, and so had the chance for which he had waited.

"Driving back in the evening from Coombe Tracey he was in time to get his hound, to treat it with his infernal paint, and to bring the beast round to the gate at which he had reason to expect that he would find the old gentleman waiting.

The dog, incited by its master, sprang over the wicket-gate and pursued the unfortunate baronet, who fled screaming down the yew alley. In that gloomy tunnel it must indeed have been a dreadful sight to see that huge black creature, with its flaming jaws and blazing eyes, bounding after its

de la grande fondrière; il trouva la cachette sûre pour l'animal, et il l'enchaîna à une niche. Puis il attendit une occasion propice.

«Elle ne se présenta pas immédiatement. Impossible d'attirer, la nuit, le vieux gentilhomme hors de chez lui. Plusieurs fois, Stapleton rôda dans les environs, accompagné de son chien — mais sans succès. Ce fut pendant ces infructueuses tournées que des paysans aperçurent son terrible allié et que la légende du chien-démon reçut une nouvelle confirmation.

«Il avait espéré que sa femme le seconderait dans ses projets contre sir Charles, mais elle s'y refusa énergiquement. Elle ne voulait pas entraîner le vieux gentilhomme dans un commerce sentimental qui le livrerait sans défense à son ennemi. Les menaces et même les coups — je suis honteux de le dire — ne purent briser la résistance de la la pauvre femme. Elle s'obstina à ne se mêler de rien, et Stapleton se trouva fort embarrassé.

«En s'éprenant d'une belle amitié pour ce drôle et en l'instituant le dispensateur de ses libéralités envers l'infortunée Laura Lyons, sir Charles lui fournit l'occasion qu'il recherchait depuis longtemps.

«Il se dit célibataire et exerça rapidement une influence considérable sur l'esprit de la fille de Frankland; il lui persuada qu'il l'épouserait, si elle parvenait à obtenir son divorce.

«Dès qu'il fut informé que, sur l'avis de Mortimer — avis qu'il appuya de tous ses efforts — sir Charles se disposait à quitter le château de Baskerville, il dressa promptement ses batteries. Il devait agir immédiatement, sous peine de voir sa victime lui échapper. Stapleton pressa donc Mme Lyons d'écrire la lettre pour laquelle elle suppliait le vieillard de lui accorder une entrevue, la veille de son départ pour Londres. Ensuite, à l'aide d'un argument spécieux, il la dissuada de se rendre à la grille de la lande. Sir Charles était à sa merci.

«Le soir, il revint de Coombe Tracey assez tôt pour aller chercher son chien, l'enduire de son infernale mixture et le conduire près de la porte, où, avec juste raison, il savait que sir Charles faisait le guet.

«Le chien, excité par son maître, sauta pardessus la claire-voie et poursuivit le malheureux baronnet, qui s'engagea en criant dans l'allée des Ifs. Pouvez-vous imaginer un spectacle plus saisissant que celui de cette énorme bête noire, à la gueule enflammée, aux yeux injectés de feu, bondissant, victim. He fell dead at the end of the alley from heart disease and terror.

le long de cette sombre avenue, après ce vieillard inoffensif! Au milieu de l'allée, la frayeur et son anévrisme terrassèrent sir Charles.

The hound had kept upon the grassy border while the baronet had run down the path, so that no track but the man's was visible. On seeing him lying still the creature had probably approached to sniff at him, but finding him dead had turned away again. It was then that it left the print which was actually observed by Dr. Mortimer. The hound was called off and hurried away to its lair in the Grimpen Mire, and a mystery was left which puzzled the authorities, alarmed the countryside, and finally brought the case within the scope of our observation.

«L'animal galopait sur la bordure de gazon, tandis que le baronnet suivait la partie sablée, de telle sorte qu'on ne remarqua que les pas de l'homme. En le voyant immobile, le chien s'approcha probablement pour le flairer; mais, le voyant mort, il fit demi-tour. C'est alors qu'il laissa sur le sol l'empreinte si judicieusement relevée par Mortimer. Stapleton le rappela et le reconduisit immédiatement au chenil de la grande fondrière de Grimpen. Le mystère demeura une énigme indéchiffrable pour la police, alarma toute la contrée et provoqua finalement la visite dont le docteur nous honora ici même, il y a quelques mois.

"So much for the death of Sir Charles Baskerville. You perceive the devilish cunning of it, for really it would be almost impossible to make a case against the real murderer. His only accomplice was one who could never give him away, and the grotesque, inconceivable nature of the device only served to make it more effective.

«Voilà pour la mort de sir Charles Baskerville. Comprenez-vous maintenant l'astuce infernale qui présidait à ces préparatifs? Cependant, il serait absolument impossible de baser sur elle une accusation contre Stapleton. Son unique complice ne pouvait jamais le trahir, et le moyen employé était si grotesque, si inconcevable, que son efficacité en était accrue par cela même.

Both of the women concerned in the case, Mrs. Stapleton and Mrs. Laura Lyons, were left with a strong suspicion against Stapleton. Mrs. Stapleton knew that he had designs upon the old man, and also of the existence of the hound. Mrs. Lyons knew neither of these things, but had been impressed by the death occurring at the time of an uncancelled appointment which was only known to him. However, both of them were under his influence, and he had nothing to fear from them. The first half of his task was successfully accomplished but the more difficult still remained.

«Les deux femmes mêlées à l'affaire, Mme Stapleton et Laura Lyons, conçurent bien quelques soupçons à l'encontre du naturaliste. Mme Stapleton n'ignorait pas ses sinistres desseins contre le vieillard; elle connaissait aussi l'existence du chien,

«Mme Laura Lyons ne savait rien de tout cela; mais la nouvelle de la mort de sir Charles l'avait d'autant plus impressionnée, qu'elle était survenue à l'heure précise d'un rendez-vous donné à l'instigation de Stapleton et non contremandé par elle. Comme l'une et l'autre vivaient sous la dépendance de ce dernier, il n'avait rien à redouter de leur part. Le succès couronna la première moitié de sa tâche; il restait encore la seconde — de beaucoup la plus difficile.

"It is possible that Stapleton did not know of the existence of an heir in Canada. In any case he would very soon learn it from his friend Dr. Mortimer, and he was told by the latter all details about the arrival of Henry Baskerville. Stapleton's first idea was that this young stranger from Canada might possibly be done to death in London without coming down to Devonshire at all.

«Il se peut que Stapleton ait ignoré l'existence de l'héritier canadien. En tout cas, il en entendit bientôt parler par le docteur Mortimer et, par lui, il apprit tous les détails de la prochaine arrivée de sir Henry Baskerville. Il s'arrêta d'abord à la pensée de tuer, à Londres, ce jeune étranger tombé du Canada, sans lui permettre d'atteindre le Devonshire.

He distrusted his wife ever since she had refused to help him in laying a trap for the old man, and he dared not leave her long out of his sight for fear he should lose his influence over her. It was for this reason that he took her to London with

«Depuis que sa femme avait refusé de l'aider à creuser la chausse-trape dans laquelle il espérait prendre sir Charles, Stapleton se méfiait d'elle. Dans la crainte de la voir se soustraire à son influence, il n'osa pas la perdre de vue trop long-him. They lodged, I find, at the Mexborough Private Hotel, in Craven Street, which was actually one of those called upon by my agent in search of evidence.

Here he kept his wife imprisoned in her room while he, disguised in a beard, followed Dr. Mortimer to Baker Street and afterwards to the station and to the Northumberland Hotel.

His wife had some inkling of his plans; but she had such a fear of her husband—a fear founded upon brutal ill-treatment—that she dare not write to warn the man whom she knew to be in danger. If the letter should fall into Stapleton's hands her own life would not be safe. Eventually, as we know, she adopted the expedient of cutting out the words which would form the message, and addressing the letter in a disguised hand. It reached the baronet, and gave him the first warning of his danger.

"It was very essential for Stapleton to get some article of Sir Henry's attire so that, in case he was driven to use the dog, he might always have the means of setting him upon his track. With characteristic promptness and audacity he set about this at once, and we cannot doubt that the boots or chamber-maid of the hotel was well bribed to help him in his design. By chance, however, the first boot which was procured for him was a new one and, therefore, useless for his purpose. He then had it returned and obtained another—a most instructive incident, since it proved conclusively to my mind that we were dealing with a real hound, as no other supposition could explain this anxiety to obtain an old boot and this indifference to a new one. The more outré and grotesque an incident is the more carefully it deserves to be examined, and the very point which appears to complicate a case is, when duly considered and scientifically handled, the one which is most likely to elucidate it.

"Then we had the visit from our friends next morning, shadowed always by Stapleton in the cab. From his knowledge of our rooms and of my appearance, as well as from his general conduct, I am inclined to think that Stapleton's career of crime has been by no means limited to this single Baskerville affair. It is suggestive that during the last three years there have been four considerable burglaries in the west country, for none of which was any criminal ever arrested. The last of these, at Folkestone Court, in May, was remarkable for the cold-blooded pistolling of the page, who surprised

temps. Aussi l'emmena-t-il à Londres avec lui. Ils logèrent à Mexborough hotel, dans Craven street, l'un des établissements visités sur mon ordre par Cartwright pour rechercher un commencement de preuve.

«Il retint sa femme prisonnière dans sa chambre, tandis qu'affublé d'une fausse barbe, il suivait le docteur à Baker street, puis à la gare et enfin à Northumberland hotel.

«Mme Stapleton avait pressenti une partie des projets de son mari, mais elle en avait une telle peur — peur fondée sur sa brutalité et sur les mauvais procédés dont il l'abreuvait — qu'elle n'osa pas écrire à sir Henry pour le prévenir de dangers éventuels. Si sa lettre tombait entre les mains de Stapleton, sa propre existence serait compromise. Elle adopta l'expédient de découper dans un journal les mots composant le message et de déguiser son écriture sur l'adresse. La missive parvint au jeune baronnet et lui donna la première alarme.

«Pour lancer facilement le chien à la poursuite de sir Henry, il était essentiel que Stapleton se procurât un objet ayant appartenu au jeune homme. Avec une promptitude et une audace caractéristiques, il se mit en quête de cet objet, et nous ne pouvons douter que le valet d'étage ou la femme de chambre de l'hôtel n'aient été soudoyés par lui dans ce but. Par hasard, la première bottine remise était neuve et par conséquent sans utilité. Il la renvoya et en demanda une autre — une vieille. Cet incident, très instructif, me prouva immédiatement qu'il s'agissait d'un chien en chair et en os; aucune autre supposition n'aurait expliqué ce besoin d'une bottine vieille et cette indifférence pour une neuve.

«Plus un détail est futile, ridicule, plus il mérite qu'on l'examine, et le point même qui semble compliquer une affaire est, quand on le considère attentivement, celui qui très probablement l'élucidera.

«Ensuite nous reçûmes, le lendemain matin, la visite de nos nouveaux amis, toujours espionnés par Stapleton dans son cab. Il savait où je demeurais, il me connaissait de vue; j'en conclus que la carrière criminelle de Stapleton ne se bornait pas à cette seule tentative contre les Baskerville. En effet, pendant ces trois dernières années, on a commis dans l'ouest de l'Angleterre quatre vols qualifiés, tous restés impunis. Le dernier, datant du mois de mai, à Folkestone, a été surtout remarquable par le sang-froid avec lequel le voleur masqué a brûlé la cervelle du domestique qui venait de le sur-the masked and solitary burglar. I cannot doubt that Stapleton recruited his waning resources in this fashion, and that for years he has been a desperate and dangerous man.

"We had an example of his readiness of resource that morning when he got away from us so successfully, and also of his audacity in sending back my own name to me through the cabman.

From that moment he understood that I had taken over the case in London, and that therefore there was no chance for him there. He returned to Dartmoor and awaited the arrival of the baronet."

"One moment!" said I. "You have, no doubt, described the sequence of events correctly, but there is one point which you have left unexplained. What became of the hound when its master was in London?"

"I have given some attention to this matter and it is undoubtedly of importance. There can be no question that Stapleton had a confidant, though it is unlikely that he ever placed himself in his power by sharing all his plans with him.

There was an old manservant at Merripit House, whose name was Anthony. His connection with the Stapletons can be traced for several years, as far back as the school-mastering days, so that he must have been aware that his master and mistress were really husband and wife. This man has disappeared and has escaped from the country. It is suggestive that Anthony is not a common name in England, while Antonio is so in all Spanish or Spanish-American countries. The man, like Mrs. Stapleton herself, spoke good English, but with a curious lisping accent. I have myself seen this old man cross the Grimpen Mire by the path which Stapleton had marked out. It is very probable, therefore, that in the absence of his master it was he who cared for the hound, though he may never have known the purpose for which the beast was used.

"The Stapletons then went down to Devonshire, whither they were soon followed by Sir Henry and you.

One word now as to how I stood myself at that time. It may possibly recur to your memory that when I examined the paper upon which the printed words were fastened I made a close inspection for the water-mark. In doing so I held it within a few inches of my eyes, and was conscious of a faint smell of the scent known as white jessamine.

prendre. Je ne serais pas étonné que Stapleton augmentât ainsi ses ressources, de jour en jour plus minces, et que, depuis longtemps déjà, il méritât d'être classé parmi les coquins les plus audacieux et les plus résolus.

«Il nous a donné la mesure de sa décision le matin où il nous a glissé entre les doigts si heureusement — pour lui, — et le fait de me renvoyer mon propre nom par le cocher prouve son audace.

«Dès lors, il comprit que je l'avais démasqué à Londres et qu'il n'y avait rien à tenter dans cette ville. Il retourna à Dartmoor et attendit l'arrivée du baronnet.

— Un moment! dis-je. Vous avez certainement décrit les événements dans leur ordre chronologique, mais il est un point que vous avez laissé dans l'ombre. Que devint le chien pendant le séjour de son maître à Londres?

— Je m'en suis préoccupé, répondit Holmes; ce détail avait son importance. Il est hors de doute que Stapleton ait eu un confident; mais je suis non moins certain qu'il a toujours évité avec soin de lui donner barre sur lui en lui confiant tous ses projets.

«Un vieux domestique, nommé Anthony, vivait à Merripit house. Ses rapports avec Stapleton remontent à plusieurs années, à l'époque où la famille habitait le Yorkshire. Cet homme ne pouvait donc ignorer que son maître et sa maîtresse fussent mari et femme. Il a disparu du pays. Or Anthony n'est pas un nom aussi commun en Angleterre qu'Antonio en Espagne ou dans l'Amérique du Sud. De même que Mme Stapleton, il parlait couramment anglais, quoique avec un curieux grasseyement. Je l'ai aperçu plusieurs fois traversant la grande fondrière de Grimpen et suivant le chemin que Stapleton avait balisé: En l'absence de son maître, il prenait probablement soin du chien, sans soupçonner toutefois l'usage auquel on le destinait.

«Les Stapleton revinrent donc à Dartmoor, bientôt suivis par sir Henry et par vous.

«Un mot maintenant sur l'emploi de mon temps. Peut-être vous souvient-il qu'en examinant le papier sur lequel on avait collé les mots découpés dans le Times, je regardai attentivement le filigrane. Je tenais ce papier à quelques centimètres de mes yeux et je sentis un parfum à demi évaporé de jasmin blanc.

There are seventy-five perfumes, which it is very necessary that a criminal expert should be able to distinguish from each other, and cases have more than once within my own experience depended upon their prompt recognition. The scent suggested the presence of a lady, and already my thoughts began to turn towards the Stapletons.

Thus I had made certain of the hound, and had guessed at the criminal before ever we went to the west country.

"It was my game to watch Stapleton. It was evident, however, that I could not do this if I were with you, since he would be keenly on his guard. I deceived everybody, therefore, yourself included, and I came down secretly when I was supposed to be in London. My hardships were not so great as you imagined, though such trifling details must never interfere with the investigation of a case.

I stayed for the most part at Coombe Tracey, and only used the hut upon the moor when it was necessary to be near the scene of action. Cartwright had come down with me, and in his disguise as a country boy he was of great assistance to me. I was dependent upon him for food and clean linen. When I was watching Stapleton, Cartwright was frequently watching you, so that I was able to keep my hand upon all the strings.

"I have already told you that your reports reached me rapidly, being forwarded instantly from Baker Street to Coombe Tracey. They were of great service to me, and especially that one incidentally truthful piece of biography of Stapleton's. I was able to establish the identity of the man and the woman and knew at last exactly how I stood.

The case had been considerably complicated through the incident of the escaped convict and the relations between him and the Barrymores. This also you cleared up in a very effective way, though I had already come to the same conclusions from my own observations.

"By the time that you discovered me upon the moor I had a complete knowledge of the whole business, but I had not a case which could go to a jury. Even Stapleton's attempt upon Sir Henry that night which ended in the death of the unfortunate convict did not help us much in proving murder against our man.

There seemed to be no alternative but to catch him red-handed, and to do so we had to use Sir Henry, alone and apparently unprotected, as a bait.

«Il existe soixante-quinze parfums qu'un expert en crime doit pouvoir distinguer les uns des autres, et bien souvent — j'en ai fait l'expérience — la solution rapide d'une affaire dépend de la subtilité de l'odorat. Le parfum me révéla la présence d'une femme, et déjà mes soupçons s'étaient tournés vers les Stapleton.

«Donc, avant même de partir pour le Devonshire, j'étais sûr de la présence d'un chien et j'avais flairé le criminel.

«Mon jeu consistait à surveiller Stapleton. Pour ne pas éveiller ses soupçons, je ne pouvais le faire qu'à la condition de ne pas être avec vous. Je trompai tout le monde, même vous, et, tandis qu'on me croyait toujours à Londres, je vins en secret à Dartmoor. Je ne supportai pas autant de privations qu'il vous plairait de le supposer; d'ailleurs, pour bien conduire une enquête, on ne doit jamais s'arrêter à d'aussi menus détails.

«Le plus souvent, je demeurais à Coombe Tracey et je n'habitais la hutte de la lande que lorsque je jugeais nécessaire de me trouver sur le théâtre de l'action. Cartwright m'avait accompagné et, sous son déguisement de jeune campagnard, il me rendit de grands services. Grâce à lui, je ne manquai pas de nourriture ni de linge. Quand je surveillais Stapleton, Cartwright avait l'œil sur vous, de telle sorte que je tenais sous mes doigts toutes les touches du clavier.

«Je vous ai déjà dit que vos rapports, expédiés sur-le-champ de Baker street à Coombe Tracey, me parvenaient rapidement. Ils m'étaient fort utiles, et principalement celui qui contenait la biographie de Stapleton. Il me permit d'établir l'identité de l'homme et de la femme; il affermit le terrain sous mes pieds.

«L'évasion du convict et ses relations avec les Barrymore embrouillèrent considérablement les choses, mais vous dégageâtes la lumière d'une façon très efficace, bien que mes observations personnelles m'eussent déjà imposé les mêmes conclusions.

«Le jour où vous découvrîtes ma présence sur la lande, j'étais au courant de tout, sans avoir toutefois la possibilité de déférer Stapleton au jury. Je vais plus loin: l'attentat dirigé contre sir Henry, la nuit où le malheureux convict trouva la mort, ne nous apporta pas la preuve concluante de la culpabilité du naturaliste.

«Il ne nous restait d'autre ressource que de le prendre sur le fait, les mains rouges de sang; mais, pour cela, il fallait exposer sir Henry, seul, en ap-

We did so, and at the cost of a severe shock to our client we succeeded in completing our case and driving Stapleton to his destruction.

parence sans défense, comme un appât. Nous le fîmes, au prix de l'ébranlement des nerfs de notre client. Nous obligeâmes Stapleton à se découvrir. C'est ce qui le perdit.

That Sir Henry should have been exposed to this is, I must confess, a reproach to my management of the case, but we had no means of foreseeing the terrible and paralyzing spectacle which the beast presented, nor could we predict the fog which enabled him to burst upon us at such short notice. We succeeded in our object at a cost which both the specialist and Dr. Mortimer assure me will be a temporary one. A long journey may enable our friend to recover not only from his shattered nerves but also from his wounded feelings. His love for the lady was deep and sincere, and to him the saddest part of all this black business was that he should have been deceived by her.

"It only remains to indicate the part which she had played throughout. There can be no doubt that Stapleton exercised an influence over her which may have been love or may have been fear, or very possibly both, since they are by no means incompatible emotions. It was, at least, absolutely effective.

«J'avoue que je me reproche d'avoir ainsi mis en péril la vie de sir Henry. Cela tint aux dispositions que j'avais prises. Mais comment prévoir la terrible et stupéfiante apparition de cette bête et le brouillard grâce auquel, à peine entrevue, elle se trouva sur nous. La santé de sir Henry paya la réussite de nos projets. La maladie sera heureusement de courte durée, puisque les médecins affirment qu'un voyage de quelques mois ramènera l'équilibre dans ses nerfs et l'oubli dans son cœur. Le baronnet aimait profondément et sincèrement Mme Stapleton, et la pensée qu'elle l'avait trompé est la chose qui l'a le plus douloureusement affecté dans cette sombre aventure.

«Quel rôle a joué Mme Stapleton? Il est incontestable que, soit par l'amour, soit par la crainte — peut-être par ces deux sentiments — son mari exerçait sur elle une réelle influence. Sur son ordre, elle consentit à passer pour sa sœur; mais toutefois cette influence cessa, dès qu'il essaya de la convertir en un instrument de meurtre. Elle avait tenté d'avertir sir Henry autant qu'elle pouvait le faire sans compromettre son mari.

At his command she consented to pass as his sister, though he found the limits of his power over her when he endeavoured to make her the direct accessory to murder. She was ready to warn Sir Henry so far as she could without implicating her husband, and again and again she tried to do so. Stapleton himself seems to have been capable of jealousy, and when he saw the baronet paying court to the lady, even though it was part of his own plan, still he could not help interrupting with a passionate outburst which revealed the fiery soul which his self-contained manner so cleverly concealed. By encouraging the intimacy he made it certain that Sir Henry would frequently come to Merripit House and that he would sooner or later get the opportunity which he desired.

«De son côté, Stapleton connut les tortures de la jalousie. Quand il vit le baronnet courtiser sa femme — quoique cela rentrât dans ses plans — il ne sut pas maîtriser un accès de colère; ce fut une faute grave, qui dévoila toute la violence de son caractère, si habilement dissimulée jusqu'alors sous ses manières froides et compassées. En encourageant l'intimité des deux jeunes gens, il provoquait les fréquentes visites de sir Henry à Merripit house et préparait pour une heure quelconque l'opportunité qu'il désirait.

On the day of the crisis, however, his wife turned suddenly against him. She had learned something of the death of the convict, and she knew that the hound was being kept in the outhouse on the evening that Sir Henry was coming to dinner.

«Le jour de la crise, sa femme se retourna subitement contre lui. On avait vaguement parlé de la mort de Selden et Mme Stapleton avait découvert, dans le pavillon du verger, la présence du chien, ce même soir où sir Henry venait dîner chez eux.

She taxed her husband with his intended crime, and a furious scene followed in which he showed her for the first time that she had a rival in his love.

«Elle accusa son mari de préméditer un crime. Une scène furieuse éclata, au cours de laquelle le naturaliste lui laissa entrevoir qu'elle avait une ri-

Her fidelity turned in an instant to bitter hatred, and he saw that she would betray him. He tied her up, therefore, that she might have no chance of warning Sir Henry, and he hoped, no doubt, that when the whole countryside put down the baronet's death to the curse of his family, as they certainly would do, he could win his wife back to accept an accomplished fact and to keep silent upon what she knew.

In this I fancy that in any case he made a miscalculation, and that, if we had not been there, his doom would none the less have been sealed. A woman of Spanish blood does not condone such an injury so lightly.

And now, my dear Watson, without referring to my notes, I cannot give you a more detailed account of this curious case. I do not know that anything essential has been left unexplained."

"He could not hope to frighten Sir Henry to death as he had done the old uncle with his bogie hound."

"The beast was savage and half-starved. If its appearance did not frighten its victim to death, at least it would paralyze the resistance which might be offered."

"No doubt. There only remains one difficulty. If Stapleton came into the succession, how could he explain the fact that he, the heir, had been living unannounced under another name so close to the property? How could he claim it without causing suspicion and inquiry?"

"It is a formidable difficulty, and I fear that you ask too much when you expect me to solve it. The past and the present are within the field of my inquiry, but what a man may do in the future is a hard question to answer. Mrs. Stapleton has heard her husband discuss the problem on several occasions. There were three possible courses. He might claim the property from South America, establish his identity before the British authorities there and so obtain the fortune without ever coming to England at all, or he might adopt an elaborate disguise during the short time that he need be in London; or, again, he might furnish an accomplice with the proofs and papers, putting him in as heir, and retaining a claim upon some proportion of his income. We cannot doubt from what we know of him that he would have found some way out of the difficulty.

vale. Sa fidélité se changea aussitôt en une haine féroce. Il comprit qu'elle le trahirait. Pour lui ôter toute possibilité de communiquer avec sir Henry, il l'enferma. Il espérait sans doute — ce qui se serait certainement produit — que toute la contrée mettrait la mort du baronnet sur le compte du maléfice héréditaire, et qu'il amènerait sa femme à accepter le fait accompli et à se taire.

«En tout cas, j'estime qu'il se trompait et que, même sans notre intervention, son arrêt était irrévocablement prononcé. Une femme d'origine espagnole ne pardonne pas aussi facilement un semblable affront.

«Maintenant, mon cher Watson, je ne pourrais, sans recourir à mes notes, vous fournir plus de détails sur cette curieuse affaire. Je ne crois pas avoir rien oublié d'essentiel.

— Stapleton, demandai-je, n'espérait-il pas, avec son diable de chien, faire mourir sir Henry de peur, ainsi que cela était arrivé pour sir Charles?

— Non; la bête était sauvage, affamée. Cette apparition, si elle ne tuait pas le baronnet, avait pour but de paralyser sa résistance.

— Sans doute… Autre chose! Si Stapleton avait été appelé à la succession de son parent, comment lui, l'héritier, aurait-il expliqué son séjour, sous un nom déguisé, dans le voisinage du domaine des Baskerville? Comment aurait-il pu revendiquer cette fortune sans éveiller de soupçons?

— La chose aurait été fort difficile, en vérité, et vous exigeriez de moi l'impossible, si vous me demandiez de résoudre ce problème. Je puis discuter le présent, le passé,… mais je me déclare incapable de prédire la résolution qu'un homme prendra dans l'avenir… Mme Stapleton a entendu son mari discuter la question à plusieurs reprises. Il envisageait trois éventualités possibles. Dans la première, il revendiquerait cette fortune du fond de l'Amérique du Sud et, sans avoir à paraître en Angleterre, il serait envoyé en possession de cet héritage, sur la simple justification de son identité devant les autorités anglaises de là-bas. Dans la seconde, il se rendrait à Londres et y vivrait le temps nécessaire sous un habile déguisement. En troisième lieu, il se procurerait un complice, lequel, après la remise de toutes les preuves exigées par la loi, chausserait ses souliers moyennant une certaine commission. Par ce que nous savons de lui, nous sommes en mesure d'affirmer que Stapleton aurait tourné cette difficulté.

And now, my dear Watson, we have had some weeks of severe work, and for one evening, I think, we may turn our thoughts into more pleasant channels. I have a box for Les Huguenots. Have you heard the De Reszkes? Might I trouble you then to be ready in half an hour, and we can stop at Marcini's for a little dinner on the way?"

THE END

«Après ces quelques semaines de dur labeur, je crois, mon cher Watson, que nous pouvons nous octroyer un peu de distraction. Ce soir, j'ai une loge pour les Huguenots… Soyez prêt dans une demi-heure… Nous nous arrêterons en route pour dîner chez Marcini.»

FIN

Printed by Amazon Italia Logistica S.r.l.
Torrazza Piemonte (TO), Italy

56281729R00105